John F Plimmer retired as a De
Midlands Police in 1997 after 31 yɩ

Throughout his career he was i
inquiries and was the senior investigating officer in more than 30 murder
cases, all of which were successfully completed.

He obtained a Law degree and Master of Philosophy degree and has
had one book, *In the Footsteps of the Whitechapel Murders*, published,
together with numerous articles in the *Police Review* and other national
magazines.

He has also been the technical adviser on a number of television drama
programmes including *Dalziel and Pascoe* and he lectures to CID Officers at
the West Midlands Training Centre in Birmingham. He now lives with his
wife and family in Warwickshire.

Robert Long was a boy soldier before joining the Coldsteam Guards.
During his service he became the Imperial Forces Middleweight Boxing
Champion.

After three years he deserted from the army to marry his wife, whom
he had known since early schooldays.

Having difficulty obtaining employment, he turned to crime and
became a professional armed robber and target criminal. He served two
lengthy terms of imprisonment as a Category A prisoner inside top
security prisons and was finally released in 1986.

During his periods of imprisonment, he became strongly connected
with various high-profile criminals, including the Kray twins, Frankie
Fraser and the Richardson brothers.

He now lives with his wife and family in the Erdington area of
Birmingham.

Plimmer and Long knew each other as children, and were raised in
neighbouring districts. Both were members of street gangs during the
late fifties and early sixties. They had similar backgrounds, living in the
same environment and attending similar schools. After leaving school
they went separate ways.

During their early thirties, they met once again, at the scene of an
armed robbery in which Long played a prominent role. He was arrested
by Plimmer, although they only recognised each other later, inside a
police interview room.

To Jonathan

RUNNING
WITH THE
DEVIL

Plimmer & Long

With many thanks for the
help & support you have given
my wife.

John Plimmer

5-6-03

HOUSE OF
STRATUS

This edition published in 2001 by House of Stratus, an imprint of
Stratus Holdings plc, 24c Old Burlington Street, London, W1X 1RL, UK.

www.houseofstratus.com

Typeset, printed and bound by House of Stratus.

A catalogue record for this book is available from the British Library.

ISBN 1-84232-523-X

Dedicated to my wife Fira, who is my rock.
To my daughters Lynda and Donna
who stood shoulder to shoulder
with their dad through thick and thin
and to my dear friend John Mills
for his faith and encouragement.

BOB LONG 2001

chapter one

It seemed appropriate if not ironic that, at that very moment, such a strong beam of light should pierce through the small stained glass window situated high above the Judge's chair. As though sent from a higher authority, it shone directly into the prisoner's face, who stood with his head lowered, trying to avoid the blinding glare. He turned and surveyed the surroundings as the old man cleared his throat in preparation for the address he was about to give. At least they'd been right about that part of it. There were no members of the press there. No members of his family in attendance. And no other nosy bastards who would only have been looking on to celebrate his downfall. They said it would be 'in camera' – only strangers and those who *had* to be there would participate in the proceedings.

'I have listened carefully to what your counsel has said on your behalf…'

He wondered if the old man knew the truth.

'…and I accept the difficulties in only having been out of prison for such a short period of time.'

Perhaps he does?

'But I must also accept you only have yourself to blame. There can be no mitigation, no matter how hard your barrister has tried. You are a hardened professional criminal. A man without conscience, one who seeks to gain at the expense of others.'

It was beginning to look doubtful. Typical though.

'Your past life as read out to the court by the Crown, shows the type of person you have become – hard and unrepentant, unwilling to turn over a new leaf. A man whose only desire is to satisfy his own personal greed, no matter what the cost.'

He definitely hadn't been briefed. The look of disgust in the Judge's eyes told the story.

'Your counsel has quite correctly put forward the point that your family are uppermost in your mind. But this latest affront to the rules by which society exists and the atrocious crime to which you have pleaded guilty, only confirm your own lack of genuine feelings towards those around you.'

The red robe paused to glance down at the papers in front of him before continuing, 'I have taken into consideration the fact that you have admitted your guilt and for that reason and that reason only, the sentence I am going to pass will be reduced considerably.' The old man paused, 'You will go to prison for seven years.'

And that had apparently been reduced, considerably. Just where do these people come from? he wondered.

The Judge then looked towards the two prison officers standing either side of the convicted man, 'Take him down. I have no doubt we haven't seen the last of him.'

*

Autumn had established itself in typical fashion. Rolling mists, heavy carpets of browns, reds and golds were now the dominant feature. The summer crowds had long disappeared together with the sound of children flying kites and kicking balls. The occasional jogger could still be seen pounding the winding paths. The smaller lanes were occasionally graced by the footsteps of young mothers, watching over their offspring, pushing prams up and down the varying gradients, in-between favourite park benches. Even the birds were busy quietly preparing for the long winter ahead. It was a scene of natural beauty, which could easily have been framed and hung on some senior copper's wall next to the row of historical training course photographs. Peace and solitude captured in oils.

But on this particular day, an eerie stillness also seemed to accompany the silence.

Cannon moved to the left, then to the right. Infantry gained ground on both flanks. The retreating army had little resistance to offer. Their heavy artillery lay in broken pieces. It would only take one more cavalry charge, down the middle. One more obstacle to overcome. One more hill to take from the enemy's grasp. The Cavaliers cheered and sang their victory hymns, as they progressed forward. But one military success would not decide the outcome of the war. The Roundheads hoped to regroup and swing the campaign back in their favour.

Four-thirty saw the dusk quickly descending. Moisture filled the air. The pastoral atmosphere was now captivating. And then, the sound of rubber on tarmac interrupted the serenity. A young boy dressed in anorak and jeans, sitting astride two metal-rimmed wheels, panting and puffing. Last year's Christmas present thrusting its way through the idyllic panorama, like one of the King's generals leading that final cavalry charge that would bring victory to his monarch.

The Roundheads were digging in. Muskets loaded. Swords at their sides. In a circle. Back to back. Gazing through the blue

3

gunpowder smoke. Watching for the enemy to come forth. The last stand. The ultimate defeat. Unless divine help from above swept down to assist them in their worthy cause. For they knew, God was on their side. A holy war that must be won. Failure, in any shape or form, could only mean disaster. Cromwell screamed at his last rear guard, 'Together men, we fight in the name of the Lord.'

As regular as Big Ben, twelve-year-old David Cheswick steered his beloved Phillips Manhattan bicycle through the park on his daily journey from school to the newsagent's, as he had done throughout most of the year. It was the shortest and quickest journey available to him. Once he'd got to the bottom of the hill he would pedal hard up the other side towards the summit. From then on it was 'easy rider', the breeze blowing in his face as he freewheeled down, through the gates and out into the street where the shop was situated. But the hill had to be taken first. Each revolution of the pedals became slower as he neared the brow.

The general knew the enemy would be waiting on the other side. Waiting to pounce at the first sight of the Cavaliers. It would be a sight to behold. But surely, the Parliamentarians were doomed? And this field of Naseby would be revered by historians, for evermore, in the King's name.

His mind continued to focus on that bloody war; an historic battle that had to be concluded on the lounge carpet beneath his father's outstretched legs. The Cavaliers had a distinct advantage. They were winning at the moment and victory was in their grasp. But he was confident Cromwell's broken army would hit back, with both cannon and venom. Almost there; just a few more downward strokes. He noticed the mist had intensified and the light seemed to be fading into a bluish cloudy tint, which always pre-empted the inevitable darkness of night.

But wait! There was a slight movement in the small copse near the top of the hill. To his left, or so he thought. Two dark whispers behind the trees. No, perhaps not. Perhaps the dimming light was playing tricks on him.

Onward King Charles! We shall soon take this hill for God and for England.

✳

He wondered whether all those centuries ago Cavaliers and Roundheads had ever enjoyed the same delicious pies his mother baked with corned beef and potato fillings. And of course, there was Sir Alec Guinness who'd played a leading role in the film. Perhaps he'd never had the good fortune to experience cooking like his mum's. But his mind was made up. Tonight, the Battle of Naseby would witness Cromwell's turn to claim victory in the same way as Richard Harris had mustered his troops, only to return to the battlefield with such vengeance and victory. Yes, he'd taken the hill. He had accomplished the principle objective. And now for the final phase of his crusade – to ride out of the park and capture the newsagent's.

Suddenly, the boy's secret world disintegrated. The battlefield was no longer there, cluttered with bright coloured plumes and silver body armour. The daydreaming had come to an abrupt end. Something violently grabbed him from behind and his highly polished machine collapsed beneath him. He felt a vicious blow to the back of his head and was dragged across the wet ground, gasping for air; shocked and bewildered by what was happening to him.

There was darkness amongst the trees. The smell of body odour was nauseating, and then...

The boy's screams and cries echoed across the park, but were never heard, except by the birds that croaked as they took flight from the trees above. And of course by the monsters who were about to become his abductors and rapists.

✳

Priestley didn't miss a puddle as he raced from the car to the front entrance of the tower block. Bastard weather! Why couldn't they build car parks nearer to the entrances, he thought. The heavy rain needed only those few seconds to drench him. As he reached shelter, whispers of steam drifted off his back, like a racehorse crossing the finishing line. This was a very unfit Jack Priestley.

'Penny for the Guy, mate?' There were three of them, just inside the public reception area. Three small Oliver Twists proudly displaying their stuffed doll. Eyes, nose and mouth drawn on a piece of cardboard with one of their mother's lipsticks, supposedly representing a face.

'Piss off,' was the reply. Not very friendly for an upstanding officer of the law, but Priestley hadn't the time. He was forgetting how he and Steve Blade had stood on street corners all those years ago, begging in the same fashion.

'Why do you always have most of the money, Priestley?' The youngster stood hands on hips, his face distorted by a look of genuine concern.

'Because I've already told you. I brought the Guy,' explained young Jack. 'And it's my mum's make-up we've used to draw its face.'

Both of them were suffering from cold and wet feet, but Blade's were even wetter due to the cardboard covering the hole in the sole of his shoe, quickly becoming a rain-sodden sponge upon which he had to tread. That wasn't helping his temper much.

Blade's punch knocked the skinnier of the two off his feet – this was his usual way of settling any kind of disagreement between them. 'Well, you can shove it. I'm not playing anymore. I'm off to Tommy Curley's bonfire anyway.'

Priestley hadn't fully realised this was a game they'd been playing. Tapping up anybody who had the misfortune to walk around 'their' street corner, for a few pence for good old Guy Fawkes. He'd actually believed they were trying to make some extra pocket money to buy fireworks. But now he had all the bounty they had collected and watched as his best mate stormed off in protest.

The Detective Chief Inspector couldn't resist a slight smile as he remembered the outrage on Blade's face. Always jumping in feet first without any thought or consideration about the situation they found themselves in. Young Steve's answer to everything was always a smack in the gob. Then he'd be off before anybody could retaliate. He turned and went back to the pathetic souls, both wet and shivering, his conscience getting the better of him.

' 'Ere. And don't get buying any bangers.'

Their faces lit up and their eyes bulged seeing the five pound note offered as a serious afterthought.

*

Well at least having done his good deed, he could now concentrate on the problems he was about to confront. He was trying to work out an answer for each of the questions she was likely to ask, trying to calculate the real reason for this particular journey, which he had a gut feeling would prove to be a complete waste of time. Question one. Why had she called him in the first place? The answer to that was simple. He hadn't a clue. The lift arrived and he couldn't help but remember the way in which Blade had tried to outfox those two baboons, hiding in the passageway. Waiting to ambush him on the night of his welcome home party. He remembered the story Blade had shared with him, a long time after the event. The way in which the recently released armed robber had sent the lift up and down like a yo-yo, trying to confuse them. He'd managed to do that alright. But being the kind of gormless prat he was, he'd got his sums wrong. There'd been three not two, the third kindly pushing a shiv into his back.

Question two. Why had she been so excitable on the phone? Perhaps he'd had an accident or his intellectual capacity had crashed, like an overloaded computer with what few brains he had between his ears, finally deciding enough was enough and he was now lying there in a coma, still scratching his arse mind you, as had been his habit since the day he'd been born. The lift stopped and Priestley stepped out onto the landing.

Question three, he pondered. Money problems? Yes, that was the favourite. It had to be. That would be it. Bladey was in the shit with his bookie and Mr Charity here had been called to the flat to help out. Well he can go and stuff himself, thought the policeman. He hadn't seen or heard from Blade for months and the cheeky git was about to put the arm on him!

'Come in, Jack.' It was more of a sigh than an open invitation.

Sammy looked very different from the last time he'd clapped eyes on her. In fact, he'd never seen her looking as dishevelled as this before. A female version of something that had just crept out of a laundry basket. But her appearance also seemed to be pitiful and perhaps even pathetic. It was obvious her long shoulder-length hair hadn't seen a brush for at least a couple of days; face pale and drawn; bags under her eyes like two chunks of liquorice. She was wearing a loose-fitting jumper with gravy stains down the front and a pair of old jeans that looked as though she'd borrowed them from the car mechanic next door.

Sammy Blade? Priestley asked himself. Or was this some lost soul from the local bail hostelry? Whatever, the big brown glistening eyes in which many a man had previously drowned, weren't there anymore. They'd been replaced by two lifeless pieces of ice. Her dark skin was now more of an olive colour, as though much of her life's essence had been drained from her. Bit heavy for just a few money problems.

He followed her into the familiar surroundings and sat in *that* chair, the one usually occupied by the man of the house. This was the very room where he and Blade had argued, debated and on occasions, fought. Where he'd lost control of his rage, only to find himself on top of the man, threatening to put him away for the next twenty years or so, having just put his lights out. She sat opposite him, upright with both hands tightly grasped together. The atmosphere was tense and perhaps a little strange. But at least she wasn't hostile so that was a good start. After all she'd invited him to call and see her, so why would she be? Yes, he was now more convinced his initial assessment had been an accurate one. Money troubles, undoubtedly; but major troubles by the look of her.

He waited for her to speak but her eyes remained focused on the Persian rug. He needed to break the ice.

'Sammy?'

She returned his gaze.

'You asked me to get here as quickly as I could. So what's up?'

He'd already noticed her lower lip trembling and she wasted little time in starting a full tearful explosion, covering her face with both hands.

'Take your time, darling. It can't be as bad as all that.'

She regained some control. 'He's gone, Jack.'

'Gone where?' It was a natural and understandable response.

'I don't know.' She shook her head. 'He just upped and went. He said he had to do something that would take a long time and then shot out through that door.'

'When?' Another purposeful question or so *he* thought. He was trying to show some sincerity, although with some difficulty. Blade had always been an enigma, even to his parents when he was a kid. Priestley remembered how they both used to disappear for hours before returning home exhausted and covered from head to toe in whatever dirt or filth they'd chosen to roll about in.

'About six weeks ago.' She was quickly regaining control of herself.

Priestley was surprised at such a length of time. Six weeks wasn't real, not as far as Blade was concerned. Normally he wouldn't leave his missus for more than a morning without letting her know where he was going, unless of course it was to serve out some debt to society. She was his most trusted servant. His right arm and all that.

'He must have said something, Sammy?'

'I've told you, Jack, something has happened to him.' The hands were clasped together again, both sets of knuckles a whiter shade of pale. 'I was hoping *you'd* know something.'

Priestley slowly shook his head, pouting his lips at the same time, a little lost for words, momentarily staring at the silent television screen that had inadvertently been left on, he saw some geezer talking about an earthquake in LA.

'I wouldn't worry too much, Sammy.' That didn't help. It didn't sound genuine. 'You know what he's like.'

'Find him, Jack.' Her tears had now disappeared but the worry and frustration remained, still evident.

'Did he take anything with him, Sammy?' That was a good question. 'Such as a toothbrush, money?' That was a stupid question.

She could only shake her head in response, her eyes welling up yet again. Life for a woman married to a professional armed robber could never be easy. It went with the territory – but married to an armed robber who was also Steve Blade, went beyond the boundaries of human logic, or so Priestley had argued many times.

He stood up to leave, those brief concerns he'd experienced when first told of Mr Blade's disappearing act now diluting. His normal feelings were slowly beginning to return. Those realistic, down-to-earth, emotional senses that had been part of his character since being introduced to the world of crime and scum. Feet on the ground; extremely practical am I; no-time-for-this-kind-of-bullshit, type of feelings.

He wondered why he was there. Why him? He wasn't Blade's guardian angel. He was just a cop, not a bloody social worker or one of those long-haired tosspots who ran about looking for missing kids. Why lumber him with her husband's misfortunes? Just because they'd been kids together and he'd locked Blade up for his last blagging. That didn't mean he was family. A voice echoed inside his skull. Perhaps you're the only one she can turn to. That brought a lump to his throat, but meaningful words had now abandoned him.

He turned towards the door and then tried to garble some kind of optimistic message. 'He'll be back, Sammy. I'll ask around.' He couldn't conceal the guilt in his voice and the tone that indicated he really didn't give a shit. But he had to persevere. 'I'm sure he's okay. I'd have heard otherwise.' Then as an afterthought, 'Let me know if he gets in touch.'

She remained seated as he made his own way to the door, disappointed at the inadequate way in which he'd handled what was so obviously a delicate situation. He remembered his ex-wife always used to brainwash him into believing he had the subtleties of a herd of stampeding bison! Always was one of her favourite sayings, repeated at regular intervals like an old record. Perhaps she was right after all. But what more could he do?

The black clouds were still belching out the torrents of rain as he drove back towards his office. He didn't feel overly concerned, but knew deep down something was wrong. Blade had known his wife for almost as long as he'd known Jack Priestley. The three of them had been brought up together in the slums, almost as part of a bigger family. And since discovering what the real difference was between men and women, the notorious villain hadn't left Sammy's side, except when he went out to rip off a post office van.

No, six weeks without a word? Alarm bells rang for a brief moment. But then the Detective Chief Inspector wondered whether *he* was becoming too soft. This was

12

Steve Blade. The scumbag of the Midlands Circuit. No, there were far more important things to think about, such as the disbandment of the regional units and introduction of their successor and his new employer, the National Crime Squad. Still, he might just have a peep at Blade's personal file. He owed that much to Sammy. His mind leapt back thirty years. To both of them walking along a busy thoroughfare, filled with black painted motor cars and the occasional white one. Funny, he thought, How people in those days only seemed to favour the one colour.

'Now remember, Jack. It ain't my fault.' Young Steve was concerned and had a right to be.

Priestley just looked at him, not sure whether the punishment would be an early to bed job, or sharp cuff round the ear off his father. As they turned the corner, both parents were outside young Jack's house. It was dusk and way past the time for reporting in.

'It's a copper, Jack,' confirmed a somewhat startled Blade.

'What? Where's a copper?' The word seemed to launch Priestley into full alert mode. He was tired. They'd been walking all day and he didn't need a shock like that one, not just at that particular moment anyway.

'With your Mum and Dad,' continued the shorter of the two. 'Look, up there, he's talking to 'em. It's not my fault, Jack.'

But Jack knew it wasn't important whose fault it was. When the coppers were brought in, that was both a clip around the ear and an early to bed job. He was right.

The small group of people, including the man in the gabardine mac and trilby hat, ran towards them. Mrs Priestley was the first to make contact, throwing her arms around the seven-year-old Jack. 'We've been worried sick. Where on earth have you been?'

Both boys had heard it all before.

'You might have had an accident and we wouldn't know. What if you'd both been picked up by a strange man?

What if...? What if...?

*

chapter two

The warehouse was packed to the gunnels. The two large wooden doors had been closed long before the first bout. Of course, people wishing to leave could do so whenever it suited them, but anyone sitting on the benches immediately surrounding the circle in the centre would have to fight their way out. A Saturday night spent at this particular promotion was for some an experience to behold. But for the majority, it was also an opportunity to relieve their gambling addictions, with money changing hands like cricket balls between bowlers and fielders.

It wasn't as though the actual size of the crowds depended upon the skill or reputation of those named on the bill. Most of the time, with one or two exceptions, the names of those providing the entertainment were unheard of. The gambling fever was the most influential factor, the call which drew them to the altar, like lost sheep. Like national newspaper reporters glued to a cabinet minister who'd just married his mistress, creating yet another vacancy in more ways than one. To George Riddell the promoter, it mattered not who the participants were, as long as every Saturday night provided a full house. And that was always guaranteed.

The two men glared at each other menacingly, their faces showing no sign of pain or fear. They slowly moved around the outside perimeter of the circle. Eyes staring, stripped to the waist, they faced each other like two awesome objects from cyberspace. With blood dripping from various orifices and flesh wounds they were looking and waiting for an opportunity to pounce. The noise from the onlookers had briefly subsided. This was a moment of respite. Each participant was taking time out to rethink his strategy, while remaining focused on their opponent's every move. One short lapse and it would be over. Hundreds, perhaps thousands of pounds lost as the loser lay, spread-eagled across the straw-covered floor.

The heavy, lingering cigar and cigarette smoke swirling around them, like that London fog in the film *Waterloo Bridge*, went unnoticed. Both minds were as one, concentrating on how to beat the other whether by fair means or foul. One thing was certain in the minds of both bareknuckled fighters; neither could stand much more punishment. They'd already given and received their fair share of brutality. But the contest could only end when one of them was down and unable to get back onto his feet.

As always, the crowd dictated the pace. The tension increased dramatically as the onlookers bayed for more blood. The physical action had to restart quickly, as the shouting was restored to fever pitch. The air was punched. The screams got louder, frustration reached a crescendo. The crowd clamoured for more action as individual punters demanded their particular man attack the other and finish the job.

'Take him now, Jackie!'

'Cripple the bastard, Punchy. He's right for plucking!'

'Come on you pair of morons. Get stuck in! I've seen stronger gnat's piss than this.'

The atmosphere was exciting but also frightening. The short interval was at an end. The battle resumed, conjuring up images of the Roman Coliseum, host to so many of the Empire's favourite blood sports. The gladiators moved closer. Fists clenched and raised. The contest was evenly balanced. The shorter of the two had been the main aggressor, trying to wear down the taller fighter's defensive guard, only to be pushed back by a series of stinging punches to the face and jaw. It was he who again took the initiative. He swerved and hooked, ducked and pounced. This time he dug deep into his physical reserve. Springing like a mountain cat he managed to deliver the full force of his fist into his opponent's face like an auctioneer's hammer. More blood. The recipient let out a painful gasp and groan which couldn't be heard above the surrounding din. Another heavy blow, accurate and perfectly timed, landed just above the heart. The knees trembled. The mind wanted to continue in an upright position; the body argued. But the bigger man's resolve was strong. He winced. He staggered. He'd been there before. When the chips were down he had that urgent inner desire to survive the onslaught.

He spat out his bloodied gum shield, the only item allowed inside the ring apart from boots and shorts. His teeth grinded together like two mechanical cogs meshing. He screamed out, more in anger than hurt, like a wounded animal that had been cornered. His knee came up and crashed into his opponent's groin. The other's knees weakened and the taller fighter took full advantage. His fist shot down from a high elevation similar to a well-oiled piston driving a machine. It had to be effective now. It was. The smaller man sank towards the floor as the blow hit the top of his head with the weight of an iron anvil. He staggered, his eyes rolling in all directions. Another crushing delivery and he went to the floor, like a fallen bird of prey.

Those who'd put their money on the smaller man to win stood in silence, as he lay on top of the straw, unconscious. Well beaten up. And well defeated. For the winning punters it was time for celebration. They roared their delight. The victor had surprised himself. It had taken everything he could summon to dispose of such a worthy opponent.

George Riddell was a proportionately built 45-year-old who had all the trade marks of a street metal-dealer with his white Sea Island cotton shirt, silk tie and heavy crombie overcoat. Over the years he'd developed a regular twitch in his neck, which gave the impression he was nodding at everybody else or agreeing with whatever was said to him. A dream subject for a young detective in an interview room!

'Did you commit this horrendous crime?' Nod from George.

'Have you committed others?' Nod from George.

'What about clearing up all the crimes on our books?' Nod from George.

But that wasn't his only problem. He also seemed to have a permanent worried look on his face. A dream subject for a port's customs officer. There had been many occasions when George had been pulled as he got off the plane from Benidorm or Torremolinos only to be found carrying a little excess duty. But this was his home territory. A warehouse full of punters. Two brave, if not dense contenders and lots of dough exchanging hands, a large percentage of which found its way into the promoter's coffers. A far cry from dogfighting and much more profitable! George had it made. A lot more exciting than the steel business although that was where his real bread and butter came from.

Illegal street fighting was a hobby in which George Riddell indulged himself. Usually at weekends, in a similar way to how other people might go fishing, horse riding, or playing tennis. George loved to see money made from pain and suffering. He was that kind of a man.

His principle source of income came from other business transactions. He was the Managing Director of a steel company, International Swarf. The organisation had been constantly discussed and watched by CID officers for years, mostly because of the characters of those individuals employed as debt collectors.

As with most large steel companies, it was common practice for International Swarf to sell a large amount of stock to an individual customer on the understanding that they would eventually reimburse the seller with the agreed cash price. That would be made over a predetermined period which would usually amount to a couple of years or so, depending upon the initial deal.

Unfortunately for the client, years were reduced to days and usually to within forty-eight hours or so. Following delivery of the merchandise purchased, the buyer would be visited by men carrying staves and, on occasions, shotguns, demanding full payment in cash. When the small business-man or woman failed to pay, both the stock purchased and the outstanding balances would be taken under threats of violence.

Almost all of those who fell victim to George Riddell's methods of business would be too afraid to report any loss to the police for fear of reprisal. One courageous man did and lost his fleet of haulage vehicles for his trouble. He later retracted his complaint after finding each of his vehicles burned out. The time it took to replace them was sufficient to put him out of business, long term. That following Christmas the man received a card with a fifty pound note inside and signed, 'A gift to buy the turkey with. Love, George.' Both weird and wonderful – that was Georgie boy.

Riddell had never had either the time or patience for honest business dealings and his survival had always been dependent upon surrounding himself with others willing to take the rap should anything fall off the rails. His weekend sporting activities went well with his character. Hard as nails. Having been bullied as a schoolboy, it was as though he constantly wore the label, 'I'll never play second fiddle again.' That was the real driving force behind him. As a businessman he could have been a lot more successful than he was. He had the necessary acumen. Highly intelligent, energetic, innovative, and ambitious – if only he could have shed those inner desires to cripple everybody he met, he would have been a lot richer.

He stood near the exit with both hands in his overcoat pockets, staring at those around him. After quickly working out the size of his percentage of the takings, he did his usual trick and cleared his throat as though in acknowledgement of having had another successful night. He then turned to the heaviest of his four bodyguards, 'Collect the divi, Ponteus, and bring it round later.'

His newly recruited minder nodded.

Riddell felt confident having Ponteus around. In fact he was the kind of man Abraham Lincoln or John F Kennedy could have done with. The fundamental requirement for the job wasn't resourced from brainpower. All it needed was a nod of the head followed by the quick transportation of muscle, to be delivered wherever directed. The fight promoter was also aware that his new acquisition might be twice the size of Jimmy Gabriel, but he wouldn't have half the bottle the little man had. But he'd serve a purpose, albeit only physical. He had no choice anyway. His previous servant was now well out of it and would be for some time. So Ponteus would just have to do.

'And fix up that meeting with Pete Owen. Tell him he's on for the third of next month and he'll have an easy opponent.'

Riddell always made his exit quickly and just seconds after the main result. He never favoured personal confrontation, probably because of all the times he'd been smacked over the head as a kid. But he knew there would be punters who'd lost an arm and a leg, only too willing to leap into action at first sight of him. So he was away, out into the night. Thanks for coming. Sorry about all the dough I've just taken from you, but you know the saying, 'If you don't like the heat...' You could hear his words well after the disappearing act.

But on that particular night and for some unknown reason, Gabriel seemed to be stuck in his thoughts. He remembered, as he drove his recently acquired Roller off the industrial estate towards the bright lights of the city, how the little man used to deal with some dickhead who wanted to argue about a result. Fast, clean and efficient. With a wry smile on his face he'd pull the complainant along the ground, before kicking him out of the door. Riddell knew in his heart how he still missed his presence.

For years Jimmy Gabriel had been Riddell's oxygen, his most trusted employee, having known him since the start.

That was before George's more successful, if dishonest exploits. He'd looked after the younger Gabriel when times had been hard for an out of work jockey and Jimmy in return had remained loyal – that was until he'd decided to enter into a business transaction on his own which proved to be his eventual downfall.

Like a ferret, Gabriel could sniff out trouble before it started and then deal with it effectively, leaving his gaffer to concentrate on manicuring his fingernails or some other menial task. But then, the temptation of a foreigner became too great an opportunity to miss. A chance to go it alone. Of course there'd be risks. But wasn't there always when the end result meant a full bank balance or large bag of readies? But this particular adventure wasn't for two. Gabriel wasn't happy at the thought of having to share with his boss. After all, if Riddell had been in on it, the former jockey would have had to have done all the spadework, in any case.

Gabriel had actually gone out and hired the boat, after listening carefully to the proposition made by the government man, which is what he'd always called the civil servant responsible for putting so much work Riddell's way. When the bowler hat made such a substantive and confidential offer to Gabriel, how could he refuse? After all, everything the government man had done for his boss had previously turned to gold – just as this particular job had done. Well, almost.

Two hundred grand had been the total prize up for grabs and he'd got that close to it, he'd already booked his ticket to another life. He couldn't remember how many times he'd tormented himself since his arrest, thinking about what might have been. If only…

The Froggies had done their bit. That side of the deal had gone down without a hitch. The stuff had changed hands. All Jimmy and the three other monkeys in the boat had to do was deliver it into the safe hands of a contact at Folkestone. There was no way the government man would be getting his hands dirty even though fifteen per cent of whatever they earned would be going his way. But then again, without him there wouldn't have been a job. He'd made all the arrangements so none of the others, including Gabriel, had been over-bothered at the time. Having said that, Gabriel retained a number of doubts about the way in which the operation had gone down.

He remembered the excitement as they approached the White Cliffs and the feelings of achievement and celebration shared amongst them all. Confident their deeds would be richly rewarded. Confident they'd be safe and free from any hassle. Confident that now the French coast had disappeared from view they'd be home and dry. He also remembered how his bottle had twitched when he saw the glare of the lights attached to the customs launch, as it pulled up alongside theirs and shouted warnings from an amplifier, before seizing everything and everybody. Only two miles off the English coast and stuffed like four pickled herrings. Unfortunately for Jimmy and his business associates, the law just wouldn't believe that a shoal of mackerel had found bags of heroin on the seabed and swallowed them. And now, the one-time Newmarket apprentice was just another con. George Riddell's right-hand man had created a vacancy – to be filled by the local friendly neighbourhood Godzilla.

Jimmy Gabriel was a slightly built man. His pointed features and receding ginger hair disguised his true character. If it hadn't been for the ugly scar on his right cheek, protruding for everybody to see the horse's hoof that put it there, he would have appeared to be the shy, quiet type. The 'I'm-a-smart-arse-that-can-disappear-into-the-wallpaper' kind of individual. There was no doubting Jimmy G's love for horses and hatred for human beings. Both feelings being equally balanced inside a mind that worked overtime on causing mayhem, whenever necessary. He enjoyed violence, especially when dishing it out and apart from his mother, Riddell had been the only person he'd ever got close to. There was at one time an old school mate, Frank Cheswick, but he hadn't seen him for years. No, he preferred to be a loner, rolling about in horse shit at every opportunity.

He'd always had a love of horses since a child and his small frame had helped to drive his personal ambitions to be a professional jockey. But humans were different in his book and they were either hated or not there. After all, he'd always blamed them for his constant failure to ever win a race. For such a small man he had an impressive list of convictions ranging from manslaughter to GBH, although never murder, which was surprising to those who knew him.

Since arriving at Long Lartin to see out his time, he'd openly refused to socialise with any of the other prisoners. Ignoring most, he snarled at others who broke into his airspace. It wasn't because he was a sulker. He'd always been a loner, preferring isolation and his own company to that of others, unless they had four legs and went 'neigh'. Any individual wanting to pass the time of the day would soon be told to go away in no uncertain terms, or would receive a violent message meaning the same thing.

✱

But now in his own cell, he had a real problem. This was different. This was a completely new experience for him. One which he was now having a great deal of difficulty resolving. He was quickly realising there was something to be said for safety in numbers, as all of his previous life flashed before his eyes. His breathing was restricted. His head rolled from side to side. The animal lying across his chest trying to asphyxiate him, wasn't really interested in a social chat or whether Jimmy the Jockey was a loner or one of Pan's People. Stan Bynar's sole intention was to rape his fellow con. He didn't give a shit about past reputations, only that somehow he had to satisfy the demanding urge that so frequently took control of him. At the end of the day that was why Bynar was in the nick; a sex pervert with the physical strength of three men. And now it was little Jimmy's turn. The deviant had been watching him for days, building up a lust to perform what was now about to happen. The wooden wedge jammed beneath the cell door, standard issue to every con, was going to ensure that his lustful objectives would be achieved without interruption. It had worked before and was going to work now. The smaller man knew of his assailant's intentions. The newspaper clippings sprung to mind. He remembered reading about Bynar's antics. After the team had emptied the security van it was always this bastard's job to drive the vehicle and two captured guards well away from the scene. He was then supposed to abandon it with both victims tied and bound on the floor in the back of the van. The problem was always Stan the Shirtlifter's habit of wanting to bugger the guards, before leaving them more shocked and disturbed than they'd been before making his acquaintance. And that left Gabriel with no doubt as to what was going to happen to his tea and sugar if he couldn't overcome the big blob of human muscle rolling across the top of him.

The back of the intended victim's head hit the concrete floor twice, as Bynar fought hard to further his advantage. Both of Gabriel's arms were pinned down beneath the heavier man's knees and he knew, with all the meanness in the world, you couldn't overcome situations like this one if you didn't possess the necessary physical attributes. A knife or bullet in the back or a broken glass plunged into the side of somebody's face was more his style – not an upfront kind of confrontation like this! Dizziness was beginning to overcome logical thought. The back of his head collided once more with the floor. The smell of bad breath was beginning to overpower him. The dinosaur's weight was becoming heavier; Gabriel's breathing more difficult. He was losing it. Any minute now it would be total surrender, no matter how reluctantly communicated. He was about to kiss his arse goodbye, literally.

Suddenly there was some movement from behind Bynar. Then instant relief. Thank God. As though picked up and thrown by a mob of invisible fairies, Stan the Shirtlifter suddenly leapt sideward, screaming and clutching at the spot where his hair had been violently yanked. Two sharp kicks in the ribcage and what had once been every security guard's nightmare disappeared out of the cell as though someone had just waved a magic wand before ramming it up his rectum.

'You alright, Jimmy?'

There was no answer. Couldn't be. Gabriel was still trying to force some air into his lungs. He managed to nod, but then jerked his arm away as Blade tried to help him to his feet.

'That dirty bastard's been eyeing you now for some time.' Blade was picking up the wedge that he'd managed to dislodge before opening the cell door. 'You're lucky I was passing, Jimmy boy, and heard the grunts.'

Gabriel's voice was returning. Hoarse, but faintly audible. 'I'll look after that pig soon enough,' he coughed. 'Don't let me keep you.'

But Blade had other ideas. He sat on the edge of the bunk and started his sermon.

'Jimmy, I've been meaning to have a word with you son, about your social attributes.' He watched the unwilling host pick himself off the floor and flood the small corner basin with water. 'You're going to be here for a long time, Jimmy, and you're going to need a mate or two, to watch yer back.'

'Disappear, Blade.' Jimmy gurgled as his head came out of the water and was thrown into a towel.

'Son, you need to listen…'

Suddenly Gabriel's hand was near Blade's throat and the unwanted visitor felt the sharp end of what was probably a Stanley knife pressing against his windpipe. His legs straightened as he rose off the bed, gazing into a pair of wild and furious eyes with a pattern of small pinpricks of blood beneath them, obviously resulting from the crude strangulation he'd just experienced.

'No, you listen,' demanded Gabriel, 'and listen good. I don't need company.' He paused, the fire remaining. 'Now are you leaving? Or do you want to get sliced?'

Blade just smiled. He mentally acknowledged what an ungrateful bastard Gabriel was and turned and walked out. This was going to be more difficult than he'd imagined.

✳

chapter three

He could no longer control his anguish. Ever since they'd found his son, an emotional turmoil of grief, sorrow and anger had been swirling around inside him, waiting to be triggered. And as soon as he stood away from the bed, still gazing at the sight of the twelve-year-old lying comatose amongst the drips carrying the drugs intended to save his life, he erupted.

Although Frank Cheswick would have been one of those rare selected individuals on Jimmy Gabriel's Christmas card list, if the ex-jockey had ever kept one, he was just as much a loner, now going through his own kind of personal nightmare ordeal. Another former street urchin from the inner-city slums. A man who would always have etched on his mind the smell of pine disinfectant; small, narrow doorsteps covered in Red Cardinal polish; and all the other niceties tattooed on the memories of those who were reared in a similar impoverished environment. The trademarks of days long past remained in one's thoughts like the stains of horse manure on the cobbled streets from the Co-op milkman's four legged transportation system.

Cheswick was a tall, thin individual with combed back wisps of dark brown hair that matched his eyes; and a lean face that was friendly enough, but now starting to show some of the scars resulting from his recent trauma. He was also a person of principle and had been since childhood. One who had always recognised strengths in others rather than taking advantage of their weaknesses. That was the real reason why in earlier days, he'd got on so well with Jimmy Gabriel. What he wouldn't give now to have the former jockey onside. He needed someone to lean on, a strong crutch to support him. His wife couldn't. She still sat there, staring at her son's pale face, incapable of supporting even herself.

The tears streamed down his face. He couldn't believe what lay in front of him. An innocent child, who had brought him so much happiness and pride. An innocent being so full of life, loved by teachers and friends alike. On his way from school to earn some pocket money he had been completely unaware of the scum hiding in the trees. Scum whose deaths would be the only way his father could feel relief from the pain he was now experiencing. He stared at the back of his wife's head, feeling the convulsions uncontrollably winding their way up from the very pit of his stomach. And then, without feeling any sense of relief, some of the pain left him in the form of a loud scream, which made his wife stand from the bedside seat and look upon him in horror. Like an incapacitated orator, he couldn't put any words together, just a long, drawn-out scream.

Two nurses rushed into the room in response to the howls coming from the distressed father. They didn't speak as he gasped for breath, trying hard to explain what he had to do.

'I have to go,' he stuttered to his wife who was now crying dry tears. 'I have to leave. Go find them.'

His wife just nodded her understanding.

One nurse placed her arm around the stricken man and tried to comfort him, but he was unaware of her presence.

✻

Frank Cheswick knew the streets as well as Jack Priestley, Steve Blade or any of the others who'd been members of that private club. And it was the streets of his childhood that were calling to him, pulling him back, for it was only there he felt he would find an understanding of what had happened to his boy and those who had been responsible.

✻

He didn't visit his son again for at least a month. He couldn't. The pain was too unbearable. Even when young David later regained consciousness, his father was absent, wandering the streets. Looking, searching, asking questions both of himself and other people. His pale, sombre face was seen in every known gay public house in the city centre. His feet carried him miles around the backstreets, until the early hours. His eyes reflected a dazed and confused look, haunted by his own incubus. The last image of his wife and son's faces constantly reminded him of the task upon which he had embarked. He had no idea what he would achieve. He only knew that he had to do something and this was the only thing that would satisfy his quest to contribute towards identifying those bastards who'd made it all so necessary.

Members of the gay community soon got to know or hear of Frank Cheswick and the torment he was going through. They offered sympathy but were rejected, sometimes violently. They tried to explain but the man wasn't listening. All he wanted was something to ease the burden which had now taken over his life.

'I'm looking for the bastard who attacked my lad in the park.'

'Which one of you lot visits Sutton Park?'

'Please help me to find the men who attacked my young boy.'

The questions were never-ending and the answers the same. Nobody knew anything.

Sadly for Frank, the only thing he avoided more than anything else was the police. They were the only people who might be able to do something for him, within the boundaries of the law. But he had no interest in that. He didn't trust them. He'd had a bad experience as a youngster, being fitted up for some trivial theft that he hadn't been involved in. Since then he'd rather cross the road and wish 'Good morning' to some notorious executioner, than a copper pounding the beat. But unknown to him, they would be his saving grace, even without his help. Individuals who were genuinely close to him, like Jimmy Gabriel, would have been able to convince Frank he needed to work with the law. But for all he knew, they were doing nothing towards finding those responsible for his lad's condition. He was wrong.

'Do you know Frank Cheswick was an old shoplifter, boss?' asked Dave Vaughan.

'Yeah,' answered Priestley, continuing to write a draft report. 'Got into trouble a couple of times as a kid, that was all. I haven't heard anything about him since they landed that shuttle on the moon.'

Vaughan was still having problems working out his gaffer's sense of humour. He wasn't alone. 'Well, it was his kid who was attacked in the park some time back.'

Priestley looked up and pouted his lips, 'First I've heard. How's that going by the way? You involved?'

'I wasn't but I am now. It was a bad attack by two pervs. The kid's still hospitalised, but my main concern is the old man. He's been wandering around the gays for the past few weeks, stirring them up.'

'With a hatchet in his hand?'

Vaughan shook his head.

'Then he's not doing anything wrong. Apart from that, can you blame him, Dave? Think of what he must be going through.'

'We've been asked to take it off the local CID because the lab's found some DNA.'

Priestley stood to stretch himself, 'Where from?'

'Semen.'

'As bad as that was it?'

'Afraid so,' answered his Detective Sergeant. 'We've got a make on it, but I need to go back to talk to the locals some more. If the DNA falls down we might not have enough to make it stick.'

'If we know him, son, pull him in,' directed Priestley. 'I don't give a shit about the DNA going down. If he's a known perv let's get him off the streets before he does another one.'

That was what DS Vaughan really wanted to hear and he nodded in agreement.

'We can always sort the evidence out afterwards,' concluded his Detective Chief Inspector.

✳

The door to the maisonette looked as though it hadn't been painted since the buildings were put up before the war. It slowly opened and a dishevelled, unshaven, middle-aged figure obviously in need of a bath, appeared.

'Yes?'

'Tony Ryan?'

'Yes.'

'We're from the National Crime Squad,' explained the Detective Sergeant. 'Been into any kids lately?'

Ryan tried to shut the door in their faces, but was pushed to the floor as the three detectives pounced on him.

'We'd like to speak to you about a little incident that happened in the park a few months ago, Tony, you nasty, horrible bastard,' explained Dave Vaughan as he was snapping the handcuffs on the big man's wrists.

Uncle Tony, as he used to be called many years before by children who would congregate at his invitation around wherever he lived at the time, was frogmarched into the crime car, together with plastic bags full of magazines and a computer used by him to take what he could off the Internet.

His life had most definitely taken a turn for the worst.

*

'Does Cheswick know?' asked Priestley.

'We left a message with his wife, boss,' replied the overjoyed Detective Sergeant.

'Well done, Dave. A good job and congratulate the others for me.'

The junior rank turned and left the office, strutting like a proud peacock. After all it wasn't every day you managed to capture such a dangerous piece of shit like Uncle Tony.

Priestley returned to the intelligence docket on his desk, a little surprised at the obvious lack of material inside. He was expecting a great deal more information on the life and times of Steve Blade, armed robber extraordinaire – the Ned Kelly of Nechells Green. He sat for a moment imagining Blade's face on the front cover, just above his name and date of birth. And then started to turn the pages over, one by one. When he reached the second page he studied the official police photograph which bore no resemblance to the one conjured up in Priestley's mind. The ugliest man on Earth would have been an apt description.

Unfortunately, official police photographs always seemed to project the worst possible image. Individuals who had to stand in front of a camera having just been interrogated for probably hours, white faced, black balloons propping up their eyes. They all seemed to be lifeless, as though taken at the subject's funeral just before he or she was planted. Or was it because each photograph was taken with the individual knowing he was about to leave society's bosom, long term? There wasn't much difference, thought Jack, between today's colour poses and those old Victorian snaps taken of bodies in the morgue, after they'd hung them up on a nail buried in the wall to make them vertical for the purposes of the old box cameras.

He turned each page carefully, examining the printed matter like a philatelist searching for a rare penny black. He reached the part that described Blade's last arrest and paused to savour that particular moment in history, which brought him face to face with his old school mate; when the horror story for all post office security vans walked out of the alley, straight into Priestley's fist. He remembered the retaliatory kick in the groin, followed by that gang of uniformed bloodhounds trapping Blade after he'd legged it back up the track, and then manacling him like some sort of dangerous animal escaped from a zoo. Priestley remembered being reminded at the time of the old Frankenstein film when Boris Karloff was chased by the town's people carrying torches of flames up towards the castle, ready to execute the fugitive once they'd caught him.

Then he found what he'd been looking for. Central Criminal Court – Drugs Importation – 7 years. His eyes rolled up towards the ceiling in disbelief. The Old Bailey? Smuggling drugs? A seven stretch? Blade? No, never. No, there was something wrong. Something very seriously wrong. His eyes returned to the document. Central Criminal Court – Drugs Importation – 7 years. If he believed what he was reading, firstly, Blade had involved himself in something he'd always hated and condemned, and secondly, he'd have to believe that Blade had gone down the steps without telling his missus or anybody else. And that just wasn't possible. Or was it?

He stood up and stared through the window at the dark clouds hovering above, ready to unleash yet another barrage of snow or hail or something just as dramatic. Perhaps it was for that very reason Blade didn't want anybody to know what he was in for, including his missus. A drugs baron might make lots of money but he certainly wouldn't be the most popular boy in town. Perhaps Blade was too ashamed to let anyone know just what a mean, nasty bastard he was? Yeah, that was probably it. He tried to picture his face, when he'd first learnt about how much dough he could make bringing a lorry load of heroin or amphet into the country. Oh, he'd really hit rock-bottom this time, thought Priestley. Lower than shark shit!

'Jack?'

The sound of his name disturbed his thoughts and he quickly turned away from the window. Carol Guardia, his lunch date, stood in the office doorway looking as pensive as ever. He'd forgotten to cancel. Still he couldn't do much about it now. There she was, patiently waiting for her escort, credit card at the ready just in case he failed to pay which was fairly normal for him! He tried to appear attentive as he listened to her latest piece of hot gossip. But what he was hearing made him wonder whether he really did look like a Disney cartoon. Normally she was a down-to-earth, practical type of person, was our Carol. But what was flowing so freely from her mouth now, could only be regarded by him as garbage.

✳

They hadn't quite reached the restaurant when Priestley decided to stop the car and turn towards his passenger.

'Carol, you really are a one-off. Do I really look that gullible?' Sarcasm wasn't his strongest point but he was certainly doing a good job now. 'Or is it that you just think I'm some sort of prize prat?'

She seemed surprised at his hostile reaction. In fact dumbfounded by it, so she just sat back and stared out of the windscreen with that usual look of frustration and anger written all over her face. He gently tapped the steering wheel with his fist. It was supposed to have been a thump, but he didn't want to overdo it. He didn't want to risk alienating her.

'Street fighting went out before the last world war.'

'So you say, Jack Priestley. So you say.' She sank further down the seat, arms folded across her chest.

'But – '

She sharply interrupted him, 'Okay, just you listen to me Mister put-it-on-a-plate-for-me-Carol. If there was an opportunity for somebody to earn thousands of pounds for doing next to nothing, would it really matter what was involved?' She took a breath, 'And how crooked it was?'

'But street fighting?' This was too incredible, even for him. But he needed to maintain some kind of credibility with her. Why? He didn't quite know why, but he just needed to. He paused and now placed both hands on the steering wheel. 'Alright, tell me. How, where and when?'

'I've told you, Jack, I don't know the details. Except that Mister Big and Mighty George Riddell from International Swarf is the promoter and they take place every weekend. That's according to my source.' Her stare returned towards the front of the car. 'And it involves mega-bucks,' she paused again. 'And it's going to be one hell of a story for me with or without your help.'

Well, he was either going to continue in her face and not have to pay for a meal because it wouldn't happen, or back off. Give a little ground as they say.

'Okay, okay,' he lifted his arm as if in surrender. 'I'll go with it, lady. Just don't blame me if this turns out to be another legend.'

Both corners of her mouth turned upwards, just sufficiently to confirm his credibility had been reinstated. 'Thanks, Jack.'

He'd be paying for the meal!

＊

Prison to Steve Blade had almost become like a second home to him. He'd served with the best of them and because of his own notoriety, was now regarded as one of the top cons. Of course, he missed his wife and daughter; the nuptial comforts and all the other advantages that went with living with such an electric current as Sammy; the violent disputes inside the flat, none of which he ever won; the violent disputes with neighbours across the landing, most of which he did. But basically, he had no problems in the nick. He'd become partly institutionalised anyway. And if he could get back out after a short stretch, like three months and with a Home Secretary's paper in his hand saying what a good lad he really was, then it would have been worth the ten grand paid and ten grand still owed.

His mind continued to analyse his present predicament, as he followed the screw towards the visitors' block with a slight grin on his face. Would he swop his life with this screw in front of him? Blade asked himself, whose head swayed in synch with the rest of his body. This one always strutted about like a cock who'd just dicked twenty hens. No thank you. There was more chance of Blade becoming Prime Minister. He couldn't imagine a more boring existence. Coming to work every day on different shifts; feeding and baby minding demented tosspots like him; then going home to spend a few hours glued to a square box, being fed by another demented tosspot whose only purpose in life was to spit out kids. No, Blade would take his chances inside. And outside? He'd just continue with his normal way of life, although perhaps in a quieter way than before.

When he first saw the apparition standing there to greet him he initially thought he'd got the wrong room. But like all good cons experienced in the art of integrity, in other words see nothing, hear nothing and say fuck all, Blade just stood there, allowing his eyes to roll over the body beautiful. He couldn't avoid the uncontrollable sigh. After all, he was only a man. One who had been deprived of any female contact ever since the Moon broke away from the Earth, or so it felt that way to him.

This was their first meeting and it must have seemed obvious to her he hadn't really prepared himself. He'd been expecting some kind of tall lanky clone in the usual dark pinstriped suit with bowler hat to match. Even the screw appeared a little embarrassed as the picture of all men's desires, with her gorgeous shoulder-length blonde hair and trim but busty figure, threw her arms around Blade's neck and dumped her tongue inside his mouth.

'Darling, will you ever forgive me?' Words spoken in a brief cessation, before the steamy supposed reunion continued.

He heard the door close quietly as the prison officer left them alone while Blade tried to imagine the smirk that must have been on the screw's face. But she continued cleaning his teeth until his right hand dropped and felt the tight little arse jumping up and down like a fiddler's elbow. But that was the wrong button to press and she backed off, hurrying across to the chair parked furthest away from the door. Blade, not even trying to hide the glint in his eye or wide grin across his face, sat opposite.

'So what's new, Steve?' The charade was over. They were alone. Now it was time for business. Nice while it lasted though, he thought.

Blade nodded and glanced up towards the ceiling. 'Do you think you could say hello again?' Just like Oliver Twist taking that empty bowl back to the counter.

He was ignored and she just sat there with a straight face, the tops of her breasts bulging out as if there'd been a silicone movement and the two implants had pushed themselves up towards her chin.

Blade shrugged. 'Need more time. The man's a hard nut to crack.'

'You've got more time,' she explained confidently, leaning across the table, moving closer towards him, letting him peer further down the silicones. 'But have you made contact?'

Now it was Blade's turn to ignore a question and he continued with an afterthought, as though talking to himself. 'I never thought I'd be asking for more time in this place.'

His blonde contact remained serious, 'My name is Joyce and we were living together in London when you got locked up.'

He nodded, still feeling the effect of her tongue on his dentistry but realising that this session was to be business only. A briefing from his first contact. What he really needed was a roll on the floor with her.

'And if anybody asks,' she continued, 'I'm just a tart who you've been using to spite your wife.'

So why couldn't she be a tart now, he thought, and give him one over in that corner next to the door? The screws couldn't see through the glass panel if they dropped their kegs just over there. His mind was all over the place. It was the effect of being in the same room with Marilyn Monroe, here. It wasn't bastard fair.

'Are you okay, Steve?' She couldn't help notice his 'far away' gaze.

'Fine.' He snapped out of his lustful desires and gave himself a mental kick up the arse. 'So, what about my wife…Joyce?' That did the trick. He was back in alignment!

'She's alright. Missing you but doing okay.'

'Does she know?'

'No,' Joyce interrupted sharply, 'and she doesn't need to. But she's alright.' She then looked hard into Blade's eyes, 'Now listen carefully…'

Here we go, thought the convicted con. Here comes the, we want you to do this and we don't want you to do that bit, and all for a miserly ten grand.

'There's a man in here by the name of Ryan.'

The name was more than familiar to Blade.

Joyce continued, 'He attacked a young boy about nine months ago. In a park…'

*

chapter four

The ball bearing hovered on the edge of the hole, as though waiting further instruction before actually dropping in. All the young dirty faces looked aghast.

Priestley remembered the mixed feelings of elation and concern, as he stood and demanded Blade's favourite glarney as the prize for winning the game.

'You can get stuffed, Priestley,' bawled the defeated ragamuffin. 'You cheated.'

But that hadn't been convincing enough to stop the winner claiming his reward with two fists and half a house brick.

How many times had that happened? thought Priestley. That had been just one of many occasions when both of them had fought like dogs, continuing to do so throughout their teenage years. But it had always been Jack who had to shovel the shit away from his mate. And here he was, yet again, obviously back to do that very same thing!

He looked up towards the main block as he parked the car. There would be Blade, sitting and scratching his arse inside one of Her Majesty's cells. He was like a bad habit in Priestley's life; a habit that had remained with him for as far back as he could remember – one that refused to find space somewhere else, like Mars or Planet Zod.

The DCI looked again at the letter he'd received earlier that morning. There was no doubting the handwriting. It was Blade's. And so was the grammar:

'Bout time I had a visit, Jack.

And how many times had he read that? He could almost hear the words being spoken.

Of course he was angry. Extremely angry at what Blade had done to get himself back inside. His lip curled every time he thought about such a happy-go-lucky chappie bringing shit into the country so it could be pedalled out to kids on the streets and perhaps even in the playgrounds. Yes, he would have to try hard to restrain himself from kicking Blade in the balls as soon as they met.

The most despised person in Priestley's mental library of criminal characters was a dope pedlar. In particular, one who imported the stuff. But he'd go along with it for now and listen to all the bullshit, even though it would probably be the last visit he would ever make to see Blade. As soon as he knew the reason for the request and unless it was something which would help the police service of this country, he intended to be out of there waving tarah for good, making his way back to his car as fast as his feet could carry him.

He walked down the corridor towards the suite of interview rooms, wondering how many of the population he'd been responsible for putting inside there. Quite a few he suspected. His worst nightmare had always been being in there with them; falling down a bottomless pit; being kicked from all sides as he fell; some criminal organisation

fitting him up and having nowhere to turn. Even the lovely
Sonia Hall, with all her advocacy skills and experience
would be unable to help him. There had been so many tales
about ex-cops doing time. Having meals doctored and
drinks pissed in. For some strange reason those thoughts
reminded him of Charlie Brockie, a fellow probationer who
worked on the same shift when he first joined the job.

He remembered Charlie having a bad time with Bill
Russell, one of their sergeants. He was sent to fetch old
Bill's cigars when he had more important things to do, like
file a report in the bin. He had to stand for hours watching
a zebra crossing, waiting to nick some poor sod for parking
in the studs and wait outside to the exact minute to book
off. He was always being given the worst traffic point,
always being given the most arduous tasks and always being
bollocked up hill and down dale for something or other.
And he remembered the hatred Charlie felt towards the
man who was making his life a complete misery, festering
for weeks, perhaps even months. Until that early morning
when the young PC was handed a golden opportunity to
take his revenge, literally on a plate, when old Bill Russell
ordered him to make his toast.

Charlie as always, obeyed gleefully and made sure the
corners of the sergeant's toast were fully buttered, as was
his supervisor's constant wish. In fact Charlie had been
congratulated once or twice on the way in which he never
left the corners of a piece of toast dry. But on this particular
occasion, as he climbed the stairs towards the canteen on
the first floor, the probationer heard a stray dog whining in
the kennels situated at the back of the nick. He eventually
presented the two pieces of buttered toast to his sergeant,
who quickly devoured them whilst dealing the cards to the
rest of the shift. Charlie watched him before walking away,

only to have convulsions in the corridor outside. What he hadn't told old Bill Russell was that he'd popped outside to the kennels and wiped the two pieces of toast on the stray dog's arse.

The sergeant was never to know that. And Charlie was never to forget it.

The escorting screw opened the door and there was Blade, sitting with both arms resting across the table. He looked glum and slightly depressed. The room was small and dimly lit, as though the prison service was cutting back on electricity. Priestley had been right about his initial concerns. He did feel an urgent need to kick him in the balls. In fact, a number of medieval methods of torture also sprang to mind.

'So here I am.' He waved Blade's letter asking for the visit to take place, noting the obvious embarrassment that hung over the other man like a blanket.

The con cleared his throat, leant further forward, grasped both hands together and used them to support his chin. 'It's not what you think, Jack. I can't say too much, but you've got to believe me.'

Priestley just stared, waiting for the usual crap to pour from Blade's mouth. Of all the audacious bastards, he thought, but he had to stay in control.

Blade sat back. 'You know I don't deal in drugs.'

That failed to have the desired effect on Priestley. It didn't exactly help to temper the senior cop's bad attitude towards him either, 'What you after? A pardon? I suppose you were fitted up?' he said in short rapid fire.

Blade had seen this kind of hostility from Priestley before and knew it would be a pointless exercise trying to argue his case any further. 'Sort of, Jack, sort of,' he said in a half-appeasing manner, wishing not to pursue the point any further. More importantly he didn't want to increase the friction that was so obviously present.

Priestley was hurt and still a little bewildered at this scumbag's recent diversion. He'd always believed and still did, that there were crimes committed by individuals that people could live with. Thieving for example, where no one except an insurance company got injured. He would condemn that but also learn to live with the culprit. But hitting old ladies over the head or sexually abusing kids was unacceptable to both sides of the fence. Bringing funny stuff into the country was also totally unacceptable to him and he'd thought at one time Steve Blade had shared those same views. Just how wrong could he get? And what he interpreted as Blade's piss-poor efforts to put the record straight with him didn't help matters. It was a habit of Priestley's to raise his eyes towards the ceiling when about to say something detrimental to someone else. And he did just that, 'Bollocks, Blade.'

There was a short period of silence during which time both men sat and looked away from each other. They were drifting apart by the second. Blade knew that Priestley was on the verge of standing up and leaving, without them having approached the real reason he'd asked to see him. He had to break the ice somehow. 'Nice one at Stratford, Jack. Read all about it in the papers.' Blade's grin was artificial but at least he was trying to ease the tension that had now enveloped the room.

'Don't take the piss,' was the short response.

'Old Shakespeare's birthplace, eh?' He sniggered trying hard to sound genuinely amused. 'Took out three burglars in their car and demolished the front of a listed building into the bargain. Read all about it. Yes, nice one, Jack.' It was working, or so he thought. This was how they used to talk to one another. The gloom was slowly lifting, in Blade's corner anyway.

'They reckon it'll take thousands to restore, Jack.' The best way to recover Jack Priestley's attention was to humour him, thought Blade. Like the time they were kids and he'd held young Jack's head under the water in the local swimming baths. And kept it under the water until he'd almost drowned. That little trick finished up with Priestley chasing him out into the street with just his trunks wrapped round him and pushing him into the snow before rolling him over and over, kicking him at the same time with his own bare feet. Blade hadn't realised until then, that it was possible for a person to turn forty-five different shades of blue!

But now, what he really didn't appreciate whilst trying to win back some favour, was that Priestley was still smarting over the incident Blade was referring to. Some of his National Crime Squad officers had ambushed a team of robbers in Stratford town centre. Unfortunately the bandit car, together with two crime cars had all ploughed into a protected building – none other than the Bard's birthplace, which had been standing there for the past four hundred years until Jack and his merry men had visited, causing tremendous damage. The attention of the national press had been well earned and at that particular time Jack Priestley's name was shit.

'Don't push it, Bladey. You didn't want to see me just to take the piss.'

Yes, this was better. This was more like the old Jack Priestley. Normal service was being resumed.

No, you're right, a bit of crawling never hurt anyone, thought Blade. 'A favour, Jack.'

Guessed it, thought the visitor. It couldn't be a parole letter because it was too early. So what was it?

'To be honest, Jack, it's not for me but I'll fill you in.'

Priestley just sat there like Father Christmas about to tell a small child he couldn't have that CD after all.

'Sometime back there was a twelve-year-old kid, David Cheswick, picked up by a slimy perv. It was in Sutton Coldfield. Remember?'

Priestley nodded, of course he did, 'In the park. Frankie Cheswick's lad. The kid was badly injured and we locked up a geezer by the name of Ryan.'

'That's him, Tony Ryan. He's a perv, Jack.' Blade liked the sound of that particular word. It seemed to have a ring of disgust about it, which was right up his street. 'I think your lads banged him up.'

'A paedophile?' Priestley said, trying to keep the conversation as up-market as possible – sometimes a major difficulty when debating a subject with Steve Blade.

'Yeah, one of them as well.'

Priestley could never work out whether Blade was serious, still taking the piss, or downright ignorant.

'He only got three years for crippling that kid, who's now in a psychiatric ward dreaming of stars and pretty colours.' Blade was genuinely snarling, 'Finished for life, Jack.'

Priestley raised his eyebrows and remembered the fuss that followed in the media. The newspapers reported it as a horrific attack which it was, and although there was widespread relief when the bastard was caught by Priestley's officers, no one was pleased with the outcome. A short-term custodial sentence. Not at all what the doctor had ordered.

'They say the mental damage done to him could be permanent and all his mother does is sit at her kid's bedside, rocking in a chair, moaning and sucking her thumb,' continued Blade.

'Wasn't there a scream because he only got three years or something? And then there was some talk about how he'd done other kids in the same way and he had a mate who wasn't caught?'

'Yeah, the other one wasn't caught, officially that is. But everybody thinks he's in here as well for doing over another kid.' Blade seemed tense. 'Mott's *his* name. Clifford Mott. But it's Ryan I'm interested in.'

'Why?' Priestley was beginning to wonder now, why all this interest in a couple of pervs.

'I'm coming to that.' Blade moved away from the table and sat back in his chair making a V sign with two fingers up to his mouth, at the same time watching the small glass window in the door. His confidence in Priestley's willingness to oblige was now fully restored. At least the senior detective had spoken to him.

A packet of cigars spun across the table and disappeared into his trouser pocket.

'Tell me, Jack. What's your feelings about the scumbags that do that sort of thing to kids?'

'No different to drug traffickers.'

That one hurt and stopped Blade in his tracks. He'd walked straight into the Lion's den, and raised the palms of both hands towards Priestley, as though surrendering the point made. Oh yes, he would love to have argued that one out all right, but couldn't. It would be suicidal. 'I'm serious, Jack.'

'So am I.'

Blade's eyes rolled and a heavy sigh communicated his obvious frustration at Priestley's negative, almost hostile attitude towards him. He began to wonder whether this exercise was going to be a complete waste of time.

'If it's any help to you, shithole,' continued Priestley, 'my feelings are the same as yours.' That was no big secret as far as Priestley was concerned. 'I'd put them all away with a flame-thrower if it was possible.'

Blade stood up and towering over Priestley spoke with an excited, but lowered voice. 'Good, Jack, good. Cos I've got a proposition for you. The bandit's in here with us.' He looked like a man about to attack somebody. 'He's on Rule 43 with the rest of the slime. Normally nobody would be allowed near him but I can arrange things differently. I know the kid's father well, so do you. Frank ain't done much in the past, you know that, but he's alright.'

Priestley had hardly moved since sitting down. 'I'm still listening.'

Blade returned to his seat at the sight of the screw's face peering through the window in the door, obviously about to enter and bollock him for moving.

He quickly leant forward with both hands on the table, his voice lowering to a whisper. 'Well, Jack, he visited me last week and asked for my help.'

'Cheswick or Ryan?' Priestley was confused and the question was genuine.

But Blade ignored it, still glancing up towards the door.

The nosy bastard had turned his head away. Springing up and down on the heels of his feet, pretending to be a copper on the beat, full of his own self-importance and arrogance.

'He wants to get in here to sort Ryan out for attacking his son. You know what I mean? And I'm inclined to give him what assistance he needs, Jack.'

'How does he propose to do that?' Priestley's eyes squinted slightly, as if a shaft of light was piercing them, but it could have been the strong smell of garlic on Blade's breath.

'With your help, Jack.' Blade smiled. 'He's going to screw a warehouse and walk in to you.'

'Is he now? And who's brilliant idea was that?' As if Priestley didn't already know.

Blade chose to ignore the question, yet again. 'He wants to get himself in here, Jack. Well, that's the general idea.'

'He's not going to get much for doing a warehouse. He's only got a bit of form for shoplifting.' Priestley looked doubtful. 'A couple of years, perhaps three or four at the most. So tell me, how could he manage to get into Long Lartin, a top security nick? He could be placed anywhere in the country. Do you want me to put him up as a terrorist or something?' he continued sarcastically.

It was a valid point and well anticipated by Blade.

'Not if he's a Cat. A prisoner, Jack.' The smile broadened, 'And that's where you come in.'

'But even as a Cat. A that doesn't mean he would automatically be transferred into here.' But Priestley already knew exactly where Blade was coming from.

'So, what do you think I've been doing all this time? Sitting on me arse?' Blade's confidence was growing. He'd almost landed his man. 'That's not a problem, Jack, leave that to me. He's not asking much.' He shrugged his shoulders, in a sort of would-you-buy-a-second-hand-car-from-me type of fashion, 'In fact, all you've got to do is what you would have to do anyway if he commits a burglary. Lock him up and then make sure you drop a line to the Home Office and have him put on the Cat. A list. I can do the rest.' Blade sat back with a smug grin. He was confident Priestley wouldn't refuse.

'And what happens when I find out this Ryan geezer has had his dick cut off in the nick?' There was genuine concern in Priestley's voice. He had the bottle to participate in Blade's little scheme. There was no doubting that. But he still felt some concern. 'What do you expect me to do, stay quiet about it?'

'Yeah. Where's the problem, Jack?' Now Blade's newly found confidence was starting to flag, although he couldn't afford to show it. 'All we want you to do is make sure he goes Cat. A. I'll look after his interests once he's got his bird.'

'Whose we?'

'Well me, then.'

There was a lengthy silent pause.

It was time to bring out the begging bowl and Blade continued. 'Look, Jack, this bastard has ruined a kid's life as well as a mother's. Come on, Jack, where's the justice in three years for a rodent like that, being allowed to carry on living in here, like a human being? He should be topped and you know it. If you gave it – '

'Shut yer mouth,' Priestley snapped. He'd listened to Blade for long enough, now he needed to think. His mind worked overtime looking for any kind of pitfall. There weren't any, not as far as he could see anyway. There wouldn't be any problem just writing a letter to the Home Office. But he would be condoning anything that might happen to Ryan, although that alone wouldn't weigh too heavily on his conscience. The only real problem for him was helping Blade. This boil on his arse, the one he'd intended to lance. That was the *real* reason for his visit. But then again, he knew the procedures for selecting a

Category A prisoner weren't just as a result of police recommendations.

He slowly unfolded from his chair and walked towards the furthest corner of the room away from Blade, before turning to face him. 'What's the difference between this geezer and somebody like you who damages the lives of thousands of kids by pumping them with poison?' He paused and then continued with obvious anger in his voice, 'How much did you draw for it, Steve? Couple of grand or was it six figures?' Now it was his turn to walk back to the table and lean over it.

'I know what you're thinking, Jack, and I don't blame you, but it's not how it seems, mate.' Blade was looking up at him, like a scolded child.

'So you've said.' Priestley was looking down at him, like a Victorian Sunday school teacher.

Blade couldn't afford to push his request any harder and decided to give his voice a rest. Priestley returned to his chair, staring at him, almost snarling. His anger outweighed any thoughts of accommodating Blade's request. He was finding it difficult to contain himself. Blade's eyes dropped to the floor, as though waiting for a noose to be placed around his neck. Priestley then stood up again and with both hands in his trouser pockets, walked to the door. It was time to leave. He didn't want to stay a second longer in Blade's presence. The screw answered the senior police officer's knock by opening the door. Blade sighed with frustration and disappointment. And Priestley turned to look back at the totally dejected figure, just sitting there.

'Okay, just this once.'

*

During the few weeks that followed the meeting with Blade, Priestley had been kept busy. The Stratford-upon-Avon incident was history and his department had almost reached breaking point with the number of assist requests made from various forces, including his own. Kidnappings, armed robberies, murders and so forth. The list seemed endless.

And then, as if that particular massive volume of work and commitment wasn't enough, news of two children having been abducted and murdered in the north of the country reached the National Crime Squad. A number of branch offices were asked to assist including Jack Priestley's. Both homicides had been recorded as separate incidents, having occurred within a two-week period of each other. However, although not formally linked as having possibly been committed by the same person, both investigations were treated as if they had been.

There were a number of nationwide inquires to be made, typical of those that normally followed such serious high profile cases. And that meant the deployment of a number of Priestley's detectives away from their own branch office, leaving the senior detective short of resources on the ground with the workload still increasing daily.

He'd forgotten about the conversation with Blade, until he answered an almost apologetic telephone call from Ernie Musgrove, a Detective Sergeant from the Stafford-shire force. The officer told him about a fairly simple inquiry involving a man by the name of Frank Arthur Cheswick. More than fifty thousand pounds' worth of precious metals had apparently been stolen from a factory on an industrial estate near Cannock. The inquiry conducted by the local law had only just started, when an anonymous call was received from a man giving details of a flat-back lorry used to take away the stolen gear. Subsequent inquiries with a local hire company quickly revealed that Cheswick had in fact rented the vehicle for the day on which the job had been pulled. When eventually seen he admitted, without hesitation, responsibility for the theft. And then, to the pleasant surprise of the officers interviewing him at his home, told them where they could find the missing metal. In fact, being the good-hearted, public-spirited citizen Frank was, he took them to a lock-up garage where it was stored.

Whilst the CID officers were celebrating, Frank asked to see Priestley. The least any Detective Chief Inspector could do in return for such kind and complete co-operation, was to oblige. How could he refuse?

'They tell me you wanted to see me?' asked the senior detective.

Cheswick sat back, staring at him and slowly nodded.

'Well, I'm here.'

'I remember you when you were just a kid. Jack Priestley from Nechells Green.' Cheswick looked extremely forlorn and a little pathetic. 'There was something about you in the papers. Local boy makes good, or something like that.'

Priestley just sat and listened. He couldn't fully appreciate exactly what this man had been going through after having a young son subjected to such a horrific ordeal, but he had a bloody good idea.

'Well,' continued Cheswick, 'my boy won't have that chance.'

Again, Priestley thought it best not to respond or even offer any kind of sympathy for fear of it not sounding genuine, although it would have been. He preferred to listen. Cheswick then focused on his hands, entangled with each other on the top of the table. He started to scratch the backs of them. A nervous irritation he'd developed over the past few weeks. And then his reddened eyes shot back to meet Priestley's.

'They tell me you can help?'

'Perhaps.'

Another long silent pause. 'This woman came to see me,' he said rather nervously. 'She told me that Steve Blade was prepared to help me get at Ryan, the man who attacked my son, if only I could get inside the nick.'

Priestley made no gesture, either verbally or physically.

'But I have to get on the Cat. A list – '

'Just stop there, Frank,' interrupted Priestley. He suddenly felt uncomfortable, Frank having already said more than he should have. Jack already knew what else the man was about to say and didn't like it. It was too dangerous. He was in a strange nick, talking to someone who was almost a virtual stranger to him and who was about to ask him to interfere with the course of justice. For all Priestley knew, there could be wires all over the place with Noddy and Big Ears sitting outside, taping every word.

'I'm very sorry about your lad and I've spoken to Steve Blade about your situation, but I'm afraid there's little more I can say to you.'

He winked at Cheswick, trying to show him some sign of reassurance, trying to let him know that everything would be alright but not knowing how the man would interpret it. He probably thought Priestley fancied him or something, being as he'd spent so much time recently surveying gay pubs! He stood to leave and was hesitant as to whether or not to offer his hand as a farewell sign of goodwill, but decided against it. He apologised once more for not being able to converse any further with the man and then left

Cheswick sitting alone, eyes starting to well up again. But Priestley knew he'd done the right thing.

✳

'Of course, you know he's suicidal?' asked Priestley.

He just delivered a bolt of lightning to the robust, red-faced Detective Sergeant. 'No, I had no idea,' explained Musgrove in a deep Welsh accent. 'Suicidal, you say?'

'He's tried it three times before to my knowledge,' lied the DCI. 'There was one occasion when my lot had him. Tried to hang himself with a belt he'd smuggled past the custody sergeant.'

'Well, I'll be damned,' sighed the overweight DS. He looked sharply at Priestley. 'And you say three times?'

Priestley nodded, 'You'll have to watch him, sarge. With all the trouble surrounding his boy and that.' Now he shook his head, 'He must be very vulnerable.'

'Well I never,' Ernie was still staring out of the window in disbelief. That wasn't his problem. His mind was trying to work out what it was he was supposed to do about it.

'Cat. A, sarge,' shouted Priestley as he walked out of the door. 'He'll just have to go Cat. A. And by the way, tell me when he's up and I'll write to the Home Office for you explaining his difficulties. Don't you worry, I'll sort that out.'

A senior officer with a heart of gold, thought the junior rank. A very unusual specimen indeed!

'Well thank you, sir. You're a proper gent,' he shouted, listening to Priestley's footsteps disappearing down the outside corridor.

✳

'I don't give a Jack shit,' cried Riddell, 'I want Owen for this Saturday night.' He quickly walked across the room and threw the office door open. 'Ponteus, get yer arse in here.'

Dumpy Caine was Riddell's main fixer. He was the man who carried his short fat frame all around the circuit looking for potential fighters who would be suitable for George's Saturday night bill. But there were occasions when Riddell would ask too much of Dumpy. And this was one of them.

The room seemed to darken as the large human citadel made its entrance.

'Ponteus will go back there with you,' explained Riddell, still sounding as though he was trying to make himself heard across the heads of a thousand people, all gathered in a market place.

Dumpy Caine hadn't moved off the easy chair. 'And what about the purse, George? That's the real blister.'

George hesitated. This was painful for him. He was hurting, badly. Hard cash to him was like his life's energy and to have to part with it, especially in circumstances when a big thick elephant brain like Owen was calling the odds, was against his nature. It was completely alien to the way in which George had been brought up. But he knew he needed the fighter there on his bill, and it had to be this forthcoming Saturday. Riddell had told everybody Owen would be the main event. If he let them down now, he'd be crippled financially, although he only thought that, not really believing it.

'Double it,' he snapped, his face changing from red to crimson. 'Double the purse.'

He turned to Ponteus, 'And if that doesn't work, smack him.'

His minder's face remained as it always did – expressionless. Just like a plastic mask.

Both Dumpy, standing at five-foot-two, and Ponteus, standing at six-foot-nine, left the office together, leaving George to wonder whether he was actually running a circus!

✳

'What's an impos…impos…imposter, Steve?'

Blade just shook his head.

Tommy the Leg (and God knows how he got that nickname), was the prison grass. A snotty nosed little germ who ran around with the library trolley, picking up whatever gossip he could and passing it onto the screws.

'Importation, you stupid little git,' answered the senior con. 'Bringing the funny stuff into the country.'

Both men stared a while longer at the card on Gabriel's cell door which read, Cat. A Importation 20 years.

In other circumstances, Gabriel's aggressive anti-social behaviour wouldn't have been allowed to continue as long as it had. Blade would have just knuckled the top of his oval-shaped head and shoved it down the nearest pan, before pulling the chain, of course. But that wouldn't fit in at all with his current plans. He would just have to bite the bullet. Go on sucking up to the little mountain goat until he'd achieved his main objective. That was becoming quite a test for him as each day passed by.

But it was the notice on the cell next to it that attracted Blade's attention, Cat. A Burglary 5 years. It was still unoccupied, but his prison nose and gut feeling told him, this had to be it. Cheswick's arrival was imminent. There couldn't be two Cat. As posted for just a five-year stretch.

'I've also heard, Tommy, he's got two wives,' Blade explained, knowingly feeding the jungle drums. 'One an old dutch and the other a seventeen-year-old page three.'

'Never,' gasped Tommy the Leg.

That should give the screws something to chew on, thought Bladey.

'And, Tommy,' he called back whilst walking away towards reception to collect one of the edited copies of yesterday's newspapers, 'I've just discovered why they call you Tommy the Leg. All yer brains have been stuffed into your third one.'

His laughter could still be heard as he disappeared down the winding steps, towards the ground floor.

Gabriel had certainly been a major obstacle for Blade to conquer. He'd tried just about everything to become acquainted with the little prick. On the landing; in the showers; when queuing for a meal and even in the prison laundry. But the man who he'd been told to target, continued to treat him just like he did everyone else, as though he carried some highly infectious disease. Even after having his arse saved by Blade, he still persisted in refusing to recognise that anything else in the nick, apart from himself, was a part of the planet. Obviously working hard to retain the Super Rat mantle, he was despised by other cons and now destined to be a loner for the remainder of his twenty-year stretch.

And then, Blade's prayers were answered. The card on the cell next to Gabriel's hadn't been misleading. The cavalry had arrived at last. There he was, standing with an escort in the reception area, looking a little worse for wear, but who didn't on their first day in that place? Frank Cheswick. The new Cat. A con, having been identified as mentally unstable and dangerous to himself and others.

And where he was going to be domiciled couldn't have been any better for Blade's purposes.

His first contact, Miss Joyce Big Bristols had done well. Cheswick wasn't a stranger to Blade and Joyce had put herself up as his representative, offering the kind of help that Cheswick was looking for. Nevertheless, he couldn't help but feel some sympathy towards the bloke. After all, he wouldn't have a clue how he was going to be used as a pawn in return for the favours about to be rendered. But there would be some recompense for Cheswick. In return for unwittingly helping Blade to breach Gabriel's armour, he would have his way with Ryan. Blade would keep his promise and ensure that happened – if only for the sake of Mrs Cheswick and her son.

He cleared it with the escort and offered to show the new inmate to the wing. There was no doubting just how tired Cheswick appeared and how quiet and reserved he was, unlike the jovial party-goer Blade remembered him to have been in the past. They'd never really spoken in depth to each other. They'd more or less been like passing ships in the night, both accepting invitations to the same various functions, but they were never talkative or really sociable towards each other. Just the occasional nod of the head accompanied by a few words of recognition.

But Blade's new employers had done their homework well. His own distant association with Cheswick had gone on for some years, but Frank's connection with Gabriel had been closer and longer, although always on a social basis rather than a business one. For them to have put those links together, and all for the benefit of Blade, must have taken some doing.

No wonder they stitched up the Russians so effectively, he thought, as both cons climbed the spiral staircase up towards the landing.

'Welcome to Stalag, Frank.' That was the usual greeting. 'So, how's things been going, mate?'

'Is he still here?' Frank only had one thing he wished to talk about and his pale, drawn face was a tell-tale sign of the distress he'd been subjected to in recent months.

'Yeah.' The reply was as short as Blade wanted it to be. He couldn't afford to allow too much chat to go on about the kind of dastardly deeds he had in mind.

'When?' That question didn't take a lot of working out, but Blade was worried that his old acquaintance would start to fret.

'You must be patient, Frank. You'll soon know. From now on don't get too close to me.' He was in the prison whispering mode. 'It might take a week or so, but you'll know what to do soon enough. Worked so far ain't it, mate?'

Cheswick just looked at Blade, but there *was* gratitude in his eyes.

'Anyway, we've got you the best suite in the house. Right next door to an old mate of yours.'

He waited for a response or some other obvious question to come back at him. But Cheswick wasn't at home. The mention of Gabriel's name would have to wait, until the new addition had gathered his thoughts.

During the next few days the new inmate did what he'd been told and managed to avoid Blade. There was the occasional exchange of words in the exercise yard or on the landing, but conversation was never prolonged. The only problem for Cheswick was his own impatience, often aggravated by the tortuous memories of his son and wife's condition, caused by one slimy piece of shit. On one occasion he stood at the bottom of the spiral staircase looking up with pleading, tearful eyes as Blade approached him from the top landing, two screws following in his footsteps. The senior con could see the man was burning up inside but could only shake his head, warning him that any conversation between them at that time, would be both futile and bloody dangerous. One thing was becoming more and more certain. There wasn't much time left for Blade to do what he had to do. Cheswick was likely to blow it at any time.

*

No previous convictions. Never been nicked, except for a few brushes with the customs for being over the top with a box of cigars or few bottles of plonk. Priestley paused and sat back, a little surprised at the fact that, on the surface, George Riddell appeared to be a straight businessman – if there was such a thing, of course. Managing Director of International Swarf, a steel company situated on railway sidings near the city centre.

He picked up the phone. 'Chris, International Swarf?'

'Mostly intelligence, boss.' Chris Barton was in charge of Priestley's research unit and what he didn't know about the patch they covered, wasn't really worth knowing. 'We've been picking things up on them for years now,' continued the young Detective Inspector. 'Bad business transactions; dissatisfied customers; things like that.'

'No police operations?'

'One or two, but not on the company itself,' was the reply. 'It's run by George Riddell and he's been known for employing a number of undesirables, such as Vinnie Grant and Jimmy Gabriel. People like that who look for work when they come out of the nick.'

Priestley sat up, 'Gabriel rings a bell.'

'He's tucked up, boss. Drew a heavy sentence for bringing some dope across the Channel.' There was a short pause before Barton continued, 'There's been something recently on Riddell. Let me just have a look at him and I'll come in and see you.'

Priestley sat back in his chair and stared at the Lowry print on his wall. He wondered how one man could make so much money for painting pictures that wouldn't be out of place on the wall of some classroom in an infant school. But he had to concede there was some magic in the one he was studying. An atmosphere. Some kind of magnetism. Some kind of magic that took his mind away from the trials and tribulations of life as a Detective Chief Inspector. Yes, he realised that's why it was on his wall.

It sounded as though International Swarf was a haven for ex-cons. He wondered why there hadn't been more on the file sitting on top of the desk in front of him. Perhaps he'd missed something somewhere?'

'This is it, boss,' Barton handed another, smaller file to his DCI. 'Riddell is on the anvil at the moment.'

That surprised Priestley and he straightened his back, quickly moving through the pages of the latest material. 'Blackmail?'

'Apparently so,' explained Barton. 'He's got this habit of selling off stock to various customers and then sending the boys round the following day demanding money which he'd previously agreed to be collected over a period of time.'

'How heavy, Chris?'

'Sawn-offs. Threats to break their legs if they didn't pay up, pronto.'

'Hence the reason for employing the undesirables.' Now things were beginning to take shape for Priestley. 'But no mention of any betting tricks or street fighting episodes?'

'No, but there have been rumours about that, mostly over in the Black Country.'

Priestley stood and walked to the window, supposedly contemplating the next move but in reality, smiling at the Chief Superintendent who'd just got out of his car and stepped straight into a foot-deep hole in the tarmac, filled with rain water. 'Life's a bitch, Chris.'

'Sir?'

Priestley turned, 'Okay. Dig a bit deeper and see what else you can come up with, mate. He's supposed to be running some sort of illegal fighting scam.'

Barton turned to leave and then stopped. 'There is one more thing I think you should know.'

Priestley was back in his chair.

'Riddell is being represented on this blackmail job by Miss Hall.'

Priestley looked up, a thousand child-like questions in his eyes, but only one that needed asking. 'Sonia Hall?'

Barton's nod confirmed it.

*

chapter five

The days soon turned into weeks. For some of the cons the process was slow and laborious. For the minority, it passed a lot quicker according to what piece of news they'd just been given, such as earlier than expected release dates or promotion to a better working environment. But there was always one ever-present common factor that stretched out like a piece of elastic, reaching all corners of the establishment – the prison's internal communications system. Everybody knew what everybody else was up to.

Blade spent most of his time watching Cheswick and Gabriel meeting and talking on the landing or in the exercise yard. From their behaviour towards each other, there could be no doubt they went back a long way; like two lost brothers. Blade couldn't believe Gabriel was capable of befriending anyone, especially in the manner in which he appeared to have taken up with Cheswick. Another tick in the box for the security services, from whom the idea had first emanated.

However, Cheswick's friendly relationship with Gabriel didn't help endear him to the other cons and he was soon made the subject of various jibes and insults. Not that he really noticed the hostility towards him – he had other things on his mind. And such triviality was also ignored by Blade, who couldn't do much about it anyway. Neither did he want to. The role he was to play in helping Cheswick to achieve his ambition meant he had to keep his distance from him, if only for a short while. But he would be patient. After Cheswick had accomplished what he'd got himself locked up for and the dust had been allowed to settle, he would be in Blade's debt. And then it would be the senior con's turn. Our Frankie, no matter how unwittingly, would repay him by persuading Gabriel that Blade wasn't that bad a person, after all. He'd soon have Jimmy G eating out of his hand. Clever bastard!

Time dragged by for Frank Cheswick and although he never really learned to completely control his frustration, he managed to act like a normal member of the prison community for most of the time. What little optimism he had was supported by the messages he received virtually every other day. At first he was surprised at the efficient undercover methods used by Blade's selected few, in getting the small dispatches to him. Short notes found their way into his hand or pocket, usually when he least expected them: whilst pushing a trolley filled with laundry from one wing to another; or underneath the door of his cell, whilst he was napping during the lunch interval; pushed into his mouth during a shower. They were like a jigsaw puzzle. An instruction written on each tiny piece of paper which was also numbered in sequence, for him to follow easily. Once he'd received the full set of instructions, he would know it was time. His time. And it wouldn't be long now. He could sense there was a light at the end of his own personal tunnel. The plan which had only been formulated in Blade's mind to accommodate one thing, revenge for Cheswick, was nearing its conclusion.

He knew there was only one more final message to be delivered and that was delivered by Blade himself, placed in

Cheswick's back pocket, whilst completing his morning's ablutions in the washroom.

It read:

AND THEN GET DRESSED AND RETURN TO YOUR CELL.
DO NOTHING ELSE.

By itself it meant nothing. But to Frank it was the final curtain. And now the scene was set. The opportunity he'd been waiting for. Every detail had been carefully considered and worked out and now everything was ready.

Another two days went by without any further contact. His big chance, all that he now lived for was just around the corner. He knew from the communications that it would probably come during one of the lunch-time breaks. He'd done his part so far and remembered to the letter every instruction that he would have to follow. The pieces of paper had long been disposed of at the direction of Blade and now all he had to do was wait. And that was the hard bit. His stomach started to churn over. Sleep had long abandoned him, and now he was aware that things were starting to move in his favour, quivers of excitement shot through his body as his nerve ends fell out with each other. But his hatred towards Ryan couldn't increase any more and he started to count the minutes as each day passed.

The normal routine was for every prisoner to be locked in his cell at 12.30 p.m. daily. Those screws who lived close to the prison perimeter would walk home for lunch whilst the few remaining, would have theirs in the officer's mess-room before returning to duty one hour later. Only a skeleton crew, usually four, would remain in the central office of the prison, each responsible for one of the four wings. One additional officer would stay in the library and a sixth officer in the security block, which was situated on the ground floor of C Wing. It was there that Tony Ryan, that dirty bastard who'd kidnapped and raped Cheswick's innocent child, could be found.

He lay on his bed, opening his mind once again to the nightmares that had been tearing him apart for so long. He thought of the filth whose twisted and violent lust had wrecked two lives; sitting in his cell, a couple of floors below him, probably gloating over his past crimes and grinning at the lousy system which had virtually patted him on the back for the pain and heartache he'd caused. Comfortable and well protected, he'd be dreaming of the day he would be released when he would be free to spread his evil shit once again. It hurt Cheswick more to think of how Ryan would have now wrapped the prison welfare officers around his little finger, telling them it hadn't really been his fault because he too, had been sexually abused as a child. He'd be praying to God with the prison chaplain asking for forgiveness. Blade had told him earlier that Ryan had a job cleaning the chapel and was now the chaplain's favourite little lamb. He wondered how many other children this specimen had attacked and more importantly, how many more he would come into contact with after his release, which wasn't that far away.

Suddenly, he heard faint footsteps getting louder as they approached his cell. Could this be it? The moment he'd been longing for? He moved his hands from behind his head and sat up, steadying himself on the edge of the bed. The footsteps stopped directly outside his door. Then he listened to the cover on the spyhole, being moved to one side. He looked up. A human eye peered at him, before the spyhole was covered up, once again. This surely was his time. The outside bolt slowly and quietly slid across and a key entered the door lock. One click and the door opened, just a few inches. He stared momentarily, frozen for that moment, as if waiting for an invitation to leave his cell, but nothing happened. The footsteps walked away and disappeared along the landing.

Cheswick looked at his watch. Twelve-fifty. Forty minutes left. At first he just sat there, frozen to the spot, the clock ticking away. Seconds, minutes were being lost. He still just sat there, staring at the open cell door. There was something wrong. He had the motivation. He had the bottle. But his understanding of the situation was the problem. What was wrong? he asked himself. Motivation: plentiful. Bottle: overflowing. Understanding: a little cloudy. His legs wouldn't move. He pressed both palms down hard on the bed. But he couldn't move. More time elapsed. All the planning. All the bad thoughts. Five years inside, for what? For this one moment. This one opportunity. But now, he was scared bloody stiff. He sighed a deep breath and lowered his head towards the floor. This was his time, he kept repeating to himself. Get yer bastard arse off this bed and go and fix that scum who raped your child.

Cheswick moved. His legs kicked out. He stood up thank Christ, and slowly walked out of the cell onto the landing, as if watching himself from a long distance away. It was as though he could see himself in some sort of dream world, sleep walking, in a place far beyond. He was on the very brink of insanity. He looked up and down, not knowing really what he was looking for. Blade's instructions must now come into play. Sweat trickled down his face and body. Think hard and concentrate on the job ahead.

There was the faint sound of radios playing in some of the other prisoners' cells and he began the long, silent walk down to the far end of the landing. His knees were trembling. He encountered each step of the metal spiral staircase, amazed he wasn't falling down them. He had to grip the side-rail with both hands.

He reached the floor below. The first floor landing. Halfway there. His knees felt weak. More sounds. Voices, coming from the wing office. The door was ajar. Christ Almighty, if anyone walked out of there now. The screws were eating and playing cards. So far, so good. He had to stand there for a few seconds, filling his lungs with air, calming himself and above all, concentrating. Pools of sweat were now forming inside his eye sockets and he wiped them with the back of his sleeve. Another flight of stairs. Jesus, if anybody saw him now. The ground floor. He had reached C Wing, his first objective and his knees felt even weaker, ready to buckle.

Now Cheswick's mind and body were in automatic. He heard a thump and nearly shit himself. He stopped, the flow of sweat increasing down his pale forehead. It had come from upstairs – probably one of the screws dropping something. He must carry on, as in Blade's carefully thought-out instructions. He saw the table with four chairs around it. He walked across, smelling his own body odour coming from his sodden shirt. He looked. He searched. Five seconds seemed like five days. There it was, inside the recess in the wall. He grabbed the small cloth bundle and spun around once more to confirm he was alone. Wrapped inside the cloth was a home-made knife with the usual tape encircling the wooden handle. The blade was about nine inches long, as sharp as a razor. Blade's instructions were to put the outer wrapping in a pocket. He did so.

His mind was now racing with all kinds of confusing thoughts. He felt disorientated. But this was his time. He'd planned it all those months ago. The nightmares. His son. His wife. That bastard, just a few yards away now. Oh yes. He took another deep breath. This was his time. He knew he had to remain focused, otherwise everything would have been for nothing. He gripped the knife and slowly walked over to the heavy metal door that led to the security wing.

'Okay, son, I'll get it.' The voice of a screw. Loud, almost shouting.

He nearly threw up, there and then on the spot. The inside of his stomach started to push upwards. He had to get control of himself, quickly. He turned to his right and saw the back of the officer disappearing towards the kitchen area. The words were obviously intended for someone else. God, how bad can it get? he asked himself. He managed to get a grip of the convulsions inside his stomach. But now, he also had to move swiftly. That screw would return any minute but this time would be facing him.

He stopped and read the notice:

NO PERSON BEYOND THIS POINT WITHOUT THE
PERMISSION OF THE SENIOR OFFICER.

He softly knocked on the door three times and it was opened, almost immediately. His heart missed a beat and his eyes popped out like gobstoppers, as he stood face to face with another screw. This one hadn't got his back turned. He was staring straight into his eyes, as he stood there.

Thank Christ the knife was hidden inside his waistband. He tried to quickly think of something to say. Why he was there? Why wasn't he locked up in his cell like the rest of the prison population? He was deflated. To come all this way and now, all seemed lost. At first, the screw said nothing. He just beckoned him inside. The door was closed behind him and the screw quietly whispered in his ear, 'You know the score, son?'

Cheswick nervously nodded, still on another planet, trying not to fill his pants. The officer pointed towards a small room that was situated next to the shower block and Cheswick softly and nervously walked across to it. The only piece of furniture inside the room was a small table. Blade's instructions came into play again. He quickly stripped off his clothes and trainers, at the same time looking into the shower area. No one there. He was alone. He placed his clothes in a neat pile on top of the table and stood behind the partially opened door. Mr Revenge then waited, knife in hand, like an eagle waiting to swoop on its prey.

The prison officer walked along the small landing, which had about ten cells on each side and stopped outside one situated about halfway up. The card on the door read: Anthony Richard Ryan. 3 years. Rule 43.

The door was unlocked and opened with a slight push.

'Okay, Ryan, shower.'

The prisoner jumped up from his bed, obviously surprised. 'We usually have a shower after tea, sir.' Very courteous.

The officer looked harshly at the prisoner, who stood about six foot. He was a 48-year-old, quite well-built with a large gap in his upper front row of teeth where two had been removed by another prisoner, shortly after his arrival at Long Lartin. He was looking a lot cleaner than he was on the day of the visit to his flat by Priestley's men. The officer was aware that Ryan had submitted a compensation claim against the prison authorities, for failing to afford him sufficient protection whilst he was in lawful custody. It was possible he would receive a few hundred pounds for his injury, but not if this particular screw could help it. The prison officer's steely eyes made Ryan nervous. He hadn't seen this screw before. He wasn't one of the usual team who looked after him and the other misfits.

'Go and get a towel and get a shower.' The command was clear and it was obvious to Ryan that this particular officer wasn't the type to piss about with. There was no doubt in Ryan's mind the slightest hesitation or failure to obey would result in a good kicking. There was no other option for him but to agree, 'Yes sir,' and follow the screw to the wing office where he was given a towel. He then walked alone, across the landing and into the shower room.

There were four showers in the communal block and a number of chairs placed against one of the walls. Ryan stripped off his clothes and threw them onto a chair. He hummed a tune to himself, another habit of a lifetime, as he turned on the circular tap. Within seconds he was soaping himself under the hot water that poured down from the ceiling with some force. Steam began to form an envelope around his naked body and Cheswick gripped the knife tightly.

He waited. And waited some more. This was his time. All the pain. All the grieving. All the fucking trouble because of this bastard. He would wait no longer and started to move his own naked body, like a midnight prowler, towards his selected victim. If his knees were still trembling he couldn't feel them. He couldn't feel anything and he seemed to glide across the tiled floor.

The man in the shower had his back to him. Cheswick was stealthily closing in on him by the second. Ryan's bare back was drawing closer and larger through the whirling, rising steam. Suddenly, the humming stopped and Ryan half turned, sensing Cheswick's presence. He was struck a severe blow to the side of his neck. The blade had entered just behind Ryan's ear in a downward movement, cutting the carotid artery. Ryan gasped and swung his body round, staring into Cheswick's eyes, his mouth wide open. But before he could make any sound, he was struck between his legs. His knees buckled and he groaned. His body became limp and he started to crumble. Anger and terror both poured from Cheswick and he grabbed the wounded man's hair as he fell onto the white tiles. This was the point at which the assailant crossed over the boundary line that divided sanity from madness. His mind was falling deeper into the dark abyss.

He would have seen the first gush of blood spurt out from Ryan's neck wound as he quickly extracted the knife, but it wouldn't have registered. Cheswick's mind had long left his body. He frantically tugged at the hair, wanting to scream at the bastard who was now under his control. He viciously pulled Ryan's head up and stared down into his eyes.

'You filthy bastard. This is for my son, David Cheswick. And all the other kids whose lives you've ruined. You filthy bastard. Go to hell Ryan. Where you belong.'

He struck the pervert underneath his chin, driving the blade upwards into his mouth, through the back of his tongue and into the base of his brain. Ryan's eyes rolled and his body shuddered. There was a gurgling sound from his throat and Cheswick released him, watching the lifeless body fall back to the floor, cascading water dispersing the blood as it now poured in torrents from the fatal wounds.

Cheswick tried to pull the knife out, but the blade snapped at the butt leaving part of it still inside Ryan's head. He moved out of the shower and stood motionless, looking down at the dead man. The one who had caused such damned misery for himself and his family. A sudden feeling of immense relief coupled with exhaustion overcame him and what strength was left in his legs seemed to evaporate. He'd achieved what he had set out to do and yes he *could* feel some elation. He'd taken his revenge and could now appreciate everything that had been done for him, as his strength slowly started to return. His mind was racing back to normality. Inside his very being, he could feel a level of contentment he hadn't enjoyed since his son's ordeal. Like a spaceship returning to Earth, he was now fully back in the land of the living.

He realised he hadn't much time. Speed was essential. He stepped beneath the next door shower and washed both himself and the knife handle. Had he left his prints on the blade lodged inside Ryan's brain? If he had, would they be found? It mattered not. Too late now. Remembering Blade's instructions, he threw the handle onto the floor and stepped out. Before leaving, Cheswick turned and stole one last look at the result of his work. He felt no guilt. He walked back into the side room and dried off before getting dressed.

The same prison officer joined him. 'Okay, son?' He seemed pretty bloody calm for a screw, considering what he'd just allowed to take place. Cheswick's teeth were chattering. Strangely though, he hadn't felt nervous at all when attacking Ryan but now couldn't stop shaking. 'I've left part of the blade in him.'

'Don't worry, son. Where's the rest of it?'

'In the shower next door.' Just uttering those few words was an ordeal for him.

'Okay, son,' the screw looked at his watch. 'Now get back to your cell. You've got ten minutes.'

Cheswick nodded and followed the officer back to the exit door. The screw stepped outside first and then beckoned him out. There were no more verbal exchanges between them.

Mission accomplished. He was back in his cell and closed the door behind him. The lock automatically shot back on and he collapsed in a heap on the bed. The footsteps returned and he saw the eye peering at him through the spyhole. The outside bolt was then replaced and the footsteps disappeared. He lay on his back, still shaking and closed his eyes. He didn't want to return to work and wondered how long it would be before the hue and cry started. It was over. He felt at peace with himself and the rest of the world. He didn't give a damn about what would happen to him now.

Ron Birch was the senior prison officer in charge of the security wing for that day and he stood in the shower block, just staring for a moment, observing the scene before him. He left and returned to Ryan's empty cell where he unlocked it and left the door open. He then quietly walked along the landing to another cell door, which was secured: Clifford Mott. 10 years. Rule 43.

He could see through the spyhole that Mott was asleep on his bed. He was a little man, powerfully built with fair hair and a matching moustache and short beard. Mott had numerous convictions for buggery and sexual abuse against children and in recent months had befriended Ryan. Another lowlife the state had to care for.

'Right, Mott, shower.' Birch's voice bellowed and the prisoner awoke, startled.

Once Mott had taken possession of a towel, he walked across to the shower block. His terrified eyes rested on the exact scene Birch had walked away from, only seconds before. He gasped at the sight of Ryan lying there, the shower still running over his dead body. Mott turned to scream for help and raise the alarm. Before his first retreating step, Ron Birch's heavy riot stick crashed down on top of his head. Mott fell backwards, naked and unconscious. Birch picked up the handle of the knife left behind by Cheswick and placed it into the right hand of Mott. He stepped back and gave everything his final consideration. He mentally reviewed every part of the role he'd agreed to play and then, fully satisfied, turned and calmly pressed the panic alarm on the wall three times. That was the signal to communicate to the rest of the prison, an officer needed assistance urgently. It took only seconds for other officers to join him. They found Birch standing over the two bodies of Mott and Ryan.

Ron Birch later made a statement to murder squad detectives, explaining how he'd caught Mott pulling the bladeless knife from the wound beneath Ryan's chin. He had no option but to subdue the prisoner with his riot stick and then summon assistance. The fact that Birch had an eleven-year-old son who had been previously raped by a child sex attacker never came to light.

Clifford Mott was charged and later convicted of the murder of Tony Ryan.

It was only a few weeks after Mott received a life sentence that Cheswick, the model prisoner, heard the result of his appeal against sentence. Reduced from five to two years, the trial judge having failed to fully take into consideration the extent of the appellant's co-operation at the time of his arrest, and the fact that he'd chosen to take the fast track through the judicial process that had followed. It was a course of action that had saved thousands from the public purse. He was a free man. In his mind the tables had been turned. Justice had been done.

'You're something special, you know that, Blade.' Whether Gabriel was being complimentary or otherwise, Blade wasn't sure and just stared at him.

'Cheswick. I don't know how you managed that, but you made him a very happy man.' He *was* being complimentary.

'As long as it stops him picking his nose in bed,' was a typical reply from Blade when embarrassed by someone bestowing praise upon him.

Gabriel sat on the edge of Blade's bunk and allowed a short pause to pass before continuing. 'No, you've done more than that. I've known Frank and his missus most of my life. We went to school together. What you've done is give him back his life.'

Blade just couldn't handle any thought of him being some kind of hero and his face reddened. In normal circumstances he'd have spat on the floor and walked out. But Gabriel's words encouraged him. He knew that George Riddell's former right-hand man was beginning to accept him, and that was the reason why he'd agreed to go back inside the nick in the first place. Together of course with the recompense already bunged him.

Frank Cheswick left the top security prison, knowing in his mind everything he wanted to achieve had been accomplished. He knew nothing of the real reasons why so much support had been given to him and if he had, it probably wouldn't have made much difference to the way he felt that day – the day he would be returned to his family. What he wouldn't forget was his recognition that he would be forever in Steve Blade's debt. Perhaps there were a few good 'uns in the nick, after all.

When he met Blade in the reception area for the last time, all the pain had gone. The anger and torment had long disappeared from his system, together with Ryan's lifeless body.

He shook Blade by the hand, 'I could never thank – '

Blade grabbed his shoulder and interrupted him, 'Frank, I can't say its been a real pleasure because in fact, you've been a right pain in the arse, my son,'

They both smiled at each other.

'But good luck and remember us all to that missus and kid of yours.'

Cheswick tearfully nodded and walked away towards his freedom.

Blade watched from the prison library, as his friend walked through the prison gates. He saw a plain-looking woman, standing with her arm around a young boy. They both embraced Frank Cheswick and all three wept openly, outside the prison gates. The man turned and looked upwards towards Blade's face and waved his last farewell. Blade held a forefinger up to his mouth and shook his head, slowly. A small solitary tear rolled down from his eye as he turned away from the window, to return to his own way of life as a convicted con with a mission.

✳

chapter six

At least the scenery was as beautiful as ever. Most of the trees that usually formed an archway above the long winding drive had lost their leaves, but were still embellished by the winter mists clinging to the bare branches like ornamental shrouds of white satin. Priestley wasn't really aware of the slight smile on his face and the glint in his eyes. He felt good to be alive, as though it was a bright frosty morning without a cloud visible in the sky. He remembered an old Supergrass he'd become involved with many years before, telling him about the effects of snorting cocaine.

'Your mind becomes alive to everything around you. Like on a winter's morning when the sky is blue above and the frost grips your face.'

'But what about the brain cells you manage to kill off and the enlarged nostrils?'

The villain had just laughed at him, 'Well, I've got a few of them to spare, son.'

*

But it wasn't a frosty morning and the weather wasn't as bright as all that. In fact there wasn't a patch of blue sky anywhere to be found. So why did he feel so good? Perhaps it was more to do with the person he was hoping to see at the club. Then he remembered his ex-wife. The beautiful and wonderful Brenda, whose big saucer-like blue eyes could capture any poor soul's heart. One in particular – the man she'd run off with.

There were some good times in the earlier days when they used to visit the club on a regular basis. He remembered the friends they met and socialised with as a couple; the stories they'd shared; the jokes and laughter that used to accompany them, no matter whose company they were in. And then came the arguments and fights which eventually led to the break-up. He still felt a little incomplete and hollow inside, a failure for not having been able to save what he'd always regarded as the most sacred thing in his life: his marriage.

As he slowly drove out of the final bend, the large mansion house appeared in front of him with its square-shaped car park occupied by the usual Mercs and BMWs dotted across its gravel surface. Bloody marvellous, thought Jack, as he walked across towards the side entrance of the club. They're all bloody German and expensive, obviously belonging to committee members attending for the usual lunchtime discussions and debates. No other member would be there as late in the year.

The interior hadn't altered much either. Still the same old dark corridors with their oak-panelled walls and framed pictures of past captains and champions, individually illuminated by overhanging brass strip lights. The dark blue carpet that always seemed to go well with the fusty smell that was restricted to the corridors leading to the various function and committee rooms. He did notice they'd changed the carpet. It used to be red, or so he recalled. Priestley hadn't visited the place for at least five years. But what was that compared to the period in which this particular building had been standing there, he thought, as he admired its Victorian architecture.

There'd been some changes to the lounge though. Where there had once been a multitude of pictures, now stood an impressive wall of glass allowing an unrestricted view of the links. There was modern furniture in a setting far brighter than Priestley remembered, with the old chandeliers having been replaced by uplights. But there was one thing that hadn't changed: the five or six committee members protecting the far corner of the bar, as though it represented that small piece of England somewhere in a foreign land. Yes, he thought, that was one cultural habit that would never be changed.

He nodded to the small group and waited to order a drink from the barman with the white shirt and bow tie. He remembered how he used to wonder at the vast amount of time some individuals would spend there, frightened to go home in case they missed something or found themselves voted out before they had chance to return.

'Well, I don't believe it.'

It hadn't taken long for his presence to be acknowledged.

'Jack Priestley. Well done.'

He wondered what it was he was supposed to have done well, and then remembered. It was the usual way in which Colin Grey used to greet everybody.

'It's been years,' suggested the boisterous treasurer or perhaps he was even chairman now. 'Thought your ticket had expired old man.'

Priestley hated being called an old man. But he was there for a purpose and not to rock the boat. He was thankful he'd kept his membership up although he was now more of a country member, not having participated in the club's social activities for as long as he could remember, certainly well before his divorce.

'Just passing, Colin.'

The handshake was strong, another small factor that had inadvertently slipped his mind. Too late now, thought Jack. His little donnie felt as though it had just been squeezed in a vice.

'Thought I'd look in and see what was happening.'

'Well, it's good to see you, Jack. Drink?' Apart from the well-established and now ageing moustache, nothing much had changed about Grey's appearance. He was as loud as ever and his portly figure had become more portly. In fact his handshake matched his build which was more like that of a retired colonel whose experiences went well back to the Somme. He was a man who'd obviously enjoyed life given the size of his belly. Both men sat down and Priestley had some initial difficulty in conversing. Most of the issues discussed were golf-related and since he hadn't held a club for five years, he was a little out of touch.

But Grey wasn't the kind of man who would let down anybody wishing to enter into a prolonged conversation, no matter what the subject. 'Bloody this and bloody that...' Still the same old complaints about the disastrous way in which the club was being run. 'They couldn't manage a piss-up in a brewery, Jack,' he bellowed, so that the group of statues in the far corner couldn't help but overhear.

Obviously he's not the chairman after all, thought Jack. Neither would he be the treasurer any longer, or even an ordinary member of that bloody historic committee they had, organising the club's affairs.

And of course, Grey couldn't resist the opportunity to name a list of committee members, the majority of whom, according to him, should have been sacked after they'd reached their eightieth birthdays.

'They go on longer than bloody judges here, Jack,' he bellowed again, the audience in the corner glaring across the room at him. 'How is Belinda by the way?'

'Brenda,' replied Priestley.

'Yes, yes, yes, of course. Well how is she?' Grey leant over and dug his elbow into Jack's upper arm. 'Bit of a cracker, Jack, from what I remember. Still doing the nuptials are yer lad?'

'Divorced,' he explained.

'What!'

'Divorced. We were divorced a couple of years ago. Haven't seen her since. Still smoking the cigars, Colin?' Priestley couldn't remember whether or not this gent smoked cigars, but still offered his packet of Hamlet.

Colin declined and changed the subject back to the inadequacies of the committee, interspersed with stories of over seventy women he'd been with since he last saw Jack. Priestley just sat and listened, not being tempted into entering Grey's private war. If he found it so disagreeable, thought the DCI, why doesn't he just go and find somewhere else to lurk about in? But he didn't have to wait long for the real reason he was there to appear.

'Here's one for you, Jack,' suggested Colin, looking across at the glass-panelled door.

Priestley looked too and there she was. The light of his life, looking as radiant as ever. He did hope that one day she'd become a judge. And he'd benefit.

She glided across the rich carpet towards the bar, more like a world-famous ballerina than a practising lawyer, wishing everyone a good afternoon in that usual, sexy, resounding voice, extremely effective in a large courtroom.

Her bright red silk blouse stood out from her black trouser suit like red-hot coals in a night-watchman's scuttle.

In Jack Priestley's eyes, Sonia Hall was as devastatingly attractive as ever and he almost forgot why he was there, thinking only of trying to get back into her bed. She saw him, smiled and then turned her back to address the bow tie who was standing there admiring her beauty, making a shiny wine glass shinier, and smiling in a way that was very different from the facial expression he had when serving Priestley earlier. Jack felt no embarrassment at just standing and leaving Colin Grey in mid-sentence. He knew a pretty woman would be the only reason the man would accept for another male to want to leave his company. He carried his drink to the bar and sat on a stool next to his former lover.

'Good God, how did you know I'd be here?' she asked, looking a little astounded and wrapping her well-manicured hands around the glass.

The bow tie stepped away, with an annoyed expression written all over his face. As modest as ever, thought Jack. And she obviously realised what a conceited impression she'd just given to him.

'I mean, what are you doing here?'

'Visiting you,' was the truthful reply.

She should have known that in an instant from his attire. With his dark blue suit; white shirt; tie to match the suit, aftershave by the gallon and so forth, he certainly wasn't there to knock a few balls around the course.

'But, how did you know I'd be here?' she repeated, eyes glistening, eyelids flashing rather than just blinking, like two red lights rotating outside a brothel in LA. But the vibes she was giving off appeared to be in Jack's favour. There was a 'pleased to see you,' look all over her face. Or it might have been a, 'glad you're here, now I can take the piss,' look.

He'd just have to wait and see. 'I remembered,' he said, throwing all caution to the wind with a smirk on his face. The one usually portrayed by men trying to elevate themselves into an irresistible position when wanting to have their way with a particular female.

'You remembered what?'

'That you came here every Friday lunchtime.'

That was one up for Sonia. Jack Priestley chasing her. Now, how she wished she'd been more liberal with the Chanel. But from his point of view, he had no doubt she would still be as unpredictable as ever before. And she proved him right. The look in her eye was definitely moving towards the I'm-now-going-to take-the-piss-out-of-you category.

'Why didn't you come to the flat?' she asked. 'Or better still Jack, ring me?'

'I thought it best to talk to you away from there,' he explained, shrugging his shoulders.

'Why was that, Jack?' Her words were sharp, 'Frightened you might find me with someone else if you knocked on the door?' Bingo. She was starting to motor now.

Unpredictable? Absolutely, he thought. She hadn't changed much after all. But our Jack wasn't that bothered. Compared with what it used to be, his passion for Sonia had long been subdued. Since he had had her door slammed in his face by that smarmy, fresh-faced kid in the dressing-gown she'd taken up with. A fellow member of chambers and all that. He really didn't need a reminder, but also knew she'd use it as a smack in the face for him. And she had done just that.

'Business, Sonia. I need a chat and just thought it better to see you away from the flat.' He was starting to feel a little less confident now.

'Then you should have rung, dear.'

It was time to move this conversation forward. He thought it best to get the questions dealt with as soon as possible. He knew. He sensed an explosion wasn't that far away. All the years he'd known her, except when lying on her back, she was more volatile than nitroglycerine being shaken up like a bottle of pop. Yes, he had to get in now. She would soon turn and run away.

But before he could start his interrogation, she helped him. 'So, what business is it you want to discuss, darling?'

Her attitude was becoming more outwardly hostile and that puzzled him. He still felt something for her, even though it was less than before, or so he wanted to believe. What he would never accept, couldn't accept, was that he loved her.

'I know this is sensitive.' It always was when he was about to ask her to breach a confidence with a client. 'So please don't take this the wrong way.' Now he was grovelling, but he felt the need to, 'I need some information about George Riddell and I understand you're representing him.'

She didn't explode which was the first good sign. In fact she just looked at him, calm and relaxed, with that Mona Lisa smile she had so often used in the past when trying to tease him. And then she winked an eye, before glancing over his shoulder and making a suggestion that almost floored him. 'Then why don't you ask him yourself, darling? He's just walked in. I'm meeting him here.'

Priestley's head swung round as fast as that girl on the bed in *The Exorcist* and there before his eyes was the man himself, heading straight towards him. George Riddell? A member of Jack's golf club? He could never accept that. Riddell stopped and nodded towards his lawyer, before his eyes met Priestley's.

'George, well done. Right on time,' congratulated Sonia looking at her watch. 'I'm not sure if you've met Jack Priestley.'

Here it comes, thought Jack.

'He's a Detective Chief Inspector on the Regional Crime Squad.'

Thank you, Sonia. You piece of shit.

'Or is it the National Crime Squad now, Jack?' she asked.

He replied with a smile and a look sufficient to open up the heavens. Riddell didn't speak. His face remained expressionless, as though still adapting to the warm air, having walked ten miles across snow-covered fields. He nodded and allowed Sonia to lead him by the arm towards the farthest and darkest corner of the room, well away from the wall of glass. She waved at the bow tie to follow, as she asked Riddell what it was he preferred.

Priestley turned and walked out, knowing he'd done the right thing: kept his mouth shut. He hoped the next time he met George Riddell he would be inside the nick.

Well that little meeting had been a disaster. Following his rapid exit from the golf club and the picture of Sonia's superior expression still painted on his mind, Priestley decided to visit more familiar surroundings. He'd easily fallen for a knockout punch and couldn't help but feel a right prick. Like a schoolboy who'd just been slung out of the bigger boy's classroom. Whatever slight feelings he had towards the lady barrister had now totally disappeared. Or at least he tried to convince himself they had. Mind you, he argued with himself, she couldn't have set him up. She didn't know he'd be there. The meeting between her and

George Riddell had been pre-arranged. But she'd still taken advantage of the situation to take the piss out of him, and that one had caught him under the belt. No, she hadn't changed. There'd be no more games with Sonia. He was finished with her. Perhaps.

He hadn't been able to confront Riddell, obviously. He couldn't. He wasn't ready yet to disclose his hand. He needed a bite at one of Riddell's fight promotions. A bird in the hand, and all that rubbish. No, he would have only frightened him off. He just hoped Sonia Hall hadn't let the cat out of the bag following his hastened departure, by telling her client that Jack had been asking questions about him. He doubted it. She was a tease alright, but not a fool. Patience was a virtue and his time would come soon enough. By the time he'd returned to the city centre, darkness was rapidly devouring what little daylight was left. Within the next few minutes it would be completely dark with only the street lights to illuminate the showers of hail and sleet now starting to fall.

The small backstreet-market public house was as packed as usual, mostly with barrow boys and other traders. But Jack noticed how unusually quiet it seemed. And then of course there was that manifestation in the corner. A part of the furniture with legs and arms attached. Each occasional movement occurring like a major incident and comprising only of an effort to raise the pint glass off the bar, drink some of its contents, and replace. There was one good thing about Jacky Benton as far as Priestley was concerned. He always knew where to find him.

The policeman ordered his drink and stood next to Benton, staring straight ahead, examining the optics on the back wall. He wondered whether or not they'd stand scrutiny from the customs men. The old man remained slumped on his stool, his only welcome being a loud rush of air from his gullet, escaping out through his mouth. Priestley didn't take offence. He knew it wasn't personal.

Benton slowly raised his head sideways, looked at Priestley once and then returned to his favourite pastime of gazing and guzzling.

'George Riddell, Jacky?' Priestley spoke softly but his question was ignored.

'Forty years, son. Forty years.' Another short belch. It was obvious Benton was very drunk and at first Priestley thought, extremely deaf.

'I don't want his age, Jacky,' the copper explained in a sarcastic tone of voice, 'I want his background.' He turned and looked towards his snout who was quietly crying to himself.

He returned Priestley's stare and then tears streamed down his face, but without the slightest of convulsions. That told Priestley, his old friend had been distressed for some time, most of the tears having already been used up.

'We've been wed for forty years, son,' explained old Jacky.

The younger man suddenly felt terribly guilty. What an insensitive, thoughtless, dickhead! Jacky was grieving and Priestley had just galloped straight into the middle of a private wake.

'She's gone, son.' Benton was hoarse and having difficulty in speaking. But it was obvious he needed to talk, even if for a few seconds. 'Cancer, Jack. Bastard cancer. Took her this morning.'

Priestley felt his own throat starting to swell and he placed his arm around the old man's shoulder. 'I'm sorry, mate. I didn't know.' Consoling words that were sincere and well meant.

Benton returned to his drink and just waved an arm in the air. 'No matter, Jacky boy. No matter.'

Priestley gave him a mild hug, 'Another time, old feller,' and reached in his pocket for the usual tenner, although he wondered whether such a paltry sum would be an insult to the man at such a moment. Benton just nodded and waved his other arm in the direction of an obvious acquaintance who'd just placed a large brandy in front of him. 'No, Jack. Stay put, son.' He stretched himself upwards and breathed a long heavy sigh. 'You're into big news there, Jacky boy.'

As though trying, with some difficulty, to return himself into the land of the living, he straightened and then stumbled off the stool. Priestley assisted and the old man returned to his original position, mumbling something about, 'Life must go on…'

'I'll come back,' suggested the copper.

But Benton was having none of it. It was the first time he'd had any kind of conversation for the last four hours or so. Except with himself. 'Sit down, Jack,' he slurred, 'and behave yerself.'

He took time out for another gulp before continuing. 'Now, Georgie Riddell? I'll tell you about George Riddell, Mr Priestley. Bastard extraordinaire.' Jacky's demeanour was picking up, starting to return to some kind of normality, whatever that was. 'A real crock of shit.' That was normality for Benton.

'You know him?' Stupid question. Course he knew him. The old man knew everybody. That was why Priestley was visiting him.

And of course, the question was correctly ignored as though it had never been asked. 'Had the same kind of upbringing as me and thee, lad.' The old man paused, 'But never wanted for anything. Mother was a brass. Father? Never knew him. Pissed off when he was born.'

The speech was being made in shorthand but the points were easily being picked up by the listener.

'Big notch now. In the steel business. But a bastard, Jack. Only those who don't know him, deal with him. Not very popular. One day your blokes'll find him in the cut with his brains missing.' Benton was now well on the way to recovery. The tears were drying up and his voice was getting stronger.

Priestley needed to ask his questions now, before the old man had a relapse and the doors to his mind closed shut again. 'I've heard he's in the fight game?'

Benton smirked, 'Every Saturday night. Down Saltley. On the estate. Bloke makes a packet.'

He suddenly turned to scold two young barrow boys who were about to start some communal singing. 'There'll be no claptrap in here tonight,' he shouted and was supported by the local gorilla, whose upper arms were thicker than Priestley's thighs and heavily tattooed with some story about a shipwreck. The two innocents were quickly cautioned but allowed to stay in the corner of the room where they sat, provided they kept their gobs shut.

Benton turned his attention back to Priestley. 'No respect, young 'uns. My missus will be respected tonight, Jacky boy.'

Priestley just nodded and waited for more information, like the student waiting for the lecture to finish.

'Get your arse down there any Saturday night and he'll be there, taking the bets. Been to one or two meself.'

'Much armour with him, Jacky?'

'One or two. He boasts about three or four monkeys, but he's just lost his main minder, Gabriel. Jimmy Gabriel. Got stuffed bringing a boat over from France or something like that.' His reddened eyes looked up again, 'Drew a score, Jack. Lot of bird.'

There was another pause and that was for Priestley's benefit, who quickly cottoned on and ordered two more drinks.

'I'll tell you what, son,' the old man continued, 'he's got Pete Owen performing this Saturday night.'

Priestley looked inquisitive.

'Peter Owen. Wanker from Wolverhampton. Strong wanker though. S'pose to have knocked out twenty-five blokes. If I'd have been younger, Jack,' Benton tried to slam his fist on the bar counter but missed, 'I'd have seen him off.'

'One at a time I hope,' said Priestley, forgetting that this wasn't the time for humour.

Benton took a long pull of his drink and the tears returned. Question time was over.

Priestley stood to make his second early exit and to leave his old friend to grieve alone once more. The old man was in good company, thought Jack. Years of working the market had brought him many friends and oceans of respect. No harm would come to him and Priestley nodded at Mr Tattoo as he walked out, who winked his eye in reply. They both knew the question and answer without having to speak. Yes, Jacky Benton would be alright, but in a day or two perhaps.

*

chapter seven

Steve Blade had made good use of Frank Cheswick's relationship with Gabriel. The support given to Jimmy G's old school mate had been sufficient to land Gabriel's appreciation of a job well done. And now Cheswick had been released, Blade was the only ally left for him to rely on. Not that he needed company that much. He'd just got used to talking to another human being and during the previous few months had developed a bond of trust with his new-found friend, Stevie boy. But the armed robber, supposedly now turned drugs baron, had always been the careful type when it came to dealing with scum like Gabriel. At first he remained wary, not wanting to show too much interest in the ex-jockey's past life, particularly the bit that involved Riddell.

The other problem of course, was that Gabriel was still the most despised con in the prison system. But Blade could handle that. His flamboyant character, supported by the willingness to chin anybody who gave him too much lip, tended to help him. Just a bit.

'Give us a couple of those sausages, Harry,' begged Blade, holding out his hand. Having missed his breakfast he'd decided to deviate from his route between the laundry and backyard and grab a few leftovers from the kitchen, as he had done so many times before. But now he had a problem. Harry, the six-foot-two cook ignored him.

'Harry? The bangers?'

The big man dropped the knife which he'd been using to cut some onions and turned to face Blade, 'You ain't getting nothing from here, from now on.'

Blade smiled and repeated, 'Harry? The bangers?'

'We've had a meeting,' said Harry, now concentrating on the cutting and slicing board.

'And?' asked Blade.

'We've decided,' the cook explained in his cockney accent, 'you're too close to the germ,' which was the nickname allocated to Gabriel by the rest of the inmates.

'And?' asked Blade again.

Harry stopped chopping, 'That's it. We've decided you're on your own.'

Blade just tutted and grabbed a couple of sausages off the tray. Harry turned on him for a second time, only now the large cutting knife was in his hand, pointing towards Blade. 'You're not 'aving them, Bladey,' he said rather nervously.

'Oh piss off, Harry,' he said, stuffing half a sausage into his mouth.

Harry moved towards him. Blade laughed and stamped on his foot. The bigger man yelped and dropped the knife on the floor. Blade then needed to make a strong point for the benefit of the others, so grabbed the cook by the back of his neck with one hand and the arse of his blue and white checked trousers with the other. The swill bin was only a few feet away and Blade managed to force Harry's head inside. Blade then turned to the others who'd just stood watching the entertainment.

'Anybody else been to this meeting? Anybody else got a point to make?'

There was silence. There'd be no more meetings, or at least no more agreement to isolate the senior con.

Gabriel heard about the small incident in the kitchen but thought it best not to make any mention of it to Blade. But he was quietly thankful for the way in which Blade had stood his ground on his behalf. During the days that followed the encounter with Harry the cook, both men seemed to spend even more time together. They talked, discussed, debated and commented on numerous subjects, most of which were related to past incidents in their lives outside the prison. Blade had even seen a smile on the other man's face, albeit only now and again but things were picking up. At least Gabriel had a sense of humour, although it would be like searching an antique dealer's loft to find it! The exchange visits to each other's cells became more frequent, the other cons looking on in disbelief. But Blade was on a mission and didn't give a shit about how the others felt, or what they were thinking. Any of them could have the same treatment as Harry got, anytime. And they were all aware of that.

Suddenly, Gabriel's own lifestyle changed for the better. Some of the minor trivialities that had plagued him since first entering the system started to become less common. Meaningless accidents, such as finding a broken razor blade in his soap and losing his footing on some grease carefully spread across a step on the spiral staircase happened less frequently. The other inmates couldn't quite work out why Blade was showing so much interest in the prison garbage. A leopard never changes his spots and they would always regard Gabriel with dislike and suspicion. But they still respected Blade's views, in particular the way he enforced them. And that was very much to Gabriel's advantage.

But time was getting short and Blade was becoming frustrated. He was satisfied he had Gabriel's complete trust and now needed to move closer to his objective. He'd reached the point where he knew he had to push the boat out further. He'd given a lot of thought to his plan and knew it would either strengthen his relationship with Riddell's right-hand man, or create other major problems for him.

The fag break was almost over and the two of them stood staring down at the contents of a large revolving drum. Looking but not seeing, which was one of Blade's favourite sayings, they were concentrating more on what each other was saying.

'I'm out of here, Jimmy,' was a statement common to many of the residents and usually made fairly openly. But whispered from the lips of a man such as Steve Blade it would be interpreted differently. Gabriel's eyes glanced away from the spinning clothes and almost did a full circle of the immediate area in which they stood, as though ensuring no one was within listening range.

Blade had already done that before dropping the bombshell.

'Wanna come?' That was the tricky part of his plan. If Gabriel agreed, Blade would have a problem he could well do without. He was banking on a refusal and held his breath whilst the smaller man stared back into the open-topped drum, quickly considering the offer made to him. Gabriel knew an answer would have to be given there and then, at that very moment or at least within the next few seconds.

'How?' was the first question.

'Back of the laundry van.'

'When?'

'Soon.'

Gabriel just shook his head.

Blade tried hard not to show his relief. He hoped that such a show of trust in Gabriel would be reciprocated and moved quickly onto the second part of his plan, trying to make himself heard above the noise of the dryers, at the same time avoiding any unwanted sets of ears.

'Might need some help outside though. Any ideas?' It was now or never, with just one minute left before the end of the break and back to work.

'Stay clear of Georgie Riddell,' warned Gabriel.

That came as a stunning blow. He was the one Blade needed an introduction to. He needed more. 'J, I'm not likely to drop in on him with half the bloody police force looking for me.'

Gabriel turned and looked at him. 'That's what I mean. He's got one on the firm.'

Bent copper? So what? thought Blade. Who hasn't got one on the firm, these days?

The return to work whistle blew and Blade, with all the cunning of a fox, placed his hand on his man's shoulder, 'Don't worry, J, I'll be okay, mate. I've got somewhere to go. I've got a sister with some stables. I'll get in there for the first few weeks, amongst the horses. I'd rather talk to them than half the wankers in here, Jim, if it's of any interest to you.'

That did the trick. Jimmy G responded in exactly the manner Blade had hoped for. Mention horses, thought the senior con, and his legs buckle. Like mentioning Jayne Mansfield's tits to half the male population.

'Chrissie Lawrence and Marty Waltham at Cheetah Express Parcels.' Gabriel said, winking an eye as he started to walk away towards the other end of the room where his work post was. Good old Jimmy G.

That was more like it. Blade felt his heart suddenly begin to pound. That was what all this had been about, what he'd been working on for weeks. Gabriel's main contacts. Lawrence and Waltham would be the boys, and in a bloody parcels company at that. He kept repeating the names in his head until they were firmly established.

His own ordeal was almost at an end. He felt relieved, but only for a moment or so. There was a new set of circumstances for him to concern himself with. Now he'd got what they wanted would they stand by him? The promises of a return to freedom without hassle. A pardon from the Home Secretary. Steve Blade would deliver. But would *they?* Of course they would, he thought. But there again, best keep his cards held tightly to his chest. He wasn't going to part with anything until he was out of there and safely tucked up somewhere, with Jack Straw's piece of paper in his hand. After all, he hadn't really nicked a load of dope. That had been *their* idea. Pity Jack Priestley didn't know that. Dozy bastard!

✳

The vehicles rolled silently through the estate. Cars and vans without lights, freewheeling whenever possible. The heavy rain helped and Priestley anticipated another five minutes before they would go in. The convoy stopped just a few hundred yards from the target. Then he made his first and biggest mistake of the night.

'Vehicle moving away from premises. Description to follow,' came across from the static observations point.

'Leave it,' ordered Priestley. 'He might have a mobile and we don't want the others inside being warned.' A reasonable and safe assumption thought the operational commander. He was wrong.

Just another couple of minutes. The tension began to increase. Adrenaline levels started to rise. Truncheons, pickaxe handles and anything else officers could get their mitts on, were at the ready. They'd all been well briefed and everybody knew what tasks they had to perform, or so Priestley hoped.

'Victor One.' This was it. The signal to go for it. Priestley replied.

'It's a go now,' was the message.

'Affirmative,' acknowledged the DCI. 'Okay everybody, nice and quietly. Move in.' For someone who hated talking into plastic machines he hadn't done too badly, he thought.

The convoy moved again. The rain poured down. Still no lights. Only wipers clearing windscreens. First left, then a right and the warehouse came into view. There must have been well over a hundred cars, vans and other vehicles parked around the building. It must be like the last night at the Proms inside, thought Jack. Fortunately the double doors weren't locked and access would be easy. He'd already gleaned that much from his covert officer inside.

Like a black mist just visible through the lashing rain, he watched a large group of his officers run along the side of the warehouse towards the back. There was no exit there but Priestley knew from past experience that once the heat went on inside, there would be individuals capable of finding their way out of a vault at Fort Knox. He remained in his car and listened to the radio activity. He saw the remainder of the black overalls and chequered hatbands pour through the large double-fronted doors, the front car park flooded with light as they opened wide.

Then came the usual riot. Shouts, screams, groans, moans and all kind of other noises common with major disorders. Wise, thought Priestley, to stay put until the

101

mêlée was at an end and some sort of civil order had been restored, which it would be eventually.

A circle of officers remained across the front entrance to stop anybody trying to leave. As if anybody would! And Jack briefly thought of what Sonia Hall's response would be once she heard about this shindig and her recently acquired, big-time client. Not that he was doing this for her benefit. He needed to put people like Riddell out of action. They were scourges on society, people who took advantage of every opportunity to corrupt and deprave. Riddell was going to regret the day he ever heard the name Jack Priestley. And, even though their last encounter hadn't been anything more than a mere fleeting glimpse of one another, tonight Riddell's short-term future would be in his hands.

The usual lists of false names and addresses were scripted. The usual attempts to leave without being invited were made. And of course, the odd punch-up between law and dissenters, adding more inevitable variety to the operation. Within a few minutes the noise had abated and the radio commentaries reduced to a minimum. Priestley decided to join the rest of them, contented that the fifty officers he'd borrowed from the force to supplement his own detectives had been sufficient. And now the moment he'd been waiting for. He wanted to cherish the look of defeat on a beaten George Riddell's face.

As he slowly walked across the front car park, in between the parked cars, looking like a solitary figure in a cigarette advert from the sixties, not that he could have lit up in the prevailing weather, betting slips and cash were being thrown into plastic bags. Individuals argued they had a right to be there. Some denied having ever been born. Others argued they'd thought it was a dog show. But not surprisingly, the two exhausted and bloodied figures slumped on top of the straw in the centre of the warehouse, remained there, towels draped across their shoulders. Motionless, silent, and not really knowing what was going on around them, not knowing which of them had won or lost the fight.

But they weren't alone in their confused state. Even Jack Priestley was about to become somewhat bewildered. The news greeted him like a .38 entering his skull. Mr Smart-arse had made a complete balls-up of it! The bird had flown. No George Riddell. The car he'd let go through the net had obviously been Georgie boy's early retreat. Lucky bastard! Damned lucky bastard!

He quickly turned to Barton. 'Go get him from home, Chris, and turn his place over. I want everything. Books, diaries, posters, whatever you find.'

'No warrant, boss,' explained the Detective Inspector, shrugging his shoulders, somewhat mystified at his gaffer's obvious desire to make this one personal.

Normally, if a villain had put one over the law they'd just let it go. There would be another time. Always was.

'You won't need one, Chris. Because you're going to arrest him under PACE.' There was a pause and Priestley immediately knew what was going through Barton's mind. 'For illegal betting, Chris.'

That satisfied the younger officer and he grabbed two other detectives, still feeling perplexed but they obeyed orders and disappeared into the dark wet night outside. How could such a highly professional and experienced superhero make such a cock-up? He couldn't believe his own inadequacy. Tosspot! This was one he wouldn't live down for a while. It hurt him more than the Stratford-upon-Avon cock-up.

*

Blade's mind was becoming full of flashing light bulbs. His agitation had already left the forces of gravity and he was floating around like a lost little sheep. The phone call had gone in two days earlier, but there was still no contact. Where was Big Bristols or any of the other cowboys who were supposed to ride into town now and shoot up the sheriff, getting him out of jail at the same time? He sat on his bed trying to remain calm, trying to convince himself that he couldn't afford to show out. They'd only have to sniff a slight change in character to assume he was planning a home visit. And that would mean a month in the block, just in case.

He'd spoken to one of those answering machines when he'd phoned. Perhaps they hadn't got the message? But there again, they told him that's what it would be. All he had to do was ring the number when he was fit and ready. Well now he was fit and ready, so where the pissing hell were they?

'Blade, visitor.'

It was music to the ears. At last, his ticket out had arrived. He wondered what she would be wearing today.

'Hello, darling.' Like McArthur in the Philippines, she'd returned. The darling of the secret service, bright red trouser suit with all the trimmings. And that perfume. My God, things were looking up! Nothing like being a little outrageous, thought the con. But he was glad to see her again, even though the reasons were different from the first time she'd visited him. This signalled his release from what was now becoming an unnecessary chore. He was now becoming desperate to get back to Sammy and his life. Gabriel had bared his soul and Blade was ready to share the knowledge. But not in the nick. He wanted that pardon first and on the outside, as they had promised.

'So, how are you, Steve?' She asked, looking very tasty but also very business-like. 'Ready for the next stage?'

'Ready and able. Just give the word.' He hadn't wanted that to sound as though he just wanted to give her one. It had been a natural comment to make. And the way in which his eyes seemed to be transfixed on her breasts, it wouldn't really help any accurate interpretation of his meaning.

'Nothing more to be done here, then?'

What she was really saying he thought was, You'd better have everything you should have or you might find yourself back in the slammer.

'It's time to go,' he insisted. 'Bags are already packed.'

If Big Bristols had shown the slightest sign of doubt about what he was suggesting he'd have taken her hostage. For an innocent man he'd been in there long enough. He'd well earned his first ten grand. But his fears were quickly allayed by the positive nod of her head. 'Be ready in the morning and just do as you're told, darling.'

He had a million questions but thought it best to remain silent and behave more like an obedient school child. After all, he was in *their* hands now.

✳

'I didn't know you had it in you, Bladey,' explained Tom Scart, who was one of the nicer screws in that particular nick.

Blade just looked bewildered.

'National Crime Squad, mate. They're here with a warrant to take you on an awayday.'

The con still looked confused.

'They reckon you've agreed to show them some of the past jobs you've pulled.'

Scart was smirking.

Bastards, thought Blade. Everybody in the nick would now think he'd gone turtle. Grassed up. Decided to help the Old Bill clear their books. He was tempted to say, 'bollocks', but then knew if he did that would be the end of route one. His ticket out. Reluctantly but convincingly, he nodded his head and reached for his prison issue coat. Scart just kept shaking his head, like a pendulum unable to stop until midnight struck. 'Never thought I'd see the day. With you, Bladey, anyway. The times, they are a-changing, matey.' That was one of *his* favourite sayings.

Big, thick, sloppy git, thought the con.

'Who's the filth?' asked Blade, thinking he should show some interest in the boys who were supposed to be taking him for a day out at the seaside.

'Told you, crime squad. If you mean, who's the senior nark with them,' the screw paused to glance at the papers in his hand, 'a Detective Chief Inspector Priestley.'

Blade felt his knees give way and gasped what might just as well have been his last breath.

*

This had been a bad twenty-four hours for Jack Priestley. Riddell had walked after they'd found him to be as clean as a hospital theatre. Not even a ticket to the fight had been found. No ledger. No diary. Sweet FA, and Jack wasn't a happy bunny. The operation had gone well but he knew the main prize had got away because he'd allowed it. And now Riddell could just sit back and cover that fat face of his with the widest grin imaginable.

Then to make matters worse, there was a phone call from the Home Office asking for the name of the police station in which Detective Chief Inspector Priestley had detained the prisoner Blade, having collected him from

Long Lartin and kept him longer than he should have. Cheeky bastards! He rocked back in his chair, mouth open, eyes bulging. He knew exactly what this was. He was in the middle of a dream. He rolled onto one cheek and pinched his arse to wake up. He didn't. Therefore, somebody was having him on.

'I don't care what Under-Secretary of State you get in touch with,' he bawled down the phone, 'I'm telling you, you've made a big mistake my little Whitehall wizard. Listen to the words carefully. Neither I, nor any of my staff have taken Blade out of Long Lartin.'

The phone went down on him.

'I don't believe this is happening.' Priestley was stunned, talking to himself. He hadn't the strength to bang his desk, which was what his brain was telling him to do, but help was at hand.

'It happened yesterday morning apparently, boss,' explained Barton. 'According to the prison, four CID officers with personal warrant cards, one purporting to be your good self, just walked in with a letter of authorisation and took him on his way.' Barton paused. 'They're not very happy.'

Priestley was momentarily speechless. His colour was changing by the minute.

Barton decided to continue the conversation. 'The letter of authority was also apparently signed by you.'

That did it. 'I'll kill the bastard.' Priestley was on his feet. His desk now felt the full force of his fist. 'I'll not rest until that dirty little bastard's back inside.'

Barton raised his hands, questioningly, 'But how did he manage to do that, boss?'

'Easy. Only he'd think of that. He's recruited some help from outside.'

Someone knocked on his office door.

'Piss off,' was the loud reply. 'He's got some of his germs to forge official documents using my name and walked. Like taking candy from a baby.' He walked back to his chair. 'And from a supposed top security nick at that!' He sat down again and started chewing his nails for the first time since he was a child. 'Right Chris, get them out. I want every drum we know he's acquainted with, hit. Every little shit known to him.' He paused and his voice lowered, 'But leave his missus to me.'

✻

On the way to see Sammy Blade his mind was still preoccupied with why Blade hadn't told her of his detention and why he didn't want her to know he was back inside the jug. There were a number of things that needed explaining. Top of the list was how in hell's name had Blade got out of a top security prison? He knew how he'd managed it physically. But who would have the know-how and facilities to accommodate such an escape? Why would he want to get out in the first place? He must have been helped, but by who? It didn't figure.

Priestley's mind searched for answers as he sped towards Nechells Green, trying to tackle the confusion that was now clouding his natural reasoning powers. Sammy was the only person in the world Blade would trust. She must know some of the answers, but did she trust Priestley sufficiently to share such information? He knew she'd been genuine at their last meeting. But would the same apply now? He'd know if she was bullshitting him.

'I've heard, Jack.' She looked a bit smarter than the last time they'd met, but there was genuine concern written all over her face, which in a way disappointed Priestley. He was hoping she'd be full of crap and fairy tales, which would confirm to him she knew where her loving husband was.

'How? When?'

'Just. It's been on all the news.'

That was quick, he thought.

'Has he been in touch, Sammy?' The question was direct enough, but the answer was as anticipated. Somehow he believed her.

'Would you tell me if he did?'

'No, not unless he told me to.'

Now he definitely believed her.

Priestley fumbled in his pockets and produced a card. 'That's my number, Sammy. Phone me if he agrees.' He intended the last comment to sound sarcastic but she obviously didn't pick that up and just nodded, holding his card at a distance, as though in dire need of spectacles.

*

Forty-eight hours passed by without any news of Blade's recapture. Priestley knew the convicted drugs pedlar would eventually get himself caught and favoured Sammy's flat as the key to finding him. He guessed he wouldn't go there physically, but he'd try and make contact with Sammy and there was only one way. The telephone had already been tapped. What the little shit would do then, guessed Jack, would be to arrange another meeting far away, but he knew that hadn't happened yet. She hadn't left the flat except for visiting local shops, according to the surveillance team Priestley had put on her.

*

Steve Blade had always been the one to boast how well he could do his bird. How he despised others who would collapse and cringe about their own predicaments and bleat about missing their mothers and wives. Priestley remembered one occasion in some public house when Blade told him that the only way to do your time was to get your head down and do it. But this time he'd failed. Broken the rules himself. Turned rabbit and legged it in total contrast to his own beliefs and prison philosophy.

But why? Perhaps things had got too much for him? He was no spring chicken and perhaps the thought of another few years away from Sammy had got on top of him? He should have thought about that when he decided to dip into the drugs market. No, he couldn't accept that Blade had been so stupid. But he had and his old mate Jack wouldn't rest now until the bastard was back behind bars serving his debt to society.

*

Priestley stopped the car and looked around him. The changes that had taken place over the years brought a lump to his throat. There was a large superstore there now, casting a shadow over the area where dozens of tiny shops used to line both sides of the street. A butcher's next to a tailor's, a chemist's next to a public house, a bread shop next to a pickle factory. This had been their playground. Their own personal kindergarten. Where the buzz and excitement that can only be found in the minds of children captivated them; where the future was discussed and planned with the utmost optimism.

His mind turned back to an old bomb peck upon which now sat a large petrol station. The young Jack Priestley was sitting amongst the rubble and dust, discussing his future intentions with a philosophical ten-year-old Steve Blade.

'I'm going to be a general, like the French geezer.'

'You mean Napoleon, Steve.'

'Yeah, like Napoleon.'

'What if you were ever locked up, Steve, for something you hadn't done?'

Blade looked down at the two milk bottle tops in his hands, each representing a famous footballer, kicking a small piece of rounded plaster in front of where he sat. Wondering why being locked up had anything to do with him becoming another Napoleon. 'What do you mean?' he asked.

Priestley turned his head sharply towards the sound of a bottle smashing on the cobbled street. 'Like that over there. What if you got the blame for smashing that bottle of milk he's just dropped off his cart. What would you do?'

'Escape.'

'How?'

Young Steve shook his head. 'I'd find a way.' The one milk bottle top, Tom Finney, dribbled the small ball of plaster around the other, which looked very like Nat Lofthouse.

'And then what?'

'Get the most trusted person in the world to get some money and we'd both leave the country.'

Priestley looked concerned and asked the next question whilst watching the milkman trying to stop his horse from stepping backwards over the broken glass, 'And who would that be, Steve?'

Blade sprung to his feet, both bottle tops secured tightly in his hands. 'It wouldn't be you, Jack Priestley,' he laughed. 'You'd dob me in!'

*

chapter eight

Had he really forgotten what good food tasted like, accompanied by a pint of real ale? Had it been that long since he used a toilet without some tosspot watching over him? Being able to speak without whispering? Had it been that long? Yes, it bloody well had been and now Bladey was going to sit back and rest on his laurels – for a short time anyway. Compared with the accommodation at Long Lartin, this was the real business; something to lie on which didn't give you backache; air-conditioning rather than dry heat coming from Edwardian radiators; the freedom to walk through a door without the jangle of keys closing it behind you. Yes, he could stay here for as long as they wanted him to. There'd be no complaints.

He read about his escape in a dozen or so newspapers, most of which were spread out on the floor.

'To make it look authentic,' she'd told him.

But he had his doubts. He'd been surprised at the amount of publicity he'd attracted and wondered whether Jack Priestley was reading the same stories. Course he was. He glanced over at Big Bristols, grafting like a television scriptwriter on the small oval-shaped table. He knew exactly what she needed and smiled to himself. Probably already getting it, by the bucketful!

His eyes focused back on the air vent in the far right-hand corner. It wasn't one of the ordinary white plastic ones most households displayed. This baby was made of brass, just like the canopy over the fire and the small rectangular table near the door, on top of the sheepskin rug. It looked like the rest of the flat – full of grandeur.

He stretched his legs further down the couch. Yes, this would definitely do for Bladey – until he got bored with it. He felt secure enough and was secure, knowing whilst in *their* company he would remain so. He imagined four masked men piling in through the solid mahogany door with machine guns, only to be blown away by Big Bristols diving on the floor, snatching some kind of military automatic from inside her bra and peppering three million pieces of lead at them. And all happening within two seconds. Who needed Clint Eastwood when she was around?

But then all the good dreams have to end sometime, as his mother used to tell him. Like a dark cloud slowly appearing above his head, his mind came back to reality – Jack Priestley. There he was, hovering, looking down at him. Like that shot in the opening scene of the first Superman film with Trevor Howard's face all over the screen. Jack Priestley. Not so much every villain's nightmare, but certainly his.

Jack was the only real problem that now existed for Blade. No matter how good these people were at their jobs, Priestley had something that could only be part of an individual's character. Something you had to be born with. Determination? Yes, bundles of it. Grit? By the skip load. Brains? Well, he never left much on the mat at home. But above all, Priestley had street knowledge. Something he doubted Big Bristols and her mates would have stored away.

He had a gift for selecting the right mount, the horse that would lead him to wherever he wanted to go. He *was* streetwise and Blade knew there weren't many coppers about with that kind of skill and experience in their armoury. He felt frustrated and disappointed that he hadn't been given the chance to tell him. Stubborn bastard. Nine times out of ten he would only want to talk, not listen.

'I thought people like me were kept tucked up in some country mansion, like on the TV.' He pulled himself up into a more upright position on the couch.

'Problem with the flat, Steve?' she asked, not looking up and continuing to write what he thought were her memoirs.

No, there was nothing wrong with his new digs. He just wanted to make conversation. 'Only kidding, Joyce,' he said, doubting whether that was her real name. He smiled and returned to his original horizontal position, both hands clasped behind the back of his head.

'Camilla,' he called.

She looked up again and smiled, very patiently.

'I bet your real name is Camilla?'

She shook her head and returned to the writing.

'Okay, Tania.'

She shook her head again, 'Read the papers, Steve,' she suggested.

He'd read the bleedin' papers twenty times over and now wanted to play. But he realised the sort of game he wanted to play was out of the question. His eyes returned to the brass air vent. No, he knew Jack Priestley wouldn't give up on him. He could see his face now, blazing mad, promising a crate of malt to the first one of his band to bring in Blade. A man of principle! A relentless bastard who would never be deterred or deflected from his task. What many would call a determined thief catcher. One without a charitable thought in his head – a pain in the arse!

Blade thought back to the time when they were hitching a ride on a corporation bus.

'I'm only twelve and I'm not paying the full fare, because I don't have to. It's the law,' explained a determined, fourteen-year-old Jack Priestley.

'You're fourteen if a day, my son,' thundered the conductor. 'And you're going to pay the full fare or I'll throw you off the bus.'

Priestley glared at the official.

Blade sank in the seat next to him. After all, this was young Jack's ball game. Blade didn't quite have the bottle for this kind of confrontation.

'You touch me and my dad will break your nose.'

That surprised even Blade. Steady, Jack, he thought. Bit over the top, mate.

The conductor was more than taken aback, and snarled. After all, this was the era in which children had to be respectful towards adults. 'Why you...'

Priestley interrupted, 'There's the fare. A child's fare, because I'm a child.' He held out the couple of coppers, he and Blade had scratched together.

The conductor's face was now crimson and he bawled, 'Right! That's it...'

'Leave him alone,' spoke up a woman passenger sitting at the back of the two kids. 'Anybody can see they're only children.'

'Madam, as the conductor, it's for me to decide whether these two little gems are children or adults.' A notepad and pencil appeared in his hand and trying to remain calm and collected, he insisted on their names and addresses.

Priestley glanced out of the window. He realised he had to delay the result of this minor argument, just a little longer and turned to the kind lady who was still looking at the conductor as though he'd just fallon off the bottom of her size 5 boot.

'Can he do that, miss? Demand our names and addresses?'

She turned on the conductor, letting him see she was armed with an umbrella. 'Anybody would think it's your money, the way you're quibbling. What did you do in the War, my lad? Suppose you was busy picking off the black market.'

The corporation bus employee was rapidly losing face, obviously starting to wonder whether he should have stayed on the Co-op milk!

'I'll have you know, madam, I did my bit. Royal Navy. On subs.'

Another glance out of the window and Priestley knew it was time to claim victory. He elbowed Blade in the ribs and quickly stood up from his seat. 'Come on, Steve, we're off.'

He turned to the conductor who was now completely deflated. 'You win, mister. We're off.'

He then flashed his eyes at the kind lady and expressed that childish look he was so good at doing, whenever the situation required it, before marching down the corridor towards the rear platform. Both of them jumped off at the next stop, where they'd always intended getting off, without having paid a penny for the trip.

✳

It was that strength of character that Blade admired most in Jack Priestley. But he was also aware that the man would come looking for him, if it meant searching the whole of the country and taking him ten years to do so. He'd witnessed the kind of steel in his old mate's make-up, which made him such a worthy adversary. But most of the time, he and Priestley had been on the same side, with one or two exceptions of course. No, he couldn't afford the risk of isolating Jack from the main plot. No matter what these sparklers said. They didn't know Priestley as he did. He would have to try and contact him; explain that he wasn't really a drugs baron; that he'd accepted a back-hander off the government people just to get some information for them. That was the only way to stop him from interfering. Otherwise he'd rather go to Siberia and face the Ruskies.

'There you are, darling.' Big Bristols had become active and broke into his daydreaming. She handed to him a driving licence and passport in some fictitious name, one he wouldn't even bother himself to remember. So she hadn't been writing her memoirs after all! He didn't have to ask the question. She could see it in his eyes.

'Just in case you're stop-checked by the police. At least you have some kind of identification.'

'Couldn't I just tell them to ring you?' he asked and was serious.

'No, that won't do,' she explained in her cultured accent, at the same time flashing her bright shining white teeth across her beautiful face.

He wondered how you got teeth that white. It was for sure she couldn't drink much coffee or smoke cigars. He remembered a saying amongst some of the old villains, 'Never trust a smiler,' meaning the one who smiled at your face was usually the one who would stick you in the back. And then came the first bombshell.

She held out her hand. 'It's been nice knowing you, Steve. I wish you well.'

What kind of bullshit was this? Where was she off to?

'You've got twenty minutes before the debriefing team arrive.' She picked up her handbag and walked towards the door. Make sure you're still here.'

The door closed behind her and all of a sudden he was alone. For the first time since walking out of the nick with the Madame Tussaud's replica of Jack Priestley. And yet, although he could leave whenever he wanted, he still felt like a prisoner; not in control of his own destiny; dependent upon these ratchet heads who'd escorted him there. Even if he did piss off, he knew he'd probably be back in the slammer before he could scratch his arse, or clean his teeth, and without Jack Straw's ticket. He got up and walked across to the table, the one Joyce had been sitting at before she'd said tarah. He saw an envelope she'd left on the top with just the word 'private' written across it. His initial reaction was to have a nose at the contents. After all, it wasn't addressed to anyone in particular, so it could have been meant for him. Could be a letter describing her true feelings towards him and her sexual desires she'd had to fight so hard to contain, whilst in his company? On the other hand, opening it might just drop him in the shit. He walked away towards the door and stood gazing at the brass fittings, again. This was getting ridiculous, he thought. A 'debriefing team'? He'd imagined he'd be just having a chat over a pint or two. Pissing Secret Squirrels!

He walked into the bedroom and inspected once more, the few items of clothing left for him in the wardrobe. Ideal if he'd been going for a month to Hawaii. Every shirt seemed to have flowers on it, with short sleeves. Perhaps he was? All he wanted was out of there and of course, the rest of the dough in his pocket. He walked back into the lounge and sat on the edge of the couch, staring into the pieces of red hot lava covering the gas pipe. He wondered what Jack

Priestley was doing. He could certainly share a pint with him now.

*

There was a sombre atmosphere in the crew room, as Priestley picked up his briefing papers and walked back to his office, followed by Barton. The murder of a young child was one of the most difficult inquiries a detective could be tasked with investigating. There were too many distractions. Apart from the obvious trauma of having to deal with it, there was always the family, distressed and usually, quite rightly, screaming for support. That in itself required all the patience and sensitivity in the world. The dangers of becoming a part of the grief that followed such a tragic loss were obvious. He'd known officers before, who'd become too close to a victim's family, forgetting what their real role was – to investigate and not to counsel. There were others more aptly trained to do that. Every detective's priority was to catch the bastard who'd done it.

Then of course there was the media. He'd already spotted Carol Guardia amongst the crowd of reporters at the earlier press briefing. She'd be phoning him shortly for a one-to-one interview and of course he would oblige. But having given an initial press conference, his habit was to then avoid them, concentrating only on the job at hand.

He sat listening to Barton describe how he'd put into operation Priestley's initial selected lines of inquiry. But the picture of the small lifeless body lying in the ditch remained uppermost in his mind. He thought of one Peter Ryan and any regrets he'd held about the help he'd given to Frank Cheswick, were dispelled. A rabid dog would be put down without any screams. That's how he looked upon these bastards. As sick as they might be, they should have the same treatment. There could be no greater pain, as far as he was concerned, than to learn that your little girl or boy had been sexually taken apart and then murdered. This was one of those rare incidents that would be treated with condemnation by both law and villains. No criminal would have any compunction about helping to find the twisted mind that had committed such an atrocity. Unfortunately for people like Priestley, it was also very rare when the 'other side' were ever in a position to help. Killers of children didn't exactly go from pub to pub boasting about their achievements.

He'd already decided this one would be a long drawn-out investigation. The search for Blade would have to wait. This was far too important and needed his undivided attention. Some other copper would have to stumble across Blade and rope him in. That's how Jack believed he would be captured; not far from home. One risk too many and 'boom', Gotcha, you little shit!

✳

Blade's briefing team consisted of one man, Richard Pike. A slightly built man in his fifties. He sported the usual attire: white shirt, dark tie, black suit. Blade wondered where this one had been all these months. This was better. This was the geezer he thought would be with him from the off – straight out of Eton; into Cambridge, because that's where all the spies come from, or so the newspapers kept telling us, thought the ex-con. Then straight into Whitehall to start a fruitful career in the cloak and dagger business. 'Have a bit of that. Off you go, old son. Take your bag of James Bond tricks with you and find out who's going to try and kill the Queen this week. And by the way, failure will get you a poison-tipped umbrella to stick up your arse before jumping off London Bridge...old son.'

Then he looked more closely at the garments and suddenly had a thought. All of these MI5 men were given undertaker's outfits to wear at the same time they were recruited straight out of Cambridge. They had to have some kind of uniform so they could recognise each other. He remembered reading somewhere about the G men in the US, having to wear white shirts and black ties, by order of Edgar J Hoover. Well, this was probably the same. The idea of bowler hats was to provide them with somewhere to put their antennae loops where they couldn't be seen. Well, they'd look bloody daft wearing straw boaters, wouldn't they?

This one had all the other attachments as well. He'd obviously been a member for a long time. His head was crowned with thick silver hair, not a strand out of place. A wonderful advert for Brylcreem, straight out of the fifties and an appearance Stewart Grainger would have been proud of. Then there was the voice. My God, he must have been a radio broadcaster for the BBC some twenty or thirty years ago.

Pike introduced himself. 'Good to meet you, Steve.' It was tenor. Probably the deepest-sounding voice Blade had ever heard, which seemed out of place with the gentleman's meagre physical build.

Blade nodded. His disappointment was obvious. This was no fair substitute for Big Bristols – he had always hoped he would eventually shag the arse off her! The bowler hat walked briskly over to the mahogany table where the lovely Joyce had been sitting just thirty minutes earlier. The envelope was picked up, opened and one page from inside read, before disappearing into the man's inside pocket.

Blade had got it all wrong. It was obviously a love letter to M here.

What then appeared to be two files were pulled out of the standard issue, black leather briefcase and Mr Pike parked himself in the easy chair opposite where Blade was sitting, with the folders resting on his lap. He smiled and nodded his head. Nice man, thought the ex-con. Couldn't imagine this geezer driving fast boats and shooting Ruskies in the head from five hundred yards with a tiny handgun which held two thousand rounds.

'Now, Steve. Where shall we begin...?'

Blade interrupted. 'What about the rest of my money?'

'We'll come to that.'

'And my free pardon off the Home Secretary?'

'All in good time.'

'I need to speak to my missus, urgently...'

'Yes, yes. We'll come to all of that, after we've had a chat about what you know.'

✱

As far as Sammy was concerned he could go and throw himself off a cliff. She'd had enough of the strain and worry resulting from a life with Steve Blade. If it hadn't been for their baby daughter, she'd have gone long before now or most certainly when he went inside without even sending her a note. And now her brave hero had shot his bolt again. No word from him and once again he left her alone and in the dark. Enough was enough.

'Mrs Blade?'

Not bad looking for a postman thought Sammy, holding the door open. Perhaps he'd be interested in taking on board an exciting and adventurous woman with only one child.

'Yes.'

He handed over the parcel and asked her to sign the usual form.

Wherever the bastard was now, she hoped he would eventually rot in hell. She should have gone off with Harry Nesbitt when the opportunity was there to grasp. She'd have all that money now, being his widow.

She had to stand on the bottom rung of the stool to reach the tin on the top shelf. It was empty, which meant another trip down to the social with the begging bowl. Or perhaps she should think more seriously about finding another Harry Nesbitt. Why not? At the end of the day, she was only in this pathetic position because her bastard of a husband had failed to provide for them. Perhaps there was something in the parcel, like a couple of grand in cash. Oh for the return of Charlie Richardson. At least he was a gent and looked out for them. Perhaps she should try and contact old Charlie?

There was more sellotape wrapped around the brown paper than they had in stock down the Post Office. This was ridiculous. She needed a pair of scissors and walked into the kitchen to search the drawers, her mind still racing. Could she beg a few quid off Jack Priestley? Heaven forbid. Now she seriously wondered whether she was losing her marbles. She'd try the social first, failing that, the pubs. Failing that...well, there was always some way of earning on the streets.

The small note read: Switch it on and follow the instructions on the back. Normally she would have treated what looked like a kid's toy as a joke but her face lengthened as she realised the note was in Blade's handwriting.

She studied closely the object she was holding. A black plastic rectangular box with a small screen and keys of the alphabet below it, like a small typing pad. It was obviously meant for sending messages, or receiving them. Or both. But how? The instructions were on the back: First, type a message and then press the green key. And wait. Even Sammy could remember that. But where would the message go? She remembered from her old part-time job down the probation office that faxes had to go to a specific number, otherwise they'd be lost. Her mind was becoming confused but she'd always been a goer, had our Sammy.

She placed the machine on her lap and followed the instructions carefully. Not knowing what to type onto the screen, she just printed the letters, HELLO. The green button was pushed and the screen cleared. After a second the words, MESSAGE SENT, appeared for a brief moment. She sat patiently waiting. Nothing. Holding the box in both hands, nothing happened. She stared at the blank screen. Nothing. Perhaps it was a joke after all. Perhaps he'd nicked it and sent it to her so she could sell it on. But how much would it be worth? She didn't even know what it was. Why couldn't the prat have sent something more useful, like a diamond ring or necklace, something that would bring in a few quid?

She'd had enough. Her neck was getting stiff. She stood up and shook the box before slinging it onto the settee. Suddenly it bleeped. Just for a second. She stood staring at it, as though expecting it to jump up and give her a kiss on the mouth. She cautiously picked it up again and read the words on the box:

HELLO TO YOU AS WELL THEY TELL ME THIS MACHINE IS TOTALLY SECURE. WE CAN SAY ANYTHING. YOUR LOVING HUSBAND STEVE.

Sammy dropped the box and yelped. She cautiously picked it up again hoping it hadn't been damaged. It bleeped, twice this time. Another message:

CAN'T TELL YOU EVERYTHING YET. NOT AS BAD AS IT LOOKS. NEED TO SPEAK TO J P. CAN YOU FIX IT FOR TONIGHT?

For a local lass brought up in the slums with the rest of them, this wasn't for real. She wanted to shout some abuse at the box, hoping he would be able to hear her. But instead, she ran across to the window to see if there was a television detector van outside or something similar. The street was empty apart from Jack's lads sitting in the car outside, where they'd been since her loving husband had done a duck. Then she sat down and drew in a deep breath. She knew exactly who J P was and he would be getting a phone call very shortly. She'd play out the role she'd been asked to perform but there was one thing about living with Steve Blade. He might be a bastard, she thought, but life was always, always on the fringe. She calmed herself once more and typed YES and then pressed the little green button.

*

He was walking out through the door, car keys in hand, having just finished for the day. The inquiry into the murdered girl was taking its toll and total exhaustion was an understatement to describe the way he really felt. The phone rang. Not now thought Priestley and continued to walk away. But there again, it could be important. He really didn't need somebody else talking a load of crap over the bugle.

'Priestley.'

'I need to see you, Jack.' It was Sammy. 'Alone and tonight.'

Strange how two short sentences can revitalise your whole inner being. 'Where and when, love?'

'Outside the Oliver Cromwell, at seven.' The phone went down.

Now he was back on track. The hours of drudgery behind that desk quickly lost their effect and his heart began to pound. This had Blade written all over it. A meeting to protest his innocence and get his best mate Jack to do some perilous favour for him. Well not this time, decided the Chief Inspector. Blade's going straight back to where he belongs with the rest of the scurvy. There'd be no more favours, not for a dope pedlar.

'Alan?' Cresswell was one of the most capable Detective Sergeants under Priestley's command, with loads of bottle to go with it. That's why he'd put him where he was, running the dedicated surveillance unit.

'Guv?'

'Still on the female target?'

'Course. She's just made a phone call from a box near the HA. We'll have the number she rang in a bit.'

'I know. It was mine. She's just phoned me.' Nice to be one step in front of his own team, thought Jack. 'Stay with it, Alan, she's meeting me at seven, outside the Cromwell. I think we'll be seeing the main target.'

The voice at the other end didn't seem to vary. 'Gotcha, guv. We'll be there.'

Priestley realised why Sammy hadn't used her own phone. It was to protect him from others listening in. But she had a shock coming. Blade had already lost his old mate.

✳

At least the weather was on Blade's side. He couldn't have picked a better night for a 'private' meeting. It was as black as coal. The sleet being driven by cold wintry winds lashed at Priestley's face as he raced across the street towards where he could see Sammy sheltering in the pub doorway. He knew that Blade wouldn't be inside and Priestley would probably be led a merry dance before coming eye to eye with him. The surveillance team would have to be on their toes. He wasn't far wrong.

As he approached, he saw her face partially hidden by a mobile phone. He greeted her with a nod of the head assuming she had already confirmed his arrival with her wanted husband. Amazing though, how some people have never got two pennies to rub together, he thought, and the kids always needed feeding but they've always got mobile phones and Sky TV!

Sammy beckoned him to follow her before disappearing down an alleyway which ran alongside the public house. She walked quickly and at first Priestley had to adjust his step, finding it difficult to keep up with her, remaining just a few yards behind. In fact he could only follow and was never given the chance to actually catch up and walk alongside Mrs Blade. She hurried across a road into the front entrance of a block of flats. Without stopping or easing the pace, she dashed straight across the ground-floor area and through a rear entrance into back gardens. It was cold, wet and muddy. The policeman wasn't too appreciative of the game being played but any doubts he might have had as to who they were going to meet had now disappeared.

Through a gate and down a narrow path which divided the gardens. It was pitch black and Priestley called to Sammy to slow down but was ignored. She was almost running now and her figure was slowly disappearing in the distance, as if being swallowed up by a thick fog. Suddenly a hooded man stepped out in front of him and grabbed his arm. He was pulled to one side and his first reaction was to drop the cheeky bastard, but he knew it was Blade. He could smell him, metaphorically speaking of course. His sleeve was grabbed and he was pulled into what appeared to be a nearby garden shed. The hood came off and there they were. Together for the first time since they'd discussed the Cheswick saga.

Blade had a broad grin over his face. 'Hello, Jack. It's good – '

Priestley's fist was fast and hard. It struck Blade full in the face causing him to collapse like a deck of cards. His mind went immediately back to his own assessment of Priestley just a few hours before, in the flat, as both of his arms were quickly wrenched behind his back. He got it absolutely right – talked a lot but never listened. He never wanted to. Before he could even draw breath, both of Blade's wrists were manacled together.

As he was violently pulled up off the floor by the detective, he tried to explain, 'Jack, don't do this. We need to talk. There's something you need to know, Jack.'

Too late, Jack had made his mind up. Like the kid on the bus having the conductor over, the same determination was still there. A stubbornness encouraged by a belief that he, Priestley, knew everything worth knowing and anything else that didn't fit into his way of thinking was insignificant. The only place Bladey was going was into the back of a crime car and it was Priestley's duty to see that such a manoeuvre was successfully accomplished.

'You gob-smacking, blinkered bastard,' raged Blade.

The copper pushed the handcuffed fugitive out of the shed, with the protests still loud and clear. Priestley's eyes had now become more accustomed to the darkness and within a minute they would be back on the streets.

'There are things I need to tell you, Jack, before you do something you might regret.'

'The only thing I regret is ever having met you, you slimy bastard.'

Not much hope here, thought Blade, but he continued to plead, 'Jack,' but his calls were to no avail. His chance had gone. He knew that Priestley was strong and angry. This wasn't what Blade wanted. He'd come this far to try and explain, in the hope that Priestley would become an ally. Instead he felt betrayed by a man who he had once regarded as a friend. Jack was a changed man. Or was he?

'What's up, Steve?'

He was shivering, white faced, petrified, crouching, partly hidden amongst the wooden crates and planks they'd collected for tomorrow night's bonfire.

'I've killed him,' cried Blade.

'Killed who Steve?'

'The motorcyclist.'

'What motorcyclist?'

'Round the corner in Henage Street.'

'How did you kill him, Steve?' asked a wide-eyed Jack Priestley.

'That big mirror over there,' young Steve blurted. 'I was carrying it across the street and he came round the corner and crashed into the gardens.'

'But how do you know you killed him?'

'Because he saw himself in the mirror and thought it was another bike.'

'Hang on, Steve. I think he's coming. He's over here mate, hiding in the bonfire,' shouted young Jack.

✳

Priestley marched his prisoner down one path and then another, until they reached the bright lights of a small cobbled side street which, due to the falling snow had now taken on a totally different appearance. But Jack knew exactly where he was and frogmarched Blade back towards the Cromwell public house. They'd only walked a few yards when the sound of a revving engine and car headlights swinging towards them, confirmed that Jack's cavalry were in attendance. He stood back and watched as Blade was pushed into the back of the police car and driven away.

Judas? No, how could he be? It was his job. And what he'd done had served the public in the best possible way, by apprehending a criminal responsible for bringing death onto the streets.

He'd already decided to make his own way back to where he'd parked his car and did so, still feeling some confusion. With his mind not really accepting what had just occurred, he continued to convince himself, he'd had no option. Blade was an escaped felon and that's all there was to it. Time to go home and get rid of his doubts with a glass of Glenfiddich. Then a good night's sleep and back on the child murder in the morning.

It wasn't until he was just a few yards away from his car he recognised the slim, saturated figure of Sammy standing in front of the bonnet. The snow was thick now and he thought of offering her a lift home, but he wasn't given the opportunity. She slapped him hard on the face and her spittle crashed against his right cheek. There were no words spoken but the message was loud, clear and painful.

She just turned, with fire in her eyes and briskly walked away. That hurt, more than he could ever have imagined and for the first time, strong doubts as to whether he'd done the right thing started to take control.

Oh yes. He was as he felt. A bag of shit. A smart-arse who'd turned his back on a friend who might very well have been in urgent need of support or help. What if Blade intended to give himself up? What if he wanted to warn Priestley about something horrendous that was about to happen? The what ifs flooded back as they had done so on many previous occasions. But this time the questions were accompanied by an overwhelming feeling of guilt. Had he done the right thing? No, Mr Shithole hadn't. His conscience wasn't as clear as he thought it would be, but he didn't know why. All he'd done was his job and he tried to force what had just happened out of his mind.

There was the murder of a little girl he had to clear up and that was far more important than any further thoughts of Steve Blade's predicament. But he was wrong again. There would be no sleep for Jack Priestley that night.

*

chapter nine

'I suppose that overgrown schoolboy thinks everything will be alright now, eh?' screamed Blade. 'Now he's let me see my missus, eh?' His face was a deep claret and he wasn't just trying to impress Sammy either.

She just sat on the other chair. Silent. Watching her husband bawl through a closed door. Nobody was there to listen and she knew that. But Steve was Steve and he'd carry on letting off steam, not caring whether anybody was there to hear him or not. And he'd just continue bawling until he'd got whatever it was out of his system. He turned and went back to his seat. It was a moment when neither could find any words to say to each other. It had all gone dreadfully wrong as far as Sammy was concerned. She'd trusted Priestley; so had her husband, who could only sit there with his head bowed, like a child in disgrace.

He looked at his wife, pleadingly, 'I shouldn't be in here, Sam. I haven't done anything.'

'Did you do what they said you did, Steve?' She'd avoided the question for long enough and felt the need to ask it, ignoring his last comments. 'Did you really do what they said, bring drugs into the country?'

He slowly raised his head and looked up at her, shaking it in defiance. 'We need to talk Sam. There's a lot you need to know about, before I start losing my mind.'

*

In appearance, Sir Ronald Chapman was everything the public would imagine a Chief Constable to be. Six-foot-eight inches tall, broad shouldered, late fifties, a slight pot belly and a strip of dark greying hair wrapped around a bald top. Integrity and honesty were written all over his face. His mere presence in the same room made Priestley wonder how anyone could have the bottle to argue with such a colossus.

'Sit yourself down, lad. It's good to see you.'

His loud, commanding Yorkshire accent was just the ticket for such a high ranking leader of people thought the DCI, as he obeyed instantly. The bigger man remained on his feet, towering over his large, solid oak desk, which curved inwards at each end and went with the job and the status. 'So how's life been treating you on the NCS, Frank?'

'Jack, sir. It's Jack.' The mistake was no surprise to Priestley. The man had a reputation for focusing on individuals for no more than three seconds. How on earth could he be expected to remember names? Mind you, thought the CID officer, he might have got the file out first, just to check.

'Jack, Jack. Of course.' Chapman showed no signs of embarrassment and turned to look out of the large window from which he could see a great deal of the city centre roof tops.

Wonderful material for an artist like Lowry, thought Priestley but personally he'd have preferred a park, or perhaps even the Brecon Hills.

'The child murder, Jack. How's it coming along?'

Priestley started to brief him. He wanted to tell him about all the hard work he and his crews had been doing over the past couple of days but was cut short.

'Yes, yes. Well, thank you for that.'

Ignorant bastard! Jack hadn't finished. He hadn't even completed his description of the scene.

But his Chief Constable had other ideas. 'So, let's see. You must be near to promotion now.' He paused, as though trying to remember the lines he'd rehearsed, although Priestley was convinced he'd never rehearsed anything in his life. Perhaps he'd been summoned for some reason other than the murder investigation he was running? The DCI began to feel a wave of optimism suddenly sweep through him. Promotion? Well now, there's a subject he wasn't expecting to discuss. The Chief turned away from the scene of urban beauty and sat down. 'Especially after that well-handled operation with Jim Nolan and the others.' He'd remembered Jack's major scoop.

The younger officer had often wondered whether locking up half the CID hierarchy would be a black mark against him. He still wasn't sure. But one thing was certain he wasn't going to be interrupted so abruptly again. He decided to keep his mouth shut and divulge as little as possible. A bit like a spoiled brat really, who'd just lost his girlfriend to another competitor. But from now on he would use his head, literally, nodding in reply to any acknowledgements required. Especially when Ron disclosed he was going to promote him to Superintendent. It had a sort of pleasant ring about it.

Chapman sat back in his chair, hands clasped behind his head – an obvious sign of an autocrat. But then, probably appreciating that Priestley had noticed the sweat stains beneath his armpits, he dropped his arms and sat forward again, placing both elbows on top of his bureau pad. 'This escaped prisoner, Jack. Brean is it?'

'Blade, sir. Steve Blade. Inside for drugs importation.' He shouldn't be asking about Blade, thought the DCI. Keep talking about the subject of promotion, he was begging in his thoughts.

'That's it, Jack. Well I wanted to discuss it more with you.' The senior officer was now looking piercingly into Priestley's eyes, obviously probing for the junior officer's most inner thoughts. Jack felt a little deflated. Promotion out the window. That man Blade again.

'Wasn't he the one who helped us with the Nolan affair?'

The introductions and niceties were over. It was obviously now down to the real reason he'd been summoned so early in the morning. 'He was, sir.'

The door opened and the chief's secretary peered in. 'Commander Pike, Chief Constable.'

Chapman leapt to his feet and strode towards the door.

Priestley remained where he was, bemused.

'Pikey, old son,' there was an air of excitement in the Chief's voice. 'Good to see you. Come in, come in.'

Pikey old son must be something special, thought Priestley. Probably an old swat from the Police College.

'Let me introduce you to Detective Superintendent Priestley.'

Jack stood up and shook the smaller man's hand. 'It's Chief Inspector actually, Commander.' Bloody well should be Superintendent though, thought Jack, still smarting after having his hopes raised earlier by Sir Ron. He'd been promised the next rank more times than he'd slept around and he thought it was about time they started to look at him seriously.

Commander Pike sat with his back to the wall nearest the door. The space behind his head was like an art exhibition in a museum; the actual wallpaper was hidden from sight by the collection of photographs, cartoons and other remnants kindly presented by various distinguished people visiting police headquarters over a period of years. That particular office always reminded Priestley of some DA's office in Los Angeles or Chicago, which always had the Stars and Stripes propped up in a corner behind the desk, waving in the wind coming from all the verbal bullshit contained in the films they made over there.

Chapman returned to his seat and allowed for a slight lull in proceedings whilst looking for what could have been his favourite lost teddy, in one of his large drawers. What all this was about was a complete mystery to Jack Priestley and for a moment, his head turned from one to the other, wondering which of them was going to open up the bidding for explanations. At last he found his teddy, in the form of a pair of nail clippers and leant over the nearby wastepaper bin, poised to commence battle with his fingers and thumbs. 'Over to you, Pikey,' he directed as the first snip could be heard from beneath the desk.

Was that, or was that not, professional delegation? Priestley asked himself. Of course it was. That's why he was a Chief Constable. There were no flies on Sir Ron. The following twenty minutes saw more changes of expression in Jack Priestley's face than there'd been in the previous ten years. Any surprise? Constantly present. Shock? Occasionally thrown in for good measure. Despair? A little. Relief? Hadn't yet been experienced. It was the only thing missing but urgently sought after.

The Scotland Yard Commander wasted few words and his briefing was fairly full and to the point. He'd already referred to Steve Blade and when concluding, returned to the same subject again. 'He's gone through quite a lot, Mr Priestley.'

And so had Jack, who was now finding it difficult to resist the temptation to forward his own description of the man. Blade, someone who would sell his own mother for ten grand. But then again, who was he to talk? He knew deep down that was a description more apt for himself than his old mate, so he declined the opportunity and just sat there, listening.

'We're now entering the most important phase of the operation.' Pikey stood up and walked towards the back of the Chief Constable so that he could face Priestley, who in turn, was thankful for the relief from having to twist his neck to look behind him.

'Your man...'

Priestley interrupted. 'He's not my man.'

'Fair enough.' Pikey hesitated looking slightly confused, before continuing as if that particular hiccup hadn't occurred. 'The next part of Blade's job is to use the information he got from Gabriel to identify those involved in the next tier up in the organisation.'

'Gabriel?' Jack was at it again.

Another interruption and by the look on Pikey's face, the Commander was starting to get a little pissed off with it.

'That rings a bell.' The name had already been mentioned three or four times before, during the early part of Pike's briefing but must have gone straight over Priestley's head.

'It should do. He's got quite a bit of form.'

'No, I mean...' Jack stopped and allowed his eyes to wander, as his thought processes took over. 'Yes, Gabriel.' He looked up at the other two men, as though startled by something that had just flown in through the window and pecked him on the arse. 'Jimmy Gabriel?'

The Commander nodded. 'You do know of him?'

'If he's the same one you're referring to, I've heard of him recently.'

'No doubt, when you raided one of George Riddell's little games.'

That surprised Priestley.

'Riddell is part of our operation as well,' explained Pikey. 'In fact a major part. We think he's the mover. The man who organises the arms going out of the country.'

'And into the hands of those Arab terrorists you mentioned earlier?' Priestley suggested.

'Well, terrorists?' Commander Pike shrugged his shoulders. 'If you believe Saddam Hussain is a terrorist, yes. But we'd like to think of him more as an adversary and a political one at that.'

There was a short pause and the Chief Constable just sat there, having finished clipping his nails, listening half interested in what the other men were saying. He gave them the space they required to thrash out the mechanics of the operation.

Pike continued, 'You see, we're not sure where the arms are being delivered to. Arabs? Chechnyans? Palestinians? That's what we really need to know, Jack.'

Priestley suspected that the Commander's use of his Christian name could only mean one thing. An invitation to jump on board HMS *Adventure* was just around the corner. It was a thought he wasn't really relishing.

'What kind of arms are we talking about?' Good question, Jack, but he really didn't give a shit and would be reluctant to become involved in anything that implicated Steve Blade.

'Military. Semi-automatic and automatic.' The Commander returned to the window behind the Chief and let Priestley gaze at his rear end for a short while.

'But that's not the real problem, Jack.' He turned once again, his face not clearly visible because of the backlight from the window. 'You see, to sell arms illegally is a criminal act, right? But to sell arms to countries which are strongly opposed to our own western allies is also political, which also means extremely sensitive.'

Priestley understood but still felt there was more to this particular Mr Pike than was being let on.

'So why Blade?'

Pike appeared to be very serious and shook his head. 'He's a proven commodity. He was successful in that recent operation involving corruption inside this force. Weren't you involved with that? A man called Richardson or something like that?'

Priestley nodded. It appeared that Blade had been given all the credit for something Jack himself had started.

'And the only way we could progress our own inquiries into what we had already confirmed was an arms dealing organisation, was to start at the bottom. We knew of Riddell and Gabriel. Been watching them for months. But couldn't infiltrate them. We need to know who's behind the wheeling and dealing. A man like Blade working covertly inside prison would create an opening for us.' He paused, 'And in fairness, he did just that.'

He leant back against the window sill, as though inviting Priestley to interrupt at that point if he so wished. But he didn't.

'What we need to do now is go further up the ladder and find out how they're getting the goods out of the country and the identities of those responsible.'

It all sounded too clear-cut for Priestley's satisfaction, but there again he was a suspicious bugger and couldn't wait to hear what prize he was going to be handed from Pike's bag of tricks.

'So, why tell me?' he asked. 'If you wanted Blade out, why didn't you just arrange another of your escapes. But perhaps this time not using my name as the dickhead who's supposed to have sprung him.'

Sir Ron coughed and Priestley apologetically nodded towards him. That wasn't the kind of expletive you used in the company of such a churchgoer as this particular Chief Constable. The Commander returned to his original seat and Priestley's pain returned to his neck.

'Because we want you to be his first contact.'

The suggestion made Priestley smile. He didn't know why really, but felt it was the most natural thing to do when being asked to manage Steve Blade in an undercover situation.

'And who's "we"?' That was a fair enough question, especially as he would be working closely with a man like Blade.

And Commander Pike nodded his head as if accepting its validity. 'Security Forces. I've been attached to SIU for some time now.'

Priestley's ignorance was written all over his face.

'The Sensitive Information Unit. To replace MI5.'

Well, that made his day. There wouldn't be many people who'd know that, thought Jack, doing his mental impression of Michael Caine. Now it was his turn to look on in earnest and he leant forward, staring directly into Commander Pike's eyes.

'Forgive me, Commander, if I seem to be acting a little flippant, but have you any idea of the kind of man Steve Blade is?'

'He's the kind of man that is of some use to us at this very moment in time, Mr Priestley. Beyond that, I'm not particularly bothered.' He smiled, 'To use your vocabulary, you don't need a man security vetted to put him inside a nick for six months.' One of Pike's eyebrows reached for the ceiling in recognition that his point had been well made.

Priestley looked across at Sir Ron and then back to Pike, 'Fair enough.'

The Commander reached for his briefcase and pulled out a rectangular box identical to the one Sammy had received through the post from Blade. He then handed it across to Priestley and explained, 'This is what we refer to as an Enigma Unit. It's similar to an encrypted personal pager and is completely secure.'

Priestley looked closely at it, in a similar way to how he would inspect a young puppy he was about to buy a child for Christmas.

The Commander continued, 'It can send messages on a one-to-one basis from and to anywhere in the world.'

Now Priestley *was* impressed.

'That particular unit is linked to one in Mr Blade's possession.' The smile returned, 'Switch it on.'

Priestley obeyed and within a second, words were illuminated across the screen:

I'VE BEEN PISSED OFF WAITING HERE FOR YOU TO CALL ME.

Oh yes, thought Jack. That's Blade alright. Winner of the academic of the year award! It was obvious he had spent the last few months studying William Shakespeare's use of the English language in the prison library.

'That same unit was used by Blade's wife to arrange the meeting with your good self, last night,' explained Richard Pike.

Priestley was still a little bewildered, trying to take everything in. His focus remained on the machine, which would keep him in touch with what he regarded as his lifelong boil on the arse. And the most terrifying thing was that he would have to be accessible, at the little git's beck and call, for not less than twenty-four hours a day. The depressing thought hit him like an enamelled stove being dropped on top of his head. He briefly imagined himself rolling over the top of Sonia Hall, with the Enigma Unit bleeping and Blade asking if he was alright!

'So, Jack.' The Commander was on his feet.

So was the Chief Constable, stretching himself.

The briefing was at an end, or so they thought.

'One thing, sir,' asked the DCI, addressing his own senior officer, 'what about the murder inquiry I'm running at the moment?'

Chapman looked across at Pike for some direction, but a shrug of the shoulders was the only assistance he was given. This was one query he couldn't delegate. 'Stay with it, Jack.' His eyes returned towards the Commander, 'I don't see how this commitment should interfere with your own management role'

Still only a shrug of the shoulder, but at least there appeared to be a slight shake of the head which indicated the Chief Constable had got it right.

*

Well, at least much of what had been shared with him explained a lot of the questions he'd been asking during the previous few weeks. He owed Blade an apology and remembered the persistence of his old mate the night before; he was trying to tell him something, whilst Jack was occupied with only the need to lock him up and throw away the key.

In fairness to Blade, Priestley wouldn't have gone through what he'd done – even if there was twenty grand at the end of it. Greedy bastard, he thought. But at least there was some relief for Priestley that Blade wasn't after all, a dope pedlar. If only he'd listened to him. It might have saved him a pisser off his missus. Must concentrate more, he accepted as he drove off the car park and headed back towards his own office.

✳

Now it was really getting cold. It was that damp kind of cold that seemed to enter the body and run straight through it like a cavalry charge of lancers, leaving its effects clinging to the bones. She'd sat there for almost an hour waiting for him to arrive. Hang about, she thought, perhaps he'd had the day off? Perhaps she should go inside and ask? But then if he heard she was waiting for him, he wouldn't come out. His car was nowhere to be seen so he must already be out. No, she'd stay where she was. Give it another hour and if she had no joy, well, she'd have to return to work by then anyway, no doubt feeling even more of a prat for having let her emotions rule her head.

✳

'I want the custody sergeant to release him now, Chris.' Priestley knew how that message must have sounded to Barton, who knew how hyped-up his DCI had been earlier about Blade's escape.

'Boss, he's already gone.'

'He's what?' He stopped the car in a bus lay-by.

'His missus came to visit him,' explained the young Detective Inspector, 'and after she'd left, we found her in his cell.'

Although it sounded double-dutch, Priestley got the message. 'You're joking?' was his loud response. 'Chris, they didn't fall for that one surely?' Jack could feel that volcano about to erupt again, but then smiled to himself. Did it really matter? Now that he knew the truth about what Blade had been doing, why shouldn't he take the piss out of the constabulary? Just to let Jack know he could have legged it anyway, without anybody else's assistance. It wasn't important now. After all, the Priestley–Blade partnership was just about to take off again. Heaven forbid.

He switched off the mobile and heard the Enigma bleep on the front passenger seat. He didn't have to look. He knew exactly what the message would be:

THANKS FOR THE HOSPITALITY JACK BUT NOT MY KIND OF ACCOMMODATION. GIVE US A SHOUT WHEN YOU'RE READY JACK AND DON'T FORGET TO SEND MY MISSUS BACK TO ME.

*

He parked his car on the back car park and placed the Enigma in the boot.

'Hello, Jack.' Her voice sounded harsh. Angry. No, more like, extremely mad. The look on her face was as if she'd just been sick in the toilets. She was as white as chalk, with both fists clenched.

He'd never seen her like this before but had a bloody good idea why she was raving. He turned from closing the boot lid and just stood there, watching her approach across the short distance that separated them.

'You bastard!' she roared and threw an open palm across his face. He winced and felt his cheek swelling like a blown-up condom. The second smack in the gob for Jack Priestley in twenty-four hours. But this one stung more than the first. He raised his arm to protect his face from the possibility of a second flyer coming his way, but she stepped away. What could he say? Nothing. He'd forgotten all about etiquette and the unspoken convention and understanding that she would have the exclusive if he ever took action on what she'd told him. He was getting pissed off though with all these furious women suddenly coming onto the scene and using him as a punch bag. He turned, feeling too embarrassed to look up at any of the windows, and walked towards the entrance.

'Jack,' she called after him. 'Why?'

He turned and shook his head not really wanting to prolong this meeting, particularly as they were both in view of every nosy bastard inside the nick. But she obviously had other ideas and walked after him.

Not another smack, he wondered. He took the initiative. 'Had no choice. I can't apologise enough, Carol.'

At least she seemed to respond and stopped just a yard or two away from him with the clenched fist opening up again.

'I'm sorry, love, I never gave it a thought,' he continued. 'And that's the truth,' still holding his cheek.

She wanted to hear more and just stood there, glaring at him.

'I'll make it up to you, I promise.'

That did the trick and the fury left her eyes. 'I'm sorry I smacked you, Jack.'

Jack relaxed at that piece of good news.

'But you almost cost me my job.'

He needed to stay calm. 'I'll make it up to you. Let's have lunch tomorrow. I'll give you an update on the murder…'

Bloody women!

*

chapter ten

'Didn't think I'd be back in here so quickly, Jimmy.'

Gabriel just sat and stared at him, expressionless. He hadn't changed.

Neither had Cheswick, apart from looking a little apprehensive. Even though he was just visiting.

You could count on one hand the number of people who'd gone to the trouble of visiting Jimmy G. In fact, with one exception, he hadn't had a visitor before in his life. The exception was when he was doing a quick twelve months for dividing some geezer's rib cage with a shiv. Georgie Riddell popped in to find out when his favourite minder was due for release. So why all the attention now? He sat and waited for the reason to be made clear to him.

Cheswick stole a quick glance at the window panel in the door, 'Blade's been to see me.'

Guessed it, thought Gabriel. He'd have put his last dime on the man Blade having something to do with it.

'He came to see me and the missus and kid. I owe him a lot Jimmy. You know that.'

Jimmy just sat patiently, frowning, maintaining the stare which was making his visitor feel even more uncomfortable.

'Well, he asked me to come and see you. I think things are getting a bit on top of him.'

'Not banged up again, obviously?' asked the ex-jockey.

Cheswick shook his head, 'But he wants to know how he can get into a couple of names you gave him. He's not sure whether they're safe or not.'

Gabriel's face changed. He smirked wondering what this was really all about. He'd allowed Blade to befriend him but still didn't trust him. He'd regretted mentioning Cheetah to him, and the names of both Lawrence and Waltham. But then he got some comfort from Riddell's absence. It meant that Blade hadn't gone sticking his nose in where it didn't belong, at the same time shouting his name all over the place. Georgie boy wouldn't have liked that too much. The fact that his old boss hadn't come bowling into the nick, demanding to know whether he'd lost his crown filling, reassured him that nothing untoward had happened. But now he was getting confirmation that Blade was still interested in Gabriel's past associates and Jimmy didn't like it. He placed his palm upwards, on top of the table that divided them. And Cheswick quickly responded with a few ounces of tobacco.

'This from Blade?' guessed Gabriel correctly.

'Yeah. He told me to tell you it didn't matter whether you helped him or not,' Cheswick smiled. 'The baccy's on him.'

Another time, another place, and Mr Gabriel would have slung the two packets in the bin. But here in the nick, it was a different story. Each strand of tobacco was a valuable asset. He sighed and shrugged his shoulders, the grin returning.

'Tell him those doors have been closed since we last spoke. So what else does he want?' Gabriel knew Blade only too well. There just had to be something else.

'He wants to know if he can use your name, and...' Cheswick paused for a brief moment. 'Just let me get this straight, Jimmy,' he said slowly, 'he wants to know, if it doesn't work out, is there anybody else he might be able to go to?'

'The crafty bastard's sent you on a fishing trip, Frank,' explained Jimmy G. 'Tell him from me, "bollocks".' He stood and banged on the door.

*

It really was a sight to behold. Exciting; pulsating; different. It was loud, noisy and energetic; headlights flashed from all directions; engines revved up; tyres screeched; air brakes hissed. The wagons were made up of heavy tractor units, each pulling its own large transportation container. Moving in and out of the loading bays, crowds of people raced from one point to another, mingling with each other, shouting at each other.

He sat there for a brief moment, staring out of the front windscreen. Although he'd seen it all before, such a tumultuous disturbance had always impressed Blade. After all, as a youngster he'd spent many a happy hour sitting with Harry Nesbitt, hiding in far distant bushes, watching a parcels company at work and nicking whatever was available whenever an opportunity presented itself. He wound the window down and sensed that even the air was different.

Cheetah Express Parcels was situated on a rural industrial estate surrounded by fields of sheep and cattle. However, the company's boundary lines appeared to be marked by the heavy diesel fumes which hung overhead, having escaped from the exhausts of more than a hundred heavy articulated wagons parked around main building.

From the sky it would have resembled a bicycle wheel, but with a rectangular centre and each lorry representing a spoke.

He steered the car towards the barrier. It was one that he'd borrowed from Ronnie Lakin, the last of his old villainous mates still prepared to help out an old con on the run. Ronnie had been looking after him on and off for years. He was still doing so. It was now nine o'clock and the night shift would only have just started. He'd been hoping that the hard slog he was about to undertake could have been avoided with one or two other names from Gabriel. But Cheswick hadn't been much help to him. Jimmy G wasn't as daft as Blade thought, obviously. So now route one was going to be the long way round.

The sight of the uniformed security guard at the barrier reminded Blade of the need to remain vigilant. He had to watch his back as he was still listed as an escaped prisoner and would remain so until *they* provided him with the necessary piece of paper stating otherwise. He'd been under the impression that as soon as he'd walked out of Long Lartin, the Home Secretary's pardon would have been immediately placed into his mitt. But the Secret Squirrels obviously had other ideas.

'Problems with red tape,' according to Pike. What a load of shite! They were the people who were running the country. Red tape? They must think his head was full of Scotch mist or something. But he'd be patient. Obviously they had their reasons. He'd give it a couple of more days and then go and point a Smith and Wesson at Pikey's head.

But yes, until that happened he'd have to stay on his toes. One bad move. One phone call, that's all it would take, and his secret service days would come to an abrupt end together with what he was really about – the additional ten grand he'd been promised upon completion! There had to be better ways of making a living but at the moment he couldn't think of any.

*

'Come for a job,' were the only words needed for the barrier to be lifted. He was directed to the administration office inside the warehouse and parked the car before weaving his way on foot around the stationary and moving heavy wagons.

'You should have a fluorescent on,' shouted somebody. But Blade ignored him.

As his eyes adjusted to the bright lights inside the warehouse, his ears also had to adapt themselves to the noise created by two or three hundred men and women labouring. They were all busy pushing parcels from one part of the building to another. Some in wheeled cages; some on palettes; some on top of hand-controlled trolleys. There appeared to be more activity inside than he'd seen around the outer loading bays. The atmosphere was intense, like a crowd at a football match, but the people here were running around in different directions, racing against the clock to get every container filled before the nightly deadline was reached.

He stood there for a moment, looking across at the huge conveyor belt running around the outside perimeter of the building. It was directing and transporting queues of items of all shapes and sizes towards the open loading bays. There was another similar construction suspended high above head height, with metal gantries built alongside the moving belt for the use of supervisors. Wherever Blade turned his eyes he saw night porters working incessantly, all with the same objective.

'Half-two's the time out.' A tall, slim, dark-skinned man with face stubble and black thinning hair stood at the side of him. 'Every trunker has to be loaded and on its way by then, otherwise they can't get the parcels out to the depots for delivery on time.'

Blade nodded his appreciation of the lesson. He could only just about hear what was being said to him. The tall man stepped closer, his gloved hands remaining inside his pockets. Who could blame him? Each side of the warehouse was open, allowing the icy winds to blow straight across the floor. That was fine whilst you were building up a sweat, running around like a headless chicken, but not very comfortable if you were at a standstill for more than a few seconds.

'I'm Lawrence. Understand you've been asking for me?'

Blade wondered whether he'd just lost his pet mouse or something, as his eyes never seemed to leave the concrete floor. At first he didn't know whether he was addressing a thick black beard or the top of Lawrence's head.

Neither man was allowed to stand still for more than a few seconds before having to move out of the way of various consignments, either rushing or crashing past them.

'Gabriel,' Blade shouted, 'Jimmy G said you might have some work for me.'

The eyes lifted, took in Blade's blue-tinted face and then returned to the floor, obviously continuing the search for that bloody mouse. Blade couldn't quite hear what his new acquaintance said, but caught the name, 'Terry', as Lawrence pointed towards a small block of contemporary offices in the far corner of the warehouse. At least he'd made some contact and that was sufficient for now. He didn't think it wise to try and enter into any prolonged conversation, although that would have been an almost impossibility in the circumstances.

Within minutes, Terry the night manager had briefed the ex-con on his work duties. They were fairly simple: shift those cages over there and then run your arse ragged until we tell you to stop. It wouldn't need the brain of Britain to sort that one out and he was quickly directed to where a load of cages, full to the brim with parcels, were standing filling a large space on the warehouse floor. So, Steve Blade was now a night porter in the parcels business. He didn't exactly feel exhilarated by the thought of what was to come and even less so when he was handed a pair of industrial gloves, to wear for protection. But here he was, from a small cell inside Long Lartin to a small corner of a freezing warehouse, lifting parcels onto the back of a lorry – all for five quid an hour on top of his already agreed bonus from his real employers. He didn't know which was the worse: here, or in the nick? One thing was certain though. You had little choice but to work hard, otherwise you just froze your bollocks off!

'New at the job, ain't yer?'

Here we go, he thought, another Bernard Manning. Blade was inside the container, towards the front, pushing what seemed to be a ton of parcels in a cage that had to be propped up against the inside wall. He turned to see a large man in overalls, sporting a ginger beard to go with his mop of hair, standing just inside the entrance to the vehicle. Looks like Bernard Manning as well.

'First time I've ever had to load parcels on a container.'

'We calls them trunkers, pal,' explained Goliath. 'Bin in the nick, ain't yer?'

Blade looked startled, not at the question itself, more at the way this nosy bastard had asked it. But he had to play it softly. Normally he'd probably favour sticking a crow bar over this dumbo's head, but now he was in, he had to keep the peace – long enough anyway, to get the information he needed.

He answered the question with one of his own. 'Who wants to know? You the local godfather or something?'

The big man moved closer towards him, his shovel-like hand extended as a sign of friendship, to which the new porter responded positively. 'No, Graham Rudge. I drive this 'ere trunker you're loading.'

'Blade, Steve Blade.'

'Listen, Steve, don't think I'm being personal,' explained Rudge. 'It's just that most of us have been in the nick. Who else do you think would do this kind of work for a fiver an hour?' The man had a point. 'If there's anything you need just give us a shout, mate.'

Blade nodded. 'Got the job through Chrissie Lawrence and Marty Waltham.'

Rudge seemed to become more at ease. 'Waltham's off tonight. Have you seen Chrissie yet?'

Another nod of the head, 'He's still looking for his lost mouse though,' quipped Blade, but he made no inroads with that one and Rudge just looked at him blankly.

A voice bellowed from outside the container, 'Come on, Victor Mature. Let's see some bloody sparks come out of that arse of yours. More chance of seeing Jupiter blow up, you idle bastard.'

Rudge smiled and nodded towards a small tubby geezer standing just a few feet away from the trunker they were in, hands on hips, very unpleasant looking.

'Don't mind the Midget. He's a wanker.'

'Supervisor?' asked Blade.

154

'Sort off. A wanker. I'll let you get on. Mustn't delay the trunker – or the wanker.' He turned and jumped back down onto the loading bay, grinning but not having a clue just how much help Blade might be asking from him in the future. One thing was certain though, Blade would be feeling very stiff in the morning!

✳

The entertainment was a bit loud for Priestley's liking. Must be getting old, he thought, as he stood in his favourite position, up against the bar. He watched Carol Guardia for a short time, laughing and performing with a group of young reporters, some with knotted bright ties around their oversized shirt necks. They were obviously there to impress the editors. Others just wore T-shirts. They were obviously the real workers who got the news in for the paper. Well after all, it was their do, so he mustn't take the piss. Or rather, it was some woman's leaving party. Some secretary for one of the editors who'd been with the paper for the past three hundred years or so. He'd only accepted Carol's invitation as an attempt to make amends for his earlier cock-up with her. It was the least he could do, having inadvertently shit on her from such a great height. But at least the shirt ties and T-shirts weren't pissing about. The small dance floor was crowded and it was still fairly early. He usually needed about five pints down him before he ventured into that particular arena. He had a habit of making a prat of himself, once he tried to swivel his hips and touch his toes.

'Well now, twice in a week, Jack Priestley.' Sonia looked devastating in a long, white, low-cut dress covered in silver sequins. When he saw the top of her breasts peeping out from the dress his mind raced back to the times when they were together and when they'd really enjoyed themselves. That was before she'd declared UDI on him. He was surprised to see her and it showed, which was probably the reason why her companion tried to make a diplomatic departure.

'See you shortly, Sonia. I need to speak to Jas over there.' She was a tall, slim woman with hair the colour of Sonia's dress. In fact she was a very beautiful woman who Priestley had difficulty in putting an age to. Perhaps early forties?

'Susan, let me introduce you to an old friend,' the barrister insisted. 'Detective Chief Inspector Jack Priestley. Lady Ridlington.' It was becoming a bad habit, her using his rank like that.

He managed to shake hands with the height of sophistication, before she disappeared into the crowd leaving himself and Sonia alone. Very romantic.

'So, Jack. Found out what you wanted to know about my client?' That was said with more than a hint of sarcasm and Jack replied with a shake of his head.

Choosing not to be drawn further on that delicate subject, he asked, 'Who's the lady?'

'Interested, Jack?' The sarcasm was still there. 'Don't be. That's Susan Ridlington. Sir Richard Ridlington's wife. Not your type. Bit upper-class, you know.'

'Am I supposed to know the name?' asked Priestley, trying to look a little superior because that was Sonia's type of man, or so he thought. But he was just showing his ignorance, or so she thought.

'The former defence secretary.'

Good old Jack! Everybody in the country knew of Sir Richard Ridlington, except Jack.

'She's a very lonely woman, Jack,' explained Sonia, 'with her husband being away most of the time on business. But she's not that lonely.' She paused and looked serious for a moment. 'She's got some kind of problem and I'm trying to find out what it is.' She lifted her arms, palms turned upwards as Jack had seen her do so many times before in court when trying to emphasise a particular point. 'I've offered to help but she tells me she's alright.'

'Perhaps she is,' suggested Jack.

'No, there's something wrong. I can feel it.'

He sympathised but really couldn't be bothered with all this women's tittle-tattle. It was time to bite back. He'd had enough of sarcastic women, especially those who were in the habit of giving him a pisser in the face. 'Well, I don't suppose she'll feel very lonely for long, Sonia. Especially with you around.' It was amazing he didn't use the words, 'Especially with a nosy git like you around.' He knew immediately, he shouldn't have said that and regretted his words the moment he spoke them. With a screaming desire to climb back into the lawyer's bed he wasn't exactly using his loaf. More like, he couldn't stop himself from banking his own little ship straight onto the rocks. Sonia smiled, adjusted her bra strap as if to frustrate him more and walked away. Well done, Jack. That's the spirit. That little gem put you back to the dinosaur era.

It was time to go. He'd had enough. He certainly wasn't going to get anywhere with his old flame. *He'd* made sure of that. And there was no one else of interest to him in the room.

'On the move then, copper?'

He was glad they'd overcome their slight differences the day before, even though the memory of his left cheek on fire hadn't quite left him yet.

'Early to bed, early to rise.' Bit corny but Priestley didn't give a shit.

'See you got to meet royalty at last, Jack?'

That was worth a smile and that's all she got as an answer, but there was more to come from the budding young reporter. He just had to be a little patient.

'Bit elusive, that one.'

Priestley stubbed his cigar in the ashtray. With its twelve-inch diameter, it was almost as big as a washing-up bowl!

'A lady with secrets, Jack.' Carol was tuning up for something.

He remained patient. It was on its way, like a speeding train whizzing through a long tunnel. He always got the full story eventually.

'But of course, you know all about them.'

Time for mickey taking was at an end. 'So let's have it, Miss Cassandra,' he suggested, still bearing a wry smile. 'What's behind that remark?'

'Only joking, Jack.'

He hadn't really noticed before, just how attractive Carol Guardia was and a number of thoughts crossed his mind. Perhaps the night wouldn't be such a waste of time after all. Then on reflection, perhaps it would. He turned to leave for about the twentieth time, but she grabbed his arm.

'There's something not quite right about Lady Ridlington. I don't know what it is, Jack, but I would love to know more about her past. I'm going to try and get an interview with her.'

'Well chuck, you're just the kind of researcher to do it.' He kissed her cheek and left.

✳

There was a buzz in the crew room as Priestley made his way through, towards his office. Whatever happened to the casualty department, he wondered. The normal early morning deathly stillness was missing. His people would usually just sit at their desks, gazing at something, unaware of events going on around them; holding their heads; talking softly with eyes half closed, allowing small flickers of light to penetrate slowly. All, except for one or two, recovering from bouts of alcohol poisoning.

But this morning was different. The office activities which didn't usually start for another two hours, were now well under way. People were laughing and joking, being nice to one another. Incredible, thought their leader. Perhaps they'd all been on orange juice the night before.

Patience had always been one of Jack Priestley's virtues and he knew eventually, someone would bring news to him. He wasn't wrong.

*

'Morning, boss,' Chris Barton looked as chirpy as ever. The only one of Priestley's officers who remained consistently boring, if not essential to the cause.

Priestley sat back in his chair and waited for his morning briefing from the DI.

'Bit of a buzz about the place, Chris?'

'That lot in there have just learned that they've won the Lottery.'

Priestley shot up in his seat.

Barton laughed and shook his head. 'Only a few hundred each,' he explained. 'Nothing for them to retire on.'

'Glad to hear it. No wonder they're all looking like they've just lost their virginity.'

'There is one other thing.' Barton looked serious, 'We've had a circular from Catchem in Derbyshire.' He placed the piece of paper in front of the Detective Chief Inspector.

'They've identified a pattern with two other child murders, one in Scotland and the other in North Yorkshire.'

Priestley looked at the circular. 'Catchem?'

'The National Child Abduction Unit, boss.'

'Of course,' agreed Priestley. He should have remembered, 'Go on, Chris.'

'Well, apparently the link between them is the motorway and they suspect it could be a sales rep, or somebody else who travels up and down the country.' Barton seemed almost apologetic in bringing such information to his senior officer's attention, particularly as the murders had taken place a long way off their patch.

'Okay, let's go down that road.' He paused to think quickly of a new strategy. That was what he was there for, what he was being paid all that money to do. It was what senior management was supposed to be all about. 'Get me a map artist. I want to know every town and village from which you can get easy access to where the girl's body was found.'

Barton didn't quite understand.

'As a short cut, off the motorway. The victim wasn't that far away from Junction 12.'

'Three miles,' confirmed Barton.

'Well, he might just be taking short cuts, but I prefer the idea that he's coming off the motorway to dump them.'

Barton nodded in agreement.

'One thing's certain though, Chris. If he is using the motorway network as they suspect, he's not snatching the kids off it, is he?'

'Right, guv.'

✳

Christ, it was a cold night. The frost didn't just nip Jack in the face it booted his backside as well. Or at least it felt as though it did. He looked at his watch. Five minutes late. And then he looked over at a small distant plot of grassed-over land at the side of the first industrial unit on his right which he was walking towards. At least they haven't built anything on that yet, he recognised.

He knew why Blade had tapped out the message on his Enigma, asking for a meet at this particular venue. During the daytime it was a hive of activity. But now, it was dark and lonely. They'd spent hours during the summer evenings just sitting on what was then a piece of wasteland, discussing, debating, dreaming. And that was well before anybody had even heard of Industrial Estates or Business Parks.

'Like Napoleon. He almost conquered the world.'
'You'll never be like Napoleon.'
'Who says?'
'It's not like it used to be now, Steve. It was different then.'

Priestley remembered the wide-open eyes of the young Steve Blade as they both sat just there, next to the hedge he was now walking towards, discussing their futures.

'So, what about Montgomery?' Blade persisted. 'He was a great soldier and a great leader of men.' He'd read that somewhere.
Young Jack was fascinated by his mate's dreaming but always thought Bladey was reaching too far towards the stars.
'Yes, he was.'

The place hadn't changed much since they were kids, except he couldn't remember it being as cold as this, the frozen grass crunching beneath his feet.

'Your sister's got holes in her drawers, Jack Priestley.'
'I haven't got a sister.'
'Well if you did, she'd have holes in her drawers.'

Only a few more yards to walk now. No sign of Blade yet. The voices continued to echo in his head.

'You can kiss my arse, Jack Priestley.'
'If your mum heard you swear like that, you'd get a backhander.'
'No, I wouldn't'
'Yes, you would.'
'Well take that for your lip.'

✳

The senior detective could still remember the blood dripping from the cut on his forehead.

'Jack, over here.'

It was only a whisper, but he'd recognise that voice anywhere. And there he was, standing huddled up inside the large doorway.

'On your own this time, I see.'

'You hope.'

Blade stepped out into the light coming from the corner of the industrial unit.

'Made a right balls-up of it last time,' he complained. 'Bit over the top weren't you?'

Priestley ignored the remark. 'How long have you got to keep up this cloak-and-dagger stuff for?'

'Until they say otherwise.'

'They?'

Blade stomped his feet up and down to try and prevent frostbite. 'The Secret Squirrels, mate. You should know. All I've been told is that I'm supposed to pass everything onto you.'

'I know. So how did you get yourself involved in this crock of shit?'

Blade beckoned for Priestley to walk around the back of the building with him, where it was even darker. 'Ten grand, Jack.'

'And that's the only reason?'

'Could there be any other?' Blade seemed surprised. 'There's another ten at the end of the job. Would you turn it down?'

Priestley just smiled, not really knowing the answer.

'I tried to tell you in the nick, Jack,' Blade continued. 'But you were too hell bent on believing I'd brought funny stuff into the country.'

'Yeah, well. There was nothing else to make me believe otherwise.' Priestley looked down towards the flagstones, slightly embarrassed.

Blade just sniffed. The cold air was irritating his nose. 'I'm into Cheetah, Jack. Loading parcels like a good 'un.'

'And?'

'Not much at the moment. Met Lawrence and Waltham. They're both on the international run.' Blade stopped and faced him with both hands dug deeply into his pockets. 'Problem is, Jack, they haven't made any approach to me yet and they don't look as though they're going to. I haven't seen either of them since the second night. Lawrence introduced his mate to me and then they both disappeared. Haven't seen them since.'

'What's involved with the international run?'

'Apparently, they just take those parcels that have to go to the airport for overseas delivery. But I haven't been able to find out which loading bay they work on yet.'

'Birmingham Airport?'

'Yeah.'

'I'll try and have a look at them from that end then. What about Gabriel? Have you mentioned his name yet?' asked Priestley.

'First night, to Lawrence,' was the reply. 'But all he did was push me off to the night gaffer.'

'Might take time.'

'I've been talking to one of the other drivers, bloke named Rudge. He reckons Lawrence and Waltham are inseparable but I have to be careful with him.'

'In what way?' Priestley lit a cigar, more for warmth than the actual smoke.

'He's a bit shifty. I don't trust him, Jack. Mind you, I don't trust any of the bastards.'

The two men continued their walk, until the path reached the back of the unit only to be blocked by some wild-growing hawthorn bushes. They both then turned to walk back in the same direction they'd come. Priestley was contemplating the next move for Blade, but couldn't think of one. He just had to stay with what he was doing and persevere with trying to get closer to the two delivery boys.

'I'll update James Bond in the morning,' suggested the copper.

'You mean our Mr Pike?'

'Commander Pike.'

'He didn't tell me that, Jack. What is he?'

'In what way?'

'Copper or member of the cabinet?'

164

Priestley laughed.

That was the first time Blade had seen that for a long time.

'Bit of both, I think.'

They decided to leave the estate as they'd come in: separately. But as Priestley walked away, he looked back at Blade, 'And Steve, try and play this one straight if you can. I've had enough of your antics in the past to last me a lifetime, son.'

Now it was Blade's turn to laugh, 'Well good for you, Mr Smart-arse. Just remember to keep your boys away from me and keep an eye on that portable screen.'

✱

chapter eleven

The fine powdery snow blew in like Arctic washing-powder, but without the blue bits. It had already completely covered the corner where Blade was working, creating a treacherous skidpan underfoot. He was constantly stamping his feet as he pulled and pushed and then lifted, at the same time running between the warehouse floor and hydraulic lift at the back of Rudge's trunker. But no matter how much effort he put into his work, he was quickly starting to look like an ice cube.

The others were well seasoned for such weather. Most of them had been working at Cheetah for years and knew exactly what was required. One cup of hot soup during the midnight break wasn't sufficient. It had to be accompanied by long johns and thermal vests with newspaper tucked beneath shirts and heavy pullovers providing the necessary insulation. It was the same during the warm summer nights when T-shirts were the fashion. The only items of clothing worn throughout the complete year were heavy gloves and toe-protected boots.

But now, Blade felt as though he was working on some scientific expedition up at the North Pole. With every roller-shutter door open around the whole perimeter of the warehouse, he might just as well have been performing on the outside car park. Not long now though, he thought.

Two more cages to go and then home. Home to a long shot of whiskey and lapful of warm bum. He still hadn't seen Lawrence and Waltham and was puzzled as to whereabouts they were working.

'Rudgy?'

The big feller walked across to him.

'Whereabouts is international mate? I can't see any place inside here that looks any different to the rest of it.'

Rudgy grinned, like the gormless git he really was, 'Over there.' He pointed towards the back of the warehouse.

Blade still couldn't see but raised his shoulders and shook his head, not wanting to appear over-interested.

'In the other unit. Over the back.'

'What other unit?'

'Come on, the midget's having his cuppa. I'll show you.'

The last thing Blade wanted to do was go pioneering on a night like this. But he'd asked the question, so really didn't have much choice.

Both of them felt their faces start to freeze and they walked in between the trunkers being loaded, Rudge leading the way. Blade followed him across the open space, past queuing wagons being mustered by security men in bright yellow jackets and thick woolly hats. Then across some grassland towards another brick-built building. But this one was enclosed, without roller-shutter doors for allowing loading access. In the few weeks Blade had been there he hadn't noticed this particular place, probably because of a copse of trees which stood between the warehouse in which he worked and this new discovery.

'By the way, Steve, you interested in making a few extra quid?'

Blade looked at the big man. He was singing his kind of song, 'Always.'

'Well, I've got a little proposition for yer.'

'I'm all ears, Noddy.'

Their conversation was interrupted by a security guard shouting and running towards them. 'Where's your jackets?' he was bawling in a very excited and aggressive manner.

Blade thought about snotting him, but then remembered his new image.

'You're supposed to be wearing fluorescent jackets out here,' the guard persisted. 'Looking to get run over or something?'

Now he was definitely going to get snotted, but Rudge grabbed Blade by the arm, sensing that his new-found mate was starting to boil over at this numbskull's attitude.

'Sorry mate, we'll go back and get a couple,' agreed Rudge. After all, it was only common sense the man was preaching.

They both turned and started to make their way back towards the main warehouse. Still within earshot of the security guard Rudge explained that the international trunker backed into the other unit through two large entrances.

'The parcels are loaded into igloos which are like big curve-shaped containers. Then they just load the igloos onto the back of the trunkers and it's off to the airport.'

'Igloos?'

'Yeah. Did you ever see those air raid shelters on the films. They gave them to everybody during the war? Made of corrugated sheeting.'

Blade didn't know whether to nod or shake his head. He decided to do neither and just continued to listen carefully, still glancing back at the guard who was still standing where they'd left him, arms folded, legs slightly apart. Like a New

York cop on point duty, waiting for them to pull out a couple of sawn-offs and take out a trunker. When they both got back to the warehouse, Rudge suggested they climb up into the cab of his trunker. As was the case with most of the wagons being loaded, the engine was still running and a wall of hot air hit them as they climbed up into the seats.

'You don't just happen to have a drop of brandy as well do you, Rudgy?' joked Blade.

'I've got something better than that,' explained the lorry driver before he lit up a cigarette. 'This lot.'

Blade slowly turned his head towards him. 'This lot?' It wasn't really a question, just confirmation of what Rudge had just said.

'Yeah. Christmas is a-coming Stevie boy and I need a hand making a delivery.'

A picture was starting to evolve and Blade's short-term future was beginning to look brighter. 'This lot?' That was a question.

'This lot.' Rudge nodded. 'Interested?'

Now it was Blade's turn to nod his head, like a baby orang-utan mimicking its mother. 'The whole of this lot?'

'Yeah,' confirmed the other. 'Well, the parcels inside it anyway,' he grinned.

That sent a few shock waves through the retired, now-working-for-the government armed robber. He just stared out through the front windscreen.

'Fuck me,' was all he could say at that particular time.

'We always have a touch at Christmas.'

A touch, thought Blade. This was more than just a perk. There'd be a few grand up for grabs and for that the government could go and blow up its own arse. Perhaps working in the parcels business could have its rewards after all. He came out of his trance and turned his head sharply towards Rudge, who now had Blade's undivided attention.

'You said, "we". Who's "we"?'

'Me and whoever is working with me.' He also began to stare out of the windscreen, still clocking that nosy bastard who'd bawled them out earlier, but he'd moved on. There were other bodies flying all over the yard, some pushing empty cages, others directing trunkers away from the roller shutters. 'It's Christmas, Steve and it's your turn. That's if you're interested?'

How could he refuse. After all, he was a thief. 'How?' was his next question.

'Piece of piss,' explained his newly-found criminal associate. 'I usually square it with one of the other drivers, but this year I'm going to have my own away.'

Blade's question hadn't been answered, but he was a patient man.

Rudge continued. 'Thursday night is the best.' His voice lowered. That surprised Blade because he hadn't bothered to lower it before, when asking him if he was prepared to knock off a thousand parcels. 'That's when we carry the most.' Another pause whilst he spun his head around, as though the whole world was sitting outside his cab, listening in. 'I go for a Jimmy Riddle at the Warwick Services. That's the first one from here on the M40 and you just get in here and drive it off.'

'How?' Blade repeated.

'I've got duplicate keys.'

This sounded too good to be true. But what about the real reason he was there? He couldn't start performing whilst on Her Majesty's Service. Could he? Oh yes, he bloody well could. As Chrissie had already explained, it was Christmas. Next question, 'Where to?'

170

'London. Wembley to be exact. Richie Blagg. He's a trusted servant. Hand him the wagon, he hands you twenty-five. Ten for you, the rest for me.'

Blade sat up. The feeling in his body had returned. He was fully thawed out now. But he had a question. 'Five extra grand for you and I take all the risks?'

'Wrong. Who's got to go through the copper's interrogation and all that afterwards?' Rudge had a point. It was a fair point at that.

Blade thought about it for a split second. 'When?'

'This Thursday, night after tomorrow.'

'Time?'

'You finish at the same time I drive away from here.'

Blade didn't need reminding of that fact.

'When you leave just make your way down to the M40. Wait for me at the first services.'

Blade couldn't see any problems with that.

'When I come out of the bogs I'll expect to see the trunker gone,' continued Rudge. 'I'll give it another half an hour before I scream and you'll be well on your way.' He looked up to the roof, 'I reckon about an hour's drive for yer.'

'That still gives them half an hour to pull me on the motorway.'

'They're not going to pull every Cheetah trunker on the road.' Rudge was bristling with confidence.

Blade wasn't, yet. 'No, but they will this one because you'll give them the details.'

Rudge had obviously been waiting for that one. A broad grin almost spread across his face and around the back of his head. 'I'll give them the correct reg. number, but this wagon will have different plates on it.'

Blade suddenly felt a wave of optimism sweep across him. 'And you'll change the plates on your way to the meet?'

Rudge nodded, still grinning. 'Told yer it'd be a piece of piss.' His face straightened. 'Just don't forget to bring the bunce with you on Friday night.'

Blade had an afterthought. 'Need a contact number.'

The Cheshire Cat gave him his home telephone number.

Yes, it could be a Merry Christmas after all.

✱

It was four o'clock in the morning when Priestley and his team first saw the trunker arrive at the airport. From Blade's earlier message on the Enigma, every trunker had cleared from Cheetah by two-thirty which meant it had taken Lawrence and Waltham an hour and a half to complete, what would normally have been a one-hour journey. So it was now up to him, to discover what exactly they'd been doing during the spare half an hour. That was the easy bit. At least now he had the details of the vehicle they were driving and would stay with it – every night until the answer had been found. But for now the cameras were busy. His team clicked away, capturing the two trunker drivers' faces. Their every movement was also recorded on video as the igloos were taken off the back of the wagon, using an airport forklift. Priestley had considered using the airport security cameras, but then thought it too risky. It was far safer to rely on their own equipment and the night glasses and lenses would do the trick.

Once unloaded, both Waltham and Lawrence followed the forklift driver into a small office where the three of them supped tea. As far as Priestley was concerned, that could only mean they hadn't stopped for refreshments en route which cancelled out any thoughts that the extra half an hour could have been used up for that purpose.

Although he couldn't be certain and he would still have to deploy the surveillance team from the moment both targets left Cheetah.

∗

The return journey only took the two night workers an hour, confirming the extra time taken on the trip to the airport. It had been a useful exercise but Jack knew this was only the start. Not that the remainder of the hours of darkness would be wasted. Not by him anyway.

∗

'So, why all the interest, Jack? Or shouldn't I ask?'

'Shall we say he wants to represent Tangiers in its bid for next year's Winter Olympics and I want to know why.'

Sonia laughed aloud and climbed back onto the bed, trying not to spill the glass of St-Émilion, which he'd brought with him.

'Well, darling,' she said with a mischievous look in her gob-stopper eyes, 'my George has probably done that because he's just had the case for which I was representing him dropped by the prosecution.'

'He's what?'

'The good old Crown Prosecutions Department, my love. They believe there is insufficient evidence to proceed any further. And what's more I agree with them,' she had a serious glint in her eyes. 'That's why, darling, I agreed to take the brief in the first place.'

Priestley was gobsmacked. Completely speechless. But he soon recovered. 'Any other good news?' he asked.

'What can I say? George Riddell is affluent. Or that's the impression he gives. He's the MD of a large steel business...'

'Which is bent,' interrupted Priestley.

'So *you* say. But what's interesting about the man, is that he always insists on paying in cash up front. Or so my clerk tells me.'

'Tax evasion,' suggested Jack.

She ignored him. 'He has told me he has interests abroad though, Jack.'

'Any country in particular?'

Sonia shook her head.

'What kind of business?'

She shook her head for a second time. 'There's not much more I can tell you, dear. Except of course, he does appear to be as interested in you, as you are in him.'

That raised Jack's eyebrows. 'But he's never met me.'

'Except the other night in the club,' she reminded him.

'Yes, but we never spoke.'

'Well, after you'd left in that huff, he asked a million questions about you.'

'Go on.'

'Where you worked and the kind of work you did and all that kind of trivial banter. Oh, and what I found to be somewhat mystifying, was whether or not you had ever mentioned...' she paused to try and recollect whatever it was Riddell had asked.

Priestley just lay there, appearing to be a little impassive but his eyes bulging with fascination.

'...Jimmy Cree, or Gable. Does that mean anything?'

✳

Another hour had passed by before Priestley left the flat and walked towards his car across the narrow road, which was now an ice rink. As he scraped the frost from the windscreen he didn't notice the dark figure of a man, standing in a shop doorway, opposite Sonia's two-storey block. Priestley's car left as the man walked across towards where it had been parked, and towards the front entrance to the luxury flats.

*

Blade stepped out from behind the pile of empty boxes at the same time Lawrence and Waltham jumped down from the cab. Mr Nice Guy was in town and he broadened his smile as they walked away from him. There was no one else around. Everyone had blown the coop some two hours before. But he needed to talk to both of them. It was time to make his own mark and he couldn't do that whilst they were working a couple of hundred yards away in a different building. So now they were back from the airport delivery. And now was the time to discuss his proposition with them.

'You all right, lads?' he shouted.

Lawrence stopped and turned, but Waltham, just like a worker having finished his shift and wanting to get home as soon as his tired legs would carry him there, continued walking.

'Marty,' called Lawrence and the other man stopped and walked back.

'Bit cold for this time of year,' suggested Blade, knowing exactly where he was coming from.

'What's up?' asked Waltham.

'Just thought I'd look in on you lads and see how things were going.'

'What?' Lawrence looked extremely puzzled.

'Haven't you got a home to go to?' That was Waltham again.

'Yeah, I have. But I'm also out of work.'

Lawrence threw a quick look at his partner and then explained, 'You've got a job, unless they've just sacked you. Is that it?'

Blade shook his head, 'I mean a proper job.' He walked to within a foot of both men and lowered his voice. 'Jimmy G told me you boys would give me an introduction into the real business.'

Again the other two looked at each other.

'Piss off, Blade,' said Waltham. 'You're in dream world.'

They both smiled and turned to leave.

'I've got ten grand to invest,' lied Blade. A last throw of the dice. A titbit, just to get their interest, like a maggot on a hook, dangling in front of the Crucian Carp.

'You're on the run, as well,' Waltham shouted back to him as both men continued to walk away.

Mission a failure. Why was it, thought Blade, all of these wankers, like Jimmy Gabriel, were difficult to get into? It was as though he had 'Supergrass' tattooed all over his forehead.

But at least he knew what he was dealing with now. Or trying to.

*

chapter twelve

During the daytime and evenings the tourists flocked to Gas Street Basin, to be propelled back in time and to be reminded of past social deprivation, when drays pulled barges and young boys heaved tons of coal onto the numerous vessels that were once pulled through an overcrowded canal system. The developers had done a magnificent job, returning the once-forgotten wharves back to their original state. Even the green slime that had sat on the surface of the water, watching the centuries go by, had now disappeared. What was once a focal point for a more commonly used industrial transportation system, was now a tourist attraction with its small, newly built, red brick bridge linking the opposite walkways.

But at one o'clock in the morning there were no tourists.

The crowds had long gone, leaving the more modern glass-fronted places of entertainment alone to enjoy their own company. The International Convention Centre and Symphony Hall stood impressively tall, like proud guardians watching over the towpaths along which a number of brightly painted narrow boats remained moored.

From the bridge, Riddell could see the barge waiting below, barely illuminated by the quaint Victorian-style overhead lamps. It could quite easily have been a scene from the late nineteenth-century East End of London, with the cobbled walkways on each side of the black shiny water. He scampered down the steps, trying not to take the quicker route on his backside, closely followed by Ponteus and another meat loaf. As he approached he nodded at the boatman who was trying to restrict to a minimum the movement of his vessel on the water. At the far end of the covered section sat the dark figure, towards which George had to clumsily make his way, down through the middle of the rows of benches. His two minders were already posted to the front of the boat.

'George.'

'Mr Grainger,' acknowledged Riddell and sat down, waiting for the lights to be switched on. He'd attended this meeting many times before and the lights had never come on until they were away from the mooring. And the same applied this time.

Grainger looked more like a middle-aged bank clerk than a senior civil servant. He was a lot smaller than Riddell, with a small dark moustache that made him look younger than his years. However, unlike his visitor who was far more boisterous and aggressive, Grainger had a natural air of authority about him that Riddell resented but also admired. Although both men were well dressed, Grainger always seemed to appear more 'executive'. It was an appearance that can only be achieved by men experienced in putting the final touches to their attire: silk tie completely flush with the top of the shirt, not leaving the slightest gap between the knot and top button; cufflinks the correct size for the occasion; socks showing no wrinkles or scuff marks; overcoat lapels pressed back without the slightest crease in them. George could never achieve that. Not all at once, anyway.

The barge moved slowly forward, cutting through the still surface of the water. The forbidding figure of Ponteus stood erect at the bow, like a Roman Centurion eyeing the footpaths which skirted the canal and the dark buildings, as they passed by.

'So, George, you came on time,' acknowledged Grainger's cultured voice, at the same time eyeing his gold wristwatch. 'Excellent.'

George just nodded. Not that he didn't have much to say, but he'd earlier eaten Italian and pasta had never really agreed with him.

'I went to a meeting with our man last night. He's been offered a new kind of deal. Landmines by the hundreds.'

George's eyes lit up, 'How many hundreds?'

'Perhaps a couple of thousand. Can you deliver?'

Riddell remained expressionless, although he was experiencing something similar to a paratrooper making his first jump. This was a new twist to the game. Firstly, he'd never had to move anything other than military weapons before now and secondly, much more importantly he had no idea of how much he could charge.

The smaller man stood and walked a few yards down the aisle.

'Its not whether I can deliver,' explained George, 'you know that already. It's how?'

'That's your problem, my man. That's why we pay you so well,' said Grainger, his voice remaining calm and positive.

'Over what period?'

'Weeks rather than months.' Grainger paused before continuing, 'There's a foreign go-between laying the ground rules. You'll meet him George, but our man is willing to pay half a million in addition to the usual financial support, provided the deliveries are made within a six-month period.'

Now Riddell was on his feet causing Ponteus to stiffen, sharply turning his head towards where the two men stood, only to relax once more after confirming that all was well.

George knew exactly what Grainger meant by the words 'financial support'. He'd never had to part with a single morsel before. Whoever it was the civil servant represented, 'our man' saw to all that. The only responsibility for George was to collect after each shipment had been safely delivered. But this new angle was testing his mental ability. He knew he hadn't time to calculate anything. The deal would be struck now or not at all. And that could mean an abrupt end to everything else involved in his illegal transportation business. And he couldn't afford that, following the recent episode when the coppers knocked on the door of one of his fight promotions.

He tried to delay matters, whilst quickly working out what adaptations he would have to make to the system he already had in place – a tried and trusted system that had been successfully used on a hundred occasions to move crates of weapons across to Belgium.

'How would I receive them?' he asked.

'In the usual way.'

'Landmines?'

'Yes, landmines, George. Do you have a problem with that?' Grainger was sounding as though they were discussing boxes of chocolates being nicked out of Cadbury's backyard.

'No, but Princess Di would have if she'd still been here.' Riddell didn't mean for that to sound insulting and it didn't. He was really trying to refer to all the adverse publicity in recent months concerning the use of landmines in conventional warfare.

It was of no matter, because Grainger ignored the remark and George knew the meeting was coming to a close because the canal barge had turned a full circle and was now heading back to where he'd boarded.

'I need your answer, George.'

'When's the first shipment?' Unlike Grainger, Riddell's voice sounded slightly agitated which was as a result of the size of the bounty involved rather than any operational problems he might have envisaged.

'Whenever you're ready, of course,' Grainger confirmed, returning to his original seat. 'Provided every consignment is delivered within a six-month period, let's say the final delivery not being later than October next year.' Grainger paused again, 'That gives you a six-month slot inside the next ten months, George.'

Riddell was still trying to look attentive but his eyes told Grainger that his mind was partly elsewhere, obviously working out the mechanics of the scheme.

The civil servant got to his feet again and, as though trying to reassure the bigger man, placed a hand on his shoulder. 'I need that nod from you, George, and don't worry, I'll have the final figures ready for you well before you start transportation. You're going to make a lot of money from this.'

'And so will a few others,' came the reply. George couldn't hide the doubt in his expression but knew this was an offer he couldn't refuse. 'We'll be ready within the month.'

Both men shook hands as the barge came to a standstill and the engines cut out.

*

Another ten grand for the festive season was too much of a carrot to dangle in front of a man such as Steve Blade. He'd toyed with the idea of not letting Priestley or his government contacts down, ever since Rudge had made him the offer, but only toyed with it. After all, they were all on steady wages. He had to get what he could when the opportunity arose, whatever crumbs fell off the table, no matter how large or small. Apart from that, he was a greedy bastard and anything for nothing usually had his label on it, anyway.

Rudge was right about Thursday nights. There must have been at least another fifteen thousand more parcels to move. And he was making sure he was doing his bit. He knew, having only been there a short time, he'd have to be very careful about his own position. He guessed that once this lot blew up, the law would want to know the names of recent employees. And then he would be presented as every young copper's dream. On the run from a top security prison. Your very own friendly neighbourhood drugs baron.

He considered going off sick after the job, but his absence from work would only get them more hyped up. No, he thought as he flashed the red light on another fifty bar-code labels, he'd just have to sweat it out and rely on Jack-the-Lad to cover him if he came unstuck. Christ, if Priestley ever found out about his little bit of overtime there wouldn't be anywhere for Blade to hide in the Universe. He shuddered at the thought.

He'd planned to stay away from the corner of the warehouse where Rudge's trunker was loaded, so made an excuse that he'd injured his shoulder. The night manager agreed for him to assist with checking the address labels for one night only, which suited his book. At least Rudge wouldn't have the opportunity to start sending signals to him or showing out in some other stupid and irresponsible way.

Blade hadn't exactly been overjoyed at the way his new partner in crime had slipped the duplicate keys to him the night before. He hadn't exactly been subtle, just tossing them at him as he crossed the yard, laughing and taunting. Clever bastard, but careless. Blade was above that. He didn't intend to blow this one. Christ, if he did, Priestley would hang him. So would the rest of the bloody country. Anyway, it was a good way of getting some credibility with the real lads, Lawrence and Waltham. And he was desperate for some of that with those two after the cold shoulder he'd experienced the other night. Once they'd heard the success story, they'd be queuing up for his services, especially with ten grand in his pocket, or so he'd have them believe. He'd done it once before with Jimmy G, why not with a couple of tosspots like those two?

The hours passed by, seemingly more quickly than ever before. Unlike any other night he wasn't in any hurry. Then the first of the trunkers started to make a move and the usual queue started to form outside the front of the building. That was a company rule. They all left at the same time whether travelling to somewhere just down the road, or to the northernmost tip of Scotland. As soon as the long convoy disappeared off the site the night porters could book off and a second convoy of privately owned vehicles would then race away.

From a distance he watched the back of Rudge's trunker pull away from the loading bay and head towards the main gate, stopping at the rear end of the long queue. The next two minutes seemed like two hours as he stood there, waiting his turn to clock out. Like a stampede, as soon as each porter had hit the button on the clock, he or she would race towards their vehicle as though the building was only seconds away from being hit by a huge comet from outer space. Every night witnessed the same spectacle. Not that he could blame them though. Who in their right mind would want to spend a second more than they had to in that dump?

His card passed through the wall machine and he was on his way; to the pre-arranged meeting place and a well-earned Christmas bonus. And what a bonus he was about to earn himself. Joy to the world and all the boys and girls, he sang as he jumped in his car.

Rudge had got a five minute start on him, but that meant nothing. Blade knew he would still get to the motorway services before him, he'd probably pass him on the way if they both took the same route.

The weather wasn't the best for thieving. It was freezing but also crystal clear. There would be no stars hiding behind clouds that night. Blade had always preferred the mucky, misty stuff, or heavy rain pouring down on everyone, persuading them to get indoors as soon as possible. He parked his own motor well away from the lorry park and walked across to the services. To his surprise the trunker was already in position, parked up by the pumps.

He waited. No sense in jumping straight in. Like a fox, his eyes skirted the surrounding area. Nothing suspicious. No law. No nosy bastards about. No sign of Rudge either. Must be taking his time in the gents, thought Blade. Everything appeared normal. He couldn't see whether he'd changed the plates or not, but he had to trust him to do something and being as it had been Rudge's idea in the first place, had no doubts it would have been done without any problems.

He couldn't stand there for too long. It would attract too much attention, even at that time in the morning. There was always the man. The one who wanted to be a hero. The frustrated copper who'd never made it because of his height, or lack of it. Or the frustrated genuine copper who was looking for something to do. He slowly approached the cab, fully alert, eyes rolling, watching for the slightest sign that all was not well. But it was. He didn't feel nervous. This was, to quote Rudge, going to be a piece of piss. A piece of beef to go with Sammy's turkey this year.

He reached the driver's door. His hand gripped the handle. Locked. Barmy bastard! Never told him it would be locked. Never mind, probably a creature of habit. He quickly ducked onto one knee, on the pretence of tying a shoe lace, but really to have another gander around. No, still quiet. Still deserted. Everything appeared to be just fine. No beads of sweat on his forehead. Cheeks of his arse tightly closed together. No problems!

The keys worked and he climbed up, still looking in front, sideways and behind. Nothing. He put the key into the ignition. Piece of piss. He kept reminding himself how Rudge had been right, up until now, anyway. All he had to do was get this thing down to the Smoke post-haste, to the Wembley address in his pocket.

Suddenly, there was a sound, like a gentle thud. Blade's heart skipped a beat and his arse leapt up from the small seat. Nothing. He wasn't hearing things. He quickly looked around the cab, sweat now streaming down his back. Nothing. Through the windows. Nothing. Except for the bloke in overalls leaving the gents and walking towards the garage reception. No wonder Rudge had taken his time. Must have been a queue. Now there was a slight trickle of sweat running down his forehead. This was always a bad sign for Blade. His fingers remained wrapped around the ignition keys, frozen. He hadn't imagined it, but it could have been one of a thousand things. Perhaps the wagon settling down, after his heavy lump had crashed into the seat? Like a house settling down after everyone had gone to bed or retired for the night, as lawyers would explain during a trial. Floorboards creaking and all that. He took in a deep breath and turned the key. The front facia lit up and he was ready for the off.

There it was again. This time he had to concentrate more on squeezing the cheeks of his arse more tightly together. This time it wasn't a thud. More of a groan. From a human being. Only there was supposed to be just one human being inside the cab – him! Another groan. This time it came from the back of the passenger seat.

'Bollocks to this!'

He pulled the seat forward and there to his amazement lay a child, curled up in a ball. He could hardly see in the darkness. He couldn't put the cab light on. He'd have the world and his brother pouring out of those services opposite.

'What's going on here?' Of all the inadequate things to say. The kid couldn't answer because it had some sort of tape around its mouth.

He wanted to remove the gag but felt like a novice about to take hold of a valuable piece of porcelain, the slightest mark reducing its value by thousands. He didn't know where to put his hands. He had to squeeze his head around the back of the seat and almost touch the small figure with his nose, before he realised it was a young girl with both her hands and feet bound together. He caught sight of her eyes. She was petrified and groaning louder and louder.

His first reaction was to run off. But what about the kid? He couldn't leave her there. But what was she doing in the cab in the first place? Then the gravity of what he'd come across hit him straight between the eyes. Good old Steve. If he drew a gun in the old West as quick as his powers of reasoning were, he'd be full of bullet holes in no time. There could be no doubting what he'd so innocently stumbled across. Rudge had picked this kid up and Blade didn't need to think too deeply as to the reason why. Of all the filthy bastards. And to think, all he was there for was to nick the wagon – on Rudge's behalf. He'd dob him in. No, first he'd kill him, then dob him in.

But there again, hang on a bit. Some logical reasoning began to return through the thick haze that was ever present inside his inadequate mind. Rudge wouldn't do that, knowing that Blade was going to nick his wagon. Was it Rudge's wagon? Shit, what he'd done was to climb into the wrong cab! Prize prat.

He searched frantically for the logbook and found it stuffed down inside the driver's door. G Rudge was on the front cover. It was his trunker all right. But something was wrong. Was *he* being set up? Bollocks to this. He grabbed the door handle to make a hasty retreat, but there was overalls, walking towards him. Shit, nowhere to go. Another groan from the kid. This was too much. He kept reminding himself that all he was, was just a thief.

He tried not to panic. Stay there. It'll be alright. Not very reassuring but he'd already forgotten about the ten-grand Christmas box. His good citizen hat was back firmly on his head and the heavy crowbar left in the passenger floorwell, held tightly in his hand. He looked towards the gents' toilet.

There was still no sign of Rudge. But the other geezer was getting closer and closer.

Why him? Why couldn't this have been a simple snatch, like they'd planned. Oh, he was pissed off, but that wasn't any good.

Think, Steve, for Christ's sake get the grey matter moving. If overalls opened the driver's door he'd get the crowbar. So what's the problem? If he didn't and just passed by, all Blade had to do was wait a short while and then leg it before ringing the filth. Better still call Priestley on that Oracle gadget or whatever it was called, in his car.

He was calming down, returning to his old self. Better and more positive thoughts came back into his head. His options were becoming much clearer now. His only serious problem was the realisation that the ten grand was slowly disappearing from view. Bollocks again, footsteps, just outside. It was overalls but where was he going? There was no other vehicle near him. Blade ducked and listened as the footsteps stopped, just outside the cab. He heard the sound of feet shuffling on the tarmac and then the cab door sprung open.

Well, there was one thing about our man Blade. When the option was clear, he took it. When there was only one junction off the motorway, he took it. And now, there was only one option. He didn't have to give it any more consideration. The crowbar crashed into the man's face as Blade leapt at him, like a leopard desperate to sink its teeth into its prey. There hadn't been enough space in which to get sufficient elevation to dump it on his skull but the shock of having been met in such a violent manner, made overalls incapable of any kind of effective retaliation.

Both men fell backwards, away from the cab onto the hard frost-covered floor with Blade on top. Now he had the space. Now he could perform to the best of his ability. All he could see in front of him was a screaming, petrified face. He would show no mercy. He never did when he was on top. Exactly the same as a kid.

The crowbar came down with a crash on top of overalls' head. He drew some comfort from seeing it wasn't Graham Rudge he was belting. What he had here was a dirty bastard who snatched kids off the streets. Another blow to overalls' head, this time causing blood to spurt down his rotten face.

Blade got to his feet and cried out as he made a serious attempt to convert his victim's ribs into chalk. Overalls also screamed out again and tried to scamper underneath the tractor unit. All that Blade could see on the tarmac in front of him was a football and he was David Beckham. Three penalty kicks in the ribs, one up the arse and another in the head. Overalls was going nowhere except to hospital, and Blade couldn't think of a better use for his metal-capped, toe-protected industrial boots.

Suddenly a pair of arms wrapped themselves around him and overalls lay on the ground in a semi-conscious state, the screams, now just muffled groans coming from his disfigured face. He'd certainly have to see a good dentist after he came out of the operating theatre!

Together with the handful of drivers who'd run across from the cafeteria, Blade pulled the terrified eight-year-old girl from out of her temporary prison. He felt his knees start to tremble as she threw her arms around his neck and squeezed tightly. She clung to him like a clam. Tears rolled down her face with her shoulders pulsating.

He remembered the ordeal Frank Cheswick had gone through and felt a sudden urge to cry himself. He tried to reassure the lass that her nightmare was at an end, and did so, but with just a few selected garbled words. For he, the terror of Nechells Green, the armed robber, who had frightened half to death so many security guards, was now openly and uncontrollably weeping.

Why him? Why was it always him who had to do the business? There was supposed to be a bloody police force for this sort of thing. And there they were. Two chequered hats climbing out of the red and white Motorway Jag. Time to leave.

He handed the little girl to one of the other drivers who had to wrench her away from him, trying belatedly to conceal his own emotions. And then, like the true hero he was, he casually strolled away into the darkness, towards where his, or rather Ronnie Larkin's, vehicle was parked, without any tax or insurance. There was no way he could afford to attract any attention to himself, for obvious reasons. He could only guess at the kind of questions they'd ask him. What? Why? And bloody how?

＊

'Jack, leave it,' she gasped.

Priestley agreed and carried on with his long awaited performance, frustration screaming from the top of his head. He'd often thought of this moment, of Blade sending a message, asking how he was, just at that critical moment. Well, he could go and stuff himself. At five in the morning and Sonia well captured, the biggest herd of buffalo on Earth wouldn't shift him now. But there again, had Blade ever sent a message just asking how he was? He must be in the shit! Damn the man.

'You're losing it, Jack. Jack, what's wrong?' There was disillusionment in her voice but Jack wasn't concentrating on the job in hand. There was a message on that damned machine and he just knew he had to read it, before he could share any further pleasure with the practising lawyer.

All the hard work coaxing her into bed, he thought as he reached for the machine. Should have left it in the car or on someone's roof. His hard-earned money thrown at a meal and the best bottle of claret he could find. But all was not lost. He turned, trying to smile and reassure her he'd be back in five seconds. Yes, that was it. All was not lost. He'd soon make up for lost ground. After all, he was a superstud, easily capable of such things!

CAUGHT YOUR CHILD KILLER JACK. MOTORWAY POLICE HAVE HIM ON THE M40.

*

Horace Machin was a 45-year-old lorry driver, later to be convicted of three murders of young children and the kidnapping of Mary Cotterill, the small girl whose life Blade had undoubtedly saved. Amazingly, Machin lived with his wife in the Scottish village of Ballater on Deeside and worked as an agency driver for a company contracted by Cheetah Express Parcels. On the night of his capture, he'd been asked to stand in for Graham Rudge and take his trunker down to North London, where he was to remain overnight, returning to Cheetah the following day to pick up another load due for transportation to Scotland. It was Machin's habit to abduct his young victims prior to arriving at Cheetah and keep them captive inside his cab whilst his container was loaded. Mary had been snatched off a street in Manchester whilst Machin was en route to the Midlands. On the night of his arrest he'd almost blown it when asked to take Rudge's trunker out. But he'd overcome his initial panic by successfully transferring Mary into the new cab without being seen, and before leaving Cheetah to deliver Rudge's load.

The first time Jack Priestley set eyes upon the man he'd been hunting, together with other forces, for the past few weeks, was in a hospital ward. Blade had done a good job on him and it took a further three weeks before Machin was fit to be discharged and taken straight to prison. Priestley was delighted, but couldn't help feeling somewhat bewildered by Blade's refusal to tell him why he was at the service station in the first place. All he would say was that he'd been following up a few hunches. But Blade was his own man. One of many faces and at the end of the day, what he'd accomplished deserved the George Medal. For once in his life Jack Priestley was proud to know him.

✳

'Steve, come in mate.'

Rudge opened the door wider, leaning on one crutch, his right foot encased in plaster. The unexpected visitor was introduced to Mrs Rudge and the four little Rudges who ran around the room trying their best to impress Mr Blade, their father's new work mate.

'Broke my foot under the car,' he said rather glumly. 'I couldn't get hold of you, Steve. But then I thought, when you saw I hadn't turned up you'd understand and call it off.'

Well, what could the bloke do, accepted Blade, and sympathised. After telling the story about the night's events he made for the door.

'One thing, mate,' Rudge said as he stood in the hallway, like the leaning tower of Pisa. 'Do you think you could put this on for me?' He handed to Blade a National Lottery ticket.

✳

chapter thirteen

Rows of weeping willows proudly displaying bunches of golden leaves, surrounded the large lake that had always been abundant with wild life for as long as Blade could remember. A clear, bright blue sky to provide the finishing touch to what could well have been a scene found inside one of those calendars advertising an engineering company. A mild day in the middle of a cold winter had brought even more ducks and geese out to play. He stood and watched them fly low across the water, some settling to wait patiently for any passer-by willing to part with whatever crumbs were about. Similar to himself, he thought.

Water had always mesmerised him, probably because he hadn't come into contact with it much as a kid, except of course in the metal tub his mother used to fill in front of the old coal fire every Friday night. All he could remember from his childhood days was mostly blue bricks, dust and mortar from the half-demolished houses, left over from the war.

Unlike most people who remembered the early sixties as being new, invigorating and exciting, Blade found that particular period in history slightly depressing. It was the era in which individuals became millionaires overnight. Buildings were razed to the ground by the bulldozers, only to be replaced by cardboard cutouts. All in the name of modernisation!

The so-called planners and developers had managed to remove every institution he'd ever been associated with, except of course the nicks. Both of the old schools he'd been forced to attend were now gone. Not that he'd ever been particularly concerned by that. His feelings of sentimentality would never stretch that far! Complete rows of Victorian terraced houses; street-corner shops and pubs; tramlines and trams that went with them were replaced by the new style matchbox shapes surrounded by green patches of grass, which in his mind represented false images of rural England. Splashes of green flicked from an artist's brush onto a piece of canvas. Only there hadn't been any artists and people had never been given a chance to express what they felt about what was going on.

What on earth had it all been about he asked himself. Except for lining privileged people's pockets. Neighbours whom he still remembered had long gone, having been moved miles out of town. Old people, his people, uprooted and dropped into rabbit hutches high in the sky, only to die off from grieving for the good old days.

But at least they'd left the fishing grounds well alone. The lakes and reservoirs remained intact. He'd often been tempted to bring out the rods and have a few relaxing hours on the side of the reservoir or river bank. If only he had the time.

He looked at his watch. It was well gone half past. She was late. Well at least he thought it was she. The message asking him to be there had been signed off by 'your favourite tart', and there'd only been one woman who had recently used that phrase – Joyce, during their first meeting back in the nick. But there again, he noticed the two suits walking towards him and wondered whether he'd got it wrong.

'Mr Blade?'

He couldn't believe it. Laurel and Hardy in pinstripes. They'd set him up, obviously not believing he'd turn up for anyone other that Big Bristols. They would have been proved right, if he'd have known.

He was escorted to a nearby bench and was soon sitting in between the two undertakers. They had one thing in common with each other – pasty faces. One slight crack of the mouth and the plaster of Paris would crumble, he thought, allowing a slight smile to show.

'We're from Special Projects,' explained the thin one. That was Laurel. 'Thank you for seeing us.'

Very polite. They could have been pools men about to hand over a cheque. There again, perhaps not. The short fat one reached into his inside pocket and produced an envelope. Must be the ten grand still owing him, thought Blade.

'These are airline tickets for yourself and your family. You leave Heathrow for Rio de Janeiro tomorrow night,' explained smiler the short arse.

'And this is the recompense owed to you,' explained Stan Laurel, before handing another envelope to him.

Blade's head was spinning from one to the other, like a top. They stood and both nodded together as though they had completed the same course in etiquette.

But Laurel hadn't finished. 'And Mr Blade, return only on the date printed on the tickets.'

'And Mr Blade,' Oliver Hardy chirped up again, 'Next time you succumb to the temptation of earning a little extra cash without our consent, the consequences might be very different.'

A threat? Oh, yes, there was no doubt in his mind that was exactly how it was meant to sound. He'd just had his tail stung by a bloody big wasp and could only sit there, flabbergasted, watching their backs as they both walked away, Laurel looking up towards the sky as if in conversation with a higher authority. Somehow they'd found out about his little scheme with Rudge. But how? Pissing Secret Squirrels!

As he stood up from the bench his mind returned to the envelopes. They were no longer in his hands and for a brief moment he panicked. Then he suddenly realised they were in his inside pocket. Another problem. Another dilemma. They'd certainly dropped a bombshell in his lap. Now he had something else to think about. Something he had to decide upon quickly. He was already betting it wouldn't be as they expected. He stood and turned right to walk away, his mind racing over a hundred thoughts. Then, as if the compass had been removed from his head, he stopped and turned left. And then, having accepted he'd become totally disorientated and unable to focus on what the hell he was doing, returned to the bench, just to sit for a few minutes, whilst he got back his bearings.

What in Christ's name was going on? he asked himself. He'd just been given the sack!

'How much more bloody snow is there to come down from there?' asked Priestley looking out of the car window, up towards the black night sky. 'This is worse than 1947.'

'Didn't know you were around then, guv,' commented Dave Vaughan in a sarcastic, piss-taking tone of voice.

The Enigma bleeped:

TANKER LEAVING NOW. MUST SPEAK LATER. URGENT.

Blade had done his part of the job but did his reference to 'later' mean immediately after this particular run or later in the morning? Priestley wondered. He replied with the question and was soon informed from the other end:

AS SOON AS POSSIBLE JACK.

Must be having problems booking his holiday, thought the copper.

'Right, Dave, they're on the move. Tell the rest of them,' directed Priestley.

In fact the rest of them had been wondering what on earth they'd been doing for the past five nights following a lorry up and down the motorway at a steady 56 mph, not really knowing what for. But they were highly trained surveillance operatives and it was not for them to wonder why. They just had to get on with the job, and all that.

It was the same route as before. Down the M5 onto the M6. A few more miles and off at Junction 4 for the link road towards the airport. They were running like a convoy, five vehicles out of sight of the target with just the one keeping it in view and relaying positions back to the team, who were anything up to half a mile behind, supporting the lead car by changing every couple of miles or so.

But on this occasion, Lawrence and Waltham didn't turn right towards the airport, but instead turned left away from it.

Priestley shot up in his seat, one ear cocked towards the radio.

'It's a left, left, left. Signposted Meriden. Under the flyover and positioning for a right on the roundabout.'

There was a pause. 'Start to move up a bit, Dave,' ordered Priestley. He couldn't afford to fall too far behind. He knew the area well and realised the trunker would only be about half a mile in front of the surveillance team, his vehicle being the last in the convoy.

'Not one,' another pause. 'Not two. Left indicator on,' another pause. 'He's taken a left, left, left, at the third exit. Signposted Meriden.'

Now for the tricky bit. The team had to be on their toes. They no longer would have the benefit of cover from other unsuspecting vehicles which they enjoyed on the motorway. The target would, from then on, be travelling along quiet country lanes at three o'clock in the morning, when any other vehicle behind would stick out like a sore thumb.

But again, Priestley's intimate knowledge of the area told him the trunker would eventually reach the village centre of Meriden.

'Tell them to put the bike in, Dave. On the small island, that's the village green.'

Within seconds a motorcyclist roared past them heading towards the rest of the team in front, and the target they were following. The radio remained silent for a short while and then, 'Duke to the team. Target in sight.' It was the bike, thank Christ, thought Priestley. 'At the Meriden roundabout. He's taken the third exit towards Coventry.'

Adrenaline was starting to flow more freely now. Priestley could feel the same wave of excitement he'd experienced so many times before since joining the force. Even he was often surprised at the buzz and kicks he still got, even though he'd won the T-shirt for operational coppering. 'That'll do. Tell them to pull the bike off now, Dave.'

A couple of miles further and the Cheetah trunker turned off into a small and very quiet business park estate. One of his officers, Geordie Baker was soon out on foot, watching from a distance. He saw the drivers of the artic being met by two other men, both wearing dark duffle coats and then made sure that Priestley was made aware of that. The heavy wagon reversed into what looked like some kind of a warehouse, before a large roller-shutter door closed down in front of it. Within minutes the sound of rattling chains came from inside and the rollers were back up, allowing the trunker to leave. As it roared away, back in the same direction from whence it came, Geordie confirmed the same two drivers were in the cab.

Things were now starting to look up as far as Priestley was concerned. He'd found the missing half an hour from the first night they'd picked Waltham and Lawrence up at the airport. And he now had the location of the unofficial en route stop made by the two men. All he needed was to find out the reason why.

∗

'I'm freezing my bollocks off here, Jack. Been waiting hours.'

'You've been waiting about an hour, Bladey.' Priestley was in no mood to listen to gripes. 'I'm desperate to catch up on a thousand hours sleep myself, so what's the problem?' What Priestley meant was that he was desperate to get some confirmation of his sexual prowess from a certain female lawyer. Then he could catch up on some sleep, if she'd let him.

'Turn the heater up then.' Blade's teeth were chattering. 'It's like working in a fridge over there, Jack.'

Although the lighting was still fully on, Priestley could see the warehouse and surrounding site from where they sat, almost deserted now, apart from a few workers clearing up after the nightly panic. There was the lone security guard still manning the barrier at the main entrance. He left the engine running for both his and Blade's benefit.

Blade described the visit he'd had from the bowler hat brigade, in the park the day before and the suggested vacation they'd insisted he take.

'Rio, eh? Lucky you,' said Priestley with a great deal of insincerity.

'I'm not going.'

That's no real surprise, thought Priestley. If you promised Blade a world cruise he'd probably turn it down, thinking there was something suspicious about it.

'Missus and nipper's going though.'

That was a bigger surprise. 'Anything for free, eh Steve?'

'I want them out the way.' Blade was obviously concerned. He twisted his body so that he could face Priestley more comfortably, 'Nobody's telling me what to do, Jack. Especially a bunch of suited-up stiff necks.'

'So, they've paid you your money, Steve?' Jack suggested with a grin.

'So what? What exactly are you getting at Jack?'

'Oh, I don't know. Just knowing what a greedy bastard you are I suppose.'

Priestley didn't really care whether Blade flew to the moon or remained where he was. He'd like to have known how his partner was going to explain Sammy and the little one turning up alone at the airport, though. There again, Blade was Blade and knowing him the way he did, that wouldn't be a problem for him.

'How did you get on tonight. Same routine?' asked the ex-con.

'They took a detour to Meriden. Spent ten minutes inside some warehouse with the letters R L Smith across the door,' explained the policeman. 'Ring any bells?'

'Meriden, eh Jack? The very centre of England. No, Smith don't ring a bell. But I suppose that's it then, Jack?'

'That's what?'

'That's where they're doing the business.' Blade sounded more motivated than Priestley felt. He was a lot warmer now. In fact he opened his side window a fraction, just to let some fresher air inside the car.

But before he could elaborate further, Priestley snapped, 'Are you definite about not taking that plane tonight?'

'Course I am. You know that.'

'Then I want you to go sick.'

'Sorry?'

'I want you to have the night off. You've got some other kind of work to do. With me,' explained Priestley. 'Now if you don't mind I've got a busy schedule tomorrow.'

Blade stepped out of the car. 'Don't forget now, Jackie boy,' he said with a smirk on his face. 'Straight to bed now, to sleep that is.'

Priestley's car took off like a bat out of hell, leaving Blade to chuckle to himself.

*

'Thank you for coming down, Jack.' Commander Pike looked more at home sitting behind the highly polished mahogany desk in his white striped shirt and bright red braces. His office looked more like a prince's study, built around the turn of the century. The small replica Georgian clock on the mantleshelf chimed four o'clock as Priestley sat back in the dark red, soft leather chair.

Heavy drapes adorned the window behind where Pike sat and the walls were covered in a sort of cloth fabric, heavily embossed with what looked like small red dragons. It was obviously to match the deep pile carpet. How different from the plain painted walls and working environment Priestley was used to, although he did suspect he'd seen the same wallpaper in a pub somewhere.

The one touch of class he'd already noticed, immediately as he walked through the door, was that Pike didn't have dozens of group photographs plastered all over the place which seemed to be the 'in thing'. Just a couple of gold leaf framed paintings that looked like original works of art.

'How did the journey down go, Jack?'

'On time. A refreshing change for Virgin.' He'd never really relished visits to London. Such a huge mass of people. Just like grains of sand on a beach, all being blown about in different directions by the wind. He hesitated when a glass of Chivas Regal was offered him but then thought, why not? After all, he was on the train so it didn't matter if he returned home as pissed as a newt!

'So tell me. Any joy so far? And how's our Mr Blade getting on?'

Priestley had to pause whilst the burning sensation in his throat, albeit not an unpleasant one, subsided. 'On his way to South America. Tonight, I believe.' He knew that Pike would be aware of Blade's proposition. In all probability, the offer would have come from him. But for some unexplained reason, Jack didn't quite feel like disclosing everything he knew, in particular the fact that Blade had no intention of leaving the country. Best to keep something up your sleeve, he decided.

The Commander didn't look surprised. 'Yes, sorry about that but there are good reasons for it.'

A box of Villiger's Export came out, as Priestley thought that Churchill cigars would have been much more appropriate, considering the surrounding décor.

'I'll explain in a short while,' continued Pike. 'But the real reason for seeing you this morning is to thank you personally for your support...'

Jack used the chrome-plated table lighter on the desk.

'...and to explain that I'm optimistic we shall get a result very shortly.' He paused for just a couple of seconds to focus on the square-shaped cigar, 'Ourselves, that is!'

The last few words were abruptly spoken and Priestley understood exactly the message being delivered. This was Pike's way of saying 'Farewell. Tarah for now!' But just like Blade, Jack wasn't there to be used in the same way as you order a dog to go back into its kennel or fetch the paper. He would now consider what the Commander obviously thought was necessary. And to do that, he would need a little time. Such as the train journey home. After all, it wouldn't be the first time he'd gone unilateral, dismissing the wishes of those above him.

*

He sat back, almost disappearing into the soft leather. His host remained silent as if allowing time for his message to penetrate Priestley's mind, without having to interpret its meaning. He needed to know whether the penny had dropped. No more involvement for you, Jack, my boy. End of the road and all that. A quick return to the daily routine and chores of crime squad management, which is what you're paid to do anyway.

'What you're saying, Commander, is that you want me to conclude the inquiries at my end?' Jack was enjoying the cigar. Made a change from the small cheroots he normally held in his mouth.

'Well, having taken your friend out of the equation,' Pike was half shaking, half nodding his head. His manner certainly appeared less confident than it had at their previous meeting in the Chief Constable's office, 'Your own role has now naturally concluded.'

Priestley should have been ecstatic, overjoyed at the release from such a heavy burden as babysitting for Steve Blade. He should have felt enthralled at the opportunity now presented, to return to a normal life without having to worry about some buzzer going off in the far corner of the room. But he wasn't – and he couldn't quite understand that. But as always, he'd play along, at least for the rest of this particular meeting. He described the operation that had taken place the night before, when he and his team had followed Lawrence and Waltham. By the Commander's response he either knew about what Priestley had told him already, or didn't give a monkey's elbow! Priestley suspected the latter, but was confused. 'You were going to explain to me why you're sending Steve Blade halfway round the world?' Bit cocky for a Chief Inspector talking to a Scotland Yard Commander attached to the Security Services but if you didn't ask, you weren't told, had always been one of Jack's mottos.

'Ah yes, Mr Blade.' Pike stood up and turned towards the window to peer across at St Paul's. From the additional creases in the back of his trousers he hadn't got his Saville Row suit on today. More like an off-the-peg job from M and S, thought the junior rank.

The Commander continued with his back to Priestley. 'Let's just say there's a security issue there, Jack.'

With Blade? thought Priestley, He couldn't even spell the word 'security'.

'Don't get me wrong.' He was now facing his visitor once again. Still standing, leaning slightly forward, fingertips only touching the desk top. The usual I'm-superior-to-the-rest-of-the-planet posture, 'I'm not saying he would deliberately sabotage our operation. But he's not like you, Jack – a trusted servant.'

Cheeky patronising bastard, thought Priestley, although thankful for the compliment, if that's what it was.

'What I mean is,' he paused to stand more erect and look up towards the carved alabaster ceiling, 'Well, I think you know what I mean. Once a villain, always a villain.'

Priestley was starting to dislike this man. 'What you mean is, you believe he would sell the knowledge he already has to those who we've been looking at?' he asked, poised to defend any further criticism of the man, who only last week, had saved a little girl from imminent torture and eventual murder.

'Exactly, Jack. You have it in one. And of course, we cannot take that risk.'

'Let me clear one or two things up for you, Commander, about – '

'Jack, he's already tried to steal a lorry load of parcels whilst supposedly working for us.'

That was an explosion for Priestley to deliberate over. Now *he* was looking up at the ceiling, blowing invisible bubbles. Of course, he realised, the motorway services where Blade had come across Machin and the girl. He was about to nick that wagon in which the girl had been kept captive. Well done, Jack. They don't come much slower than the way he felt. No wonder these goons wanted him tucked up on the other side of the Atlantic!

The look of self-satisfaction on Commander Pike's face said it all. Have a bit of that, before trying to defend your two-faced, so-called friend.

Time to get back to a more hospitable climate. Not that this had been hostile. Jack stood up to leave and shake hands. He'd heard enough but remembered to take what was left of his cigar with him.

✳

chapter fourteen

The hour and a half journey back to Birmingham seemed like a full tour of duty for Priestley. All he could do was stare out through the carriage window in dismay. His most urgent need and uppermost desire was to wrap his hands around Blade's neck and string him up from the nearest lamppost, like the way the Italians bumped off Mussolini. But he would only do that after he'd tortured the man, like the English King did to Mel Gibson in the film, *Braveheart*.

He started to wonder what it was all about. Was there anyone in this world he could trust? He sat for a while just pondering that question and couldn't find an answer more positive than no, there wasn't. He'd done so much and been so successful in his career, but there had been a cost and he was still paying the price. During the years he'd given his all to policing, he'd forgotten what life was really all about: living with other people and communicating with others on a daily basis. He suddenly realised that, without a friend in the world, he obviously hadn't been very good at it. He could feel a major sense of sadness and disappointment slowly beginning to overcome him.

The midday newspaper resting fully open on his lap, served as a suitable prop to let the girl sitting opposite him know he wasn't really interested in pulling down the zip which ran from her low neck-line, down to her pelvis. And then there was that bloody alarm! The one that was now beginning to test his nerves, with each buzz. He'd forgotten to leave the Enigma with Pike. He snatched it from the leather compartment, trying to imagine what the wording of the message would be:

ALL'S WELL JACK. THINK WERE GETTING THERE JACK. HAVE MADE TREMENDOUS INROADS INTO THE TARGETS JACK. GO STUFF YOURSELF JACK I'M BUSY DOING A FOREIGNER.

Oh yes, Bladey had taken the piss all right, in his usual habitual thieving way.

He stared down at the screen:

WHAT TIMES THE MEETING TONIGHT JACK?

He couldn't type the reply quick enough, his two fingers hitting the keys as though each represented an insect about to take a lump out of him:

GET STUFFED YOU HORRIBLE DOUBLE CROSSING SHIT.

Jack felt better.

But there was something else bothering him and it wasn't Blade's criminal mind or conniving character – he could live with that. After all, how could he expect anything else from such a narrow-minded weasel? No it was something more important than Blade's life-long practice of ripping everybody off.

✳

Sonia was late. The message left on her answering machine said it was urgent. As the garage doors automatically lifted up she got back out of the car and retraced her steps, having forgotten her handbag. Silly moo, she thought.

She was soon back at the steering wheel and slowly reversed out wondering what all the urgency was about. And outside of working hours too.

She glanced at her watch as she manoeuvered towards the main road. Just past six. He'd said he would be there at six. She quickly worked out the length of time it would take her to get there and realised she'd be twenty minutes late. Still, it was a girl's prerogative to keep a man waiting. No matter what the circumstances.

*

Priestley was a professional investigator, experienced in the ups and downs of detective work. Those working for the Sensitive Information Unit would be no different. A detailed debate started to take place inside his head. He knew that the objective was always to find out who had committed the crime. Or had a crime even been committed? And if so, what were the circumstances? He'd been about to provide a few of those answers for them. But suddenly, they had other ideas and he didn't believe for a minute Blade's departure from their way of doing things had anything to do with it, contrary to what Commander Pike had suggested.

Like Sonia Hall, and Carol Guardia if it came to that, the one thing that annoyed Priestley more than anything was being kept in the dark; being led a merry dance without knowing why; being regarded as some kind of pawn in a bigger game of chance; being treated like a prize prat!

Pike had gone to the trouble of paying Blade a lot of money to get information from Gabriel. That was both logical and acceptable, thought Priestley as the train entered a long tunnel and he was suddenly faced with his own reflection in the carriage window. In return, and in fairness to Blade, he'd repaid them by providing the information they were after. He'd virtually established the methods used, or part of the methods at least, to transport arms out of the country. So, being the little bastard he was (after all, thought Priestley, he is an armed robber) he then tries to do a foreigner across them. So what? He's a natural born little shit, who thrives on ripping off people (and Post Office vans) thought Jack. If they'd just left him alone, with Priestley sitting in the wings watching over him, then they would have had the complete result. Of that, he had no doubt.

✳

Her watch told her it was ten past now and she felt confident the twenty minute delay wouldn't be prolonged any further.

She pushed the car up to sixty. And then seventy. Seventy-five. And then remembered the long winding hill, just half a mile away. She eased off on the throttle and pressed the on button for the CD player. She was in the right mood for some classical. Then her mind had to focus on whatever the problem was that would soon be recited to her. She slowed down at the top of the hill, and wondered how dear old Jack was getting on in London Town.

✳

He was starting to wish now that he was in a position where he could pull that girl's zip down. She smiled as she looked up to catch his eye, examining her upper frame. He went back to the newspaper, embarrassed.

You don't just splash out twenty grand and then take his legs away from him, just for trying to nick a load of parcels, thought the DCI. He was convinced they'd have considered that possibility before approaching Blade in the first place. Unless of course, they were that naive. And the timing. It couldn't have been more inconvenient. They were now on the brink of delivering a package that would have taken the complete shroud off the operation. He kept thinking of Pike's laisser-faire attitude when he was telling him about the warehouse at Meriden. Surely that kind of information should have at least made him arch his eyebrows; or put a glisten in his eye; or just wriggle about and scratch his arse? But the response had been completely and utterly negative.

Crap. Can't be right. But why? And George Riddell? What role did he play in all this? Priestley wasn't the kind of person to leave things undone, even if it had been Tony Blair telling him to piss off!

✳

She had to be extra careful to avoid the cars parked on both sides of the road, as she started the descent, down towards the crossroads at the bottom of the hill. Mucklows Hill was well known by the locals. About a mile in length, it was very steep. As soon as she reached the double yellow lines the road became wider and the bends easier to negotiate.

Then her mind was completely thrown off balance, by a kind of fear no one could describe. Her foot pressed hard against the rubber block, but without any response. She slammed the brake pedal hard, up and down as fast as she could. There was still no response. She crashed the gear lever into second, which increased the noise of the engine but had little effect on the sixty miles per hour she was already doing. She whimpered. And then, cried. And finally, screamed.

✳

It was the lingering mist carrying a frosty nip in the air, which made the Birmingham canal system a place to be avoided on such a night as this. The temperature must have dropped another ten degrees since their last meeting only a few nights before.

Ponteus was the only minder present and stood in his usual position at the bow, searching the waters for any sign of shark fins. Riddell made his usual entrance, down the aisle, towards the back of the boat. It soon became apparent that Grainger preferred not to introduce by name the foreign-looking gentleman sitting at his side. However it was obvious the fight promoter was already known to the stranger – a man of Arabian descent. He was a representative of those who were willing to put the cash up, not to Riddell directly, but for the services he'd been asked to provide.

'Our friend here wanted to meet you in person, George,' explained the civil servant. 'But of course, all financial business will be dealt with by our own party.'

George wasn't too bothered about knowing the identity of 'our own party'. As long as 'our own party' kept paying the rent, which he'd been doing successfully for some time now. Long may he reign, no matter how anonymous he wished to be.

'My people require five thousand items,' confirmed the negotiator. He spoke good English and was well-educated. George could see that by the look on his face. He was good at weighing people up and if there'd been the slightest chance of making a bet, he'd have wagered the Arab had spent some time at Oxford. He'd have been totally wrong of course.

What the big fellow did notice were the two heavy bags of coal beneath each of the stranger's eyes, indicating to George the fortune teller, that he'd been putting in some long hours recently.

'After that,' continued the Arab gentleman, 'who knows?' intimating there could be further business between them if this first little venture proved to be successful. 'Can you deliver to our Belgian contact, Mr Riddell?'

Straight to the point, this one, thought George. Obviously a man with limited time on his hands.

George looked towards Ponteus, standing upright in his usual position, with the mist swirling around his head, like something out of *The African Queen*.

'As I've already told Mr Grainger, of course I can. Have I ever let you down before, Mr...?'

He hadn't met this gent before and George was trying to establish whether he'd financed the previous operations. But he was just ignored. The Arab slightly waved his hand in front of his face, like swatting a fly, as though deflecting the question. It was a signal to confirm that his own name and provenance would remain a mystery.

'How?' was the next question asked by the stranger.

Riddell's eyes returned to the statue-like figure of his tall, well-built minder.

'In the same way as I've moved other items for you in the past.'

'Can that be done, George?' asked Grainger.

He was still wondering whether or not the Arab was 'our man' but somehow doubted that. If he was the principle financier, why show his hand now? No, he was convinced the man was as Grainger had said, a go-between, sent to deal with 'our man' by those wishing to purchase the goodies. Not that it should bother George. As long as he was paid for his work, that's all he was really bothered about.

'Yes, it can be done,' Riddell coolly stated in answer to Grainger's question. 'We'll use the same system as before. Probably move about two hundred each trip, according to the size and shape of them.'

The movement of whatever the number of landmines required, was Riddell's business, and his alone. Once handed over to the Belgian contact his responsibility ended there and the boys here just had to worry about paying him. Or at least Mr Anonymous did, who'd never been to one of these happy-go-lucky meetings. He sat upright, trying to look a little more impressive, before continuing, 'Is there a problem, gents?' he asked, 'or something I should know about?'

Now Grainger was looking up towards Ponteus. Fine figure of a man. He must have felt embarrassed at all the eyeball attention he was being given.

But Mr Arab remained still and focused. He hadn't taken his eyes off Riddell. 'If there was a problem, Mr Riddell, you would be told. There isn't.' He paused for a short while. 'But we are, shall we say a little concerned at the nature of the items.'

'You mean all the recent publicity surrounding landmines?' suggested George.

The Arab nodded. 'Yes. You see, because of that fact you have just referred to, they are more in demand now than ever before.'

'Which means the price has rocketed?' George was no mug and was picking up the situation fairly quickly. Not bad for a back-street thicky. There again, he'd always managed to stay one step in front of his competitors. That was why he successfully ran a steel company, even though it was a bent one that relied on muscle rather than accountants. But neither the Arab nor Grainger responded. George had now become aware that the concern being shown by the other two was more to do with these particular shipments being more valuable to them than if he was boxing up gold bullion. The other consideration which George wasn't party to, was that failure to deliver now would probably mean the Arab being wasted, by whoever was due to receive the merchandise at the other end. No wonder they'd arranged this meeting at such short notice.

Riddell repeated the figure given to him by Grainger at their previous meeting. 'Half a million?' He wasn't bothered about the Arab listening.

Grainger nodded.

'Then gentlemen, concentrate on the financial side of things,' and just to let them know he knew what he was on about, 'and of course, the transportation from Belgium, to wherever they are destined to go after that.' He paused again. 'Leave the movement of the stock to my good self.'

That's all they wanted to hear and both cast brief looks of mutual acceptance towards each other.

Ponteus answered the mobile, as he walked alongside his employer, towards the steps that would lead to where the car had been parked. He just grunted to whoever had made the call and replaced the phone back into his inside pocket. 'Mr Riddell. It would appear you need a new lawyer.'

✳

Blade was standing in the middle of the deserted country lane, as a furious Jack Priestley drove towards him. He saw his outline in the headlights and was thankful the two-faced git had managed to keep the meet on time. As he approached, he could see the friendly look on Blade's face, a sort of revered smile. So he revved up the engine and drove straight at him. After all, he'd only turned up just to run the bastard over. Missed! Blade managed to dive out of the way.

Never mind, thought Jack, I can always cave his head in with the pick-axe handle in the boot.

'What the fuck was all that about?' screamed Bladey, as he pulled himself out of the ditch, trying to get back onto harder ground.

'I'll show you,' replied Priestley and let him have it full in the face, returning the retired, armed robber back into the thicket on the far side of the ditch.

Blade didn't move. He didn't want to. He just lay there wondering how he could get back up without having another demolition job done on him. His nose was broken. He ascertained that from the throbbing and needed to tell the lanky lawman who was still standing there like John Wayne, poised to deliver another swipe. Time to put it on a bit. He groaned and moaned and then went rigid and silent.

'Get up, shithole,' was the first demand.

No way, thought Blade. Of all the things he might be, they didn't include being suicidal.

'Eh, arsehole. Get back here.'

Silence, and stillness. That was the only response Blade wanted to make, although he couldn't piss about for much longer. The blood was starting to fall down the back of his throat and soon he would have to cough it up.

'Then stay there, you double-crossing termite.'

What on earth had upset this man? thought Blade, lying like a corpse. But he wasn't going anywhere until Mr Silver Star either cooled down or pissed off.

'Right, freeze to death,' shouted Priestley, who then turned and walked towards his car.

Blade immediately acknowledged that the lawman had a point. This wasn't the place to play heroics, stuck in a hedge at one in the morning with your balls slowly turning to icicles. He groaned a little more than he should have done, to sound genuine and then gasped Priestley's name as though he wanted to make a will before passing over to the other side. The car engine started up and the headlights were illuminated. Blade was up and out of there like his backside was on fire.

Priestley stopped and jumped out of the car, grabbing him by the two lapels.

'Jack, you're upset,' stuttered Blade.

Jack screwed his face up, trying to rid himself of the overwhelming anger he felt. He let go and stepped back to the driver's door.

Blade cleared the blood from the back of his throat.

'I know all about the parcels business, Steve,' roared Priestley. 'If you ever do that again across me, I'm out of it, permanently.'

What could Blade say? He couldn't deny it. Obviously his old mate had been talking to the same blokes who'd sent the suits with the airplane tickets.

'Is that understood?' asked Priestley, his voice still full of some aggression, some remorse.

Blade just nodded and coughed up more blood. Bastard copper! Priestley was a lot calmer by the time they arrived and drove down the lane leading to the business park. What Blade wasn't aware of, was the dilemma Priestley had faced during most of that previous evening. After a lot of deliberation, he'd made up his mind to continue with his own investigations without the official backing. But what that also meant was Priestley would now be like a coiled spring. It would be like standing on a precipice, having to make extra certain, he or they didn't fall down it. Only a gut feeling had driven him in that direction and only his own professional investigative ability, supported by Blade's bottle, would prove him to be right or wrong.

They'd both sat in silence following the tidal wave of apologies and verbal regrets made by Blade. But now this was different. This was business. Priestley was doing the job he was paid to do anyway. Blade was there because of the excitement and loyalty he still felt towards his old childhood friend. There was also the smell of more easy money in the air. He didn't know what or when it would present itself but he just sensed that, if he stayed on board there would be further cash recompense. Also, he knew in the back of his mind that Priestley offered him some protection, if he was ever caught out trying to make a bob or two outside the legal perameters. Blade would do no physical harm to anyone unless it was well deserved, but at the same time he wouldn't say no to an easy buck if the opportunity came along – as he'd proved so many times in the past. It was in his nature, like the time they made him the biscuit monitor at school.

'What's that down your trousers?'

'Mind your own business.' Blade had been attracted to the bright colours printed on the pencil box, rather than its contents. The last thing he ever wanted to be was an artist. But since being given the responsible job of selling the penny

dodgers and bags of crisps at break-time, he'd been enjoying the freedom of the stockroom, where the goodies were stored.

'You've been nicking stuff from the stockroom. I've been watching you.'

'So what?' Blade was embarrassed because he'd been found out. And by this squirmy git, which hurt him more than anything, 'It's got nothing to do with you, Priestley, so mind your own business.'

'You'll take whatever that is back.'

Blade stopped and swung round, almost falling over the piles of bricks and planks of wood they were climbing across. Materials which had once been part of some poor sod's house. 'I'm not going all the way back there now. Anyway school's finished. There won't be anybody there.'

'Yes, there will and you're going to take that back to where it belongs.'

The shorter of the two boys knew that Priestley was in one of those moods. He would be unrelenting until his demand had been met. He wouldn't dob him in, but Priestley would certainly punch him on the nose. But Bladey had to put up some sort of a show. He couldn't just surrender. 'And I suppose you're going to take them off me, if I don't take them back?'

Priestley just nodded and raised his clenched fists, but for some unknown reason, Blade didn't feel like fighting on that occasion. A rarity, indeed. But, knowing that negotiation would be a waste of time and not preferring the only other option left open to him, he eventually succumbed. There would be other times when Jack Priestley wasn't there, doing his laudable best to become the new Head Prefect.

'Over there. It's the one with the corrugated roof.'
Blade just nodded and Priestley doused the headlights.
'Just drive round the front, Jack.'

The warehouse was quite a large building, which backed onto a canal. It was big enough to contain three or four juggernauts and access could be obtained around the complete circumference, along a footpath covered at the rear by overgrown thistles. Both men knew that inside, there would undoubtedly be a small office compound, but Priestley was more concerned about the alarm system. That's why Blade was there with him.

They both surveyed the front of the warehouse as they drove past, noting there was no sign of life or even the dimmest light showing through from inside.

'Looks lifeless, Jack,' said Blade, now satisfied that the bleeding had stopped, although he daren't touch his aching nose. 'We need to get closer.'

Priestley parked well away from the building at Blade's direction. The situation was perfect. Complete darkness except for a few, well-spaced street lamps. The only potential problem they might have to deal with was patrolling security guards, but they weren't really perturbed about coming across one. The majority to quote Blade, looked but never saw anything.

He'd already spotted the alarm box at the front just to the side of the roller-shutter doors, but knew he could only access it from the back and across the roof.

'I hope that corrugated sheeting holds my weigh, Jack, otherwise you'll have to pick up the pieces.' His voice was low, almost a whisper as they made their way towards the canal at the back, Blade gripping tightly onto a small bag and Priestley carrying the box which contained the camera.

This was Blade's home territory and Priestley would have little advice to offer. He was reminded of that fact when he watched and saw how quickly the other pulled himself up onto a ledge, just short of the roof itself. Blade had used the top of a fence to overcome the first few feet, but the onlooker was bemused and puzzled how he'd managed to scale the distance between that point and where he now was. All Priestley could see was a flat surface with nothing to hold onto or grip. Must have spider blood in him, thought the DCI.

He was soon up and over the eaves, disappearing from sight. That was the signal for Priestley to walk briskly back to the car and watch the artist do his work from a safe distance. Before he'd even gently closed the driver's door, Blade was hanging upside down from the roof at the front of the building, pumping foam into the alarm box.

Then they were faced with major problems. It had to happen. It was as predictable as the weather. Priestley saw the headlights first and the usual beads of sweat started to appear on his forehead, as they always did when he was faced with a situation he had no control over. His brain became addled. He had to think quickly. Initially, the problem was his own position. Would he be seen where he was parked up? It was doubtful. Should he drive off? Out of the question. Apart from having difficulty in explaining what he was doing there, he couldn't leave Blade stranded, no matter what, although the idea was tempting and brought a mischievous glint to his eye.

The second problem would only present itself if the vehicle belonged to someone visiting the warehouse legitimately. If that were to be the case, they would have to deal with the situation as it unfolded.

The third problem was, if a friendly security man was doing his rounds, then everything would depend upon how vigilant the patrolman was. He drew some comfort from the thought that it might be a police car. That, he could handle, but as the lights drew closer he soon realised it wasn't.

He was fortunately tucked away at the side of an old builder's skip where he could remain unseen, unless the vehicle deviated off the road and drove directly towards him. He ducked his head down, praying that Blade had now seen the danger. The vehicle drove past, still crawling and manoeuvered up to the front of the building. Priestley glanced through the front windscreen and could see it was a security patrol, his heart rate now racing like a greyhound leaping out of trap one. He could see Blade, still hanging from the roof, frozen, just above the alarm box and got some relief from the thought of the burglar holding his breath whilst he shit himself.

The uniform was out of the small white van, focusing his beam on the roller-shutter doors. Then the moving circle of light crept up towards the alarm box and rested on the top of Blade's head. Priestley gulped as his throat tightened. Fear gripped both his body and mind. He had no excuse. No reason for him being there, watching another man scuttling the alarm system. He had to do something quickly. He slowly and quietly opened the driver's door, his hand shaking. Then a sigh. The beam went down the wall and the security man returned to his vehicle. Blade had got it right. They look, but don't see. Thank God!

'Jack, I was shitting myself.' The van had long gone and Blade was like a convicted man who'd just been given a reprieve whilst standing over the trap door. 'At one time I started to slide, you know. Thank Christ that box was firmly fixed to the wall otherwise I'd have slid head first, down on top of him.'

Priestley had his it-never-bothered-me-cos-I'm-a-hero look on his face and calmly said, 'Well, he's gone. Let's get on with it.'

The roller shutter was opened within a second. One twang of the crowbar and it moved. The problem was, Priestley only wanted it lifted a few feet, sufficient to climb underneath. But the momentum took the complete mechanism charging upwards, the shutters hitting the top of the doorway with a deafening crash. Both Priestley and Blade acted naturally and ran to the side of the building to wait and see if anybody had come to investigate what sounded like the start of World War II. But the estate was deserted.

They had to move quickly. Blade shone the torch whilst Priestley measured the spot on the warehouse floor where he thought the back end of the trunker would stop. It was on that point he needed to focus the camera. Once that small operation had been completed, he then needed to decide on an appropriate site for the camera to be fixed covertly. That wasn't so easy but eventually he decided upon the flat roof, which covered a small group of offices near to the front entrance. The complete camera unit was only about an inch square and to reduce even further the risk of it being discovered, Priestley placed a small piece of black cloth over it, leaving just the lens free to record the scene below. With a wide-angled lens he was confident that they would be able to see at least two-thirds of the warehouse floor. His only worry, which was always the case when using equipment such as this, was to know whether or not it was working. Because of the covert nature of the facility there was no red light showing. He would only know when trying to receive the signals relayed back from the camera housing from some far-off position.

But Priestley was fairly contented with the night's work and patted Blade on the shoulder as they made their way back to the car. Blade wondered whether he should now take advantage of Priestley's friendliness towards him, by kicking him in the bollocks. They'd met with the copper sticking him into a hedge and were now parting like-long lost brothers. Funny bloke that Jack Priestley!

*

It had turned four by the time Jack reached Sonia's flat. He knocked several times before thinking she'd had an away night somewhere. Waves of jealousy started to sweep through him. He pictured her lying next to a bloody toy boy or some wig and robe. But what could he do? She was a free woman, she could do whatever she wanted, no matter how much hurt he felt.

*

chapter fifteen

'What time is it, Chris?' Priestley was still half and half.

'Eight o'clock, boss.'

Christ! He'd only just got to bed.

'Sorry about this, gaffer, but I've got some bad news.'

He sat up, legs half out from under the duvet, 'Go on, mate, I'm listening.'

'Sonia Hall was involved in an RTA yesterday evening, at the bottom of Mucklows Hill.'

Jack was now fully awake and trembling. 'How bad, Chris?'

'It's serious, boss. She's not dead,' he hastened to add, 'but pretty bad by all accounts.'

'How did it happen?' Priestley was already walking towards the bathroom.

'Speeding, apparently. According to the traffic lads, witnesses reckoned she was flying down the hill just before she demolished a traffic light, and then ploughed into a wall.'

'Where is she?'

'City Hospital. Intensive Care Unit.'

＊

Carol didn't know why she felt so nervous. She'd been chasing Lady Ridlington for weeks trying to get an interview about what it was really like living with such an eminent former member of the cabinet. And now here she was, standing at the front door, waiting for the lady to invite her in.

It was just an early morning phone call to the office. She couldn't believe it.

'I do believe you've been trying to contact me?' And then came the invitation, 'You must call and see me today, what about for morning tea and we can break with tradition and have some muffins?'

How could she resist muffins? And in the middle of the morning as well! Quite obviously the interview would become a secondary chore. But not for this female reporter. Lady Ridlington had always been a bit of a mystery, since she first moved into the community a long time ago. Everybody wanted to know just what made her tick. There were rumours about some dark sordid love affair in the past. And then there was the one about an illegitimate child living in some distant place, not knowing that its parents were famous. But up to now they were nothing more than rumours. Carol was going to give Lady Ridlington the opportunity to deny them, or so she planned.

This is too much, thought the young reporter, particularly after ringing her so many times without getting an answer. With her notebook in hand, she gazed up at the large oak door with the brass fittings. And what's more she had arranged to be at every function Sue Ridlington had attended during the past few weeks. Oh those dear old ladies with their beads and track-suit bottoms, thought Carol, and not even getting so much as a glance off the person she was chasing. Now here she was, with an invitation to enter the lady's living-room and conduct the biggest interview of her career so far.

Suddenly, she felt a slight quiver of disillusionment. Could this be some sort of practical joke? Someone like Jack Priestley for instance, having her over? He'd often sent her packing to some major fictitious incident, just to sit there and watch her turn up with a cameraman in tow. He had a weird sense of humour. But then she realised, in fairness, this wasn't Jack's style. At least, she hoped it wasn't.

She heard footsteps from inside! The door slowly opened. 'Miss Guardia. Do come in.' My God, thought Carol, she's joined the jogging bottoms brigade. But Lady Ridlington also had the top to match in bright pink cotton with flashes of light blue across her small bust. The reporter doubted that she had ever broken into a sweat at anytime during her aristocratic life.

'So, Lady Ridlington, shall we start with your childhood?' Good old Carol, straight into the deep end, as exuberant and industrious as ever. The woman hadn't had time to ask whether her visitor preferred tea or coffee with the muffins. But the young reporter was inside the lair and wanted to extract as much as possible in the shortest time available, before the bubble burst and she found she'd only dreamt what was happening. She wasn't bothered about etiquette or the usual niceties that had to be observed, and in fairness you could give the tea and other bits and pieces to the Afghan hounds.

Note pad out, pencil poised, she was all set for what she knew was going to be tomorrow's lead story.

'Do you like the French windows?' asked the lady of the house. And what a house it was. It was not actually a mansion, but certainly close to it with twenty-six acres of ground surrounding it, which was small compared to the neighbours who lived about a mile down the road, separated from the Ridlington's by vast areas of agricultural land.

'What, pardon? The windows?' The reporter had just been derailed. Not used to having her interviews directed by another person, especially away from the subject she'd already prepared her mind to address. Carol's obvious excitement and unease was causing her some embarrassment, although Sue Ridlington didn't seem to mind.

She just sat there, calm and collected, as though she'd been giving interviews to the press three times daily for most of her life.

'The view,' the hostess paused as though to admonish herself, for not having been more clear in her initial question. 'I'm sorry, my dear. We've just had the door frame extended to accommodate a better view. What do you think?' She smiled, almost laughing, her obvious intention was to support the young reporter and put her at ease, like an older sister.

Carol had to calm down quickly, before she made a right prat of herself. And she did so, by standing up and walking across to the windows. She looked out, trying to be sincere but all she could see beyond the bottom of the large garden was a field, a hill with a group of elms on the summit and three hundred head of sheep. She didn't bother to take in the garden, not really knowing a tulip from a daisy.

The door they'd walked through earlier, opened again and in walked a middle-aged woman, who was both smart and attractive for her age.

'This is Mrs Eden, Carol,' explained Lady Ridlington. 'She helps with the housework but also makes the most delicious snacks. Now come over here and see what we've got for you.'

The reporter really did want to get on with the interview. She didn't give a toss for Mrs Eden or her delicious snacks. But she'd play along – for a short while anyway. After all, these people came from a different solar system to herself.

'Ah, blueberry muffins and cinnamon toast. I hope you like them. They're my favourite.'

Carol just nodded avoiding the temptation to glance up at the ceiling with that I'm-now-getting-well-pissed-off look she was so good at portraying from time to time.

'They're made from a special recipe used at the London Ritz, you know.'

That was it. Enough was enough. The pencil was losing its sharpness. 'Lady Ridlington, can we discuss your early childhood? Where were you born, for example?'

Silence, for what appeared to be a long time. And then the lady answered. 'Quite a long way from here, my dear.'

'Where did you do your schooling?' Carol asked, before the other woman could continue talking again about French windows or rock cakes.

Lady Ridlington moved to the edge of her seat and placed both hands on her lap. 'Tell me, what do you think of someone who blackmails another?'

One could only guess at the kind of vibrations that shot through Carol Guardia when asked that question. It was quickly becoming obvious that she wasn't there to do an interview about Lady Ridlington's past life. But this was fascinating stuff.

'Shoot them,' was the instant and only reply she could think of, trying to slow down the pace of her thoughts so she could be more logical. As an afterthought, she asked, 'Are you being blackmailed, Lady Ridlington?'

'Sue, my dear. Please call me Sue.' She laughed but it wasn't genuine. 'Of course not. But I'll confide in you, I have a friend who is.'

There it was, staring her in the face, like being the first reporter to discover Watergate. The exclusive story of a lifetime. Or perhaps just for this week, anyway. She sat speechless, not wanting to divert the lady away from what she was about to disclose.

'I don't know all the details but I'm aware that you are closely connected to a Detective Chief Inspector Priestley and I was wondering whether you thought he would be the right man to confide in?'

It's happened again, thought Miss Guardia. Jack Priestley's back in town. But she had to maintain a high standard of interest.

'Jack Priestley, Lady Riddlington, is completely trustworthy.' And with her reporter's hat on suggested, 'If you like, I could arrange a meeting with him.'

'No thank you, dear. Now where were we? Ah, yes, my childhood.'

✱

The top of her head was covered with bandages. There were a number of drips coming from various parts of her body, leading to machines, computers or just bags of clear liquid. And yet the most concerning thing for Priestley was a small strip of plaster over each of her eyes.

'We have to keep her eyes closed to stop them from drying up,' explained the nurse in answer to his question. He nodded, finding it difficult to speak. Just seeing her lying there, made him realise just how much he felt for this woman. Yes, she was more than a friend to him. He hadn't really known that, until now. He only wished he could change places with her.

'Chief Inspector?'

He turned and saw a small pale-faced elderly woman standing at the foot of the bed. He'd never set eyes on her before but knew instantly this was Lady Hall, Sonia's mother.

She motioned for him to follow her outside.

'Jack Priestley?'

He nodded as he sat next to her on a bench in the corridor.

'I'm Louise Hall.'

He shook her hand.

'My daughter has spoken of you many times, Jack. If I can call you that?'

'Of course.'

She sighed, obviously concentrating hard on controlling her inner emotions. 'Would you like a cup of tea? They have a machine down there. I could fetch you one.'

'No thank you, Lady Hall. I can't stay long,' he said almost apologetically, for he knew all she wanted to do was try and keep herself busy, as all little old ladies do during times of trouble.

'Duty calls, I suppose?' she asked.

'Yes, but I'll be back.'

'They say she's in a coma and it could be some time before we know how serious it is. I wish her father was still alive.'

Priestley knew she wanted someone to talk to. She needed someone to talk to. The job could wait a little longer. It wouldn't go away without him.

'He was a great influence on her, you know Jack. He was a judge and from the time she was a little girl he always said she would one day follow in his footsteps.'

He had to ask the question, either of Sonia's mother or a member of the medical team assigned to her daughter, but was fearful it might not sound the way he wanted it to. Silly really, he thought. 'Is she going to be alright?'

Lady Hall placed her head on his shoulder and cried.

In return, Jack pulled her closer to him, offering all the support he could. This was indeed his darkest hour.

*

'Inspector Brayton...'

'Its Barton, madam.'

'Inspector Barton, when do you expect him in?'

'I'm not sure, Lady Ridlington. Can I ask him to phone you?'

'No, I've a busy schedule today. I'll try again later, thank you.'

The Detective Inspector looked out of the window and watched Priestley walking across the car park, looking just about as solemn as he possibly could. In fact, he'd watched his car come in whilst on the phone to Lady Ridlington, but assumed his boss wouldn't be in the mood to talk to the likes of her just at that time. Barton knew that the next few days would be very difficult for Jack Priestley. Although his DCI would have to concentrate hard on the job in hand, he would never be able to get Sonia Hall out of his mind. He could only try and make the best of an awful predicament. But Barton also knew, they both had a strong team of people behind them.

Priestley had considered looking at the warehouse in daylight to see whether it was used during more sociable hours and for genuine business purposes. But then he thought it would be too risky. They would only have to see his face and, whatever they were up to in the early hours, would be moved elsewhere. No, it would be best for him to wait. Keep the surveillance on Lawrence and Waltham and when they next visited the place, monitor the camera. The batteries lasted for three weeks anyway, so he had plenty of time. Beyond recognising that small fact, he felt hopeless. His mind was in turmoil, as though his very soul was lying back there on that hospital bed.

The phone rang before he'd reached his chair. It was as though it had been waiting for him to arrive.

'Mr Priestley?'

'Yes,' replied Jack with a melancholy sounding voice.

'Inspector Greatrex off traffic, sir.'

'Yes, Inspector?'

'I understand you have an interest in Miss Sonia Hall?'

'She's a friend if that's what you mean?' Jack propped his head up with his hand.

'No sir, that's not what I mean.'

Cheeky bastard, thought Priestley. He was slowly returning to his old self.

'What I mean is, I understand you are doing an inquiry that involves her?'

'No, that's wrong. I'm not doing any inquiry involving Miss Hall.'

'I do apologise, sir. Obviously I've been misled. Sorry to have bothered you.'

'Hang on, Inspector. Why do you ask?' He was sitting up straight again, now.

'Well, it might not be of any interest to you now, but I'm dealing with the accident she had yesterday.' He seemed to be hesitant to continue. 'Well, we've just had the car examined and it looks as though the brakes have been tampered with. I was wondering if there was any light you could throw...'

'Where's the car now?' demanded Priestley.

'At the Central Garage.'

'I'll see you there in half an hour.'

This was Riddell, he thought. He knew it. That bastard George Riddell. He knew she shouldn't have become involved with that scum, even though she might have thought she was only doing her job.

✻

'Boss, this might interest you.' Chris Barton had a look of excitement in his eyes as he walked into the office, as though he'd just been told he was a direct descendant of the Duke of Wellington.

'Not now, Chris,' he pleaded as he reached for his coat and car keys.

'The message you left me on the voicemail for me to check on that warehouse.'

Priestley remembered. He made that request over the mobile whilst driving across to the hospital. 'Go on then, Chris.'

'It might have the name R L Smith written all over it, but it's leased to International Swarf!'

A faint smile appeared on Priestley's face. And then broadened into a fully developed grin. 'Well done, mate. Get hold of Pete Stringer for me, would you? It's time for him to go in.'

✻

Carol Guardia was more than disappointed at her recent failure. She felt totally deflated. She had been promised so much and yet achieved so little. She read through her notes for about the fiftieth time, as she sat face to face with her word processor. Sue Ridlington had given her an interview, but her evasiveness had produced just a page of notes. There wasn't enough to fill half a column, never mind half a bloody page as a leading article.

An exclusive interview with Lady Ridlington, by Carol Guardia – I was born; I then went to school; skipped University; met my husband and then married him. We have both lived happily ever after. And by the way, all those rumours are a load of horse manure. Some article!

But Carol was no fool. She might be young, perhaps even a little inexperienced, but she knew exactly when she was being used and the conniving lady had on this occasion, used her. She'd appeared to be more interested in Jack bloody Priestley than what the reporter had been asking her. She was convinced the interview had just been a smokescreen to find out whether or not the aristocrat should invite the local crime squad man to her bed.

The only thing she'd said about Sir Richard was that he was standing down from Parliament at the next election. Fine, but the problem was half the bloody nationals had already printed that piece of news two weeks earlier. She stood up and walked across the newsroom towards the door. Might just as well get it over with now, she thought and knocked before entering, waiting for the biggest rollicking off her editor yet. One that she just felt would destroy the rest of her day.

*

'You see where the pipe is supposed to connect to the slave cylinder?'

Priestley grunted.

'Well,' continued Greatrex, 'It wasn't attached at all.'

'Couldn't it have just come loose?' Priestley had to be sure.

'Yes, it could. But look at the end of the pipe. If it had come loose, the end would show marks. Even if it had worn, although the car's only twelve months old, there would still have been signs of wearing.' He held the torch closer to the pipe he was discussing so that the DCI could see more clearly. 'But it's been cut. Cut cleanly through with a knife or something like that.'

Both men stood erect and moved away from the wreck that used to resemble a motor car.

'But how did she manage to drive from her home to where the accident happened?'

'She would still have had some pressure on the brakes, until the fluid in the pipe had been fully ejected out,' explained the Traffic Inspector. 'And that would have happened when she reached the top of Mucklows Hill.'

'So, according to what you're saying, the accident could have happened anywhere between her home and Mucklows.'

'Yes, it was unfortunate she lost control as she was going down such a steep descent.'

'But, at the end of the day, this is sabotage?'

'Yes, that's right. There's no other reason for it, sir.'

*

Priestley was convinced Riddell was behind the disturbing news Greatrex had just shared with him. But he needed proof and knew just how difficult that would be. One thing though, there would be no going back now. It would be all or nothing as far as his own career was concerned. He needed to talk to Blade.

✳

The boys were back in town – the men in suits and overcoats this time. Blade hadn't realised until it was too late. They'd already eyeballed him as he drove onto the car park. He felt like kicking himself for not having guessed they'd be putting in a visit at his home address. Must be getting old, he thought.

He left his own car and walked across to the black Rover. He could have just run inside the tower block and locked the door behind him, but knew they would have just kept him and the neighbours awake all night, banging on the bloody door like a pair of debt collectors. Or fired a missile at him through the window, from one of those funny square-shaped helicopters.

'How's it going then, men?'

Laurel and Hardy were both sitting side-by-side on the bonnet, like the Brothers Grimm.

'It's three in the morning,' he reminded them. 'Don't you blokes ever sleep? I've only just left work.'

'Missed your flight, Mr Blade,' stated Laurel.

'Yeah,' Blade nodded, 'thought I'd let the missus and nipper have a break on their own instead.' He smiled, 'On the government, of course.'

The short fat one, Oliver Hardy opened the rear door nearest to where Blade was standing. 'Get in,' he demanded, as though he just been made King of England.

You can piss off, thought Blade. 'Go catch some Ruskies,' he suggested before turning to walk back to the tower block.

'You don't want to see your wife and child then, Mr Blade?' asked Stan Laurel, the taller, more polite one.

Blade turned, fire in his eyes. 'Again?'

'They're not in South America, Mr Blade,' explained the same man. 'They missed the plane.'

Blade stepped up towards the man who was speaking, but then thought twice about grabbing the lapels of his specially tailored, made-for-the-winter, overcoat.

'Where are they?'

'I suggest you do as my colleague has just suggested. Jump in the car.'

He had no choice. But these people weren't supposed to act like a bunch of gangsters. He'd been through that before. But these were secret agents, guarding the country against foreign espionage and all that crap. No, he thought, they weren't supposed to act like this at all. But he got in the car.

*

'Mr Priestley, we meet again.'

This was the second time he'd visited the golf club and in such a short period of time. Jack wondered whether they'd start putting him up for election to the committee.

'It's Jack,' he explained as he showed Lady Ridlington to a small table and chairs situated in one of the window bays.

She stood and admired the view outside. A large chunk of golf course stretched out in front of her, still covered in the heavy frost that had been present since early morning, touched by the golden rays of a mid-afternoon winter sun. It really was a picture-postcard setting.

She smiled at him and took her seat, keeping the magnificent view in front of her. 'Sonia Hall? Have you heard?'

Obviously Sonia hadn't confided in her anything to do with Priestley, otherwise she wouldn't have had to ask that question.

He nodded.

'Do you know how she is? I've heard the poor girl's next to death's door?' She seemed to be genuinely concerned.

'She is very poorly, Lady Ridlington,' but that was all Jack was willing to commit himself to.

'I do hope she recovers. A wonderful, dear lady.'

There was a short period of silence between them, until she started another conversation.

'You're a Chief Inspector, Jack?'

'I am.' Right so far, he thought. Why did he also feel that he was about to be cross-examined?

'And what do you do, Jack?' was the next question.

'Chief inspect,' was his reply and they both laughed together.

'I am sorry,' she apologised. 'Forgive my inquisitiveness, but I come to you with a very serious problem.'

He knew he wasn't there to discuss her husband's recent announcement relating to his retirement from politics, unless of course, he was after a part-time job in Jack's administration office?

'I would like your word that I have your complete and total confidence,' she said.

'As long as you're not planning on robbing a bank,' he quipped.

The drinks arrived and she felt a little embarrassed, drinking vodka in the middle of the afternoon when the senior detective was only having an orange and lemonade. She had a four-wheeled carriage parked outside the front with an engine attached to it. She wished she could reorder but it was too late, so she downed the drink in one gulp, which made even Jack squint his eyes a little.

'I needed that,' she said, feeling that she had to offer some kind of an excuse for her over-indulgence.

He watched her place the empty glass back onto the table.

'Jack, I'm being blackmailed.'

Lucky girl, thought Priestley. It seemed to be the in-thing these days.

'And I don't know where to start my story.'

'Try going backwards, starting with the most recent event.' That would be different, he thought. It would also help her to remember more clearly.

'Well,' the vodka hadn't quite worked yet. She was still looking uncomfortable. 'The last call was yesterday morning. He wants me to pay him a hundred thousand pounds.'

And Jack thought she was going to talk about raffle tickets for one of her many charitable ventures. 'By when?' he asked.

'Saturday night. He wants me to take it up to Nottingham and wait at a telephone kiosk inside the entrance to the railway station there,' she paused. 'You don't know how relieved I am telling you that.'

'And if you fail to pay the ransom?' This was the hard bit but Priestley had to know.

She'd anticipated it, obviously and looked up towards another waiter, beckoning him over to them. The previous order was duplicated, only the vodka was to be a large one, with just a splash of lime.

Lady Ridlington then looked straight at Priestley and with a slight nervous stutter in her voice, told him, 'You see, Jack, I used to be a man.'

Priestley, looked across the room to make sure there wasn't a crowd of people hidden away, waiting to pounce and shout, 'Gotcha'.

'A man?' he asked, unable to think of anything else more suitable to say at that particular moment. He was just appreciative that they were sitting down, when she – or he, broke the news. If he'd been on his feet, he would have collapsed. The shock and disturbance in his eyes were obvious – something she was expecting.

'It happened many years ago,' she explained. 'I thought we'd managed to keep it confidential,' she sighed, 'but obviously not.'

'We?' asked Priestley.

'Richard and I, Jack.' She looked perturbed. 'You don't mind if I call you Jack do you?'

'Of course not.' He couldn't very well object when the news she was sharing with him, albeit from necessity, could possibly destroy the rest of her life, if ever made public. It was then, he realised what a hell of a traumatic experience she must have been going through. He felt quite proud in the knowledge that she was displaying the utmost belief in his trust and integrity. He also realised that now she'd told him, he'd become compromised. His principle aim now could only be to protect her and her husband.

'That young woman from the papers, Carol Guardia, seems to think a lot of you, Jack.'

'We've known each other on and off.' He wasn't impressed and wondered what was really behind that remark. Perhaps just trying to convince herself that he was the person she should be talking to.

'I worked for Richard before the operation,' she continued. 'Does that shock you?'

He'd have problems denying it, because the look on his face was as if he'd just seen a three-headed man walk into the room and threaten to blow the place up with a bucketful of semtex! But he did and shook his head, trying to hide the lower part of his face with his right hand stroking his chin.

'Well, there's not much more to tell you,' she paused before continuing. 'I went to America for the plumbing job, if you know what I mean.' The smile she produced helped Priestley more than it did her. 'And when I returned some two years later, no one knew. I married Richard, and Graham Allsop, which was my real name, disappeared without trace.'

'Just like Lord Lucan,' he quipped, but she didn't appreciate the humour and the smile dropped.

She took a third sip of her second drink, obviously pacing herself more. 'You can imagine what will happen if this gets out now.' Her eyes quickly surveyed the room again and her voice lowered. 'Particularly as Richard is leaving Parliament very soon.'

'I appreciate what you're saying but if this had to come out, there couldn't be a better time.' He qualified what he said. 'I mean, with your husband's retirement the damage would be minimal.' He had a quick afterthought. 'Embarrassing, but minimal.' He didn't really believe that but was trying to offer a morsel of comfort to her.

'Not when he's just been offered a secure and very well-paid job working for the Foreign Office.' She placed a finger to her lips. 'And that is highly confidential.'

Priestley shuffled in his chair and sat forward. 'Okay, let's get down to business,' he suggested with a business-like air. 'I take it you want me to try and catch the finger who's putting the arm on you, without making it public.' He suddenly realised his mind was back at work and he was talking to her as though she was Steve Blade. He apologised and continued, 'Someone, somewhere Susan, other than yourself and Sir Richard, knows about your change of life.'

'I've thought about that, Jack, and apart from the hospital staff in Illinois, there's nobody else who could possibly know.'

There was something else though. Priestley could see her pondering and decided to remain silent for a short while.

'Unless there was somebody working at the hospital at the time. And now, they've come over here, hoping to cash in?'

'What about documents?' he asked. 'There must have been hospital records?'

She smiled and nodded her head, looking more at ease now. 'Yes, lots of pieces of paper. They're quite insistent that you complete every form necessary. Private medical schemes and all that.'

'How did you pay? Through a private scheme?'

'No, cash up front. A lot of money, Jack.'

He didn't doubt it. 'From your own account?'

She knew where he was coming from and answered back, fairly sharply, 'There was no charity. The money was my own. I lived like a pauper for a long time before and after the operation.'

He didn't doubt that either. To have gone through such an ordeal was testimony in itself to the strength of character this lady possessed. He had nothing other than admiration for her. He nodded thoughtfully. 'Can you raise the cash?' he asked, trying to focus his mind on what course of action was the best to take. Already a skeleton plan had sprung to mind, but it was no different from the one used by most coppers when dealing with an attempted blackmail. This one would have to be a lot more covert and the officers he would use on the operation, selected for their ability to keep their mouths shut. And that meant in their homes as well as the police canteen.

'Already have it.'

'Do you intend to pay it?'

'Why do you think I'm talking to you, Jack? I'm not a complete fool. I know he would come back for more.'

Wise woman (or man) thought Priestley. He suddenly noticed her face become softer and her eyes filled with tears. She was begging for help, obviously having gone through so much already.

'Okay, fine. You must understand, Sue, I had to ask. The skeleton had to come out of the cupboard. But only as far as I'm concerned. Details of your past private life are your business and it will remain that way.' He was sounding like some sort of psychiatric counsellor, 'All I'm interested in doing is catching the man who is trying to blackmail you. Now then, I want you to tell me everything the blackmailer has said on the phone to you.'

'All of the conversations have been taped and they're locked away at home.' The smile was back but a little nervous this time. 'Living with a Cabinet Minister, you see. Every call to our home is taped.'

'And monitored?'

'Only by one of us.'

'Then what are we waiting for?'

They both stood to leave.

*

There'd been no change during the day. He held her hand and stood at the bedside, looking down into her pale face. Her mother was still sitting on the same bench outside, as though frightened to enter the unit in case there was bad news waiting for her.

He leant over and whispered into her ear, as a small tear ran down his cheek, 'I love you.' Words he hadn't used for years.

*

chapter sixteen

Peter Stringer had been a specialist surveillance operative for the past ten years and knew all about trying to dig holes in frozen earth. He'd tell people it was a knack he had. What they wouldn't know was that inside his box of tricks, he had a small gadget that would churn up the earth without so much as a murmur. The silent digger had helped him out of a number of difficult situations whether it was frozen soil or hard-baked clay he was digging. It was an instrument he'd managed to adapt himself. In fact, he'd often thought about patenting it and he would have done if it hadn't been for the sensitive nature of the work he undertook. But it should work tonight, he thought. It was cold, but he'd known worse nights than this for digging in.

'You look more like a balloon than a balloonist,' commented Ray, his support driver. He was referring to the arctic-type clothing the officer had wrapped himself in. At the North Pole or on the Moon, his appearance would have been the same. It had certainly cost enough. The suit had been specially tailored and had everything from pockets to keep his drinks and food cubes in, to a water bottle to stop himself from pissing down his leg.

'Final check, Rolo,' suggested the driver.

'Just done it,' answered Pete. 'Everything's fine. There's only the radio and I'll test that with three bleeps on the hand-held as soon as I'm in position.'

Ray fully understood and nodded his agreement. He also had a great deal of experience in supporting Rolo and other operatives like him.

The small nondescript van reached a crossroads. Both officers checked their watches and agreed on three minutes to two, before continuing. The cover of night was essential for insertion but it would inevitably mean that Stringer, or Rolo, which was not only his nickname but also his radio call sign, would have nothing to watch for a few hours. But he was used to that and couldn't remember the number of similar operations he'd been tasked with. He just hoped there'd be no dogs. They were always the main problem.

The lead car sent a message over the radio, 'All clear at the front.'

The tail also confirmed, 'All clear at the rear.'

Travelling about a hundred yards in front and behind, their jobs were to ensure there were no people or other traffic within sight of the vehicle from which the covert would be dispatched.

'Just a few more yards,' declared Ray reducing his speed to exactly twenty-eight miles per hour, the speed at which officers like Stringer had been trained to disembark.

Like a parachutist waiting for the green light, he opened the rear doors and looked towards the back of the driver's head.

'Your deal, Rolo, and the usual best of luck, mate.'

That was the signal and without any acknowledgement, Stringer rolled out of the back of the van as he'd done on so many occasions before. Within a few seconds he was on the other side of a hedgerow and his initial job now was to get into position. And that meant a short walk across a field, over the fence and into George Riddell's back garden.

The moon was silvery and full. But that didn't bother Stringer. He knew that his camouflage guaranteed his disappearance as soon as he stopped moving. It took a long time for him to reach his objective, stealthily manoeuvring around the perimeter of the field, not wanting to attract any attention to himself, even at two o'clock in the morning and in the middle of the countryside. He was highly trained and practiced what he'd learned to the letter, no matter what the circumstances. Failure to do so could cost him dearly. His mind went back to dogs again, remembering the time he'd spent only a few hours in bushes opposite a country Post Office which was supposed to be attacked by a gang of armed men. As he lay there with just his face above the ground, a friendly neighbourhood mongrel on his evening stroll, stopped and cocked his leg up. Stringer's training dictated that he remained absolutely still at all times, but when the canine pissed all over his face the copper had great difficulty in brushing it aside. Then there was the time he'd been placed in a cemetery to relay back, through a microphone, a conversation between two known villains attending a funeral. He'd actually got to within a couple of yards of the main group without being seen and that gave him tremendous motivation. If ever he'd been caught, he had no doubt his balls would have been hung up on the gravestone.

It was widely accepted he was the best at his job. He was one of only twenty-two trained operatives in the country and Jack Priestley had always acknowledged how lucky he felt having Rolo as part of *his* team. An ex-SAS soldier who, when not operationally deployed, trained others on top of the Brecon Hills. Rolo was an ex-military man with a very understanding wife. One who didn't complain about the state of his clothing when he returned home, covered from head to foot in all kinds of anti-social, stomach-churning filth. There had been the one exception he recalled. After spending four long days and nights buried up to his ears in a dung heap, she immediately set fire to his clothes in their back garden, costing his Chief Constable a small fortune in replacements. But who could blame her? All the Persil or Daz in the world wouldn't have got rid of that stench.

He was surprised to see the downstairs lights still on, as he slowly and cautiously scaled the fence. He was lucky. There was a thick hedge running alongside the interior of the wooden structure. That gave Rolo excellent back cover and he got to work digging his hole, like a human mole desperate to obtain shelter before being discovered. This was the only time he'd be exposed. Once dug in, the rest was easy. As he managed to deepen the hole, which could possibly be his abode for a long time to come, he periodically glanced at the house. A large five- or six-bedroomed detached with just three bedrooms and one toilet window on the upper level and a lounge, possible study and kitchen on the ground floor. The lights appeared to be coming from the kitchen and downstairs lounge. Much to his relief, it seemed there would be no dogs on the plot. Thank Christ!

His briefing had been no different from the norm. Video and record everything you see whilst in position. He would sleep during the day and observe at night. There would be no relief officer, trying to extract him for the purposes of a replacement could endanger the operation. Once in his dugout, there he would be expected to remain until further notice. Days, possibly a couple of weeks. The only exercise he would get was movement inside his new-found home. A wonderful thought for a normal person – but Rolo, like his colleagues, wasn't actually normal.

There, he was soon in. Only his head protruded above ground level. And with his blackened face covered by part of the garden hedge, he was invisible – to other humans anyway.

He made the transmitter pack under his armpit comfortable. A wire that led from the transmitter was connected to a button, which Rolo would keep in the palm of his hand throughout the remainder of the operation. That was his lifeline, his only contact with his backup. He pushed the small plastic button three times. The reply came through the tiny, almost invisible receiver in his ear.

'Got you, Rolo. Reading eight.'

If Rolo had pressed multi-clicks on the button, the reply would have been completely different. That was the signal to say that the covert was in trouble and needed immediate assistance. Three clicks meant yes to a question. Two clicks, no and one click, don't know. Another three presses told his back up they had a successful two-way link. From now on he would only use the designated coded signals. He made sure his equipment was where it should be and focused the camera. Now it was time to help himself to a hot cup of soup from a tube, just as the astronauts used to. And then, just sit back and enjoy the view, video at the ready.

*

At first Priestley couldn't understand why Blade wasn't there. He'd waited an hour at the spot where they usually met, before driving over to Cheetah, but there'd been no sign of him there either. First Sonia, now Blade. He hoped he hadn't been involved in some accident as well. But then saw the old Renault he'd been driving about in parked outside the tower block. His initial instinct, as he walked across the crisp frozen snow towards the entrance, was to go up and kick the idle bastard out of bed. Then he had second thoughts. He realised he'd been giving the geezer a hard time lately and the bloke was probably too exhausted to come out to play at that hour of the morning. It wasn't everybody who flew around shagging at three the morning. He stood still for a brief moment, considering the options. He needed to get some shut-eye as well. He reminded himself of the busy schedule he had in front of him with Sue Ridlington's little job. Yes, that was it. He'd give it a rest for tonight and get hold of Bladey tomorrow. He turned and walked back to his car.

Then, for no particular reason except it had started to snow again, he looked up towards Blade's window on the fifth floor. A curtain moved. Or did it? There was no light, just a slight movement. Could be the window's open and a draft was responsible. He shielded his eyes from the falling flakes with his hand and then…a face. He was only looking straight out of the bloody window at him! What's his game? Priestley wondered. He jumped into the car and sent a cryptic message over the Enigma:

WHAT'S UP DICKHEAD? GONE SHY ON ME OR SOMETHING?

That should do the trick. Jack felt better. Just to let Blade know he'd seen him hiding behind the curtains. He started the engine and drove away. Funny git that Blade. Never known him act up like that before. That's if it was Blade. He stopped the car, looked at the screen on the Enigma. There hadn't been any reply. The shithole's up to something, guessed Priestley and turned the car around.

'If you don't open this door, I'll break it down, Stevie boy,' he shouted, banging it even harder. 'What are you pissing about at?' Normally Priestley would walk away, not concerned in the slightest about the little game Blade was playing. But things were different at the moment. He didn't trust him. And with the job they'd both agreed to do together, it was important to Jack that his boil on the arse didn't double-cross him again.

The bolts came off the inside and the door slowly opened. It wasn't Steve Blade standing there. It was Ronnie Lakin. One of the few servants Blade regularly trusted.

'Mr Priestley. You'd better come in,' suggested Lakin with a grim look on his face.

Priestley was dumbfounded and followed Lakin into the empty lounge, wondering what little gem was going to be thrown his way during this particular visit.

'Where is he, Ron?' he asked with concern. 'Is he ill?' He looked towards the bedroom door along the corridor, knowing if Blade was ill, it was serious by the look on Lakin's face.

'I don't know, Mr Priestley,' explained the other man, as he sat down. 'I was coming to see you in the morning. He's been putting me up here for the past few nights. I've been kicked out by the missus, see.'

Priestley nodded and listened.

'He's been using my motor.' He suddenly stood up. 'Can I get you...'

Priestley shook his head and waved his hand.

'Well, last night, I heard the motor pull up and then the sound of Steve talking to somebody. Well, I looked out of the bedroom window like I just did with you.' He broke off to tell Priestley that he was a light sleeper. 'Well, I saw these two blokes bundle him into the back of a car and I've never seen him since.' His face looked more glum. 'I reckon they've done him in, Mr Priestley.'

The questions shot out like a machine gun from Priestley's mouth.

'Did you get the number of the car?'

Lakin shook his head, 'Couldn't see it from up here.'

'What time was this?'

'About three o'clock. The time he usually gets back from work.'

'What colour was the car?'

'Dark. Might even have been black. A Merc I think.'

'What did the two men look like?'

'One tall, one short.'

'How were they dressed? Smart, scruffy?'

'Smart. They looked like a couple of violin cases. Dark overcoats, collar and tie, you know the type.' Lakin was obviously genuinely worried about Blade's safety and stopped Priestley from asking any further questions. 'I mean, it wouldn't be so bad if Sammy was here but she's pissed off to South America, you know.'

'Yes, I know,' replied Priestley. 'Perhaps that's not a bad thing.' He'd already made it. Put it together. These were the two goons with the plane tickets Blade had met in the park. And Jack knew exactly what to do about it. He was already doubting that Sammy and the nipper had been allowed to make that plane.

He was still seething over the Blade business when he reached his office door and headed for the phone. There wasn't anything he could do in that direction, not at that very moment anyway. There were other pressing matters to get on with, such as Lady Ridlington's payout of a hundred grand. But he'd sort it eventually. He was confident no harm had come to Blade, provided it was the two goons who'd offered him the holiday, because they worked for Pike, the very man he intended to roll over the desk as soon as he got the opportunity. But right now, other things had to come first.

'How many, Chris?' Priestley asked as he dialled the number.

'Six and a bike,' was the reply. 'You sure that's going to be enough, boss?'

'It has to be,' he confirmed. 'I have to keep this one very tight. Can't afford to spread it all over the department.'

Barton just shrugged his shoulders but the fact he was concerned was obvious. To do a full surveillance on a moving target and all the way to Nottingham and God knows where to from there, would in his opinion, require double the number of resources Priestley was requesting. But he was the boss and had named those he wanted selected. In Barton's mind, Jack Priestley had many strengths and possibly the one that stuck out more than anything was the fact that he knew his people, both individually and as a group. There wasn't much Barton or anyone else for that matter, could tell him about any of their strengths and weaknesses, including his own. So if the gaffer said just six, then just six it would be.

'You've got the number, Reg. I just need the tap putting on,' Priestley explained down the phone. 'Yes, and relay it to me in the car.'

Barton moved to make an exit but was waved back by Priestley before he replaced the handset.

He quickly looked down the list of points he needed to cover and told Barton to wheel his special team in. 'By the way, Chris, is Rolo in?'

Barton turned and nodded, 'Went in last night.'

Priestley was flying by his pants. This had to come off and it had to come off today. He hadn't got the time to piss about with a blackmailer who would spend the next fortnight making demands on the phone.

'Right, you lot,' he said with his DCI's voice. 'We're going to test your surveillance capabilities and skills in knowing how to keep your mouths shut.'

Priestley explained to the five males and one female officer the sensitivity of the operation they were about to embark on. He was more than aware of the dangers they themselves faced each time they became involved in an operation such as this. And for that reason they deserved to know as much as he did. Therefore, his briefing was full and complete, and included the fact that Lady Ridlington would be carrying a hundred grand in genuine readies. However, he had decided to keep the reasons for the blackmail to himself. That was one thing they didn't need to know about.

Arrangements had been made for air support to track a transmitter that would be in the briefcase holding the cash. That was always a risk. Priestley knew that the blackmailer could purchase a cheap electronic device from any high street store, to help detect such a device. But that was a risk he was willing to take in these circumstances.

After the briefing it was question time and only one, the usual one, was put to him. 'Do we get any paid overtime for this, boss?'

He couldn't remember how many times before he had asked that question. Priestley just looked studiously at Dave Vaughan, the Overtime King as he was known to the rest of the team, and wondered whether to agree to the officer's disguised request or just tell him to sod off, emphasising the fact that they were performing for both Queen and country, and all that bollocks.

'I mean, it's on Saturday night, guv,' persisted the officer.

But the Detective Chief Inspector was in a charitable mood. 'Okay. You'll all get paid overtime.'

There were smiles all around except from Vaughan, who remained serious as he tried to clarify, 'Time and a half that is, boss?'

Enough was enough. The team quickly vanished before Priestley could fully stretch himself out of his seat, with the intention of grabbing Vaughany by the throat. The laughs echoed down the corridor, but that was typical of Priestley's people. Yes, these were good kids and he knew they'd do a job for him, no matter what.

He'd arranged to meet Lady Ridlington in the Carpenters Arms, his own pub where he frequently met Blade. It was secure and as it was Saturday afternoon, he couldn't take the risk that the blackmailer might be watching her home address.

The licensee's wife, Doreen, had always been friendly and accommodating in the past and this was no exception, allowing Jack and his new-found lady friend the use of her back room, where they could carry on with whatever business they had in private.

'Press this as many times as you like,' explained the senior detective, 'But remember, only if you think you're in trouble.'

She hadn't missed a word of his briefing and now sat, quietly enthralled by what he was saying to her.

'Remember. It's an emergency safety valve for you.'

From his choice of words, it appeared obvious to her that he'd carried out similar briefings on this particular equipment many times before. In fact she was wrong. He was just used to briefing people.

'If you do press this button the operation is over.'

'Why, Jack?' those had been her first words for sometime.

'Because we'll know you're in trouble and everyone will come to your assistance.' He paused and then realised this wasn't another police officer he was talking to and needed further explanation. 'Once we show out to the blackmailer, the job's over.'

'And you think he might be watching me?'

'I'm convinced he will.' That didn't help her confidence much. He noticed the concern on her face and tried to lighten the moment. 'But don't worry. I don't think for a minute anything will go wrong.' Too late, Jack. The damage had already been done. But she is a big girl now, he thought. At least she was smiling.

'Oh, and wear something bright,' suggested Priestley.

'A red scarf?'

'That should do it.'

'Won't that make it easier for the blackmailer to see me though, Jack?' It was a good point.

'Yes, but it'll also make it easy for us.' That was a stronger point.

This time she chuckled. He only hoped she'd be in the same good humour in twenty-four hours time.

＊

Priestley felt like a man about to participate in a professional game of world chess. He knew the stakes would be high but he was not aware of either the strengths or weaknesses of his opponent – a faceless individual who would undoubtedly dictate the pace of the game during its initial stages. A man whose every move would have been carefully planned, possibly rehearsed, over and over again, confident that, not only would he take possession of the money demanded, but would also take it without being caught. A formidable foe. A worthy opponent for Jack Priestley and his team to play against.

There wouldn't be much difficulty in building up a profile of the kind of enemy Priestley was about to face. His starting point would be the fact that the blackmailer had chosen a first contact with his victim, some sixty miles north of where she lived. That was his chosen territory. It would mean to the professional investigator, that either his opponent was extremely clever, attempting to execute his plan in an area strange to Lady Ridlington, even though it could also be foreign to himself. Or, and more likely, he possessed some, if not a great deal of local knowledge which would give him a distinct advantage. And that would be one of Priestley's first lines of inquiry, no matter what the outcome of that day's operation. However, although everything seemed to be initially in his opponent's favour, Priestley could also build into his part of the game certain contingencies in an effort to redress the balance. He'd already arranged for a covert phone tap to be put on the kiosk inside the railway station. Agreement had been reached with the telephone company to then relay the initial conversation between the blackmailer and victim back to him, over an earpiece. At least that would guarantee he could overhear the first instructions given to the victim. The first difficulties would become apparent after that call had been made. The chances were, they would then be in the dark, having to rely on mobile surveillance only.

The second issue recognised by Priestley as a strength was the fact that the blackmailer wouldn't know the police were involved. He might suspect it, therefore introducing some safety factors of his own, to be implemented as the operation progressed. But he wouldn't be sure and that, Priestley was hoping, might make him careless in playing one of his moves.

But above all, there were the dangers that would exist for the victim herself. She'd refused to allow a trained police officer to accompany her, even if he was concealed on the back seat of the car. Priestley had listened to the blackmailer demanding she travel alone on one of the tapes. That in itself created another dilemma for the officer in charge. He considered the possibility of fitting a covert radio transmitter inside Lady Ridlington's car, or even on her person, therefore providing a communications link through which she could relay back to him what was happening. But then he acknowledged that the risk to her own safety would be far too great. If she made physical contact with the blackmailer and he discovered she was wired-up, well, who knows what the scumbag would do? Her life wasn't Priestley's to play with.

The wire in the briefcase would have to suffice and the air support surveillance facility called in, if everything went to rat shit on the ground.

He knew that she was only the pawn and would have a fairly rough ride along the way. How dramatic her role would be depended upon the two main players. The blackmailer and himself. He could do no more. Everything he could think of to minimise the man's chances of success, had been done. And now the game was on!

*

The convoy left the M1 at junction 26 with time to spare and slowly followed the blue BMW Z3 Roadster towards

Nottingham City Centre. By the time they'd reached their destination, the weather had turned into a blizzard, as the car pulled up onto a car park opposite the front of the station. That would make it difficult to maintain an eyeball on the Z3 and give the blackmailer a distinct advantage. Priestley wasn't happy at all and called to the others to stay on their toes.

Sue Ridlington remained seated in her car.

'She's doing what she's been told to do, guv,' commented Vaughan. 'Staying put, until the right time.'

'Another five minutes yet, Dave,' confirmed Priestley.

'Weather don't help much.'

That was an understatement and Priestley looked at his sergeant with a kind of sardonic look, as though here sitting next to him was a day release from one of the local hospitals. And that reminded him. He hadn't inquired about Sonia for an hour and went to dial the number before deciding against it. He'd give it another hour this time. Might bring them both some luck.

Priestley called to Anna Beecham, the only female officer he had on the job, 'You inside the main hall, Anna?'

'Affirmative, boss.'

'Stay with it.'

She didn't really need to be told that but Priestley was starting to get itchy feet. This was different from other jobs. There were a hundred big ones involved in this and to lose that would only result in him and his team having more than egg over their faces the next day. And an additional worry was the fact that failure would bring the old school tie out. That well-known group of arseholes who came out of the lace curtains at every opportunity to scream and criticise from a great height. The people, who themselves, had never done a stroke before in their lives.

'She's moving, guv.'

Both Priestley and Vaughan watched as Sue Ridlington, briefcase in hand, bright red woollen scarf wrapped around her neck, slowly walked across towards the front entrance before disappearing from sight, in the blizzard.

'Have you got her, Anna?'

'I've got her boss. Moving towards the kiosk. Standing outside now. Reading a paper or magazine.'

Priestley's earpiece was already in position, provided by technical support who would also be monitoring the call back at his office. Vaughan shouted for radio silence at Priestley's direction and the tension could almost be seen. Seven o'clock struck. The airwaves remained silent. So did the telephone. Five past. The situation remained unchanged. Ten past seven, now. Still nothing.

'Think he's had us over, boss?' asked Vaughan.

Priestley didn't reply, preferring to maintain his full concentration on the small receiver inside his ear. Another five minutes and Priestley could see his DS was getting restless, shuffling his arse about and scratching the back of his head. There'd been no contingency made for the blackmailer failing to make the initial call and Jack wondered how long Sue Ridlington would wait, until deciding to return to her car. He didn't have to wait long.

'Target on the move, boss.' It was Anna Beecham again. 'She's heading towards the exit, briefcase intact. Looks as though she's given up the ghost.'

Bollocks, thought Priestley. He pulled the earpiece out.

'Eighteen minutes past pissing seven, Dave, and she's thrown the towel in, already.'

Vaughan nodded, 'He's having her on, Boss. I couldn't see him phoning now,' he added sympathetically.

'Phone's ringing, boss,' it was Anna Beecham again. 'She needs to come back and answer it. I can't get to her.'

'Dave!'

Vaughan jumped out of the car and walked quickly but without running, towards Sue Ridlington who was just stepping onto the pavement outside the front entrance. Priestley put the earpiece back into position and could hear the familiar ringing tone.

'Go back and answer the phone,' whispered Vaughan as he walked past her, straight into the front of the railway station as though making his way towards the newsagent's stand to purchase the latest edition.

Lady Ridlington scurried back towards the kiosk, still gripping onto the briefcase, as if it contained her whole life. It must have rung a dozen times and was still ringing as Priestley looked around, convinced she'd been watched by the man he most wanted to meet himself.

'Where are you, you bastard?' he said, but there was nothing or no one looking anything like suspicious.

'Hello.' She'd made it.

Thank Christ, thought Jack and sighed as he listened to the conversation.

'Have you got it with you?'

The voice was exactly the same as the one he'd heard on Lady Ridlington's tapes. No real accent. Difficult to put an age to. Obviously disguised, as though the shithole was talking in an echo chamber. It could even have been a woman, although Priestley doubted that.

'Yes.' Her voice was nervous which was understandable. It wasn't every day of the week you had to go through something like this. It was a piece of drama straight off the telly – whether or not you were a member of the aristocracy or some poor unemployed bastard.

'Listen carefully. You're being watched and we know you've got the coppers there.'

'Bastard,' spoke Jack to himself again.

Vaughan was only just making his way back through the snow, towards him.

Priestley knew this was a try-on. The shock treatment to see how she would react. The bastard really didn't have a clue whether the law was on side or not.

'You cheeky bastard.'

That surprised Priestley. She was good!

'You can always trust a thief,' explained the victim in a rather irate manner, 'but you can't trust a liar, Mr whatever your name is.'

Shithole had been well admonished. Good girl. And to think Jack was worried about the way she would perform.

'Please don't speak to me with a forked tongue. Do you want to do business with me or not, my good man?'

There was a long pause before the reply came and Priestley couldn't help but admire this lady's guts. Perhaps she was still a man after all, in drag?

'Follow these instructions carefully, Mr Allsop.'

That was a point well made. Touché. The blackmailer had never used her previous name before and Priestley immediately felt a wealth of pity for her. She must have now felt devastated as that particular punch had landed well below the belt.

'Have you brought the tape recorder?'

'Yes,' The authority had gone from her voice.

This bastard was nasty but his words had secured the effect he'd intended.

'Walk out of the front entrance and turn left. Walk two hundred yards and go into the telephone kiosk there and you will find a tape underneath the shelf. Follow the instructions on the tape.'

The phone went dead as Dave Vaughan jumped back into the car.

Priestley broke radio silence and repeated the blackmailer's instructions to his team. Both he and Vaughan looked in the direction she had to walk. But it was hopeless. Even without the ongoing, heavy, wind-driven snow, they wouldn't have been able to see the next stopping point from where they were parked.

'She's going to lift a tape from inside the kiosk and play it for further instructions. Anyone not understanding this?'

There was no answer from any of his team.

'Right. Anna stay where you are. Do not follow target.' Priestley couldn't be sure that shithole wasn't watching his victim and if that were the case, any person following Sue Ridlington out of the railway station would become suspicious to him.

'Understood,' was the reply from Beecham.

'Cornet?'

DC Roger Price, whose call sign Priestley was now calling, responded.

'Stay close to the second rendezvous. I'm hoping she'll leave the tape for us.' Then as an afterthought, 'Have you the equipment on board?'

Jack knew that some of his crime cars had built in tape recorders but wasn't sure about Cornet's.

'That's affirmative.'

'Everyone else,' Priestley continued, 'keep your positions. And stay bright. He might just be goosing for us.' In fact, thought Priestley he could be sitting in a car, watching from the same car park on which they were holed up! He looked around with some urgency, but saw nothing unusual.

His use of the surveillance jargon was improving with each operation and Jack was quite proud of the efficient way he could now direct his resources over that bloody wireless set. Mind you, it had taken him long enough and not before he moaned incessantly. Something about talking down a plastic trumpet?

✳

Lady Ridlington put the small tape into her recorder and hit the play button. Her hands were shaking as she heard the same unearthly voice piercing her eardrum and penetrating her mind.

'Go back to your car and follow the one-way system to the first roundabout. Follow the B684 towards Arnold. Stop at the first telephone kiosk after the third roundabout and you will find further instructions written on paper underneath the shelf.'

Although still mesmorised by the knowledge that this man knew her name before she'd married Sir Richard, she still had her wits about her and dropped the tape at the side of the car as she stepped inside.

'Tape's on the ground, guv. In the road.'

'Leave it, Cornet.' Priestley directed. 'Wait until she's out of sight. He could still be here with us.' He then ordered the rest of the team to follow Ridlington, just in case.

How did this man know so much about her ? It must have come from the hospital she'd attended in Illinois. Her hands were still trembling and she couldn't swallow. She kept telling herself to get a grip as she drove steadily on, counting the number of islands. The small electronic button given to her earlier, was secured to her wrist, but hanging loosely from her palm. She was praying that Jack Priestley was right behind her. But her rear view mirror revealed nothing and she suddenly felt very much alone. Isolated. Vulnerable to this psycho who was about to relieve her of the contents of the briefcase on her front passenger seat. The temptation to press the panic button was almost irresistible, but she fought it.

Cornet relayed the contents of the tape to Priestley who immediately directed his biker to overtake them and try and make the next rendezvous point before Lady Ridlington or the rest of the team did. Despite the appalling weather conditions she unknowingly remained in sight of the first eyeball car and everything thus far, was going according to plan. Priestley had won the first two rounds. They were still with her. Once the biker got into position at the next kiosk, it would be his responsibility then to cover the victim and relay what was happening to the rest of the team.

Priestley was confident that, if the instructions were on a written note, she would do as before and drop the piece of paper for the police to find. The same would apply to another tape. But if the blackmailer phoned her there, they would then be in Queer Street, having to rely on their own initiative and mobile surveillance skills. The other concern, which had been tormenting him since the start of the operation was that the closer they got to the point where the money would be taken, the more vigilant the blackmailer would become.

'This is more for breeding bleedin' polar bears in than doing a surveillance, gaffer,' commented Vaughan.

But Priestley was at that point when he heard only that which he wanted to. His mind was well occupied. Noting, analysing, considering every possibility which might suddenly open up before them. He knew that this particular Mr Shithole had been busy. He was a schemer and planned his strategy well. He wasn't just going to surrender himself. There must be a bite at the end of the tail, a set of circumstances whereby he could take the money without any danger to himself. But all they could do at the moment was follow the BMW soft top.

✱

'Duke's in position, guv.'

Priestley was relieved to hear the biker's voice. So was the rest of the team. Round three to the coppers.

'The target will be with me in a couple of minutes. There's no problem here. In a nearby farmyard, opposite the T K. Good eyeball.'

Everything seemed to be going well, thought Priestley again. Perhaps too well.

✱

She'd almost driven past the telephone kiosk before seeing it through the curtain of snow. It was unlit and that worried her. She stopped and stepped out of the car, leaving the headlights on. Everywhere seemed deserted and now she started to feel her mouth becoming dry with fear that couldn't be repressed for much longer. She had to stay focused at all costs. No matter what. She went inside. At least the light reflected off the freshly fallen snow helped a little. She felt under the shelf. There was no note.

Suddenly the door opened and she felt her arm being tugged violently.

266

Her first thought was that she'd unwittingly left the briefcase in the car and she then instinctively pressed the panic button in her hand, perhaps a thousand times in the following five seconds.

'Get back in the car. Do as you're told and you won't get hurt.' The voice was different. Older. More personal. More like a human's voice than that horrible echo she'd had to listen to for the past couple of weeks, both in her own home and then up here in this strange land.

He kept pushing her until they reached the car and made sure she was in the driver's seat, before he ran around the front to the opposite side. That was the first real glimpse she had of him as his body broke through the two front headlamp beams. A balaclava covered his head and he was wearing what looked like a dark green anorak. If only she could tell Priestley.

The door slammed to and there he was, with her, sitting at her side. She felt sick with fear. If she'd ever needed a copper to turn up, this was it. Even an RAC vehicle recovery man would help.

'Drive,' was his first order.

She tried to obey, fumbling with the ignition keys. They fell onto the floor.

The hooded man's head spun sideways and then to the rear. 'DRIVE!' he bawled, obviously agitated. And then the engine started.

*

'Target in sight. Out of car, to the T K.'

There was a pause and Priestley told his people to hang back. He'd estimated they were only a quarter of a mile away from her and didn't want anybody crashing in, just in case their man was watching.

Then the multiple clicks over the intercom. Priestley stared at Vaughan. Vaughan stared back.

'It's a strike, guv,' yelled Duke excitedly.

'What do you mean, it's a strike?' demanded Priestley.

'A geezer has just jumped over a fence at the back of the T K and...hang on guv, he's got the target and he's taking her back to the car. I'm going in, guv.'

At least the hand-held button had worked.

'Stay where you are, Duke,' Priestley screamed back, at the same time signalling Vaughan to get their vehicle moving. 'Think of the woman. He might be armed.'

No one had thought of that particular situation and that put the adrenaline levels through the roof alright, as cars sped along to where the Z3 was parked.

'Talk to me, Duke,' said Priestley, trying to stay as calm as possible. Wishing he had a cork stuck up his arse. 'What's happening now? We're ten seconds away from you.'

'They've taken off, guv. I'm following. It's a left, left, left, after the T K. About half a mile past.'

Every member of the team was listening to the biker. Pulses were beating hard as they raced to try and catch up. The snow was getting thicker. Wiper blades were switched to maximum. The tyres slid from left to right.

Within seconds of the last transmission, the first police car was negotiating the left-hand turn. Priestley and Vaughan were behind that one.

'Keep talking, Duke,' requested the DCI but there was no answer from Duke. He called again, and again. Still no answer.

The hooded man sat with the briefcase on his lap. His head was turned, staring through the woollen slits at the solitary light behind them, quickly drawing closer and closer. He could hear the motorcycle engine now and knew they'd got company. There must have been six inches of snow on the narrow country lane and it was getting thicker. His pursuer only had two wheels. He had four. His confidence remained high.

*

The police motorcyclist was an experienced rider and realised anything coming the other way would be a major problem. Duke had to stay there and wait for his opportunity. The Z3 was swerving from left to right, obviously as a result of the petrified driver.

Sue Ridlington had been told by the hooded man to stop at the next crossroads, where she hoped and prayed that was where he planned to get out and leave her, minus the briefcase, of course. But that was the last thing on her mind. Now, he could have the money. All she wanted was this ape to vanish. She was silently screaming inside and her driving sense had completely abandoned her. All she was doing was aiming the car around one bend, then another, and another. She hadn't noticed the biker behind, which was now almost touching her rear bumper.

Duke's chance came after the BMW had negotiated a right hander. He cut across and was soon level with the driver's door. He quickly glanced at the horror on Sue Ridlington's white face. The hooded man also recognised an opportunity and reached across, forcing the steering wheel out of the woman's control. He violently swung it to the right, pushing the vehicle directly into the side of the biker. Nothing could be done. The young police officer was catapulted off the road and made a hole in a nearby hedge.

The woman screamed and through instinct grabbed the wheel back, at the same time hitting the brakes. The momentum of the car shifted onto the front wheels and the vehicle turned over and over and over, with both the victim and her blackmailer entangled together inside. It eventually came to rest on all four wheels, in an upright position. Minus the soft top.

She was lucky. They were both lucky and it wasn't until she was standing there, hands to her face screaming loudly, that she saw him slowly climb out still holding the briefcase, like the phoenix rising from the ashes. He walked towards her with his free arm held outwards, as if asking for help or intending to throttle her. She continued to scream and it was then that Jack Priestley captured his prey, clubbing him to the ground.

Game over. Checkmate.

Jack removed his balaclava and gave him the news. 'If my lad dies, you'll never walk again.' And he meant it.

Dave Vaughan quickly ran up from behind. 'Watcha, Vinnie. Fancy seeing you here.'

*

chapter seventeen

Vincent Grant was a tall 35-year-old with very short, light brown hair, swept back and receding at the front. He had the sort of pale complexion that would turn like a ripe tomato in the sun and his wiry build resembled a park paling. In fact, George Riddle had nicknamed him Biro.

He sat forward in the chair, elbows leaning on both knees. Head bowed, glazed eyes staring in disbelief. This hadn't really happened to *him*. Examining the minute scratches on the light amber-coloured floor tiles, didn't afford him much comfort either. The door to the interview room opened and Jack Priestley signalled for the uniformed officer to leave, before sitting opposite Grant. Dave Vaughan sat in the third chair by the door.

'So, how's George Riddell these days, Vinnie?' asked the Detective Chief Inspector.

'I want a solicitor.'

'There's one on the way, son,' explained Priestley. 'I understand the one you've nominated.' He turned his head and looked towards Vaughan, 'I don't think you'll go short in that department. I should think half the legal profession is queuing up to represent you old pal.'

Grant remained silent, still studying the scratches on the floor.

'I just thought we'd have a chat before we brought the tape recorder in and started all formal like.'

Grant looked up for the first time. 'I'm not saying anything until I've got my solicitor here.'

'And I don't blame you,' snapped Priestley. 'Blackmail for a hundred grand. Attempted murder. Kidnapping.' He grinned, 'Shouldn't think you'd want to talk to yer own mother, mate.'

Grant's eyes returned to the floor and he sat motionless, still using his knees as arm rests.

'Twenty stretch? Twenty-five? Maybe even thirty if the papers blow it up, which I'm sure they will once it gets out,' explained Priestley.

Grant shook his head.

'At this very moment, I suggest you need to talk to us more than anybody else alive today.'

Still silence.

Priestley pulled his chair closer to Grant, leaning forward in the same posture as the man who had earlier been his opponent. He spoke in a quiet voice, 'I think, son, you need all the help you can get.'

Grant glared at him, 'Go stuff yerself, copper.'

'Okay,' Priestley stood and walked towards the door, signalling Vaughan to stay where he was. 'Go face the judge on your own then, Vinnie. See where that gets you. I just thought you'd be interested in one or two deals I had in mind.' He sighed, as though he was the one facing such a heavy sentence. 'But, if you're not interested, go face the rest of your life washing the dishes or working in the laundry. Personally, I don't give a shit. My job's done.' He opened the door to leave.

'What kind of deals?' asked Grant, in a less aggressive voice.

Hooked like a big fish, thought Priestley. He returned to his chair. 'Well, I'll be quite honest with you. I won't be sending a letter to the judge saying what a good lad you really are.'

Grant smirked, but at least he was now paying some attention to Priestley's words.

'I won't pretend, Vinnie. You're well and truly in the shit.' He raised his hand level with his chin, 'Up to your neck in it. But a little help from you now and in five, six years time, you might just be looking for some parole. An early release if you play your cards right in the nick.' The chair was pulled back to within inches of Grant, 'Parole my son. I've done it before and I can do it again.'

'Parole?' Grant appeared to be genuinely interested. He hadn't heard this angle being used before. It was usually all about whether he'd get bail or not.

'Yes, parole,' confirmed Priestley, 'A letter of recommendation to the parole board. Works wonders. Ask some of your mates who've enjoyed that particular privilege in the past.' He paused. 'Trouble is, nobody likes to admit having had a leg up, in case people like you start to wonder why.' Another pause, 'But it goes on and you'd be a fool not to take advantage.'

Grant's mind was starting to become active again. Life was returning to his eyes. He was slowly climbing out of that barrel of black tar he'd earlier been drowning in, not wanting to come out after his world had been shattered on that lonely road, just outside Nottingham.

'In five years' time you'd have forgotten all about me,' he suggested. 'I'd just be another statistic to you.' Vinnie was beginning to sound intelligent.

'You're right,' agreed Priestley. 'But when the letter arrives from you asking for help, I'll remember that Vinnie

Grant was that bloke who sat in the interview room back in Birmingham, and helped me out as best he could.' Jack's voice was still quiet. Convincing. Sympathetic. Trusting. 'And then I'd write the letter, son. A letter that could give you back five years or more freedom.'

Even Vaughan was beginning to believe his gaffer was genuine. Priestley wasn't lying.

'What do you want from me?' Grant sat back in his chair, 'You said yerself, I'm in the shit. How much more do you want to stick on me?'

Priestley shook his head, 'No, no, no, Vinnie. It's got nothing to do with what we've got on you. Just a few smaller issues I want to clear up. Like how did you find out about Lady Ridlington's skeletons in the cupboard?'

That amused Vinnie and he smiled, which meant that things were looking up for the two detectives.

'Read it in the newspaper.'

That one floored Priestley and now it was his turn to sit back in his seat. 'The newspaper?'

'Yeah,' Grant was looking a lot more optimistic now, talking in a much more friendlier manner than before. 'I was in the nick and there was an article describing how this geezer had gone to the States and had a sex change. Graham Allsop.'

'But she didn't marry her husband until well after that. So how did you put the two together?'

'Her picture was in the same article. A sort of before and after kind of thing,' he explained still smiling. He was feeling a bit of a smart-arse, in actual fact. It was becoming obvious to him that they knew less than he did.

Priestley still looked confused.

'I saw her a few months ago.' Grant's eyes went up to the ceiling, to give his brain a chance. 'I think she was at some sort of charity do me and the missus went to.'

The only charity do he'd go to, thought Priestley was one that gave everything away for nothing. He sighed for the second time during that interview and turned to look at Vaughan who was just sitting there like a statue – taking everything in. He'd come into the conversation if his gaffer wanted him to.

'So you then decided to give it a whirl?'

'Well, at first it was just for the crack. But when I saw how nervous and upset she got, I thought I'd get serious.' His face changed again and the smile vanished, reminding himself that his attempted extortion had in fact failed.

Priestley glanced again at Vaughan. That was the signal.

'Why Nottingham, Vinnie?' asked the Detective Sergeant.

'Born there. Know it like the back of my hand,' replied Grant. 'I doubted that she would know it as well me and just thought it would make it easier.'

There was a knock on the door and a uniformed sergeant appeared. 'Excuse me, Mr Priestley, but his solicitor has just arrived.'

The senior officer nodded, 'Okay, I'll be out there in a jiff.' He stood as the door was closed again. 'One more thing, Vinnie, and by the way, I'll put that letter in for you when you come up for parole.'

Grant appeared to be assured. He believed Priestley but on the other hand, he didn't have any other choice.

'What about Riddell? Was he involved?'

Grant laughed again, 'You must be joking. With what he's doing, he could make a hundred grand by just getting out of bed.'

'What, by trying to kill women in car accidents?'
Vaughan was aware of the sensitive nature of the question
being asked in front of Priestley, but they couldn't afford to
miss an opportunity like this and he was confident his DCI
would appreciate that.

'You mean the barrister?' asked Grant.

Vaughan nodded.

'Take a lot to prove that,' suggested the prisoner.

'I think you're right but it's a shitty thing to do, don't you
think?'

'Yeah, I know. One or two of the others weren't too
happy about it.'

'In what way?' Vaughan still had the floor.

The smile was back on Grant's face again, 'When we all
read about it in the newspapers.'

It was evident that line of questioning was going
nowhere and they were running out of time. As soon as
they were joined by the solicitor, Vinnie boy would just 'no
comment' everything asked.

'So, how is Uncle George earning all that money,
Vinnie?' asked Priestley.

He just shook his head, 'No, it would be more than my
life's worth, Mr Priestley.'

Priestley knew there wouldn't be any more news on
Riddell's antics, although this bloke was the one who would
know all about the big man's escapades. If only he could put
him under some kind of hypnotic drug, he wished. But then
again, if he could it would be a totally different system of
justice he worked for, and nobody wanted that. Except the
hardest of coppers – those who walked about in imaginary
jack boots. Both he and Vaughan left him to discuss his own
personal mess with his solicitor.

✱

'It's coming apart at the seams,' shouted Riddell. 'First the jockey and now Biro. Anybody else thinking of waging their own individual war?'

The group of men just stood there, not really feeling the frost biting at their extremities, too frightened to be seen not paying attention.

'I can't be living with this,' he roared on, 'We're on the brink of making a lot more dough and some of us are too bastard greedy to wait.' There was steam literally coming from his mouth but only because of the cold air.

He'd called the meeting and as usual, held it in the middle of the field at the side of the warehouse. That was the only place in which he felt he could speak about confidential matters without some nosy undesirable bastard listening in.

He turned to Ricketts and Khan, two of his principle performers. The two who got paid more than any of the rest of them. 'Mitch, you and Mo will pick the first load up next Thursday at the usual time. And don't get trying to put the screamers on some bird or pulling the funny stuff into the country in the meantime.'

Mitch and Mo just shook their heads and both smiled.

'And you two,' pointing towards Waltham and Lawrence, 'The usual with the igloos.'

They too confirmed his orders like nodding dogs.

'And the rest of you. Any more deviations and this operation will close down.' He stared at everybody individually. They'd all got the message.

'Which also means that the rest of us will be out of work. Which also means, we'll be coming to look you up.' He turned and walked away as briskly as he'd approached them earlier.

*

Priestley stood alone, holding the spare key tightly in the palm of his hand. He felt tired, washed out, exhausted. He badly needed a break, so did his officers. But this wasn't the time. He looked around the room and then at the oil painting hanging over the fireplace of Mr Justice Hall, sitting there, looking down at him almost accusingly. Had he dreamt all this? The thought had crossed his mind once or twice before. Was he in the middle of a nightmare? He realised it was for real when he felt the emptiness around him. Everything was how it had been on his last visit. Except she was missing. And that to him, was the most important thing.

He walked into the kitchen and noticed a cup half filled with coffee. She'd made that and hadn't had time to finish it. He picked the cup up, wanting to caress it, hold it close to him, as it was probably the last thing she touched before leaving the flat. Then the phone rang. It didn't help him much, having to stand and listen to her recorded voice answering the call.

'Sonia, it's Colin Renshaw from number five chambers. Perhaps you could come back to me as soon as you get this message. Bye.' The phone went down.

Perhaps she'll never hear that message, thought a very depressed Jack Priestley. He sat down and pressed the playback button. He didn't notice there were nineteen unanswered messages. The call just made was the first to come out of the tiny speaker. Then a number of different people ringing up for whatever reason. He didn't listen to them all, he was too busy thinking about better times. There was some geezer from the gas asking if her boiler was still working okay; the plumber wanting to know the most convenient time to call and check on a newly fitted tap; then some bloke with a quote for decorating costs –

over two grand for just wallpapering a flat, seemed a bit heavy to Priestley.

'This is George Riddell, Sonia. I need to see you urgently. Can you meet me at The Bistro in Halesowen, at six prompt. It's very urgent. It might be too late now.'

Priestley was up off the chair. He pressed the button, which told him that particular call was made at half past five the day she had the accident. She was going to meet George bloody Riddell when she had the bump. He picked up his mobile.

'John, what was the exact time of that accident?'

'Quarter past six,' replied Greatrex.

'Any more on the car?'

'No sir. I've had a vehicle inspector look at it, but I don't think he'll give us any more than we already know.'

'Thanks, I'll be in touch.'

He sat down again, trying to calculate times and speeds. Priestley wasn't a mathematician but guessed she would have got home between half past five and six o'clock – which meant she would have responded to that message almost immediately. Sonia must have thought the meeting was urgent.

Riddell had used the words, 'urgent' and 'perhaps it's too late now'. But he knew his Sonia. She must have had dozens of messages like that every week of her working life. So why go chasing out at the first shout from a bloke like Riddell? There was something else. Something they'd discussed at an earlier meeting. There had to be. Something which led her to believe that Riddell was in serious trouble or needed her help as a matter of life and death. But she hadn't mentioned it to Priestley on the night they'd discussed Mr Shithole. Which meant she'd spoken to Riddell again, after talking to Jack about him. Possibly during the day of the accident. Whatever had happened, it smelt to him like a set-up. Riddell had deliberately created the kind of panic in her mind which caused her to put her foot down to make that six o'clock meeting. And she would have been more hyped up if she'd been late. But why? She'd already got the bastard off one blackmail charge. Why try to kill her? It just didn't make sense to Priestley. Unless...

He stood and made for the exit after snatching the tape from the answering machine. He needed to put something to the test, but he had one other priority first.

✳

'I really don't give a toss who's in with him. I need to see him, now.' The fire in his eyes was reflected in his outraged voice and Pike's secretary, who was a stalwart when it came to handling difficult customers, just repeated, 'Then you'll just have to take a seat and wait, Mr Priestley.'

He knew it would be a lost cause if he didn't do what was being suggested, so he parked his rear on one of the three easy chairs leaning against the wall. Unlike Pike's inner sanctum, the outer reception area in which Priestley now found himself, resembled a doctor's waiting-room and the woman behind the telephone could easily have been an ex-mercenary from the Congo.

The door opened and some snivelling little clerical assistant, as Priestley decided he was, came walking out and disappeared through the exit, which the policeman had walked through a few moments before.

Jack stood up and walked towards Pike's office.

'Mr Priestley?' shouted the secretary but Jack was having none of it. Within a second he was in, staring at Commander Pike's back as the older man was just returning to the comfort of his chair.

'Hello, Jack,' greeted Pikey in his usual cordial-sounding voice.

There'd be no Chivas or Villiger's for Priestley on this occasion.

'Where is he?' asked the copper.

Pike didn't answer. He just stared, looking a little nonchalant.

'And don't play games, Commander. If I have to I'll put this on the front page of every newspaper.'

That struck a chord and Pike started to shake his head. 'I take it you're referring to Mr Blade, Jack?'

'And his family,' added Jack.

Pike lifted the telephone and dialled a number, much to Priestley's surprise.

'Remember our most recent discussion,' he said to the person on the other end. 'Well, we need it to be implemented with immediate effect.' He replaced the receiver.

'What you and your band of golden angels have done is illegal and immoral.' Priestley was still flying.

'Heard you had a good result last night, Jack. Congratulations.'

The condescending bastard, thought Priestley.

He leant over the desk in such a threatening manner, Pike moved his chair back a few inches, the forefinger on his left hand pressing a red button situated out of Priestley's view, although the DCI had noticed the movement and guessed what he'd done. But he'd had a bad few days and wouldn't worry if half the Household Cavalry came charging in through the door.

'If they're not free by the close of this afternoon, tomorrow's papers will print history in the making.'

Pike smiled. 'Jack, you're out of your league. You're also treading on extremely dangerous ground.'

'Fuck you, Commander. You and your little army of cherubs.'

Those weren't really the appropriate words for Jack to use as a description of the people who worked for Pike, because the two gents who'd just walked in and were now standing behind him had the physique of Sumo wrestlers.

'That was your Chief Constable on the phone, Jack. He wants to see you upon your immediate return to the Midlands.' He looked at that gold wristwatch again, 'Which I believe should be in two hours from now.'

Both of Jack's arms were immobilised.

'And, Jack,' continued Pike, 'be very careful how you tread in the future.'

Was that a warning shot? No, more like a warrant of execution by the devilish look in Pike's eyes.

Jack had rocked the boat alright. He'd stung Pikey, old boy, on his left tit and he could be sure the Commander wouldn't give him another opportunity to sting the other one. He'd probably gone over the top a bit. After all, Blade was only a villain. But in Priestley's mind, it didn't matter a hoot what Blade's past was. He had the same rights as everybody else and they didn't include being kidnapped.

It was nice of the two heavyweights, Tinker and Tucker to escort him to the train but they needn't have bothered, thought Jack. There was no way he was going to let up on this one. They'd have to take him out and shoot him first. Or throw him off some cliff. Then he started to worry. Perhaps that was exactly what they had in mind.

There followed another shitty train journey home with his mind once again in torment as he tried to work out what game was being planned and who the players were. He phoned the hospital. No change – again.

George Riddell had a motive for trying to bump off Sonia Hall. And Priestley was guessing it was himself and his own association with the lady. After all, everything had been fine for her up until the smarmy git had seen them together that night in the golf club. And what was it she'd told him? Riddell had been asking her whether or not Priestley had ever mentioned Gabriel or a similar name. He stared once more out of the carriage window. It was quickly becoming a habit. If Riddell thought that she'd been talking to Priestley about him, then he'd be worried that she knew something damaging to the Riddell empire, something that, in the hands of a crime squad officer could be disastrous for him. But she hadn't disclosed anything. Or had she? He thought on, trying to remember every word of their conversation.

She'd told Jack that Riddell had some interests abroad. So what? Didn't make him a woman killer. That was probably his arms dealing in any case. He always paid his bills in cash. Didn't make him the biggest tax fiddler since Al Capone. And if it did, so what? Surely he wouldn't try to murder for it? Priestley was convinced that Riddell had mistakenly thought that Sonia knew something about his business that could harm him. And his biggest venture at the moment, according to the Secret Squirrels, was that bloody arms exportation racket. The more he thought of it, the more he knew the answers would only be provided if he closed down that operation, with Riddell caught right in the middle of it. He had to concentrate on the warehouse in Meriden. Priestley then started to wonder why Pikey had demanded he see Sir Ron on his return to Birmingham. And then it came to him. He had a bloody good idea why.

*

'Jack, this is a bad day for me.' The Chief Constable wasn't about to promote him. That much was certain. 'I've had to order an investigation into the way you handled the blackmail case yesterday.'

That was a story beyond belief. Four hours ago he was a hero, 'Why?'

'Jack, you know why. You didn't tell the local Nottingham Police you'd be on their patch. Never mind not bothering to tell them about the serious nature of what you were doing.'

Priestley couldn't believe what he was hearing. The operation had gone down as one of the most successful in police history and he was now getting a bollocking for having done it.

Sir Ron stood and shrugged his shoulders, 'Of course – '

Priestley interrupted him, 'And who's doing the investigation Chief Constable? Commander Pike of the Yard?'

'Damn your insolence,' screamed Sir Ron. 'You're not in a position to question the ethics of all this.'

The look of disgust on Jack's face remained fixed.

The Chief Constable returned to his seat, obviously agitated about what had to be done. And Priestley knew exactly what was about to happen.

'Jack, I'm going to have to suspend you from duty.' He couldn't look the junior officer in the eye and stared at his blotter as he spoke. 'You're suspended from duty as from now. There's an officer from complaints outside waiting to take your warrant card. Now get out!'

Jack wondered if he should refuse to go, just to see the Chief Constable's reaction. He'd probably crumble into dust at having his authority challenged, or he'd probably throw Jack out of the window. Still, it was hypothetical and he turned and left. At least he hadn't had to go through all that pissing about, listening to how much the Chief regretted his actions and how badly he felt and all that tripe.

But now Jack was Mr Priestley in the true sense of the word. And he felt sick to the stomach.

*

'We've just heard. Through the grapevine, boss.'

Priestley knew that Chris Barton was being genuinely sympathetic and nodded, at the same time continuing to clear out his desk, placing everything into three Tesco bags his secretary had given to him. He hadn't brought a suitcase with him to work that morning. He didn't know he was due for the bullet. He'd thought then he was going to get a knighthood!

'Boss,' Barton was still standing there in the doorway. 'If they can do that to you, after what we did yesterday with Grant and Lady Ridlington.' He raised his hands in a friendly gesture, 'Well, what could they do to the rest of us?'

Priestley could see the look of anguish on his Detective Inspector's face and turned to reassure him, 'Chris, it's not –'

The junior rank interrupted him, 'No, boss, you don't see the point I'm making. We don't even know why you've been suspended.'

'If you want to know the truth, Chris, neither do I, mate. But I'll find out. I promise.' Jack winked at him. He'd been down this path before and there were others close to him who had more serious problems.

*

chapter eighteen

'I want to know, boy,' demanded the headmaster, 'Who fired that rocket at the window?'

'Honest, sir, I've said, sir, I don't know, sir.' This was only the third time young Steve Blade had been addressed by the head teacher and on the previous two occasions, he'd had a wallop across the backside.

'You must know, boy, you were there.'

'But I wasn't, sir.'

'Mr Rogers caught you walking away.'

'What I mean, sir, is I didn't see anything.'

The headmaster walked over to the glass cabinet and reached inside. 'Split end or straight stick?' he said, giving Blade a choice of two, both options causing tremendous discomfort when swiped across a full set of fingertips.

'I think this is more serious than you realise, my lad.' The instrument of discipline was carefully placed on the study desk, beneath the nose of the shivering boy. 'Someone aimed that firework at the laboratory window deliberately. The damage was extensive. Now, I'm not having rate payers' hard-earned money wasted as a result of some childish prank.' He raised his voice, 'Do you understand, boy?'

'Sir, sir,' cried Blade, tears beginning to roll down his cheeks, 'It was Jack Priestley. I overheard some other kids saying it was him.'

The room was much the same as it usually was. Perhaps a little more crowded, thought Priestley as he entered, in search of his favourite informant. He knew most of the faces, by sight. They were all hard-working barrow boys, whose day usually finished when everybody else was just settling into work.

'So, how have you been getting along, Jackie?' he asked Benton, aware that the old man would be still missing his old dutch.

'Glad you popped in, Jack.' He appeared to be much brighter than the last time Priestley had set eyes on him. More sober for a start. 'You were asking about Georgie Riddle?'

Priestley was amazed his old snout remembered. The usual nod went in for the drinks to be set up and Priestley, as always, obliged.

'I overheard a couple of his blokes talking the other night. In here.'

'In here?' that surprised the crime squad man. Riddell's men, using a market pub – very unusual, to say the least.

'Yeah,' continued Barton, 'Mo Khan and a kid called Ricketts. Never seen the one geezer in here before but Khan used to work in the Fruit and Veg.'

Priestley paid for the drinks.

'They were talking, Jack, about having to pick some stuff up for Georgie Riddell from some army depot. Lea Marston or something like that.'

'Long Marston?' suggested Priestley.

'You're right. Long Marston.' Benton nodded looking pleased that he'd managed to get something right. 'They've got to pick the stuff up and were moaning about some prat upsetting Riddell and then having their money docked or something like that.'

'That's interesting, Jackie. Did they mention the name Vinnie Grant?'

'No. That doesn't ring a bell with me either.'

Priestley had initially gone in there to relax for an hour or so with Benton. Perhaps even to get drunk and try and snap out of the gloom he'd been experiencing of late. But that had now lifted. The old man's news had the same effect as his favourite cream cake. He could feel the sheckles creeping up his neck once more, driving the dose of the fuck 'em's out of his mind.

The usual crumpled ten pound note was carefully placed into Benton's palm, the remainder of his pint downed in one gulp. Then he walked off into the sunset, just like the Lone Ranger but this time, without the silver star pinned to his chest. He had that gut feeling Riddell and his bunch of creepy crawlies were drawing closer. But there was something else he needed to do. He had a promise to fulfill.

*

'Carol?'

'Jack.'

He hated having to use a mobile whilst driving, but this was urgent and couldn't wait. In any case, he only had five minutes left to get to the meeting with Barton which he'd arranged earlier.

'I need to see you, later tonight.'

'That sounds interesting,' said the reporter with a seductive sounding voice. 'Yours or mine?'

'Neither. Carpenters Arms. And be careful of your phone at home.' He switched her off before she could ask why.

*

He was only a few minutes late getting to Barton. The park and reservoir were both deserted, except for the occasional pram or wandering stray dog. There weren't any fishermen around the huge water hole but Priestley didn't expect any – not when it was minus five degrees. He could see Barton walking along the path where in warmer weather, the anglers sat, casting their lines out as close to the middle of the water as possible. He noticed the large inlet pipe was still in place, which joined the adjacent canal to the reservoir. The memories started to pour back.

'That's my keepnet you've got there, Steve Blade.'
'Oh, piss off.'
'I'll tell your mother you're swearing.'
'Then piss off again.'
'You've never had a keepnet of your own, so where did that one come from?'
'Mind yer own pissing business.'
'I'll tell yer Mum.'
'Piss off. Anyway you owe it to me.'
'How's that?'
'I told the headmaster I shot that firework through the window, so you wouldn't catch out for it.'
'Did yer really Steve?'
Blade nodded, his face illuminated with self-pride.
'Alright, Steve, you can borrow it then.'

'Thanks for coming, Chris, it must be difficult.'
'You might be suspended, boss, but you're still our gaffer.'
Priestley really did appreciate the risk Barton was taking. He was putting his own career on the line: just being seen with Priestley could bring about his own suspension. They

walked along the long footpath that skirted the perimeter of the water. Fleeting glimpses of the past hit Priestley like asteroids falling from the sky. He stopped on the first bend and slowly surveyed the scene, remembering the number of roach he and Blade had caught there with their cane rods.

'What do you think of my new reel, Jack?'
'You've bin and nicked that.'
'I haven't nicked it.'
'Well, where did it come from then?'
'That's my business.'
'Why is it every time I have something, you think it's bin nicked?'
'Because I know you, Stevie Blade.'
'Then come with us, Jack.'
'Where to?'
'The shop. It's empty. They're moving out and some of the stuff's still in there.'
'A fishing tackle shop?'
'Yeah, down Dartmouth Street. All the back's open, Jack. You only have to walk in and help yourself.'
'Piss off, Bladey.'
'I'll tell yer Mum you've bin swearing.'

Priestley outlined everything to Chris Barton. This was the man he was hoping would be his first contact with the force during his period of suspension. He needed to know and deserved to know. The Detective Inspector listened carefully, expressionless as they walked a full circle of the fishing ground.

'Why are you crying, Steve?'
'I've just hit Davy Copestick with a brick.'

'Why?'

'Cos he nicked my fishing rod.'

'So, why you crying, Steve?'

'Cos he's kept it.'

'How's that, when you hit him over the head with a brick?'

'He hit me back!'

'So, now you know it all, Chris. Why the surveillance on the trunkers and how Blade and his family have now disappeared from sight.'

Chris was no longer expressionless. He found it all fascinating. 'Arms though, guv. Exported. No wonder the Squirrels are involved.'

'But how and to what extent is what we have to find out, Chris.'

'Surely you don't think they're in with the running of it?'

'No, mate, I don't.'

They walked a few more yards before Priestley carried on talking, 'But there's something missing. Something wrong. The way they've been acting since we started to get close. There must be more than Georgie Riddell running this thing. I'm beginning to wonder whether he's being looked after.'

'You mean protected?'

Priestley nodded. 'Could be. I'm not sure though. It's only a guess at the moment. Like so many bloody things have been just recently.'

'But you can understand their hostility when Blade decides to nick a lorry full of parcels right from under their noses,' explained Barton.

'Yes,' agreed Priestley, 'but not to the extent where they'd chop off their main supply of information, which we were rapidly becoming.'

'Well, guv, you know all of us will back you.'

That reassured Priestley. He knew Barton was a good man but wasn't sure how he'd react to this particular predicament. At the end of the day, he too had a career and was well thought of in the force. In fact he'd probably make Superintendent before Jack did, that was if Jack stayed in the force long enough to see it happen. At the moment he wasn't exactly the strongest candidate for promotion.

Suddenly, the younger officer stopped and looked hard at his senior colleague. 'That's it. Now it makes sense.'

'What does?'

Rolo clocked a foreign-looking geezer visiting Riddell's place last night. He only stayed a few minutes but Rolo reckons it looked as though they were in deep conversation with each other. And, after the foreigner had left, apparently Riddell made seven phone calls.'

'I should have put an IOCA on his phone,' declared Priestley, annoyed with himself for having gone to all the trouble of inserting a covert and not even bothering to tap Riddell's phone.

'What about now?' suggested Barton.

'Too late. Remember I'm offside now and I've a funny feeling if anyone else suggested it, they'd be told to get stuffed.'

'But that's not all, boss,' continued the DI, 'Rolo's back-up got the number of the foreign geezer's car.'

'And?'

'It was blocked.'

'The registered owner?'

'Yeah. Not even a reference.'

'Then unblock it, Chris,' suggested Priestley. 'That could be important to us.'

'I will now. I must be honest, guv, I never gave it a thought, but it seems to fit in with what you've been saying.'

Priestley looked at his watch and gave his apologies to his DI before running back to the car. He was late for the hospital.

*

Dogs, bastard dogs, thought Rolo. He hadn't a clue where these two had come from. He looked at his watch. Five past seven. He'd seen Riddell come home about half an hour ago, and now, with these two about to create merry hell, he could only hope that the man of the house was alone. He could handle that, but if there were a couple of bodyguards hanging about, Rolo might have a slight problem. Both Dobermans barked and snarled, moving slowly closer to his face. He sank further down the hole, but these were man-trained and weren't going to give up. He knew his situation had now become perilous and all because of a couple of bastard dogs.

The decision was an easy one to make and he thumped the hand held button repeatedly, hoping that his support could extract him before somebody decided to come and look at the rabbit or whatever it was had attracted the canines' attention.

Then the barking stopped.

'Hello, what have we here?' asked a deep voice.

The covert policeman remained still and silent, his head buried as far down into the hole as he could get it.

'Ponteus, I want all of this cleared, including the hedge.'

Rolo had never heard Riddell's voice before so wasn't sure, but when he peered over the top of his dugout there was the man himself. Standing approximately a yard away from the top of his head, he was shouting his orders to the black heavyweight.

'Too many rabbits bring disease, you know.'

Thank Christ, thought Rolo.

'Just confirming, Rolo, you want out now?'

Two clicks answered Ray the back up.

'Just confirming a negative. That's a no, no, no.'

Rolo pressed the button three times in answer, confirming he'd had a change of mind.

'I'll arrange for the man at the weekend,' suggested Ponteus.

'You'll arrange for him tomorrow,' corrected his boss.

It would appear in any case that Rolo's stay at the Riddell residence was to be terminated earlier than expected.

✳

'So, there you have it. Another drink?'

She just sat there motionless, staring at the table in front of her.

'Another drink?' asked Priestley, as he stood to make his way to the bar.

'And you want me to print that?'

'Yep. Of course, that's if you think it would make a reasonable story.'

'Reasonable story? Jack, it's dynamite.'

'Then, Carol, let's just call it quits. It'll make up for that street fighting saga I let you down with.'

'Oh, it'll do that alright,' she said, still looking as though she'd walked away from some air disaster. I'll have to discuss it with the editor.'

'Of course. Another drink?'

'But it'll take up half tomorrow night's edition.'

He gave up and walked away, ordering the same again at the bar.

'Jack. I think I've just fallen in love with you.' The glassy eyes were still transfixed on the table of empty glasses.

'Carol, they all say that.'

*

The growls soon turned to barks and Rufus was up on his hind legs, stretching the chain restricting him to its full length. Just a few more inches and he would be able to sink his teeth into the intruder.

'Why do you keep tormenting the dogs, Steve?' asked Indiana, or at least that was the name Blade called him, obviously taking the piss.

'If that dog barks once more at me, I'll kick its bollocks in,' said Blade.

'You don't like dogs, then?' remarked the suit, with a sadistic grin on his fat face.

Blade just walked away, back towards the main house. It was getting dark and the cold night air was beginning to come down. He stopped halfway across the lawn and looked up at the mass of stars above. He remembered the time he and Sammy had sat together, trying to identify which one belonged to each of them. He was certainly missing her and what he wouldn't give now, just to be back in her arms. He'd put up with the fights and everything else that came with her.

The warm air hit him as he walked into the main hall. Pluto, the other monkey supposed to be guarding him, was sitting at the side of the fire. He just raised his head in acknowledgement of Blade's return from his daily stroll around the gardens and then returned to the newspaper spread across his lap. The only thing that was stopping their prisoner from falling into a deeper depressive state of mind, was his constant planning and scheming about how he was going to get out of the place. If it hadn't been for the half a dozen killer dogs and that electrified fence that ran all around the perimeter, it'd be a piece of piss. But why should he complain? He remembered mentioning to Big Bristols when they first pulled him out of nick that he would have preferred to stay in a mansion, like on the films. Well, now they'd accommodated him – and in Ireland of all places. Well at least, he thought he was across the water, because they'd flown him there. And he knew he wasn't on the Costa Brava, because of this bastard cold weather. He sat opposite Pluto and stared at the butt of the gun, protruding from the shoulder holster. 'Ever use that?' he asked.

The man just threw a quick eyeball at him. 'Only on little shits like you,' he said.

Sounds just like Jack Priestley, thought Blade, must be all tarred with the same brush.

'Charming,' he replied. 'You being a man of the law as well.'

*

CORRUPTION AT THE HIGHEST LEVEL
It is believed that a senior National Crime Squad Detective Chief Inspector has been suspended from duty following allegations of corruption. The officer, according to a police source, was at the time investigating a number of senior government officials. Inquiries were being made into individuals suspected of being involved in the recent scandal of Questions in the House for payments.

It has also come to our notice that a man, whose identity cannot be disclosed, has recently been abducted by members of the British Security Forces. Allegedly, the man was assisting the police at the time of his abduction and there is grave concern for his safety...

'Ron, I'll screw this bastard of yours to the wall.' Pike was out of his tree with rage. 'Have you read the article?'

'Of course, but is it true, Pikey? That's the thing.'

'Of course it isn't bloody true, Ron. Why do you think I've suspended him? Or rather, you've suspended him?'

'Then, why are you so bothered about it?'

'Well,' stuttered the Commander. 'Well, it could be damaging to our own inquiry and to the department as a whole, Ron.'

'Listen to me, Commander Pike.' The Chief Constable now had his official copper's hat on and there was more than a hint of authority in his voice. 'One of my best officers is now offside, because you allege he was interfering too much with an extremely sensitive investigation being carried out by your department.'

'And I want to thank you for that, Ron. The Home Sec's aware, you know, of your valuable assistance.'

'Pikey, listen to me and listen well. I wouldn't swop Jack Priestley for ten of your people and what's more, I don't believe he would do anything to interfere with the course of justice – not deliberately anyway.'

'Just a couple of more weeks, Ron,' begged the Commander. 'And then you can do what you like with him.'

'You were supposed to provide evidence for me to consider, Richard. Evidence, that would support the suspension. I'm still waiting. And now you're telling me I can reinstate him in two weeks' time?'

'Ron, there's a great deal at stake here. Even I'm not fully aware of the details. You know how problematical things can be in Whitehall.'

'No, I don't Richard. I've made my decision. I really do believe I owe an apology to Chief Inspector Priestley. He'll be reinstated forthwith.' The Chief Constable slammed the phone down and for the first time for a while, felt like a Chief Constable should feel.

*

They both stood at the bedside, hand in hand. Like mother and son, staring at the one person they both held dear.

'Lady Hall?' It was that young consultant again. 'Could I have a word?'

Priestley supported her with his arm, as they both followed the doctor out of the room.

'I'm afraid there's been no change in your daughter's condition.' He looked very sad but was trying to be truthful. 'We're now moving closer to the point where a decision has to be made.'

Priestley knew what was around the corner, but didn't want to interrupt.

'We don't know whether or not your daughter will survive once we switch the machine off.' He seemed to stop short of what he was really going to say. But Priestley sensed that was deliberate, to allow Sonia's mother to digest exactly what he was trying to say to her.

'You're going to switch the machine off, doctor?' the feeble voice asked.

The man in the white coat just looked at her, sympathetically. He was just doing his job and Jack appreciated that. But surely this was the worst part?

'You see, Lady Hall, the longer we give her this kind of assistance, the weaker she'll become and the chances of her survival reduced.'

'And what are those, doctor?' Priestley spoke for the first time.

'Very slim I'm afraid.'

'When do you intend switching her off?' That sounded harsh but Jack was used to sounding harsh. He'd never been one to choose his words, neither had Sonia. They'd never had the time or patience, either of them. For a brief moment the doctor didn't seem to want to answer the question. He sighed and then, looking directly at Sonia's mother, said, 'Now.'

Even Jack felt devastated. He would be there at the end but he doubted his own ability to remain strong for this little old woman, who seemed to have clung to him during her hour of need. All thoughts of Riddell, Pike, the fact that he was a suspended officer, even Blade's predicament, had now left him. He would now leave the police force and spend the rest of his life trying to avoid the pain and suffering he'd had to witness over so many years. Even if it meant living in a cave in Southern Spain, satisfying his hunger from the fish in the sea!

✳

chapter nineteen

'When do you think we'll know, Jack?'

'Sorry?'

'Whether she'll live or not?'

He took hold of her hand once more and tried to find some words to reassure her. But there weren't any. There was no doubting that Lady Hall was a woman of strong character, like her daughter. But what could he do or say in circumstances such as this? At any moment the consultant would come through the door and tell her that her daughter had passed away peacefully. And that was all there was to it. Except of course there would be the score to settle with the man who put Sonia there. That would be done after Priestley had submitted his resignation.

'She always belonged to her father, Jack. She was his daughter. When she was a little girl she was a real tomboy and I think that's what made her be so close to him.'

'Was the Judge able to spend much time with her when she was small?' asked Priestley.

'Oh yes. He adored her. They were inseparable.' She glanced towards the door of the room her daughter was in and Priestley quickly turned, expecting the worst. But there was no one there. Perhaps a noise she'd heard?

'He was a member of Lincoln's Inn, you know, and every now and again he would take us both to some of the lavish dinners.'

He could see she was reliving the moments that she so obviously cherished in her memory.

'Oh, those were happy times,' she sighed.

'And that's how the seeds were planted which eventually led her to the Bar?'

'Oh, yes. She worshipped her father and wanted to do the same as he did. I remember Jack, he used to take her on the circuit with him. She'd sit in the public gallery, watching and even learning at that early stage.' She looked up again at the door.

Priestley heard the movement this time and saw the consultant standing there.

'Would you like to come in now?' the doctor asked. 'The machine went off some three minutes ago.'

✳

Priestley felt a shiver run through Lady Hall's body as he helped her off the bench, his own legs were trembling. This was to be the worst moment of his life. One that he would take to his own death. He fought hard to keep some control over his emotions as they both followed the consultant into Sonia's room.

She looked no different. Peaceful. At rest. A few tubes remained, but the breathing apparatus had been removed. There were two nurses messing about with various pieces of equipment around the bed. Priestley accepted they were unplugging everything, ready for the next poor soul who would be in need of similar help.

Then he noticed Sonia's chest moving. Breathing? By herself? He looked quickly towards the consultant who was standing there, smiling.

'Yes, she's still comatose, I'm afraid, but at least she's supporting herself now.'

Priestley thought he saw a slight movement in Sonia's face. He did. She was breathing by herself. And he knew that this fighter, this stubborn, strong-willed girl wanted so much to reach out and grab life for what it was worth. It was all too much and he fought back the tears as he watched Sonia's mother weep with joy.

＊

'Don't you pair of bastards ever do this to me again,' Blade bawled from the back of the car. 'It ain't right. You lumps of shit taking me away from my missus and kid. You ain't heard the last of this, yer know.'

Oliver Hardy turned and glared. That was enough for Blade. They were only just around the corner from where he lived and perhaps he was overdoing it a bit. The black Rover pulled up and Blade shot his hand out for the door handle, but it was locked. He sat impatiently, waiting for Laurel to walk around the car and open the door from the outside. It took hours. Then he was out.

'I said you lot ain't heard the last of this. Bastards!' he shouted as the car drove away.

He shrugged his shoulders, his face full of a mixture of concern and relief. He turned and started to walk towards his block of flats. But then stopped in his tracks. He stared to focus more on the entrance. There they both were, waiting for him. Sammy, and his daughter. He laughed and cried. And then held both arms out. This had been worse than any nick he'd been in.

＊

'Welcome back, gaffer.' Priestley could see that Barton was genuinely pleased and so were rest as they piled into his office, the men shaking his hand and the women kissing him on the cheek. He was still a bit emotional and bit his lip. He opened his briefcase and took out a sheet of A4 paper whilst they all stood there and watched him. He held it up in front of the small group of puzzled faces and tore it into sixteen pieces before throwing it in the bin. It had been his resignation but they didn't know that. All they saw were his wet eyes and broad smile on his face. Jack was back and they had better bloody well watch out!

'Today, my children, is a good day,' he stated with eyes full of life and energy, 'and we've all got a job to do. A bloody big job. So let's get on with it.'

They all chuckled and turned to leave, happy to see the master back in the chair.

'And, by the way,' he called, 'thanks for your support.'

'Just hang on, Mr Priestley,' shouted his secretary from across the corridor. Then she entered his office with two glasses filled with malt whiskey and ice, one for himself, and a glass for Chris Barton. 'They've all chipped in. Welcome back, gaffer,' she said planting yet another kiss on his cheek.

And then the *coup de grâce*. He picked up the telephone. It was Lady Hall. 'She wants to see you, Jack.'

He ran out of his office to hide his tears of joy. Boys should be seen but not heard, especially when they want to cry!

✱

It took sometime for Jack to recover and get himself back into shape. He'd managed to avoid a public emotional outburst but Barton and Di well understood the pressure he'd been under.

His DI thought he'd let the Chief Inspector savour the moment before updating him on the unwelcome news, but Priestley had already recognised the look of concern in his younger colleague's eyes.

'Let's have it then, Chris. We can't party forever.'

'We've had to pull Rolo out.'

'When?'

'Last night. Riddell was going to do some gardening and it would have put our man in some peril.'

'Okay, mate.'

Barton could see that Priestley was considering other options.

'I still want the front watched though, Chris.'

'There's a light on his front drive. We could always stick a camera in there and microwave it back,' suggested Barton.

Priestley nodded. 'That would do nicely, as they say in the advert,' he said. 'Who was Rolo's back up, by the way?'

'Ray Giggs.'

'Action Logs?'

'Yes, he's brought them in.'

'And the only geezer seen at Riddell's house is this Arab guy?'

'Apparently so, but I'm going to debrief them both later.'

'Anymore on the Arab's car, Chris?' asked Priestley.

'You won't believe this but it's a Foreign Office vehicle.'

Priestley wasn't really surprised and just smiled. 'Do some research on the Army Depot at Long Marston, Chris.'

'Anything in particular?'

'Yes, the kind of gear they store there and general background. But try and do it without letting the Army know.'

That brought a smile to Barton's face, 'Welcome back, gaffer.' He knew that trying to find out information about a Ministry of Defence Establishment without telling them was like trying to fly a plane around the world, without having ever been off the ground before.

'And, by the way, Chris, anymore on Cheetah?'

Barton shook his head. 'We've kept the surveillance on the two targets but so far they've just made direct trips to the airport and back.'

Priestley winked, 'Well done, mate.' He stood up. 'I'm off to the hospital.'

As he walked towards the door his secretary called to him, 'There's a parcel come for you this morning, Mr Priestley.'

'Leave it Di. I'll look at it later.'

She understood why he appeared to be in such a hurry.

*

Blade had never felt so bitter about anything before in his life. Usually, no matter how much pain and discomfort was bestowed upon him, he had the ability to put any grievances behind him. But this time he'd been scarred. To take him away from his family and then deprive him of his freedom, not having done anything to deserve such incarceration, had deeply hurt him. Just because they'd paid him twenty grand didn't give them the right to interfere with his life, for reasons only known to them. But now, as far as he was concerned he had another reason for throwing shit at them and he wasn't going to let it go, no matter how much power they had.

*

'I need to know, Jimmy.'

'Thought you'd have sent the errand boy again?'

Blade wasn't pissing about. He wanted to get into the very core of Riddell's organisation with or without Jack Priestley's help, although he suspected Priestley would agree to what he was trying to achieve. He always preferred to work from within rather than on the outside.

'You're a cheeky bastard, Blade,' said Gabriel. 'You come here expecting me to hand you a passport into something I no longer have any shares in.'

'That's the very reason why I'm here, Jimmy.'

'Well, go blow yourself up. I'm not giving you anything to do with Riddell's operations.' Jimmy G remained expressionless and he waited for any further response from Blade.

There wasn't any. His visitor could see he was wasting his time and stood to leave.

'Sit down a minute,' suggested Gabriel, 'I want to explain something to you.'

Blade did as he was told, ready to listen carefully to the news he was about to be given.

'You have to get it into your head, you just can't walk into Georgie Riddell's office and be given a job. Not the kind of job you're after. You need a stake to begin with.'

'I've got some dough to invest,' stated the ex-con.

'No, that's it, see, you don't understand. I'm not just talking about a nest egg. Trust, Bladey. He has to be able to trust you which means he needs to have known you for sometime. And with you that's not the case.'

'But if you…' Blade was sounding anxious.

'No wait,' interrupted Gabriel. 'I'm not deaf. I know what you're trying to say but it wouldn't work. If things went wrong my balls would go down the pan,' he paused, before continuing in a softer voice. 'Would you take that risk with me if the boot was on the other foot?'

Blade knew he'd lost. Nice try but a wasted one. He was going nowhere with this geezer.

'Okay J. I know what you're saying, mate. Fair enough.' He went to stand for a second time.

'No wait. I'll tell you what I'll do, and only because of the help you gave the Cheswicks. I'll drop a note in, addressed to the man, explaining what you've done. Come and see me tomorrow and I'll have it for you.'

Blade's face changed. His concerns disappeared and he held his hand out to shake the other man's.

'Piss off, Bladey. This is for Cheswick, not you.'

True to form Jimmy G, thought Blade, very true to form.

*

This was just how he remembered Christmas mornings as a child. He felt like a child. Excited. Stimulated. Happy. And looking forward to seeing those big brown eyes again. Her mother was at her side as he entered the room. His first impression was that she looked no different from before, except her eyes were open.

'Jack,' she whispered and flopped an outstretched arm onto the bed, for him to take hold of.

'Try not to talk. You've had a rough ride, lady,' he said, unable to conceal his joy. Not that he wanted to. She was alive. She was there, speaking to him. That would be sufficient for now.

'Have you two met?' asked Sonia, her weakness showing through her voice.

'Yes, we have,' replied her mother. 'Hello, Jack.'

Priestley nodded, noticing that all the worry and stress had now left Lady Hall and she looked radiant. Her daughter's partial recovery had been an instant tonic for both of them.

'Jack,' whispered Sonia again.

'Sonia?' he said, holding her arm with both hands.

'I love you too.'

*

chapter twenty

Jack Priestley sat opposite Sir Richard whilst Lady Ridlington poured the tea.

He was a short, stocky man, his high colour reflecting many years of good living and copious amounts of port and brandy. Even in his own home, apparently relaxing, his white shirt and silk tie gave the impression he was prepared to give a speech in front of the cameras at short notice.

'I can't thank you enough, Chief Inspector, for what you have done for both myself and my wife.' Sir Richard was obviously sincere in his gratitude and Priestley felt extremely humble at having been invited to the Ridlington's to meet the man.

'I did a job I'm paid to do, Sir Richard.'

'No, it was more than just that,' explained the former Defence Secretary moving forward to the end of his chair. 'You dealt with a very sensitive situation, in the most confidential way. You are a gentleman, sir, and I will be forever in your debt.'

Priestley felt a little embarrassed. This was unusual for him and felt the need to change the subject as quickly as possible. 'I understand you are to retire, Sir Richard, at the end of this present Parliament?'

'Yes, quite so,' he took a cup filled with tea from the small, highly polished, antique table which stood between them. 'But there's no peace for the wicked, don't you know. I do believe I shall be as busy as ever, even without my Parliamentary duties.'

Priestley smiled. For him, that was the end of that particular conversation. There wasn't anything he had in common with a Member of Parliament, except of course to talk about the world's strife and starvation, deprivation in the inner-city areas and all that sort of thing. But this wasn't the occasion to raise such matters.

'I've written to your Chief Constable.'

Priestley looked up, as though he hadn't quite heard what had been said.

'Just a letter expressing my gratitude and of course, that of my wife. I hope you won't mind?'

'It's very kind of you, sir.' He wondered whether it was that which had got him reinstated. He didn't suppose he would ever get to find out.

But time was getting on now and he felt the need to leave. He was starting to feel uncomfortable with all of these accolades being thrown at him. A couple of gulps of tea and he'd be out of that door as quick as his legs could carry him. He'd done his bit now and was ready to take on the next challenge.

*

The place looked deserted. Everything seemed to still be in place. A few buildings scattered around. There was the gatehouse and the usual checkpoint at the barrier. But there was no guard, which surprised Barton. He decided to stay in the car and just watch to see if there was any activity. The place reminded him of one of those ghost towns in an old cowboy film. The only thing missing was bushes of tumbleweed rolling up and down the empty roads. He wondered where the name Long Marston had come from, or any of the names around there, if it came to that.

But then before he could develop any ideas, he heard an engine revving and saw a small American-type jeep driving down what appeared to be the central driveway which ran through the centre of the site. He watched as it stopped and the front passenger in a swaddy's uniform, jumped out to lift the barrier. The jeep then drove out past the gatehouse, turned left and he had to duck out of sight as it drove straight past him. At least there was still life down on the farm, even though this place was supposed to have been closed down months ago.

*

'Whoever sent it must have brought it to the front counter downstairs, this morning. There's no postage mark on it.'

Very astute, Di, thought Priestley. She'd been doing secretarial work on the crime squad for too long. But he was puzzled as to why the parcel would have been delivered by hand. He was soon to find out.

As he opened the top flaps of the brown cardboard box he could see, whatever it was had been covered in plastic packing material. The sort of stuff that's a right pain in the bum to handle – thousands of small individual pieces of polystyrene, and then underneath that was a small circular disc, about four inches in diameter and three inches in depth. It was made of some kind of green-coloured light plastic, with serial and batch numbers stamped all over it.

'What on earth's that?' asked his secretary.

He ignored her and held it up, closely examining the rounded sides. And then, like a spontaneous bolt out of the blue, it hit him. He was holding a landmine up to the light of his window. After he'd realised what little gem had been sent him, he gently placed it onto the carpeted floor and stepped towards his secretary in the doorway. 'Di.'

'Yes.'

'Phone and ask the Bomb Squad to visit us, a.s.a.p.,' he directed, not taking his eyes off the harmless-looking object.

'The Bomb Squad?'

'Yes.'

'Right away.' She wanted to ask a million questions but had learnt one thing from her experience of working for Jack Priestley, *you* didn't ask the questions, *he* did.

'And Di,' he said, still staring down at the small disc.

'Yes,' she was beginning to sound apprehensive now.

'Arrange for a bucket of sand to be brought up.'

✳

No letter had accompanied the item and the Bomb Squad later confirmed their attendance had been unnecessary, in the same way as the bucket of sand on top of which they'd found the mine. The device hadn't been primed, but there was no doubting the item had found its way to Jack Priestley from some military installation. More for Jack to chew over.

✳

Considering International Swarf was supposed to be a major steel business, there didn't seem to be that much activity going on.

Blade parked at the front of the building and could see the door to the reception just in front of him. There was a large opening on his left that obviously gave access to a huge warehouse or stock area. He walked over and looked inside. The place was full of metal shelving stretching from floor to ceiling, but as he'd suspected, it was half empty with very little steel occupying the spaces provided.

*

'What you after, cock?' asked the voice from behind.

Cock? thought Blade. He hadn't heard that expression for years. He remembered as a kid listening to his father address people as 'cock', or 'cocker', as a form of endearment, but the look on this bloke's face suggested he wouldn't try to befriend anybody. He'd got prison overalls written all over his unshaven, thin face. The eyes of the devil scowled at him as he tried to explain. He couldn't remember ever seeing such a black look on a geezer's face before. This one certainly must have had a hard life, he thought.

'Come to see Georgie Riddell.'

'And who are you?' asked the mortician.

'Blade,' was all our man would disclose. The atmosphere between the two of them didn't appear suitable for Christian names.

Cheerful Charlie just gave him a slight nod, the smirk on his face indicating to Blade that he already knew who he was.

'Wait here.'

He wasn't going anywhere.

Riddell studied the note signed by Jimmy Gabriel, appearing to read it over and over, before dropping it in front of him on top of the desk.

'So, you're after a job?'

Blade nodded.

'According to yer man, you've been on the trot for some time now?'

'Yep.'

'What have you done since walking out?'

'Nothing,' answered Blade. 'That's why I'm here.'

'Can't use yer,' Riddell said with a grin. 'Wouldn't be worth the risk.'

'I can drive heavies,' explained the job applicant. 'And I can keep me gob shut.'

That didn't work. Wasted words.

'Can't help you.'

Blade looked disappointed. He'd played the role well but to no avail. A man with forty kids to bring up and no money, not even a bit of social, being on the run and all that. If that couldn't persuade his man to help him out, nothing could.

He turned to leave.

'Tell you what, Blade. Come back in a couple of days. I'll have another look at you.'

Pennies from heaven. There was a gap in the big man's armour. He must have a vacancy somewhere because his last words had been voiced with what sounded like sympathy. But Blade knew that would be a false impression. Riddell was a double-dealing rattlesnake, who only received. The man never gave, not unless it was an investment and Blade couldn't see himself as that. Not in Riddell's eyes. But he'd been given some encouragement, so he'd play along and hopefully infiltrate what he knew was a top professional criminal organisation.

✳

Priestley needed an early night. One advantage to come out of Sonia's present situation, was the regular opportunity to sleep. Apart from that, he'd hardly missed a night with the surveillance team, following Waltham and Lawrence. It would just be his luck, he thought, for the trunker to make the Meriden Warehouse just on the night he wasn't there. But now he needed the break.

He almost trod on the envelope on the floor as he stepped inside the door. All it had written on it was, 'Mr Priestley'. There was no postmark, which got him thinking. He cautiously ran his fingertips along where the flap was stuck down. And then along the top, bottom and sides. The slightest indication of wires would have brought in that bucket of sand again.

He considered picking up the phone and asking the bomb squad lads for a repeat performance, but then realised there was no need. If the person who was trying to communicate with him, had wanted to make a human sacrifice, he'd have done it with the landmine. That's of course if this particular enclosure had come from the same person. It had:

Mr Priestley,
I'm returning a favour. The people you should be looking at are dealing in the illegal transportation of military weapons. They are selling landmines to a foreign country. Look at Cheetah Express Parcels. You will only know me as Roger. I shall contact you again in the future.

Roger the pissing Dodger, thought Jack, And returning a favour. What favour? He couldn't remember being Uncle Holly to anybody just lately, but it was obvious the writer knew him. It was obviously from way back in the past. Well, a friend indeed. As he knew so much the person was obviously close to Riddell.

Having failed to remember anybody from the category of favours bestowed on him, he tried to build a mental profile of Roger. The man was cute, there was no doubting that. He'd provided Priestley with sufficient information to confirm he knew what he was talking about by referring to Cheetah Parcels. The idea of putting forward the name Roger was to guarantee if it came on top, he could declare he'd been helping the police. Yes, very cute indeed. But it also told Priestley something else. The man was obviously in a position for which, if it did come on top, he could be locked up. Roger the Dodger was playing his cards both ways, or so Priestley thought.

There was one thing though, worrying the senior detective. How did he know his home address?

*

Nicholas Carpe still looked the same as he had when Priestley first met him. A corpse on legs with dazed, staring eyes and a white face with an appearance that resembled someone who had just come out of make-up, straight onto the set of a horror film.

The DCI still felt somewhat overawed in the presence of a man who had done so much to earn the respect of his soldiers whilst on active service. And this lad had been on a lengthy period of active service, most of which had been spent diffusing bombs tied to dead people dropped off in deserted country lanes. And he was still a captain and still attached to the Bomb Disposal Unit in Hereford, although now he had been given a training role. Must be bored to tears, thought the detective as he held his hand out to greet him.

'It's good to see you again, Nick.'

'You too, Jack.'

Both men sat in the same café window where they'd previously discussed a bent soldier, known to Carpe for his skills in disposing of illicit drugs some time back. That meeting had sparked off a major inquiry resulting in half the CID senior management team in Jack's force going to prison.

'You've lost a little weight, Jack,' suggested Carpe.

'Not deliberately, Nick,' was the answer. 'I've just had one or two pieces of bad news lately. I suppose that's what's done it.'

'Well, this must be rather important for you to travel all the way down here, obviously not just for a chat.'

'You're right. I'm interested in your depot at Long Marston.'

'What is it you want to know?'

'I wanted a few questions answered in confidence, Nick.'

'That goes without saying, otherwise you wouldn't have bothered to come,' he sipped his coffee. 'So, ask away.'

'I know it's an ammo dump but what kind of munitions do they keep there now?'

'None, officially that is. It's been closed down for sometime now, Jack.'

Priestley sat back, away from the table. That would explain Chris Barton finding the place half deserted, to use his description. 'But are there still people on the base?'

'Yes, absolutely. We still have munitions there, Jack, but they're mostly for destruction. We no longer keep live stores at Long Marston.'

'You say for destruction, what kind of munitions are you talking about, Nick?' asked the Detective Chief Inspector.

'Automatics, semi-automatics, stuff we would have brought back, for example, from the Gulf. Stores which are now outdated, items in need of repair.' He glanced away, trying to think of how he could paint the best possible picture for his visitor. 'Landmines, Jack. Since this country signed up to reduce the number of landmines used in conventional warfare, following Princess Diana's campaign, many of those previously shipped into sensitive areas have been returned.'

'And they would be transported to Long Marston?' asked Jack, who was now beginning to paint a picture of his own.

'Yes.'

Priestley reached for the brown paper bag on the floor beside him and produced the landmine sent by personal delivery to him. 'Would that be one of them, Nick?'

The Captain just glanced at it. He'd not only seen hundreds of items such as this before he'd also been responsible for diffusing them. 'Yes, in all probability. I don't know whether it's come from that particular base, Jack, but I could soon find out for you from the serial number.'

The questions continued, Jack feeling a bit like a quiz master on television. 'What kind of mine is this?'

'Anti-personnel,' replied the expert without any hesitation. He was winning at the moment and the score was about ten–nil.

Next question. 'What other types of landmines are there?'

'Oh dear. Do you want the full list, Jack?' asked Carpe smiling, almost laughing.

'Just the ones handled at Long Marston.'

'All of them, Jack. You see, this kind of device isn't sent for decommissioning at specific bases just because of what it is.'

318

Priestley could see the Army captain was trying to keep things simple for him to understand and he appreciated that.

'The majority would go to Long Marston no matter what shape, size or function. Another coffee, Jack?'

Priestley nodded and, whilst Carpe went to repeat the previous order, sat in deep thought, still trying to fathom out the reasons for Pike's behaviour. He remembered reading about Stalin's post-war Russia and wondered whether we were really that far away from it. People like Pike and those he worked for shouldn't be allowed to take people out of circulation just because the idea appealed to them. And then, what would be the next step if someone decided to complain? Shoot them on sight? Have them banished together with their families, to some far distant land? Oh, no, this wasn't Jack's idea of England at all. And he had a bloody good idea it wasn't anybody else's either.

Carpe returned with two coffees. 'There are anti-tank mines and other devices designed for various modes of transport and anti-personnel explosives of various shapes and sizes.' He looked towards the paper bag into which Priestley had returned his own personal weapon of destruction. 'That one for instance is only a small one. It would blow your foot off, just sufficient to put an enemy soldier out of action. But there are mines which do that and also send a charge about eight or ten feet into the air, exploding again and killing anything within a twenty yard radius.'

'It's not primed,' explained Priestley rather naively.

Carpe laughed, 'I should think not Jack. Even you, old man, would drop in the shit carrying one of those about, primed up.'

Priestley appreciated the joke, 'But how would I get something like that made active?'

'The primers are always transported separately.' Carpe leaned forward. 'What I mean is, they might be contained in the same crate, for example, as the mines themselves, but the two wouldn't be joined together until required for use.'

'So if I had a crate of these things,' the quiz master was still in full flow, 'I could expect to find the primers inside as well, lying at the side of the mines?'

Carpe nodded, 'You could, yes.' He had a pensive look on his face. 'Jack, what's all this about or am I not supposed to know?'

'You're not supposed to know, Nick. But I'll tell you.' Priestley then explained to the Captain what he suspected. That there was a distinct possibility landmines and other munitions were being smuggled out of the Long Marston base and sold abroad. Carpe didn't seem surprised. In fact, pink elephants flying through the air wouldn't surprise this man. He'd just about seen it all.

'But, I shall have to ask for your complete confidence, Captain. For the time being, anyway.'

'Most certainly, Chief Inspector. Just give me a call if I can be of any further assistance to you.'

'You've already been that – more than you know.'

✳

George Riddell had been busy doing his sums. Because of the nature of what he'd been asked to shift, his mind had been working overtime and he'd decided the going rate wasn't enough. The current cost of his services was well below the risk factor and George had decided to up the price. He wondered whether Grainger and whoever Mr Big was, were both pissing themselves laughing at him.

Whatever they were charging the Arab must leave them sitting fairly tight and secure, whilst he was dodging all the bullets. Or at least his boys were.

'I'm a busy man, George, and this is out of the ordinary,' said Grainger, looking more concerned than Riddell had ever seen him before.

'Then I shan't keep you long,' promised the fight promoter. He knew exactly what was causing Grainger to have ants in his pants – the fact that he himself had called the meeting. Before, Riddell had always been at this man's beck and call. But now the tables were turning.

'Excellent.' Grainger stood up and walked towards the bow.

'I want another five per cent on top of what we agreed before,' demanded Riddell.

Grainger stopped and turned around. George was ready for any argument the other man might put up in opposition to his proposal. He'd thought it out and was anticipating a strong rebuttal. But much to his surprise, it didn't come. Grainger just slowly walked back towards him and calmly stated, 'Okay, George. I'll put it to the man.'

'We're delivering the first load on Thursday night. I need to know before then.'

The civil servant nodded, 'Okay, George. You will.' He pulled the front of his overcoat so that it became tighter to his body, in an attempt to reduce the effects of the icy cold breeze lifting off the water. 'Now, is that all you wanted to see me about?'

Riddell quietly nodded and Grainger leapt off the side of the barge and disappeared into the night.

*

chapter twenty-one

'So, there you have it, Jack. Tomorrow I'm going back to see Riddell and I'll tell yer now, I'll have the inside track on his complete organisation within a week.' Blade's face was beaming. Priestley's was more solemn. Not that he disagreed with what his mate had done. He was just undecided whether or not Blade should be allowed to continue down that path. He was doubtful and it showed as he stared wide-eyed at his pint.

'Don't tell me you've got a problem with that,' said Blade. 'You could be pissing about with this for the next month or more, whilst Pike and his bunch of tossers snatch the rug from under yer feet.'

'I'm not in competition with Commander Pike,' explained Jack.

'Aren't we?'

'That's a dangerous game to be in, Steve.'

'I'm frightened to death,' said Blade sarcastically.

'Listen to me.'

Lecture time again, thought Blade. He knew Priestley would eventually have the final say, so he might just as well shut up and let him have the floor.

'I know what you're trying to do, Steve. But I'm not sure that we need to be on the inside now.'

'If they *are* moving stuff through the parcels company, Jack, you still don't know how.'

'But I'm hoping the camera will tell us that,' explained Priestley. 'Once that wagon driven by Waltham and Lawrence makes for Meriden, we'll see exactly what they're up to.'

'But you don't know when that's going to happen, Jack.' Blade had just had an instant rethink. For a second he'd forgotten about the few scraps that might fall from Riddell's table when Jack and his merry men moved in, and he needed to be there to pick them up. Now he had to convince Priestley more than ever, there was a need for him to be there on the inside. Not that he'd tell Priestley what was in his mind, obviously!

'But, we're following the lorry, Steve, every night. And as soon as it makes another wrong move, we're back in business.'

'But, what if they're not performing any more, Jack? It might be that they've made their last drop and all you lot are doing is watching nothing.'

Priestley hadn't told Blade about the anonymous letter and free sample sent to him through the post. He didn't feel there was a need for him to know that much.

In a similar way, Blade hadn't let on to Priestley he'd been to visit Gabriel in the nick. If he found that out, he'd probably shine like a neon light again. He could hear his words now, 'You've probably compromised the whole operation, you dimwit,' or words to that effect. But it didn't matter because he wasn't going to find out, not from Blade, anyway.

'Steve, I don't want you to go in there. Stay at Cheetah. You can be of much more help to us there. Keep Waltham and Lawrence happy and carry on relaying back to us the times they leave with their trunker.'

'But...' It was no bloody use, the boy on the bus again! It wouldn't have been unusual for Blade to agree and then totally ignore what Priestley was suggesting. But he could see the logic in what was being said. There probably wouldn't be anything to cream off anyway. Perhaps a few unpaid cheques; a couple of landmines or Magnum 45s. A total waste of time and effort. Then he had another idea.

'Okay, Jack, you're the boss. No chance of a sub is there?'

'You cheeky bastard, you've just pulled twenty grand off Tony Blair.'

Blade had to chuckle, 'How's that Sonia Hall by the way?'

✳

Barton handed the small buff envelope to his DCI. It was obviously from the same man who'd sent the previous one to Priestley's home address. 'Are you sure you don't want us to send this to Forensic?' he asked.

'What would be the use, Chris?' was the reply. 'It wouldn't tell us anything. And I'm not so sure we need to identify this geezer.'

Priestley read out the short note inside:

Mr Priestley,
    You should be ready for this Thursday night.
                                                    Roger

Di walked into the office, followed by Richard Pike. 'Commander Pike, Mr Priestley. From...'

'I know where he's from, Di. Thank you.'

Priestley offered Pike a seat, not bothering to try and hide the surprised look. He had good reasons for disliking this man but he was a senior police officer after all. He hadn't exactly earned Jack's respect, but his rank warranted some recognition, no matter how small.

Pike took off his sheepskin overcoat which Priestley thought was a little out of date – surprising for the man about town, this particular gent purported to be.

'I've no Villager's or single malt to offer, Commander. We have to manage on what we get off the empties returned to the outdoor, up here.' There could be no mistaking Priestley's resentment.

The other senior officer just smiled. 'Thank you for the thought, Jack,' he said in his softly spoken Oxford accent.

'Tea or coffee?'

Pike turned to Di who was standing in the doorway, 'Tea please, no milk, no sugar.'

'Lemon?' asked the secretary.

Pike was amazed and didn't really know whether she was imitating her boss, or being serious. He thought he'd play along with it. 'Yes, please.' What he didn't appreciate was that the lady herself could only drink tea with a slice of lemon in it. It was a habit that went all the way back to her teenage years.

'I've come to apologise, Jack.'

That was a bigger surprise to Priestley than seeing him walk through the door of his office.

'Shall we just say, I had very good reasons for what I did with your friend Blade.'

'He's not my friend. He's an armed robber who just happens to be an acquaintance,' snapped Priestley.

'Yes, I know all about the Priestley–Blade relationship and the way in which you were both children together.'

'Kids,' snapped Priestley again.

'Kids,' repeated the Commander.

'Yes. You see, Mr Pike, up here there's a difference between children and kids. Children are normal. Kids – which we were – aren't.'

Pike was intrigued, 'Do explain.'

'We were infant tyrants, Commander. Children who were close together, and highly principled, but with different outlooks on life. We were children who knew how to earn a bob or two by thieving as well as being honest. Kids, you see.'

No, he didn't see, except the harshness in Priestley's eyes.

On the other hand, Jack knew he was just being awkward. His mood dictated he argued with everything Stalin here, said. But he was also fully aware, there would be no advantage gained by feeling that way.

Pike let it go. 'Well anyway, Jack, as I was saying, I had good reasons for trying to keep Blade away from what we were trying to achieve. And I still feel that I took the right course of action.'

'But?' asked Jack.

'Well, I know that you are now, shall we say, in possession of information that would save my department a lot of time and money.'

Priestley stood from his chair, 'No, Commander, that's not the reason you are here.' He turned his back on Pike and looked out of the window, in the same way as Pike had done to him back at the Yard. 'I don't trust you, Mr Pike. You speak with a forked tongue.' He turned, expecting to see outrage on the Commander's face.

But Pike was smiling and acknowledged Priestley's concern by directing his junior to return to his seat, with just a wave of his hand. 'Can I be frank, Jack?'

Priestley could see why this bloke had got the job. 'I wish you would,' he said. 'I'm really getting pissed off with all the bullshit you people throw at us, as though coming from the sticks makes you believe we're living in the last century or something.'

'Point made, Jack, and point taken. I need to give you the complete picture.'

The door opened and Priestley's secretary walked in with two cups of tea, one with a slice of lemon. Pike could see she hadn't been taking the piss and acknowledged his thanks with a nod of his head, before she turned and left again.

'Our operation has been ongoing for the past year. And, yes, we are aware that George Riddell has been, shall we say, arranging for the exportation of arms, as I've already told you.'

Priestley slurped his tea. It was a habit of his when he wanted to let someone know, he wasn't a happy individual.

'What I haven't told you is that Riddell is paid by a fairly high-ranking civil servant, Jack. One who we've only recently identified.'

'And his name?' asked Priestley. He wanted Pike to show that he was willing to share any so-called confidential information with him as an olive branch, a sign of mutual trust. Not that such a sacrifice would make Priestley trust him anymore. Pike was on the bottom rung of the ladder as far as Jack was concerned and there he was going to remain until the DCI was utterly convinced the security services weren't going to continue taking the mick.

'I can't give you that, Jack. Not at the moment.' He'd just dropped off the bottom rung. 'But what I will share with you, is the fact that last summer one of our operatives infiltrated Riddell's organisation, before being killed in a car accident. Ring a bell?'

Jack didn't like what he'd just heard.

'You can check it out if you wish,' suggested Pike. 'His operational name was Bill Smythe and the accident happened on your Aston Expressway, last August.'

'I'll take your word for it, Commander.' Priestley had a funny feeling he knew what was coming next.

'He was murdered, Jack. His – '

'Brakes on his car had been tampered with,' interrupted Priestley.

'In the same way as Miss Hall's were,' continued Pike. 'Only she was lucky, Jack.'

'So, you and your department want revenge?'

'No, Jack. Not revenge. We lose agents all the time. It's part of the job. The role of my department, or rather that for which I work, is purely government orientated. We focus on any individual or organisation that is a threat to the constitutional running of this country.' Pike stood up and admired the framed Lowry print whilst he continued to explain further, 'Political extremists; terrorists; those who support terrorists and so on. Do I make myself clear, Mr Priestley?'

'So, why tell me all this, Mr Pike, having already fobbed me off previously?'

Pike swung round to face him, 'Because I underestimated you Jack, and because your Chief Constable seems to think you're the kind of officer whose arse drops golden bricks.'

The words were so out of character for Pike, but he was now talking Priestley's kind of language and had just got himself back on the ladder.

'Goddamn it, man, I need you to work with us, not in the opposite direction.' His words were fairly dramatic but he'd spoken them with the charm and coolness of a man who was a Commander and held a highly respected position.

Oh, yes, Jack could definitely see why this bloke got the job.

'I need you on board, Jack. The operation is now entering a final phase and I couldn't afford to have any loose cannons.'

Jack smiled. That was more like it. The truth. Pike had just moved up the ladder a couple of rungs, but hadn't yet reached the one that would encourage Jack's complete co-operation.

'So, what would you like me to do, Commander?'

Pike returned to his seat and finished his tea before continuing. 'Work with us, Jack. That's all. Join forces with us.'

There was a brief moment of silence between the two men. Priestley was trying to convince himself that he should disclose all he knew to Pike. As for the Commander, well, who could possibly know what devious thoughts were going through his disciplined mind?

It was Pike who broke the ice. 'This Thursday night, Jack, George Riddell is going to move two hundred anti-personnel landmines.' He paused to watch Priestley's reaction. There was none.

Jack was surprised that this man obviously knew as much as he did, perhaps more, but he was an old hand at this kind of game and thought it best not to show out in any way, not just at that moment, although he had a feeling Pikey knew that Priestley was already aware of that little gem.

'And?' asked Jack.

'I would like you to take him out.'

'And?' repeated the DCI.

'Any papers or documents you recover, bring them to me and I'll take it from there.'

'The police do their job and your Secret Squirrels finish it. Is that what you're putting on the table, Commander?'

'No, Jack, it's not an option. It's the way we work. It's how we *should* work, each of us looking after our own area of responsibility.'

'And you also know you leave me without any choice. You've got me over a barrel, Pikey.'

'We work together, Jack.'

Priestley knew he was right. It wasn't for him to put his big foot into matters that didn't concern him. After all, no matter what his personal feelings were about Pike and his team of faceless bloody wonders, they were trained and experienced in dealing with threats to national and international security. Jack was well out of that league. To play awkward now, could create more than a few major problems for him. He also had to think of those next door – the officers who worked for him.

'Okay, I'll take the operation Thursday night and give you whatever we recover, as well as a full debriefing on what we find.'

Pike just stood and smiled. 'Welcome aboard again, Jack.'

He held out his hand which Priestley shook, at the same time asking, 'How's Roger by the way, Commander?'

Nice try, but it was obvious from his face, Pike had no idea what he was talking about.

*

The car slowly drove up to the front of the house and stopped. Riddell sat in the back and waited for the door to be opened.

'Leave the car in the garage tonight, Ponteus,' he ordered, 'I might want it later.'

The big man grunted, as he usually did, not putting more than two words together at any given time, except once a year – Christmas morning when he opened his presents!

'And don't rush in the morning. I've got some work to sort out for tomorrow night.'

Another grunt and Riddell heard the car's wheels roll over the gravel as he walked through the front door.

*

He made his way into the downstairs lounge to answer the phone and then flopped into a large easy chair, one that Rolo had watched him occupy on so many occasions before.

'Yeah?'

'You've got the increase, George.'

The phone went down and Riddell just smiled, his demands having been met. Wise people, he thought.

*

The large black figure switched off the lights and walked towards the garage exit with the remote control that opened and closed the doors, in his hands. Suddenly he felt a devastating blow to his groin and like a Goliath, temporarily paralysed, fell to his knees momentarily disorientated. Before he hit the ground a heavy chain was wrapped around his neck and he was yanked up and pinned to the garage door mechanism, unable to move and unable to breathe.

He'd already dropped the remote on the floor and the hooded figure picked it up and pressed the button. Immediately, the chain around Ponteus' neck tightened, stretching him up onto his toes. His hands grabbed the links as they dug into his flesh, but to no avail. The man stood in front of him and just said, 'Hello,' before pressing the button again. He was jolted another six inches upwards, his feet now clear of the floor, kicking out wildly in desperation.

His captor just stood there. The chains moved another six inches and the bodyguard's head hit the top of the mechanism with an almighty thud. Ponteus was about to die, or so he thought.

He looked down and could see the man standing there, silent. Slowly nodding his head to the left and then the right, like a child watching a Punch and Judy show at the seaside.

'Well, mister, you won't be taking time out again to arrange a little accident for a certain female brief,' said the voice. 'If you don't die now, you will if I have to come back. Enjoy the rest of the evening.' The man turned and walked away, taking the control box with him.

*

George's phone rang again and he waited to empty his mouth full of food, before answering it. Presuming it was Grainger again he said, 'Yeah, I know. I got the message already. What you after, a big thank you?'

'Best go and see to your man,' the voice said. 'He's hanging around your garage, shitting himself!'

Riddell ran from the house and heard the commotion before turning the corner to see his man hanging. Ponteus was desperately pointing towards the mechanism against which the top of his head seemed to be pushing.

'Where is it?' Riddell shouted, searching frantically for the remote control.

Then he heard a car engine start up at the bottom of his drive and ran back to the front of the house. There on the front step was what he'd been searching for. Ponteus would live, just about.

*

Blade laughed loudly to himself as he raced towards the motorway. This had been his game. This was what he was good at. That sadistic streak always seemed to come out of him whenever an opportunity presented itself.

He didn't know whether Ponteus had been responsible for Sonia Hall's accident or not. And he didn't much care. The big man had been selected because the chances were he had been the one. The main thing was, a message had been delivered, one which helped to balance the books a bit. Soft as shit though, thought Blade. At least he'd tried to even the score a little. All this inactivity, particularly where Riddell was concerned, had been driving him balmy. He'd never had the same degree of patience Jack Priestley had always displayed. But he was only just starting to enjoy himself. He still had to sort out those bastards who'd held him prisoner. They'd be a different kettle of fish though. He had to find them first and that wouldn't be as easy as flying the first space shuttle.

*

chapter twenty-two

'Glad they've got a lift,' commented Riddell, who was more interested in keeping the cold out than admiring the view. And it *was* bloody cold at nine hundred and eighty-four feet above the ground.

'Have you been to Paris before, Mr Riddell?' asked the Arab.

George shook his head, 'And I'm not staying long either.'

'Ah, yes, tonight is a big night for you, is it not?'

'I have to get back so why bring me over here?'

'I would have thought that was obvious,' remarked the Arab. 'Just look at the view down there. You can see the River Seine in all its majesty.'

George grunted something that sounded as though he was agreeing but really didn't give a toss. He'd been on the road since five that morning and the Arab was right. He did have a long night ahead of him.

'You haven't got me up here to share the view.'

The Arab seemed to ignore the remark, 'Is everything ready?'

The tour of the Eiffel Tower and its magnificent views was at an end. It was time for business and to discuss the real reason the Arab had asked Riddell to cross the channel for this particular meeting.

George nodded again, 'But I have to be close at hand when things kick off,' he explained.

'Of course, so I won't keep you for longer than is necessary. You must be wondering why I've asked you here?'

'The thought did cross my mind.'

'Well, I've been asked to put a proposition to you that doesn't involve those who are currently negotiating between us.'

'Grainger?'

The Arab just looked with a slight nod of his head, 'Shall I go on?'

'I'm listening.' George kept turning his head to make sure Ponteus was on his shoulder but he wasn't. The minder was having a neck transplant!

'My people want this deal to be concluded within five weeks.'

'What's the total?'

'A thousand.'

That was a smaller figure than George had been anticipating which might mean he'd get short changed by the people he worked for, Grainger and his boss, whoever that was.

'That's two hundred a week starting from tonight. It shouldn't be a problem. We're geared up for that,' he explained.

'And then a new contract,' suggested the Arab which lit up George's face as if winter had disappeared and it was now a beautiful spring day.

'We want you to deliver the same total again, within the same period.'

'For how much?'

'Double what Grainger is paying you.'

'Half a mill?'

The Arab nodded and George knew exactly where he was now coming from. He'd overheard the figure of two hundred and fifty thousand being mentioned by George at their meeting with Grainger. What he was doing now was cutting out the middle men and saving himself a lot of money. At the same time, George was gaining much of what Grainger and his firm would have been getting. It made sense. It was good business and Riddell showed his enthusiasm by shaking the Arab's hand.

'Have a safe journey back,' the Arab said with a wide grin across his face.

It wouldn't be long before Riddell would be able to buy the Eiffel Tower for himself!

*

'You could say it's a truce, but I'd prefer to call it a new partnership.'

'Jack, they'll just shit on yer like before.'

'They know as much as we do, Steve, and I still think there's a lot more to this.'

Sammy interrupted their discussion with a tray of coffee.

'My main interest now is to get hold of Riddell, if only for setting up Sonia,' continued Priestley.

Blade looked at him sheepishly although Priestley didn't notice. What he'd done the night before hadn't been to get accolades off Uncle Jack, or even to seek revenge for Uncle Jack's bird. It was purely for selfish reasons – to inflict some agony on some overgrown boy scout, although he knew in his own heart, Ponteus was well distanced from that description.

'But there's something more, Steve. That's why SIU are involved.'

'Such as?'

'If I knew that I wouldn't be so concerned about tonight.'

'Jack, whilst we're sitting here they're probably up that telephone pole outside with a camera on us now.' He looked around the room. 'They're probably also listening to every word we're saying. Dirty double-eyed bastards.' He shouted the last few words so that anybody standing outside, five floors up with a trumpet attached to their ear could catch what he said.

'Probably,' smiled Priestley.

'Well, I'll be there, mate. As always. Faithful to the end.'

'Got something for you,' Priestley said, reaching into his jacket pocket. He handed a mobile phone across to Blade. 'The battery's charged by the way. And don't get blasting the bill through the roof.' Those were wasted words and the look on Blade's face signalled just that.

✳

He might well have been at the centre of the universe. There were people from all walks of life either sitting around the nude statue watching the waters cascade down from the fountain or rushing across the square from one end to another. It reminded Jack of The Steps in Rome, only the weather wasn't as nice.

✳

The note had said one o'clock and it was now five past. Priestley sat patiently not knowing where to put his eyes and wishing he'd bought a paper to read or something.

'Hello, Mr Priestley.'

'Roger?'

Cheswick nodded enthusiastically and sat down on the cold stone wall next to him. 'Sorry about all the secrecy but you can't be too sure.'

He looked a lot better than the last time Priestley had seen him, in some grubby interview room over in Staffordshire. He'd put on a little weight and his face was like a sheep farmer's, weathered and tanned. Probably due to the cold spell, thought Jack.

One thing was certain though, Priestley had been wrong on his thoughts about the author of the letters having worked for Pike. Cheswick was most certainly not a secret agent.

'How's the boy?' asked Jack.

'Not so well,' was the answer. 'He's still having nightmares Mr Priestley. They reckon it could take years before...well that's really why I'm here. To return the favour.'

'The favour? Right,' said Jack, now realising what Cheswick had meant. He hadn't really picked it up before, the thought of him being instrumental in getting a bloke on a Category A list, being regarded as a favour hadn't really appealed to him. But now he understood.

'I haven't got much time,' whispered Cheswick. 'I've been working for George Riddell over at International Swarf since I got out, thanks to Jimmy Gabriel. But tonight he wants me to help out in one of his warehouses in Meriden.'

'I got your messages,' confirmed Jack.

'I don't know many details but we've all been told to be on our toes. I've got snippets from some of the others. I know he's moving a load of landmines out of the country.'

'What role are you going to play?' asked the crime squad man.

338

'Oh, nothing really. I've just been told to help out with some loading and unloading. I'm not sure what the set up is.' His head spun before continuing, 'But the main reason I wanted to see you is because there isn't much time left.'

Priestley continued to sit, looking away from him but listening to every word.

'Last night somebody tried to top Ponteus.'

'Ponteus?'

'He's one of Riddell's heavies, never leaves his side. But one of the lads had to go over to Riddell's place to pick up Ponteus and drive him to the hospital.' Another spin of the head before continuing. 'Well, he overheard Riddell blaming the attack on the lady barrister whose car was fixed.'

Now Priestley's stare was aimed directly at Cheswick.

'Well, apparently it was somebody who thought Ponteus had done it. I'm not sure of the details. Anyway it wasn't him.'

Priestley was just hoping now that someone wouldn't come out of the crowds and put a bullet in his head, like he'd seen so many times on the films, just as the informant was about to name the main player. So he started to look around nervously where they were both seated.

'According to Riddell it was an Arab and he told Ponteus he'd sort him out in the morning, that's today,' explained Cheswick.

'An Arab?'

'Riddell was going over to Paris this morning to meet him. Don't ask me why.'

Priestley was already trying to remember where he'd heard of an Arab being involved in this lot, before. It was sometime just recently. Then it came to him – Rolo.

'Why tell me all this, George?' Priestley had almost forgotten Cheswick's first name and then it had hit him like a flash.

'Because I owe you one for what you did, Mr Priestley. And I don't want to go back inside. Not now, anyway. Me and the missus are happily settled down, looking after our lad. And there's nothing in the world I'd do to upset that.'

Priestley gently shook his arm and smiled, 'I can understand that son. Don't worry. Have you got a mate working there with you?'

Cheswick was puzzled at the question and shook his head.

'Is there anybody you could trust amongst the others?'

He shook his head again. Ken Evans is the friendliest. He's a Welsh kid, but I wouldn't trust any of them really.'

'Then you and Ken Evans will come in with the rest but I'll give you both the back door afterwards.'

He still looked confused and Priestley qualified himself.

'If you were the only one to walk out of this, don't you think it'd look bad? With two of you, it offers you a little more protection. Savvy?'

Cheswick got the message.

'You best get off, just in case,' suggested Priestley, again looking around at the crowds of people flying past.

'Thanks, Mr Priestley.' Cheswick stood and was soon gone, like the other half of a magician's act.

*

'Two things, Chris. Firstly, did we pull a big geezer from Riddell's fight scam by the name of Ponteus?'

'No, boss, that's his right-hand man but he wasn't there when we hit it. I presumed he'd left with Georgie boy.'

'And the other is, ask Rolo if we got any snaps of the Arab he mentioned visiting Riddell.'

'I can tell you that now,' explained Barton. 'He did and we've got them.'

'Good, I'll pick it up later.'

*

The four men sat, listening, knowing that this particular delivery was going to be special. Riddell had never before called them to a meeting before a job. He'd always spoken to them individually or in couples.

'Are we all absolutely geared up for this now?' he asked, sitting on top of his desk looking as haggard as a man who'd just flown halfway across Europe and back.

They all looked at each other and then nodded.

'There's one problem, Mr Riddell,' spoke up Chrissie Waltham. 'We've got a bloke named Blade working at Cheetah. He's been pestering us a bit for work.'

'He suspects we're doing something outside the norm, and wants a part of the action,' explained Marty Lawrence.

'How did he get the job at Cheetah?' asked Riddell.

'Jimmy G sent him to us.'

'He's been in here to see me. I think he's just a pain in the arse. Did you know he's on the run from the nick?'

Both Lawrence and Waltham nodded.

'I don't think he's a problem,' stated George. 'If Gabriel sent him, he should be alright. I might even take him on-board, eventually.' Then the big man grinned, 'Or get one of you two to bump him off.'

'What about the unloading?' asked Mo Khan.

'That will be the same as before. Just make sure you get it there,' said Riddell.

'That's what's worrying us,' explained Mitch Ricketts. 'It took too long last time. They were still pissing about unloading us when the parcels wagon landed.'

'I've got an extra man this time, so don't worry. It'll all be done on time.' He stood and walked behind his desk. 'Any more queries?'

The four drivers shook their heads in unison.

'Then let's make sure we deliver this one,' said Riddell. 'If it goes well, there's going to be a lot of big bonuses lads, in the near future. This is the first of a lot of work coming our way.'

Riddell had always believed in practising a need to know policy and although Ricketts and Khan were both aware of the nature of the goods they would be collecting from Long Marston, Lawrence and Waltham didn't. All they had to do was make sure that whatever the load was, it would be delivered to the airport.

*

'Did you just happen to visit Georgie Riddell's place last night?' asked Priestley.

'Jack, what would I be doing going over to Riddell's place?' He stroked the top of his daughter's head with his free hand, holding the phone with the other.

'Ever heard of a bloke named Ponteus, Steve?'

'Yeah, why he's not dead is he?'

'No, but who is he?'

'Riddell's new right-hand man.'

'But where did he come from? What's his background?'

'I'll have to try and find out for you, Jack.'

The phone call ended and Priestley started to make his way back to the office, still trying to come to terms with that niggling feeling that Blade was holding out on him.

'Why, he's not dead is he?' Funny question to ask, thought Jack.

*

Priestley's briefing had taken a couple of hours. And that was exceptional for him. He'd always believed that the more you tell the troops, the less sticks in their minds. Always keep it short, simple and effective was one of his basic principles since first stepping into police management. But this particular operation would be different.

He'd planned to create four surveillance posts. Three would be static, one at the Army depot, the second at the warehouse of R L Smith in Meriden and the third at Riddell's home address, using a camera fitted inside a lamp post covering the front door and driveway. The fourth part of the operation would be the mobile surveillance on Lawrence and Waltham.

He required the three static teams to be in position as early as six o'clock that evening. The mobile team which he'd be running with, taking the two Cheetah drivers along the outward bound route ever since the operation had started, would go in later as they had always done. He'd run again with them, and the Tactical Firearms lads would follow from a distance. It would be Blade's job to do the usual and give the off when the trunker left the Cheetah warehouse.

He'd almost forgotten about the last piece of the jigsaw when Nick Carpe, accompanied by another bomb disposal expert, walked into the room. The Captain had agreed to support Priestley, the idea being for both soldiers to take part in the operation. What Jack Priestley didn't want were his own officers messing about with explosives. Both men would accompany the DCI who felt the need to be armed in addition to having the firearms lads behind him.

The Long Marston static surveillance would be known as the Orange Team and managed by Detective Sergeant Alan Cresswell. Chris Barton would take care of the Green Team at Riddell's house. And last but not least, the Meriden warehouse would be covered by the Red Team, led by Ralph Darling, another of Priestley's more experienced Detective Sergeants. That additional team would be needed to keep a watchful eye over proceedings at the warehouse before the Cheetah trunker arrived there, and also as back-up to the Tactical Unit once they'd led the way. Everything was now in place. All he had to hope for was that the information he'd been given was correct and they'd all be playing ball tonight.

*

Riddell sat in his office feeling the warmth from the log fire. Ponteus stood by the door, arms folded, looking like a polo mint with his neck encircled by a white heavy support. Apollonius of Tyana, only without any movement from his shoulders upwards. There was no doubting, if he'd been in a private medical scheme he wouldn't have been there. The fact he couldn't speak didn't matter. He never found words very useful anyway.

'Keep an eye on the warehouse,' ordered Riddell. 'Let me know if you see anything out of the ordinary. No matter what.'

The minder nodded and left George to contemplate the hard cash that would soon be winging its way into his overseas account.

*

The sky was as clear as the crystal vases Brenda his ex used to keep on the dressing table. That would mean the temperature would drop well below freezing, with heavy frost covering the roads. That was a dangerous situation. It was good that they would only be following a heavy trunker, rather than speeding like a bunch of idiots chasing some prat in a Formula One model.

Carpe and his corporal sat in the back of the crime car, which was driven by Dave Vaughan. The first job Priestley had to do was check on the other teams. They all replied positively, with both cameras working at the Meriden site and Riddell's home. It would be an hour before Blade would call to say the trunker was on its way with Lawrence and Waltham.

'Orange to Purple.'

'Go on, Alan.'

'We've got some movement here, boss. Two headlights moving out of the depot, coming towards us. Wait one.'

The radio went dead and Priestley and the other two teams waited patiently for Cresswell to come back.

'One enclosed army truck just driven away. Confirm you don't want us to follow, boss.'

The last time Priestley had done that, he'd let Riddell escape through the net. But this was different. He knew where the truck was going, if the information was right. There was no need to take any undue risks.

'Take five out, Alan, and then make you way over to back up the others, later.'

'We'd be interested to know who was driving that truck, Jack,' explained Carpe.

'You'll know soon enough, Nick.'

✳

Riddell was about to leave for home when the phone rang.

'Enjoy the trip, George?' It was Grainger and by the sound of his voice he was a little put out, thought Riddell.

'What trip?'

'Paris this morning. I'll meet you at your place in half an hour.' The phone went down and Riddell stood there, just for a moment, staring at the handset. He was contemplating his next move.

He took his overcoat off and placed his briefcase back on the stool near to the door. Another log went on the fire and he retired to his favourite chair behind his desk. He wasn't going anywhere. Let them stew, was his initial reaction. He laughed to himself wondering whether the home contingent would now meet the same prize money as the Arab had offered him, earlier.

✷

'Purple to Green, any news yet Chris?'

'No, boss, the house is still in darkness. Outside lights on though. Must be on a timed mechanism or something.'

Riddell was missing and Priestley wondered whether he would show at one of the other surveillance points. He wasn't over concerned, knowing that once they found the mines and whatever else would be netted inside the Meriden warehouse, Riddell would have nowhere to go.

'Green to Purple.'

That was going to be news of Georgie boy arriving home, he hoped.

'Go on, Chris.'

'We've got one male at the front door. He's rung the bell, knocked on the door and he's now standing back having a gander at the rest of the front.'

'Description,' asked Priestley.

'Short, slim, early forties, small moustache. Smartly dressed with overcoat, white shirt and tie. You won't believe this but he's carrying an umbrella. Looks like his accountant.'

'What, at half two in the morning?'

'You never know, boss,' replied Barton. 'They work some funny hours, these accountants, especially the bent ones. He's walking away.'

'Car?' asked the DCI.

'Not yet. He's left it down the drive. We'll try and get it for you.'

*

'Nothing more on our lorry, Jack?' asked Nick Carpe.

'Red to Purple.'

Priestley turned and smiled, 'This'll be him now.'

'Go on, Ralph.'

'The roller-shutter doors have opened. The Army truck has arrived and they're backing him in.'

'How many Ralph?'

'We've counted six males at the warehouse. One driver and a passenger inside the truck.'

'Number of the truck, Jack?' asked Nick Carpe from the back of the car.

'There's one other thing, boss. We've got a stranger on the plot. One black male with, what looks like a collar wrapped around his neck.'

Ponteus, thought Priestley, somebody's tried to hang him or slit his throat.

'Probably his collar's too big, Ralph,' suggested the DCI, mockingly. 'Have you got the reg. number of the truck?'

'Affirmative,' was the reply. 'The shutters are now down again with the truck inside. Switching to the camera.'

There was another anticipated pause in proceedings.

'We have a good sighting on the monitor, boss.'

So they should have, thought Priestley, so they should have. He'd put it there himself.

'They're all busy, boss. Running all over the place. Tail gate is down. Two males inside the back. Others seem to be forming a human chain. One crate out of back of truck. Large crate. No colour. It's being handled and placed on the floor at back of the building, out of shot.'

'Give me the final count, Ralph. What's the stranger doing?'

'He's just left, boss. I think he's having a gander around the area. Probably looking for us.'

Priestley smiled.

'Do you think they know we're here, Jack?' asked Carpe.

'No, otherwise they wouldn't be.' He turned around to face Carpe and his colleague, 'But they're usually on their toes. It's a common thing. The man we're looking at is one of Riddell's minders. He's probably been sent by Riddell to scout around and then let him know if there's anything out of place.'

His mobile rang.

'They're on the move, Jack, as normal,' It was Blade.

'Right, Steve. I'll catch you tomorrow, thanks mate.'

✳

'What shall we do if these two don't make the warehouse, boss?' Vaughan was in one of his pessimistic moods, as he drove behind the boot of the last of the surveillance team.

'Probably go back on the Co-op milk, Dave.'

✳

Lawrence and Waltham drove at a steady sixty down the M6 towards the airport. Then as usual, they came off at junction 4 towards the airport. As they approached the island, from where they would need to go in the opposite direction to get to Meriden, Priestley held his breath, not believing for a minute they'd go directly to the airport, but Vaughany had made a valid point earlier. What if...?

'It's the second exit towards Meriden.'

That was a relief and both Priestley and his Detective Sergeant punched the air as though in celebration, much to the surprise of the two in the back.

'Game on, Nick. Tonight's the night,' explained Jack.

'Let's hope so,' replied Carpe.

It was about time the good guys had a bit going their way and Priestley could feel that old adrenaline going up again.

✳

'Red Team.'

'Go on, Ralph.'

'Rollers are opening up again and the Army wagon's leaving. We've counted twenty crates, boss. They're piled up out of camera shot towards the back of the warehouse.'

'Right, as per briefing Ralph, let them go and stay where you are.'

'Jack, I won't be able to ID those drivers in the morning,' explained Carpe, with some obvious concern in his voice.

Priestley nodded, 'Ralph, release the bike and one crew. Get them to take the wagon back to the depot and lift the drivers from there.'

'Gotcha, boss. By the way, your vehicle is now in sight. The rollers have been left up.'

'Thanks, Jack.'

'No problem, Nick. I should think they'll have some explaining to do when you get into them.'

'With twenty crates and probably ten mines in each crate there should be something like two hundred in total. Not bad for one trip, Jack.'

'Would the primers be with them?' asked Priestley.

'I'm fairly certain, yes.'

*

'Cheetah trunker arrived and is being backed in.'

'To the team then. Hold your positions.' He called to the Firearms Inspector who should have been in the Range Rover just behind him, 'Mack, your lads ready?'

'Affirmative.'

'I'll call it.'

*

The forklift unloaded the first igloo off the back of the trunker and Cheswick, together with the others started to unload the parcels as soon as it was on the floor.

He smiled to himself as he stood and watched the large chipboard panels that formed a false floor, being pulled out leaving a hollow bottom.

*

'Seven crates have gone into the floor of the first igloo, boss. And now they're placing the parcels back on top.'

Priestley's eyebrows made an arch, 'Piece of piss really. Unless its drugs, who's going to search a parcel company's consignments? And if they did, all they'd find was parcels.'

Dave Vaughan nodded with a similar grin on his face, 'Unless they stripped the igloos completely.'

'Yep, but could you see that happening, Dave, to a well established parcels company that's been sending stuff through the airport for years? It'd be like turning the Post Office over.'

'Do you think the company's involved, gaffer?'

'No, I don't. Okay, Mack,' called Priestley back down the radio, 'It's all yours, mate.'

✳

The second igloo had almost been filled when the roller-shutter doors suddenly flew up and the men in black appeared, introducing themselves with shouts, screams and the appropriate demands. Within seconds, all the workers were faced down on the floor with handcuffs placed on their wrists.

✳

Priestley stood and watched as the Captain and his Corporal opened the crates and started to inspect the items of war, all neatly packed.

'That's one of your primers, Jack,' said Carpe as he held the small item up in his hand, just as Priestley's mobile went off.

'I've just had the Green Team on, boss,' explained Dave Vaughan, 'The accountant's back.'

'But no Riddell, Dave?'

'No, boss.'

'Tell them to lift the accountant and I'll send a team from here to International Swarf.' He was starting to wonder why on earth he hadn't done that at the beginning of the operation. Work was the last place he thought Riddell would be during the early hours, but now it was the only option left.

He turned to survey the scene once more. Yes, it had been a good job well done, but there was more to come. There had to be.

*

chapter twenty-three

At first, Riddell's face was a picture of disbelief, confusion and madness. His world; his dreams; his empire had now been dissolved and were quickly disappearing like muddy waters running down a drain.

'Meet me on the Great Barr car park, Ponteus.'

His first reaction was to run out of the door, but then he remembered and returned to the wall safe. He knew he had to stay calm, think logically and he would soon be out of this mess.

He managed to stuff all the notes into his pockets. His briefcase was already full but he had to make sure nothing was left behind.

*

As he raced down the stairs disturbing thoughts sped through his mind, hitting him like pricks of infra-red light.

Could it have been the Arab? Had he set him up? If so, why? Surely he stood to earn more than Riddell? Perhaps Grainger had stuck him in? But then, wouldn't he be committing professional suicide? And then again, he hadn't long phoned him, concerned he was double-dealing with the Arab. That was sufficient motive to do the dirty. Perhaps it was Grainger? Perhaps he was acting under orders? None of it mattered anyway – George was going to kill both of them anyway, just as soon as he could return after things had settled down a bit.

He ran out of the door and went flying across the pavement, head first, tripping over a size-nine industrial boot with metal toe caps.

'Hello, George,' said Blade, 'you seem to be in a bloody awful hurry, mate.' He bent over and picked up the briefcase before returning his sights back to the fallen man. Blade winked at him, tucking the briefcase under his arm, 'You'd best be off then before the boys in blue arrive, eh?'

Riddell scampered to his feet and pulled a gun out from beneath his overcoat, 'I'm going nowhere without that, you thieving bastard.' Another small blip. Blade should have known the man would be carrying, on a night when he was responsible for moving so much gear.

He let the case slide to the ground before being ordered to step back half a mile. He could have kicked himself. This was the second time a well-planned, brilliantly worked-out escapade of his had shot through. And with all that secret bloody service training as well!

'Don't worry George, I know you'd use that thing. I'll be a good boy,' Blade assured him, as Riddell regained possession of his worldly goods and started to back away towards his car.

He was still standing scratching his head when the crime squad people arrived. 'You're too late,' he told them. 'He's pissed off with my...sorry, I mean *his* money.'

✳

The overgrown polo mint was still waiting patiently in the black Rover when Riddell jumped in the back. 'Aston, Ponteus, get me to the yard at Aston.' That was George's safe house. His slaughter. A small back-street yard that was as safe as Buckingham Palace used to be. One he'd kept up his sleeve, until now.

It was there he kept his most treasured artifacts and he couldn't afford to leave them behind. He intended to collect them before going on to catch the plane.

His directions to the pilot's wife were simple and concise, 'Get the lazy bastard out of bed. I need that plane up within the hour, tell him.'

He then turned to Ponteus who was travelling at a steady thirty so as not to attract any unwanted attention, 'Ireland I think. That's where we'll go for our short break.'

He then sat back and sighed, appreciating that Ponteus' earlier phone call had probably just saved him from drawing about twenty years. He smiled thinking of Gabriel. He'd been within a whisker of joining him. But what about that cheeky bastard Blade back there, at International? What was he doing there? He looked at his watch, four-thirty. How come Blade had been there obviously intent on taking his capital away from him? He'd have to think about that one later because he was almost there now. He'd already made his own contingency plans for a situation such as this a long time ago. Apart from the big fella driving and one of his men to whom he'd given a job to, the day before, he knew there could be no one else aware of his yard in Aston. And he was extremely confident no one knew of his private plane, which was about to help him disappear. No, George Riddell had managed to escape by the seat of his blue and white striped underpants, but only just. Only the Arab was now in the forefront of his mind.

*

'He's in the front office, boss,' explained Barton. 'The lads found him standing outside the front of International

Swarf. He told them that Riddell had just left and had a gun or something, so they decided to bring him in.'

'Who's this geezer Grainger? Has he said anything yet?'

'Haven't spoken to him, boss, but he must have some clout. He was on his way back to a top of the range Merc when we picked him up, outside Riddell's house.'

'Not an accountant then, obviously,' joked Priestley.

'We searched the car and there were more papers than you find at a ticker tape ceremony,' explained Barton.

'What we done with them, Chris?'

'All bagged up in the crew room.'

'Okay, lets get sorting before the vultures land. I'll go and get rid of Blade.'

*

He followed Jack into the office, muttering something about what he would have done if Riddell hadn't pulled the gun on him. 'Jack, he would have used it. I moved towards him and he pulled the hammer back. I was that much away from copping one in the chest,' he indicated a distance of about one sixteenth of an inch with his forefinger and thumb.

'What were you doing there, Steve?' asked Priestley. 'I'd have thought you would have preferred to have gone home to Sammy after you'd finished work.'

Blade grimaced and shook his head, 'Jack, I can't explain it. I was on my way home when I suddenly had this feeling that things were going right and that Riddell would be hiding somewhere, inside International Swarf,' he paused, 'I suppose I just followed my nose. I almost had it blown off mate.'

Priestley smiled, 'Okay, get yerself off home.'

*

It was still dark when Ponteus drove into the yard. Warmer air had started another fall of snow and the black tarmac was just starting to white over as the car stopped. Riddell didn't wait for the door to be opened, he just leapt out of the car with the keys in his hand and ran, still carrying his briefcase across towards a small modern building. He unlocked the door and switched the alarm off, just inside the small corridor. Within a minute the lights were on and George was opening another wall safe. He placed some papers into another briefcase he'd found under a desk, before opening a small black bag which had been stored towards the back of the safe. He slowly let the eight large diamonds fall into the palm of his hand and counted them. Satisfied, they too went into the second briefcase. He was ready now. Everything he needed he had. Except a three-month vacation, which he was now set to take.

*

He closed the safe and turned to see Ponteus standing in the doorway with a long black barrel pointing at him. Two 9mm pieces of lead entered George's brain, killing him instantly. The former minder then placed the weapon into George's hand, not even bothering to unscrew the silencer. He emptied the dead man's pockets, placing everything into the second briefcase before calmly walking out, luggage in each hand and locking the outer door behind him

*

The snow was getting thicker now as Ponteus walked across to the Rover and switched the engine off, leaving the keys in the ignition. He then walked out of the yard and pocketed the gate keys having secured it first. Everywhere seemed so still and peaceful as the large falling flakes silently came to rest on the ground.

He walked up to a bottle green coloured Jaguar parked some ten yards up the road and climbed into the back. The Arab accelerated away.

*

Priestley couldn't believe his luck. A leather bound ledger showing payments made to Ridlington over the previous two years. But more importantly, inside the back cover was a wad of bank statements, records of an account in the name of R W Ridlington.

His chair slid back from the desk and Barton, sitting opposite him responded to the noise by glancing up, only to see a look of shock on his DCI's face.

'Boss?'

Priestley stared at nothing.

'Boss, you alright?'

'No wonder they wanted to keep us out of this, Chris.'

'Boss?'

Priestley's eyes slowly rolled towards where Barton was sitting. 'He's only been running the show.'

'Who?' asked the DI.

'Sir Richard frigging Ridlington. That's who.'

Barton rushed across to look at the same ledger and accounts Priestley had been examining. 'Christ almighty, R W Ridlington, Sir Richard – '

'Walter Ridlington,' interrupted Priestley.

'The papers, Jack.'

Both men quickly looked up to see Commander Pike standing in the doorway.

'I've only just got to bleedin' bed. Who are you anyway?'

'I've told you, Carol Guardia. I'm a reporter and friend of Jack Priestley's.'

'Well, go and bother him then.' Blade put the phone down and turned over.

'Out of my way, Commander,' ordered Priestley as he barged past Pike.

'I'm now taking over this whole inquiry, Priestley,' shouted the senior ranking officer.

'Please yerself,' answered Jack, as he stormed out and turned left only to bump into Laurel and Hardy blocking his route out of the nick, like two pieces of granite in the Claerwen Dam.

He turned back 180 degrees, only to face Pike who'd followed him out into the corridor. 'You arresting me?'

'No. Let's sit down and act like responsible adults Jack. You've only got half the story. Wanna hear the rest?'

He nodded and returned to his office.

*

'I'll kill that bastard milkman. Tell him to piss off Sam. I'm on nights.'

His wife slowly unfolded herself and walked, still in another world far away, towards the front door that sounded as though it was about to be demolished.

'Alright, alright, I'm coming,' she coughed as she undid the bolts.

'I'm Carol Guardia, I need to speak to your husband urgently.'

'And I'm Zsa Zsa Gabor and I don't,' said Sammy still half asleep. She went to close the door but it was pushed back towards her. That woke her up. This cheeky young filly was now in the hallway.

'You'll be out of this flat within an hour if you don't do what I tell you, missus,' Carol bawled.

Now Sammy was wide awake, not terrified but a little stunned by the strength of this woman's tongue. 'Steve,' she shouted, 'you'd better get your arse out here, like yesterday.'

*

'So, you see, Jack, it's extremely delicate and if not managed correctly could cause a tremendous amount of harm to the Government.'

'The Arab tried to kill one of my closest friends.'

Pike shrugged his shoulders.

'Why do you always do that?' asked Jack, screwing his face up, 'when you hear something you don't really give a shit about?'

'Jack, it's all about a little give and take, both in love and in war.'

'Bollocks, little man. I want that bastard and the man to give him to me is Ridlington.' Jack slumped in his chair and then with a lowered voice continued, 'Look, I don't give a damn what you do with Ridlington or any of the rest of them but I can't just walk away, knowing the man who tried to kill her.'

'But he doesn't exist, Jack.'

'What do you mean he doesn't exist? He's more alive than me or you. One of my men saw him visiting Riddell. I've had it from a good source that he pissed about with Sonia's brakes,' he stood and leant over Pike. 'And you told me yourself, he's bumped off one of your men.'

Pike shook his head, 'I didn't say that Jack. Riddell was responsible for that.'

There was a short pause between the two of them, during which time Priestley walked to the door to check on the two lumps standing outside in the corridor. They were still there, so he returned to his chair.

'Look, Jack, I understand how you feel but let me tell you about this supposed Arab.'

'There's no suppose about...'

'Jack, he's a privileged individual with diplomatic immunity throughout most of the civilised world. He's a shadow who works across a wide plain, occasionally rising to the surface, sometimes here and then sometimes there, and then sometimes, somewhere else. He doesn't exist officially and yet he's a linchpin. One who can be extremely valuable, not just to this country's Government but also to the French, the Germans, the Spanish, the Americans.'

'I don't believe this, you're talking in riddles, Pike,' said Priestley shaking his head.

'Jack, damn you, he's one of us.'

'So why has he tried to kill my bird?' Jack snarled back.

'I don't know the answer to that. It's quite obvious he wanted you, and probably us, to think it was Riddell, being as the other man used the same m.o. to see off our agent. Why? I just don't know, Jack.'

'Then Mr Secret Service man, I'll tell you why. To get into Riddell's favour. That's fucking why.'

Priestley lit up a cigar whilst Pike sat quietly watching him.

'Because my woman was getting too close to me,' he said in a quieter, more restrained voice. 'Because they knew I was getting too close to them.' Jack paused, 'And that was because of you dear Commander.'

✳

His eyes were heavy and bulging. And as he'd already told his wife, he was a night worker now, earning an honest living but not being able to get his fair share of sleep because of this cow standing in front of him.

'He's a big lad is our Jack,' he explained.

'I know all about that, but they're going to blow him up.'

Blade could see there was sincerity in her eyes and no matter how much he thought this was a load of crap, at least she believed it.

'Steve, I've been knocking about with a bloke named Mo Khan. He's been giving me all kinds of titbits about Riddell and his organisation. I've passed most of it onto Priestley. But yesterday Khan had to drive Riddell back to International Swarf. Something about his normal driver being sick or something.'

At least this had a ring of truth about it. Blade thought of the man with the enlarged dog collar.

'And on the way he told Khan to meet another man this morning who would give him the details of arrangements they'd already made to put some device inside Priestley's car.'

'Who's the other man?'

'He wouldn't say, but he wanted me to warn Jack.'

'So, why haven't you?'

'Because I can't get him. I've tried his flat number. His mobile and even the nick where he works, but he's been out of touch and nobody seems to know when they'll hear from him again. That's why I've come to you.'

'So, where does this Khan geezer live?'

'Over in Bordesley Green.'

'Give me a minute. I'll get dressed.'

*

362

The atmosphere was less hostile. The steam had gone out of the conversation and Priestley sat there looking like a German Shepherd that had just been tamed by its master.

'Alright, Richard, I'll play it your way.'

The look of relief on Pike's face was something else, 'Well done, Jack, I thought you'd see sense eventually.' He stood up, 'Listen, what I'll do is ensure you're made aware of the full result of the operation and then write a letter of thanks personally to both Sir Ronald Chapman and the Home Secretary.' He smiled as he walked towards the door. 'You'll be getting the next rank before you know it.'

Where had he heard that one before?

Pike called his own two minders in and they scooped up all the papers taken from Grainger and put them into polythene bags.

'And what about Grainger?' asked Priestley.

'Leave him to us, Jack,' suggested Pike, who was now standing in the doorway. 'But I promise you George Riddell and the rest of them will be tried before a court of law.'

At least that was something, thought Priestley, who just nodded before turning to Barton, 'Put the kettle on Chris, it's been a long night, mate.'

Another look of reassurance from the Commander and he was gone, Laurel and Hardy close behind carrying armfuls of polythene bags.

*

Blade stood on the opposite corner whilst Carol knocked on the front door of the small terraced house. He wasn't watching her perform. He was concentrating on the upstairs windows, being the kind of street-wise type of bloke he was. What he had anticipated happened. The front upstairs bedroom curtain moved, only slightly but sufficiently to tell him someone was at home.

She knocked again, only harder but still there was no answer.

'Watch yer back, luv.'

She stepped aside and before she knew it, was following Blade into the front downstairs room, the door hanging off its hinges.

She got the distinct impression that the retired armed robber and secret agent had been there before. It was the way he appeared to be at home in surroundings that were strange to her. He waltzed straight through an inner-dividing door, into a back room and up a flight of stairs. In fact he hadn't been there before, just a hundred or so houses similar to this one.

Khan was standing in a nightshirt at the top of the stairs, looking half frightened to death.

'Having a lie in?' asked Blade. 'Sorry about the door, I've got someone who wants to see you.'

'I've only just been kicked out of the nick,' explained a very distraught Mr Khan.

*

Barton sat sipping his tea, looking across at his DCI who was obviously oblivious to what was going on around him, which was very little since the heavy mob had left.

'I suppose that's it,' suggested the Detective Inspector.

'Is it?' snapped back Priestley.

Barton looked concerned, 'Guvnor, you're not...?'

Priestley unlocked the bottom drawer of his desk and took the statement of account from it, before walking across the office to collect his overcoat.

Now Barton was getting more concerned, 'Guvnor, after what you said...'

Priestley just winked and headed for the door.

'You're not going to see...?'

His DCI nodded.

'Do you want me to take your firearm back to the armoury?' That was the real reason for Barton appearing to be more concerned than normal.

'I'll drop it in later, Chris. And don't worry, I've got my feet back on the ground now.'

*

He drove the longest route to the Ridlington home, thinking, analysing, trying to separate logic from fantasy. The picture of Sonia lying in a coma was ever present in his mind. The George Riddells of this world, making huge amounts of profit by undermining the wishes of society itself, apparently too readily assisted by those employed to protect the country from such men. And all because of one man – an Arab whom he needed to see urgently. One who, if Pike was to be believed and Priestley had no cause to doubt what he'd been told earlier, had the protection of every government in the Western World. A wheeler-dealer who invested in human life for what appeared to be all the wrong reasons.

Priestley could only think now of this scumbag crouching beneath Sonia's bonnet, cutting the brake pipes, hoping and praying she would be killed in the inevitable accident. And when he was found out he was allowed to move on, at the drop of a hat, without any interference. Diplomatic immunity, Pike had called it.

And there was the man himself. A person responsible for helping lead the country down the supposedly correct path, at the same time filling his own bank account by unlawful and immoral means. A man who'd been knighted by the same country he'd sold out to some enemy power. One who walked daily in the public eye, accepting all the accolades that went with his office. And the cheeky bastard, thought Priestley, is about to take up another position inside the Foreign Office.

*

He was quite taken aback when Sir Richard himself answered the door, 'Chief Inspector, do come in.'

Priestley trod the usual path into the lounge and was surprised there didn't appear to be any sign of Lady Ridlington. In fact, with the exception of Sir Richard, the large residence appeared to be deserted.

'Can I offer you something?'

'No, thanks,' replied Jack and handed to the former Cabinet Minister a copy of the statement of account showing payments made to Ridlington. 'I'm here in an official capacity, Sir Richard.'

He took the sheet from Priestley and stood for a short while, frowning, reading the printed matter.

'My God. You have been busy.' He turned and walked across to the French windows.

'Do you deny you've been involved in illegal arms dealing, Sir Richard?' asked Jack.

'I deny nothing.' He walked across to an easy chair and signalled for Priestley to occupy the one opposite, 'Please.'

'Let me explain one or two things to you,' suggested the detective taking advantage of the other chair. 'This inquiry is out of my hands now. And perhaps that could be a good thing as far as you are concerned,' he added. 'But I have a personal interest which has to be resolved and my going to the press and blasting your name all over the front pages will only be avoided if a resolution is brought about.'

'Money?' asked Sir Richard looking somewhat aghast at the thought that this officer might be cashing in on the knowledge now in his possession.

Priestley ignored him, 'The Arab.'

The politician looked relieved which was surprising since the bunging of a bent policeman would have been far easier than having to sort out the man Priestley was chasing. Sir Richard's eyes told Jack he was deliberating whether to admit knowing the Arab or deny any knowledge of his existence.

'You have just completed a deal to export landmines out of this country,' stated Priestley, and the impact of that short statement showed, just as he anticipated it would.

His host sighed and placed his head into his hands, as the door opened and in walked Lady Ridlington.

'Jack, it's good to see you, I do believe...' suddenly she stopped in mid-sentence, obviously recognising the less than cordial atmosphere in the room, her husband's look of despair and the policeman's stony face. 'Oh dear, I'm sorry. I do seem to have come in at the wrong time. Is everything alright, dear?' she asked her husband.

'Could you bring us some coffee please, Susan?' he mumbled still staring down at the carpet, cradling his head.

✳

'You're a scab,' bawled Khan at the reporter, 'bringing the law here.'

Blade slapped him again with one hand whilst keeping him pinned up against the wall with the other. 'If you call me the law again, you'll never be able to have children.'

The man became less tense and Blade slowly allowed him to come back down off the ceiling. 'That's better. Now then, I want you to listen to me carefully, because this is very important,' he said still keeping a hand pressing against Khan's chest. 'You're going to tell me who the man is you're supposed to meet,' he nodded but got no response, 'where you're supposed to meet him,' he nodded again, still no response, 'and at what time.'

'I don't know nothing. She's a scab,' he bawled again pointing his finger at the reporter.

Blade turned to Carol, 'Will you excuse us for a moment, darling?' and then marched Khan into the front room, slamming the door behind him.

She was about to have a quick nose around, when the first piece of furniture hit the other side of the door dividing her from where Blade had took his new found acquaintance. She then heard a number of expletives being shouted by both men, some of which she'd never heard before, and then screams, obviously from Khan. There was the sound of more furniture being thrown around and then, as though being a final throw of the dice, a sort of high-pitched wail similar to the noise she imagined a wolf would make. And then, a short period of silence, as she stood staring at the door.

*

It slowly opened and Khan was the first to reappear. His face was bloodied and swollen. There could be no doubting, given an hour or so, he would become unrecognisable.

Blade followed with a slight grin, 'Ever heard of a bloke named Ponteus, Carol?'

It had been a long time since Blade had scaled a fence or wall as high as this one but he had to help the lady over first.

They both then quickly hurried across the yard towards the office building, Blade looking for the usual guard dog to suddenly come running out snarling and showing his teeth. But there wasn't one.

'There's another half an hour to go before the meet,' explained Carol. 'If what he told you is the truth.'

'It was the truth all right, don't worry about that. I'm just surprised I didn't know about this place. Good old George – always keep something up your sleeve.'

'I think we should wait down the road and watch from a distance,' she said rather nervously. 'I could take a snap of him with the explosive in his hand and then follow him. Jack could use the photograph in evidence and...'

'I think he's already been here, chuck,' said Blade, looking through the window.

She looked and saw Riddell's body sprawled across the floor, lying on its back with two holes in the forehead. She gasped and then reached for her mobile phone.

'What yer doing?' asked Blade rather loudly.

'Phoning the paper.'

'No yer not. You must be joking.'

'Why, this is a big scoop.'

'I don't give a shit what it is, let's speak to Jack Priestley first,' Blade suggested. 'You blasting this all over the papers might put him in more peril.'

'And how are we going to get hold of him?' she asked, knowing that her paper was going to get this story whether he objected or not.

Blade just smiled and pressed the button on his own mobile. 'There are ways you know.'

✳

chapter twenty-four

Whatever the time of day or night it was, the airport concourse and its many buildings were always surrounded by people and luggage. Just like the contents of a large box of dolly mixtures, holiday makers, business people, and all other kinds of travellers, infiltrated by airport employees, stood shoulder to shoulder at one of the world's many crossroads. All shapes and sizes, colours and nationalities, together for as long as it took to catch the next plane. Outside, the taxis constantly came and left, like black streamers stopping, unloading and then driving away to join the back of the queue, whatever the weather.

He stood there at first, watching the people paying their fares before searching for tickets and pulling their individual pieces of luggage into the main terminal. He had a pensive look on his face but his eyes were quick and sharp, hastily flicking from one scene to another. Priestley was on full alert, not really knowing what he was looking for and if he found it, not knowing what he would then do. He pulled his mobile out from his inside pocket.

'Riddell's gone for a permanent lie down. Two in the head.'

'Where?' asked Priestley.

'You wouldn't know it, Jack. It's a small yard in Inkerman Street.' Blade then gave him a brief description of what had happened, posing no surprises for Priestley, who just listened, his eyes still surveying the activity around him.

'Do me a favour, Steve, let DI Barton know. He's in my office.'

'Where are you now, Jack?'

'I went to see Ridlington earlier and he told me a number of interesting things. There's an Arab involved in this arms dealing business since the start and Ridlington's been paying for his services.'

Jack started to walk slowly into the main terminal building.

'He tried to kill Sonia and put the blame on Riddell because I was getting too close to them.'

'Who is he, Jack?' asked Blade.

'According to Ridlington he's got twenty different names. It appears nobody knows his original identity or which country he was born in, but I intend to find out. Unfortunately, Steve, the geezer's got more protection around him than our Royal Family. And it's all from us!'

He stepped onto the elevator and started to make his way towards the upper level, head turning, eyes watching all the time.

'Again, according to Sir Richard, whenever the heat is switched on, our friend makes for a private charter and flies out into the sunset like a vulture going home.'

'You at the airport now, Jack?'

'Yeah. I don't hold much hope though.'

'Then get the Army out, Jack. I need some sleep,' insisted Blade, 'I'll come back to you later.'

There was no sympathy from Jack. He too needed sleep, but couldn't afford the privilege just yet.

Priestley checked the restaurant areas, then the shopping arcades, the cafés, the newsagents and bookshops, the terminals and everywhere else inside the building. He saw plenty of Arabs, together with Europeans, Americans, Chinese, West Indians, Asians and every representative of every bloody country on the map. His was a hopeless cause.

'Lost yer plane, guv?' It was Barton with Vaughan standing behind him.

'Thanks for coming, Chris. It's good to see you.'

He explained what had apparently happened to Riddell and the DI instructed Dave Vaughan to inform the local police.

'He won't be hanging around here, guv,' explained Barton. 'He'll be airside if it's a private plane he's going out on.'

'Christ, Chris you're right.' He raced through the nearest customs terminal, waving his warrant card with Barton following closely behind, and charged through each of the departure lounges. There was still no sign of anything that would make his blood pressure go up.

✳

He stood in a corner staring out and looking down and across a tarmac apron, which had a number of small private aircraft parked on it. He saw one man walking towards a small plane with a briefcase handcuffed to his wrist. Must be the Crown jewels, he thought to himself.

He turned and looked at Chris Barton who stood next to him, expressionless. Priestley knew exactly what his young DI was thinking – that this particular exercise was a complete waste of time.

'I'm beginning to agree with you, Chris.'

'Boss?'

'That we're wasting our time.'

372

Barton just nodded and then answered his mobile. 'Good grief.' There was a pause. 'He's with me here now.' Another pause, 'When did this happen? Okay, catch you later.'

Priestley waited for the news, wondering whether they'd just found the Arab's body hanging out of Steve Blade's window. Barton explained. They'd found a body all right but not the Arab's. Sir Richard Ridlington had just hanged himself.

Jack felt deflated, exhausted and with no other avenues to charge down. What more could he do? He'd been just a pawn and was now starting to realise that was all he could ever be in his present position. There would always be others to play the tune. Perhaps one day...? Perhaps.

'Okay, Chris, I surrender. Let's get back to life as we know best, mate.'

Both detectives walked back towards the customs terminal, Priestley in particular with an astonishing look of defeat written all over his face. A stranger would have thought he'd just had an accident. To say he felt low was the understatement of the year. His eyes hadn't stopped flashing around like two blue lights, but inside he realised he'd been on a fool's errand. Enough was enough. It was time to go home and make a fuss of his Sonia. Only then would he be able to take stock of all that had happened and perhaps offer some kind of accurate description of events to his Chief Constable.

Suddenly, at the other end of the terminal lounge, he saw two shadows disappearing down the flight of stairs that led to the apron. Pike, and one other? He wasn't sure. He stood for only a second.

Barton hadn't realised his DCI was no longer behind him and continued through the customs gate.

'Well I'll be...' he whispered to himself. There they were, Laurel and Hardy. As large as life itself and walking towards the same staircase where the two shadows had just disappeared. Priestley was some fifty yards or so away but there was no doubting those were the boys all right. Bill and Ben the burial men.

He quickly ran across to the large window at which he and Barton had stood only minutes before. He saw two men walking across the apron towards a number of small aircraft. He hadn't been mistaken, one was definitely Pike of the Yard.

He tried to focus his eyes further, squinting, trying get an ID on the Commander's mate. At first he couldn't make him out because the man's back was to him and then, one sideways turn of the head. Yes, like a camera snapping a moving object, he had him. An Arab-looking gentleman. Mr Frigging Jackpot! 'Come 'ere, yer bastard,' he whispered again.

✻

Priestley took three steps at a time as he charged down towards the outside exit and when his feet finally reached the tarmac, he could see the two SIU agents in front, walking away from him. In front of them was Pike with his little diamond at the side of him.

'The double-eyed git,' snorted Jack, who then unholstered his Magnum and ran forward, like a brave fusilier but without anybody else behind him. It didn't matter. In fact he hadn't given a thought to the fact he was about to take on board the Spook Department, all alone. Used to be the same when he was a kid!

✻

Both of the suits were shocked at being bundled to the ground as he fled past them.

'Pike,' he shouted.

The Commander turned, surprised to say the least and perhaps a little pale in the face all of a sudden. He then turned towards the Arab and placed an arm around his shoulder, obviously trying to hurry him towards the waiting transport. As they continued to walk briskly, almost running away from Priestley, Pike appeared to be talking to his wristwatch.

Priestley stopped dead in his tracks and pointed the gun at both men. 'Pike, if you don't hand him over I'll blow his brains out. Yours as well if needs be.'

The demand was clear enough and Pike decided to show willing by standing still. The fact he was within Priestley's range might have helped him make that decision. The Arab also stopped but kept looking away from the armed crime-squad man whilst Pike just turned and stared at the DCI.

'I told you, you're out of your league, Jack,' he called back.

But Jack's concentration had been diverted elsewhere. It took only a glance for him to identify the plane they were hoping to board.

From out of the darkness of a Piper Comanche appeared the towering figure of Ponteus. He seemed to walk down the three steps in slow motion as Jack unbelievingly, looked on. Yet another piece in the jigsaw? Perhaps, the final piece. Ponteus? Riddell's right-hand man? One of them? Astounding.

But Jack had another more pressing problem. Ponteus reached the bottom of the steps and took up a stance, which immediately informed Priestley he was well and truly in the shit. Legs apart, crouched forward, arms outstretched with both elbows locked, his body forming the triangle taught to every professional firearms man throughout the world, to achieve maximum accuracy.

He didn't have time to assess whether or not the gun was in both hands in order to stabilise it when being fired. He raised his own gun towards where Ponteus stood, before feeling the thud in his chest.

They say you never hear the bullet that kills you. Jack Priestley heard this bugger and a second that he knew had also hit him, but he didn't know where.

Oh, this lot are bloody good, he thought, the bastards, as he felt his legs turn to putty and, again as if in slow motion, his body started to curl up as it moved closer towards the deck, gun spilling from his hand. He was grounded like one of those big Canadian Firs collapsing down from the sky. We salute those who are about to die.

*

He found himself lying face downwards and managed to lift his head just in time to see the Arab boarding the plane. Ponteus was obviously satisfied with the work he'd done because his gun had disappeared and he just stood helping the foreigner up the steps.

When he reached the top the Arab turned and looked at the fallen policeman. There was just that briefest meeting of their eyes, like two stars in the night, light years away from each other, but also visible to one another.

And then the clouds came down and darkness fell all around, like it was the end of the world, the end of civilisation or as they say in the films, the end of life as we know it.

*

'Jack, Jack, come on, son.' It was his old mucker trying to revive him with his garlic smelling breath.

'Bladey,' the wounded man said, 'you don't have to try any harder to kill me.'

There was also Carol Guardia standing over him, her eyes peering down from behind two hands partly shielding the tears rolling down her face.

And then that bloody burning sensation in his chest as the two in white coats lifted him onto the stretcher. He rolled his head sideways and caught a glimpse of the tubes running from his one arm, drips already in position. Perhaps he wasn't going to die? Why would they go to all this bother if he was about to become a corpse he asked himself, before lapsing back again into unconsciousness.

*

She sat stroking the beads of sweat from his forehead. With her lovely perfume mixed with Blade's garlic breath, it was like a Bombay flower garden inside the back of the ambulance.

He sat searching his pockets until he found Jack's wallet. He opened it and took out a ten pound note.

'What do you think you're doing?' asked the paramedic.

Blade placed the note into his own hip pocket and turned to the medic, 'He's the closest mate I've got. But if he's going to die, I'm having back the tenner I borrowed him in the Carpenters Arms, a two stretch back.'

* * *

www.houseofstratus.com

Email: sales@houseofstratus.com please quote author, title and credit card details.

Hotline: UK ONLY: **0800 169 1780**, please quote author, title and credit card details.
INTERNATIONAL: **+44 (0) 20 7494 6400**, please quote author, title and credit card details.

Send to: **House of Stratus Sales Department**
24c Old Burlington Street
London
W1X 1RL
UK